Volume XIV

THE TRUMPET AND THE SWORD

PETER DANIELSON

BCI Producers of **The White Indian,
The First Americans,** and **The Holts.**

Book Creations Inc., Canaan, NY • Lyle Kenyon Engel, Founder

BANTAM BOOKS
NEW YORK • TORONTO • LONDON • SYDNEY • AUCKLAND

THE TRUMPET AND THE SWORD
A Bantam Domain Book / published by arrangement with
Book Creations Incorporated
Bantam edition / January 1992

Produced by Book Creations Incorporated
Lyle Kenyon Engel, Founder

DOMAIN and the portrayal of a boxed "d" are trademarks
of Bantam Books, a division of
Bantam Doubleday Dell Publishing Group, Inc.

ISBN 0-553-29495-4

Published simultaneously in the United States and Canada

Bantam Books are published by Bantam Books, a division of Bantam Doubleday Dell Publishing Group, Inc. Its trademark, consisting of the words "Bantam Books" and the portrayal of a rooster, is Registered in U.S. Patent and
Trademark Office and in other countries. Marca Registrada. Bantam Books,
666 Fifth Avenue, New York, New York 10103.

PRINTED IN THE UNITED STATES OF AMERICA

OPM   0 9 8 7 6 5 4 3 2 1

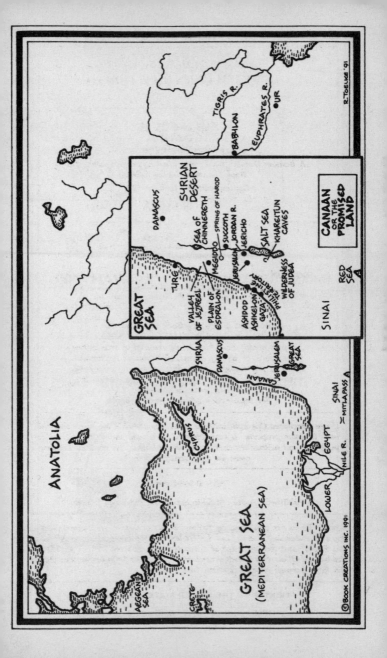

MANY GENERATIONS OF
THE CHILDREN OF THE LION

*
KHALKEUS OF
GOURNIA
(THE MINOTAUR)

MAI = SETH
*   *

NUHARA = THEON
*   *

*HELA   *GRAVIS

*
KHIAN = RHODOPE
(DEMETRIOS
THE
MAGNIFICENT)

KETURAH = IRI
*

*APEDEMEK = NEFTIS = BAUFRA
*

TIRZAH = PEPI   *MICAH   *NIMSHI   TALUS
*   *

CHILD OF THE LION *

© BOOK CREATIONS INC. 1990

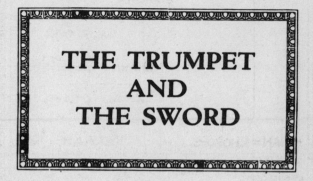

THE TRUMPET
AND
THE SWORD

Prologue

The hailstorm struck suddenly, like a lion swooping down upon an unsuspecting lamb from the jagged cliff. The soft, kindly desert night was transformed into a caldron of pain and wind and cold. When the stars seemed to have been plucked from the sky and hidden by a monstrous hand, the men, women, children, and beasts of the caravan formed a circle, huddling together in terror against the fury of the storm.

Then the familiar chant of the Teller of Tales cut through the fierce wind and calmed the gathering. "In the name of God . . . the merciful . . . the beneficent . . ."

The tall, gaunt, aged man stepped into the circle of firelight. He was naked except for a doeskin wrapped around his waist, and yet the cold did not seem to bother him. His long white hair whipped across his face, and his eyes burned with the intensity of embers in the night.

He picked up two pieces of stone from the ground and struck them together violently. A string of sparks shot upward, and suddenly, as if by the sparks' signal, the wind died and the hail ceased. With surprising grace the old man flung the stones far out into the night and glared at his audience. A child began to cry but was quickly hushed by his mother.

"Listen to me with every fiber of your being," the Teller of Tales warned. "Hear now the tragic tale of the Children of the Lion. Hear how Home, their island headquarters and sanctuary, was discovered and destroyed and how their once-mighty network of trading ships was shattered. Hear how the Children of the Lion rose from defeat and despair to challenge once again the powers of darkness and betrayers in their midst."

The old man raised one arm and pointed north. "Hear also of the powerful new magicians who called themselves Phoenicians and who, with demonic energy and cunning, controlled the very waves of the Great Sea."

The Teller of Tales clasped his hands behind his back and walked the perimeter of the circle, staring hard at the faces of his listeners, challenging them to look him in the eyes. But none could meet his gaze.

At last he spoke again. "Hear now how Yahweh's people, His chosen people, began to cower before the bejeweled Bedouin lords, just as you cowered before the dangerous, unpredictable force of the hailstorm. Hear how Yahweh plucked a fool from among His people and transformed him into a spiritual and military giant.

"Hear how the Children of the Lion, bruised and bloodied, reaffirmed their pact with the Israelites, as they had in the days of Moses, then Joshua, and finally Deborah the prophetess."

An eerie sound carried through the night. The people moved closer to one another and scanned the darkness beyond the firelight. Had it been a jackal's cry? Or a hyena's? Or a rogue lion's from the Nubian plain?

His voice became harsher. His eyes narrowed to mere slits. "Hear how a woman from Babylon empowered the winged creatures of the sky to do her mysterious bidding in the Holy Land. And listen carefully, my children, as I tell you of the new god-man, Dionysus, who rose from the ashes of Greece. His powerful tentacles tried to challenge Yahweh and to extirpate the famous birthmark of the Children of the Lion from the face of the earth."

At the edge of the circle a young man rose and held out a goatskin flask for the Teller of Tales.

The old man took it and drank. "Water!" he called out. "Sweet, clear water. The drink of soldiers."

Another flask was offered. The Teller of Tales drank from that one, also. "Wine! Strong, bracing wine. The drink of lovers."

He dropped the flasks to the ground and said nothing for a long time. His body was erect and motionless, and his eyes were closed, as if gathering strength. When he spoke again, it was in a powerful, low, rhythmic voice that seemed to penetrate the audience's psyche like a spear.

"Remember their names, children. Remember them well: Talus. Gideon. Tirzah. Theon. Blood. Dionysus. Cotto. Zeeb. Oreb. Listen to the wondrous deeds of soldiers and lovers who, armed with trumpet and sword and their wits, are thrown violently together in a new world, where the gods themselves are in conflict."

PART
ONE

CHAPTER ONE

Canaan

The donkeys moved slowly on the path, stepping gingerly on the sunbaked earth. What little vegetation remained from the effects of the drought was burned brown by the relentless heat. The trees by the side of the path were too stunted to provide any shade for the beasts or their riders.

The lead rider, called Gideon, dismounted and drank sparingly from a small bladder of water. "We'll rest here," he told his servant, Purah.

Gideon looked too poverty-stricken to have the luxury of a servant, and his appearance did not deceive. His robe was tattered and filthy. A short sword hung in a worn scabbard on the belt that secured his robe. On his back were a bow and a quiver with only two arrows remaining. His once-magnificent leather sandals with high straps were now missing many thongs and as a result flapped loosely on his feet. Around his neck was a plaited rope, which was attached to a trumpet.

His tall frame was haggard and thin; the brown, gold-flecked eyes were deep in the skull. His soft brown hair was matted with dust and sweat.

"Bring me some dates," he ordered Purah, who had just climbed off his own donkey and was standing on the path.

"There are none left," Purah said, removing his master's shield from his back and hanging it on the donkey. The servant's feet, shod only with palm fronds, were scorched by the hot earth.

Purah had been with Gideon's family for many years. He had been treated well during their long-past days of affluence and now remained to share what little they had. He wore a tattered skin around his middle, and two water bladders hung around his neck. He was a small, wiry man with eyes that squinted. His face was lined from the sun and the wind, and his long oily black hair was fastened with a leather thong at the nape of his neck.

"It is meat, not dates, I want anyway," Gideon responded. He thought for a moment, then added, "Maybe I'll eat the donkey." He laughed uproariously at his own joke.

Purah smiled grimly. "Sir, wouldn't it be better if we moved on? There is no food to be found here, and we are too close to the river. The Bedouins have been raiding this area often."

Gideon pulled his sword from his scabbard with a flourish. "Shame on you, Purah, to be frightened by the Midianites. I am here to protect you. If we see an enemy, I will make soup out of him." He waved his sword dramatically and menacingly in a circle, then slipped it back into its sheath.

Purah watched his master's antics in patient silence.

"The trouble with you, Purah," Gideon continued, "is that your fear of the Midianites prevents you from thinking straight. You believe they are the cause of the Israelites' problems; but it is the drought that has once again destroyed us as a proud people. The land has dried up; the rains have vanished; the flocks have died.

Look at me! Ten years ago I was feasting with my family on the booty from Hazor. Now we are all starving. We have been forsaken by Yahweh and by the land. As for the Midianites, they are just mosquitoes who have crossed from the east bank of the Jordan because there is no more blood to suck there."

Purah replied with his usual deference, "Yes, my lord, you are right. My mind is clouded by fear."

"And you sound sad as well," Gideon remarked. "You need to be cheered up. And music is the only thing that can make a person forget an empty stomach."

Purah shuddered. He did not think he could survive another assault from his master's trumpet. Not now.

"Perhaps, sir, you should preserve your strength for the journey back," Purah suggested fervently.

"Nonsense. Music gives strength to musician and audience alike."

Purah closed his eyes and leaned wearily against his donkey when he saw Gideon put the horn to his lips. If only he could find some acceptable way to stuff up his ears . . .

The first sounds from the horn caused Purah to feel even more despair. Gideon was playing an Israelite march that had been composed during Joshua's time. It had always given Purah a headache. If he had to listen to Gideon's trumpet, he preferred the southern love songs. But Gideon did not know too many of those. Purah shut his eyes tightly, gritted his teeth, and tried to think about a refreshing bowl of cool goat's milk, something he craved but had not tasted in months.

When the piece was finished, Gideon smiled broadly, very pleased with himself. He let the trumpet hang loose on the cord around his neck and started to mount his donkey. "Now that the music has refreshed us we can journey again, Purah. Mount up! Mount up!"

But Purah did not move. His entire body had become rigid as he stared directly down the path.

"What's the matter with you, Purah? Mount up!" Gideon ordered. He slid off his donkey again as if planning to shake his servant out of his sudden torpor.

"Your sword, sir!" Purah whispered desperately from between clenched jaws.

Then Gideon turned and saw what had transfixed his companion. It was a fearsome sight. Two immense white camels were kneeling shoulder to shoulder on the narrow path not more than fifty feet away. They were adorned with magnificent woven bridles and halters. Their limbs were muscular and lean, their eyes were clear, and their beautifully shaped heads were held erect. And on the back of each beast sat a Midianite warrior.

The Bedouins wore long black robes, and white sashes covered the lower half of their faces. From the left ear of each man dangled brilliant gold earrings, hammered fine into intricate patterns and burnished carefully until they captured the sun's light and reflected it in shimmering waves.

"Your sword, sir!" Purah hissed again urgently. The servant's hand rested on the edge of his master's shield as he waited for the sword to be drawn. Then he could bring the shield up.

"Maybe it would be better to talk to them," Gideon whispered back.

The Midianites easily swung their long legs over the backs of their kneeling camels and started to walk toward the two Israelites. Curved swords were sheathed in jeweled scabbards on their backs, and each man carried a dagger at his waist. They wore nothing on their feet, so they moved silently, like predators.

Purah's hand began to tremble, and his heart was beating so fiercely he thought it would leap out from his chest.

"Run, Purah! Run!" Gideon shouted, and they wheeled around to flee—only to discover that a dozen other Midianites had emerged from the sides of the path to form a circle around them. The Israelites stopped short, trapped.

A Bedouin left the circle, strode up to them, spat forcefully in their faces, then screamed, "Kiss the ground, pigs! You are standing before Oreb and Zeeb, warlords to King Zalmunnah." The Bedouin's curved sword cut through the heavy air an inch from their faces.

Purah could feel the hot wind from its path, and he and Gideon fell to their knees and kissed the ground, holding their mouths against the hot baked earth until they choked and their eyes were filled with dust. They were well aware of the men to whom they were bowing: Oreb the Raven, a one-eyed butcher, and Zeeb the Jackal, whose right hand was twisted into an ugly claw from a childhood mishap. Gideon and Purah knew of these two most feared Bedouins whose names had come to symbolize torture and death among the Israelites.

"Have mercy on us! For the love of God have mercy upon us!" Gideon begged. "We have nothing of value. We are just two humble travelers searching for food for our starving children." He held out trembling hands in supplication.

The two warlords strode arrogantly around the prostrate Israelites, ignoring Gideon's plea and inspecting them as if they were livestock.

"They are worthless," Zeeb said in disgust. "Zalmunnah wants gold from this raid."

"I say we bury them alive up to their necks and let the ravens pluck out their eyes," Oreb suggested.

"We don't have time," Zeeb responded. "I'll slit their throats and be done with it." He drew out one of his daggers and dug the point into Gideon's bowed neck.

"Wait," Oreb said. "There's a horn around his neck. It might be amusing to have this Israelite play for us." Oreb turned to his Midianite troops and called out: "Do you want to hear a song?"

They shouted their approval of Oreb's idea. One of the troopers shouted, "And let's see a dance."

Oreb dragged the two Israelites to their feet. "This pig will play," he ordered, pointing at Gideon, "and this pig will dance."

Purah had never danced a step in his life; but in spite of his fear-weakened knees, the moment he heard the first cacophonous notes from Gideon's trumpet, he began to leap up and down and sideways, trying to imagine the steps of a dancing girl. He ground his hips and swung his pelvis. He shimmied his shoulders with his head thrown back. He wiggled his rump and kicked his legs and twirled.

The Midianites jeered and hooted and threw dirt and stones at the pathetic pair.

When the performance was finally over and the trumpeter and dancer fell exhausted to the ground, Oreb and Zeeb kicked them into near unconsciousness, accompanied by the cheers and laughter of their soldiers. "Come back again," Zeeb yelled at them, "when you have learned some new tunes."

The Midianite troops mounted their white racing camels and followed Oreb and Zeeb northward, where there were still crops to be stolen, livestock to be slaughtered, Israelite women to be raped, and gold to be unearthed from hidden caches after their owners were tortured into disclosure.

As the camels raced effortlessly over the parched land, the Bedouins' beautiful earrings tinkled in the dry, hot wind.

CHAPTER TWO

Island of Home/Aegean Sea

The young man Talus stood with bowed head before the freshly dug grave. There were now two graves on that mountain trail: One was Keturah's, his mother, who had died two years before. The newly dug grave was for Phorbus, Talus's adopted brother. There had not been much left of poor Phorbus to bury. The sharks had taken chunks out of the body before it had washed up on shore.

Talus wept softly as he remembered his brother's last days. Phorbus had become delusional and then totally insane, believing that his long-dead lover, Myrrha, was swimming across the Great Sea to him from her battlefield grave in Troy. And then one morning Phorbus had climbed to the highest point of their uninhabited part of the island called Home, leaped into the sea, and swum out, supposedly to join his beloved.

Talus stepped back from the grave and looked toward the brush that lined the trail. He spied some yellow wildflowers and plucked a handful to scatter on both graves. Then he jogged down the trail, his short, broad body eating up ground in easy strides. He had the same sloping, powerful shoulders his father had had, the great armorer Iri of Thebes, who had died trying to rescue his family from captivity in Troy.

When Talus reached the small shack where he, his mother, and Phorbus had lived in total isolation from the other residents of Home, he rummaged frantically through the root cellar until he located an old bronze sword, an anvil, and a pair of prongs. He dragged these to a small outdoor bellows and began to fire it, working furiously to get the blaze hot enough so he could work and keep his mind occupied. He did not want to dwell on the frightening fact that now he was totally alone. Memories were all he had left—memories and two graves.

How different it had all been ten years before, when the three of them had miraculously escaped from burning Troy and reached the island home of their kinsmen—Children of the Lion. They were expecting the wealth and privileges and respect due them as the family of Iri of Thebes. They were anticipating the acceptance, love, and protection of Khalkeus of Gournia and all his retainers.

But upon their arrival, they had gotten nothing but ten years of hardship, near starvation, and isolation . . . ten years of living with the bitter knowledge that they could never leave their island prison because they had no ship, no money, and no contact with Khalkeus and his court. They built themselves a crude hovel, using materials found on the shoreline. Their shack was on the desolate end of the island, and they had been forced to live like wolves, eating gulls and rodents and roots and berries. No wonder Phorbus had lost his mind and his mother had wasted away from sadness.

Talus worked the bronze sword for hours, beating it into various shapes. And then, when he was totally exhausted, he picked up the now-useless weapon and flung it as far as he could into the woods. Then he sank down on the ground beside the small forge and slept.

When he awoke he found himself staring at bowls of olives and cheeses and small pieces of salted meat set onto the ground not more than five feet from him. He stretched and looked up to see the two young visitors who had brought the food. The twins stood silently a few feet behind the bowls. It was almost impossible to tell the brother and sister apart.

During these missions of mercy they just stood at a distance and watched him eat voraciously. They always seemed to enjoy seeing him devour the food. No matter how many times they brought him the food and no matter how pure their intentions, the twins Hela and Gravis inadvertently made him feel like a swarthy savage, like a leopard in a cage. He was barefoot and grimy and long-haired, and his only garment was the skin of a mountain wolf. The twins, however, were dressed elegantly and identically in expensive lemon-yellow linen tunics, which almost matched the color of their carefully trimmed golden hair. They wore calfskin boots beautifully embossed with beadwork.

It was difficult for Talus to accept the fact that the three were blood relatives, but he knew it was so; the beautiful twins before him were the children of Theon and Nuhara, and they bore the same lion's-paw birthmark on their lower back as he did.

Talus chewed a small piece of tasty meat. It was more delicious than anything he could scrounge up on his own. Phorbus, while he was sane and alive, had accepted food from Hela and Gravis with bitter reluctance.

"Guilt offerings," he had told Talus. "It was their mother, Nuhara, who told her father, Khalkeus, that we are imposters. It was the greedy Nuhara who prevented us from seeing Khalkeus and pleading our case that Iri's fortune—his share of the Children of the Lion's commercial enterprises—is rightfully ours. She would never have gotten away with this if poor Theon were alive! But now Nuhara's children secretly bring us food to assuage their guilt."

Phorbus is dead, Talus thought philosophically, *and I am hungry, and I don't really care why Hela and*

Gravis bring the food. The only thing he was sad about was that they seemed unable or unwilling to converse with him.

Talus finished the food, licked the bowls clean, and brought them to his benefactors.

"Next time, please bring me some big fat juicy grapes, red ones," he requested. His eyes twinkled with offered friendship as he handed the bowls back.

Talus suddenly realized that he had never been so near to the twins. Up close, their eerie beauty was almost overwhelming. And they smelled beautiful, as if they had bathed in wildflowers. Talus found himself unable to look away from their gaze. He glanced from one to the other and then back again. A growing excitement filled his heart, as if he were embarking on a journey that promised both great beauty and terrifying danger. Their eyes were magnificent wells of—

A sharp pain abruptly stabbed through his right leg, and he collapsed to his knees. Convulsed, he held out a hand for help, but neither twin moved. The pain vanished as suddenly as it had come, and he stood up. But the pain came again—this time putting his left leg into spasm. He fell flat on his face.

What was happening? He looked up. The twins were staring straight ahead, their lean, majestically clad bodies ramrod straight. He was awed by their presence and wondered if he had ventured too close to them physically and they had rightly responded with some demonic power to thwart his arrogance.

"What are you?" he cried out. But the twins had turned and were moving off to begin their long trek back to the populated, civilized part of Home. Talus could see that they were holding hands. He shuddered.

"What are the people in the square saying?" Nuhara asked the young, dark-skinned woman kneeling beside her chaise.

"They are frightened," replied the young woman, whose name was Allomander. She was painstakingly painting her mistress's toenails with a mellow red dye imported from Egypt.

Nuhara smiled contemptuously and folded her arms across her breasts. She was still wearing her sleeping robe. Although her lustrous black hair had specks of gray and her small, perfectly formed face was lined at the mouth and brow, she was still a very beautiful woman. "Of what are the fools frightened? Plague?"

"No, my lady. It's just that many of them haven't received their wages in weeks. They are starving. Many are in danger of being put out of their homes."

"Is that all?"

"No, my lady. They are frightened because they see so few ships in our harbor. The walls of their dwellings are crumbling, the warehouses and shops are falling into disrepair, and even this palace, which was once so magnificent, has become ugly to the sight."

Allomander's explanation was cut short by ferocious sounds in an adjoining room. A man was shouting, and then objects crashed against the walls and floors. Servants screamed and wept. Nuhara and Allomander listened but did not move to investigate. They knew that Khalkeus of Gournia—head administrator of the commercial empire of the Children of the Lion . . . chosen successor to the great Demetrios . . . a legend in his own time for his daring and cunning as a feared high-seas pirate—was drunk again.

"My father is obviously enjoying himself," Nuhara noted without concern, and then returned to her questioning of the servant. "What are they saying about me?"

Nuhara rarely left the palace. The small villages and squares that radiated from the palace to form the inhabited section of Home were alien territory to her. She had never even entered the warehouses or the workshops or the accounting offices—the lifeblood of the vast shipping concern.

"Nothing, my lady, except that you are still beautiful."

"Liar!" screamed Nuhara. Enraged, she lashed out with one well-formed foot and sent the bowl of precious dye spinning across the room.

Allomander, splattered with the dye, stood trembl-

ing by the chaise. She was afraid to speak and afraid
not to speak.

By concerted effort, Nuhara calmed down. She
remained quiet for a long time, then she carefully
removed from her neck a single strand of beaten gold,
so fine it seemed to be made of tiny golden raindrops.
She dangled it in front of the young woman. "If you
tell me the truth, it shall grace your neck," Nuhara
whispered.

Allomander, wide-eyed, her face stained red, gulped
and straightened. Possession of such an expensive and
beautiful ornament was beyond her wildest dreams.
"The people say, my lady, that you never really
mourned Theon when he was lost at sea. They say that
the only man you ever loved was your father, Khalkeus
of Gournia. And they say that you are destroying
Home."

Nuhara dropped the necklace onto the floor. After
the young woman grabbed it up and ran from the room,
Nuhara clapped her hands. Within seconds a eunuch
named Strabo appeared, bowing.

"Clear this mess up," Nuhara ordered, pointing to
the spilled dye, "and then bring in someone who can
finish my toes properly."

Strabo, a huge man wearing a sailor's vest and a
scarf around his thick neck, bowed and trotted off to
do his mistress's bidding.

Nuhara sank back into the chaise. *What fools they
all are*, she thought. *They think I am the worm destroying the golden apple. What would they think if they
knew that the worm is a god, and my drunken father
is the priest of that god?* She closed her eyes and,
frightened for a moment, wrapped the robe tighter.
It was, she knew, a very treacherous game she was
playing.

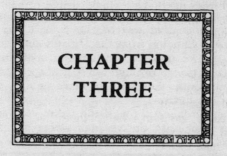

CHAPTER THREE

City of Ur/Kingdom of Babylon

The moonlight filtered through the veranda, but Luti was still wide awake. She stared at her sleeping lover. What was his name? Umm, Sostre. Yes, Sostre— a good name, a sturdy name.

His naked body was beautifully muscled. She had selected him from among the workers in her fields. The fields were similar to those owned by the priests of the goddess Astarte, where she herself had worked as a young woman before achieving the wealth and status befitting a heroine.

Luti blew softly on her lover's neck. He twitched slightly but did not awaken. She laughed quietly to herself. She would enjoy Sostre's lovemaking a few more times; then she would give him some coins and send him back to the fields. That way everyone would be happy, especially herself. Taking a succession of lovers was more appealing than dealing with the boredom and servitude of marriage. Many men had tried to marry her, and why not? She was one of the wealthiest people in southern Babylon. Her mentor had been the late, great Drak, a scientist and philosopher, astrologer and mathematician, of the first order. Drak had known many profound secrets. And she, Luti, was praised in song and story as the woman who had single-handedly stolen the innovative war chariot from Canaan. The vehicle saved Babylon from the Hittites and the Assyrians; the chariot had cut through the invaders' forces like a sharp sword through aged goat's cheese. Yes, many men wanted her hand in marriage . . . and the control of her fortune.

A sound echoed through the hallways of her villa and wafted out onto the veranda where she and her lover lay. Luti tensed. Was her son awake? She listened carefully. No, it was just the wind. Named after her mentor, her son, Drak, was ten years old and the focus of her life.

"Luti . . ." Sostre was awake. He whispered her name five more times as if it were a melody and then buried his lips between her breasts.

"Do you really want to make love again?" she asked, laughing.

"Why not?" he replied. He sat up to caress her head and face. "You are very lovely," he whispered.

"Thank you."

"Even that strange mark—that lion's paw—on your buttocks is beautiful."

She smiled but did not respond.

He drew her close and nibbled her earlobe. "Why are you sending me back to the fields so soon? Have I not pleased you?"

"Of course you have pleased me—far beyond my expectations. But I must make a long journey."

"May I ask where you are going?"

"To the Anatolian Steppes, far north of here."

"Why?"

"Look at me, Sostre: my black hair, my copper coloring, my high cheekbones, and the strange slant of my eyes. I am not a Babylonian. My mother was a nomad from the steppes. That I was told by my mentor,

Drak, many years ago. He also explained how I may have come by certain powers I possess. But there is much more I must find out. I am going north in an effort to recover my heritage. I have been planning for years to find out exactly who I am—for my boy's sake if not for my own."

"Then," Sostre noted sadly, "you may be away from Ur for a long time."

"Yes, but I will call for you again when I return."

Passionately, roughly, he pulled her close and kissed her eyes and mouth and breasts and stomach. His hands and lips were feverish with desire. She rose to meet him, and her body pressed against his. She clawed his back as he entered her, and the first waves of love seemed to lift her up and up and then down in a dizzying spiral of joy. . . .

"There are only two hours until dawn, Sostre. You must go now," Luti urged gently.

The young man kissed her and left without another word. After he had gone, Luti carefully rearranged the cushions and tried to sleep. But it was futile. From where she lay she could hear the water softly lapping against the marsh grass on the east bank of the great Euphrates River. The sound brought back a flood of memories . . . after working in the flax fields she used to wander aimlessly by the river . . . she would wait for hours in the marshes to catch sight of the migrating geese and swans in spring and fall . . . she became aware of the mystery and power of the birds—their magical ability to predict the future and transform the past.

At last she realized that no matter how she tossed and turned, no matter how many times she rearranged the cushions, sleep would not come. Resigned, Luti slipped on a tunic and left her villa, taking the narrow path that led down to the marshes. It was dark, but the remaining moonlight mingled with the tiny finger of nascent sunlight beginning to appear in the distance. A warm, silken breeze played across her face.

Reaching the water's edge, she pushed aside the

marsh grass and placed one foot in the water. It was cold. She moved back to the bank and lay down in the stillness.

Suddenly, a shadow seemed to block the moonlight. Luti sat up, erect and alert, her heart pounding.

A magnificent blue heron materialized on the water's edge. It placed its stately foot exactly where she had placed hers.

Even in the near darkness, the color and form of the bird took her breath away: the long undulating neck, the delicate but powerful torso, the long and slender legs so perfectly formed that they seemed to have been sculpted by a god or goddess. Luti felt an enormous surge of love for the heron. Her mentor, Drak, used to tell her: "Wisdom cannot endure without beauty."

She closed her eyes. A pulse began to drum in her temple . . . a hypnotic beat. Her link with the blue heron felt so strong, it crossed all barriers of time and space and specie. It was as if the exact spot in the water where they had each placed a foot was actually a whirlpool through which all men and beasts must travel in order to experience enlightenment and oneness with the universe.

Then Luti's body went unexpectedly rigid. Cold sweat broke out on her forehead. The heron was in mortal danger—she could sense it. Its beauty was about to be destroyed. She stood quickly and silently, in a trancelike state. The blue heron was motionless, one foot raised out of the water.

Without thinking, Luti picked up a small, smooth stone from the bank, and gathering her body into a whiplike spring, with an enormous burst of strength she effortlessly flung the rock into the water. An instant later, a huge predatory eel, which had been stalking the blue heron from beneath the water, shot to the surface and fell dead upon the embankment, its grotesque head smashed by Luti's unerring missile.

With a slow, heavy beating of its massive wings, the heron flew off, and Luti started back to the villa. It was growing light. She wanted to bathe and see her son, and she was thirsty from her night of lovemaking.

She meant to walk quickly on the narrow path; but the more she pushed herself, the more she seemed to slow down. Then, trembling and drenched with sweat, she stopped completely. She knew for a certainty that someone else was in grave danger, just as the blue heron had been. Someone else was about to be destroyed by a predator. The vision of a face exploded in her skull: *Micah! Micah!*

The vision stole her strength. She wanted to fall down and crawl away. For ten years she had kept that handsome, intense visage locked away in the depths of her memory. She had tried to wipe out all recollections of her lover, the man who had fathered her child in a few desperate moments of stolen passion on the floor of a damp cave in the Judean desert. But now the dam had broken. All the memories were flooding back: their chance meeting, the danger, the disclosure of the identical birthmarks that marked them both, and finally, her betrayal of Micah in order to obtain the war chariot for Babylon.

She realized that her love for him had never wavered, no matter how long and how hard she had tried to repress it. And she knew that Micah was in mortal danger somewhere in Canaan.

The vision of his face remained so real to her that she reached out to caress it and found only the morning air slipping through her fingers.

"Be strong, my beloved," she whispered in the dawn, "for I will save you as I saved my blue heron. Wait for me wherever you are, for I am coming."

CHAPTER FOUR

Tyre/Lebanon

Nimshi stared at the unrolled calfskin scroll on his desk. It contained a message from the island Home, written in the usual picture code. Deciphered, it read: "Cancel all orders for wheat. Break all leases for warehouses in Tyre."

He crushed the skin angrily, picked up his crutches, and hobbled to the window. He was naked; he never dressed until he had to, because any kind of fabric irritated the inflamed stump where his left leg had been amputated years before.

Nimshi flung the shutters open and stared out across the harbor. Seconds later, as the pain in his stump began to rack his thin body, he had to grasp the sill to keep from crying out. He cursed the morning. It would be hours before the Safe Haven Tavern opened . . . hours before he could find the dancing girl Cotto and obtain some black-market *shepenn*. Only that blessed opium derivative could ease his pain, and only strong wine could lift his despair.

After he had cursed the morning and his stump, he vilified his brother, Micah—the cause of all his misery. Nimshi had not seen Micah in ten years, not since they had returned from Gaza after their romantic but disastrous quest to find a new life.

Both were Children of the Lion, members of the famous clan of armorers, so it had seemed to Nimshi that a bright future lay ahead. In fact, Nimshi had given up a fine position as Theon's Tyre representative for the clan's shipping empire in order to start a new life with Micah. But Micah had destroyed the dream of a fresh start in the south. His unpredictable outbursts of murderous violence prevented them from plying the age-old metalworking arts of the Children of the Lion. Without provocation Micah had instigated the fight that had resulted in Nimshi's leg wound. And because of Micah's lawlessness, the brothers had been unable to seek immediate medical attention. Blood poisoning radiated from the wound. Eventually the leg had been amputated, so as to save Nimshi's life.

Where was his bloodthirsty brother now? Nimshi wondered bitterly. Dead, probably—and good riddance.

Beads of sweat stood out on Nimshi's brow as he stared out at the harbor again. Work gangs, supervised by the Phoenicians in their long white gowns and manicured beards, were beginning to unload the ships. These Phoenicians, Nimshi decided, were a mysterious lot. Of all the Sea Peoples, newcomers from the lands surrounding the Great Sea and beyond, the Phoenicians were now the most influential. Their power on the coast kept growing, but Nimshi knew little about them except that they were smart and ruthless. He knew they pursued their pleasures—sexual and otherwise—as enthusiastically as they chased their profits. But did they really come from the north, from the land of the Hittites, as people reported? How had they developed their simple but ingenious alphabet system, which gave them an enormous advantage over all their competitors? With this alphabet they could quickly convey a great deal of important information on a single piece of papyrus.

Another wave of pain suddenly engulfed Nimshi,

and he was forced to leave the window and hobble to a small stool. He lowered himself carefully, then started to plan how to carry out the instructions he had received from Home: cancel all orders for wheat and break all warehouse leases. As a Child of the Lion and the family's commercial representative in Tyre, Nimshi had the option to question the orders if he thought them counterproductive. But what would be the point? Khalkeus and his advisers, who ran the enterprise from Home, would not listen to him. They never did. For years every move they made was ill conceived. They were turning the world's most powerful shipping cartel into a joke. And the Phoenicians were laughing as they picked up the pieces in their fast, skillfully designed, and well-manned ships.

The situation had deteriorated so drastically during the past year that Nimshi's commissions had been cut in half, forcing him to run up huge debts with the Phoenician moneylenders. Strong drugs and potent wine cost money—big money.

In disgust, Nimshi dragged himself back to bed, where he tossed and turned until the sun was directly overhead. Then he dressed slowly and left his rooms to execute the orders he had received from Home.

At four in the afternoon Nimshi entered the Safe Haven Tavern and pushed through the curtains that led to the private cubicles. His crutches thumped across the floor as he entered his customary room, sat down on the edge of the bed, and waited for Cotto. There was nothing in the small space except the bed, a small wooden table, an oil lamp, a pitcher of water, a chamberpot, and a very worn jackass skin.

Nimshi leaned forward and rested his head on the crossbar of the crutches. He closed his eyes and drifted off in a half sleep.

"Does it hurt bad, Nimshi?"

The breathy voice startled him, and he looked up, wide-eyed, to see Cotto standing in the doorway. She was wearing her dancing costume, even though her performance did not begin until late in the evening.

Her delicate sandals had tiny bells fastened to leather straps. Her diaphanous tunic shifted slightly as she breathed, first exposing her lovely breasts and then concealing them. Her nipples had been stained red, to appear even more appealing to the tavern's patrons. A silk ribbon held her long black hair, and black and red daubs of color accentuated the flawless white skin of her face. Her beauty made Nimshi feel more despairing than ever. "Come," he pleaded, "sit by me."

"Soon," Cotto agreed, "but first we have to ease your pain."

The young woman vanished for a few minutes, and when she returned she was carrying several bowls, utensils, and a bladder of wine.

He watched as she prepared the *shepenn*. First she crushed the tiny, dried, brittle leaves and stems, added water, then blended in various herbs. She heated the mixture over the oil lamp's flame. When the consistency was correct, she added a pinch of salt to cut the bitterness and brought the small bowl to Nimshi. He swallowed the contents in one greedy gulp. Then Cotto handed him a bowl of strong wine, which he drank almost as quickly.

Nimshi lay back on the bed, wheezing and coughing. He closed his tearing eyes and waited for the drug to take effect. Cotto sat on the bed beside him and ever so gently stroked his forehead. "There, Nimshi, soon all the pain will be gone. Soon all will be well. Would you like to sleep now, or would you rather tell me about your day?"

Nimshi took her soft, elegant hand between his bony, clawlike ones and weakly told her about the letter from Home and the instructions contained therein. He realized that she would relay the information to her employer, the Phoenician Navan; but he did not give a damn. Nimshi felt little loyalty to Khalkeus, and it was Cotto who obtained the *shepenn* for him. It was Cotto who had talked the Phoenicians into lending him money. Cotto, in fact, was the only person who understood his suffering and tried to alleviate it, at least for short but blessed periods of time.

The dancing girl slipped her arm behind Nimshi's head and helped him to sit up. Her tunic parted, and he placed his feverish head against her naked breast. Before he slept, he whispered to her: "We are all great metalworkers, artists. We Children of the Lion are magicians who work with fire and iron and gold. One day, dearest Cotto, I shall make a gold brooch for you, so beautiful and so exquisite that . . ." His voice trailed off.

Cotto slowly and carefully lowered his head and shoulders to the pillow. She stood up and stared down at him. She felt only pity and loathing.

It was dark when Nimshi awoke. His mouth was bone-dry and had a sour taste that always followed his drug use. But his pain was gone. Cotto had left two bowls of watered wine by the bed. He drank them both, relieved himself, grabbed his crutches, then went shakily into the main part of the tavern.

Cotto had just finished her act, and the rowdy, drunken sailors were flinging coins onto the stage to show their appreciation. Seeing the men with their brawny, whole bodies and sunburned faces with handsome, reckless grins made Nimshi feel bitter and inferior. He fought his way to the bar by flailing out with his crutches and ordered another bowl of wine. Cotto would not be able to obtain drugs for him for two days, so he would have to get drunk and stay that way to make sure that his pain would be bearable.

Around him were lusty seafaring men who had come from afar, lured to the booming port of Tyre by reports of high wages on the brand-new Phoenician ships that plied the Great Sea routes. Nimshi drank steadily, trying to ignore the foreigners' stories and conversations. He was heartily sick of sailors.

Finally, when the din was too great and his eardrums ached, he struggled through the press of bodies to the end of the bar. Nearer to the door, this area had the fewest drinkers.

He had almost achieved his goal when one of his crutches slipped on the wine-drenched boards beneath him, and he fell hard against a group of Cypriot seamen. Enraged, the sailors flung him toward the center of the room.

Luckily, two strong hands caught Nimshi before he crashed to the floor and gently helped him stand and balance. The same capable hands then restored his crutches to him.

Nimshi found himself staring into the eyes of a powerfully built middle-aged man wearing a merchant-captain's insignia on the front of his open blouse.

"Do you want me to get you a space at the bar?" the stranger asked.

Nimshi could not answer. His hands trembled, and the blood drained from his face and neck as he stared aghast at the stranger's face.

"What the matter, friend? Are you ill?" the stranger asked.

Nimshi reached out to touch the man, then drew his hand back quickly, as if the flesh had been burned. "Is it you? Is it really you?" Nimshi croaked in a terrified voice.

"My name is Zeno," the captain said, confused.

"Your name is Theon!" Nimshi screamed. "You have returned from the dead to judge me and all your kinsmen. You have risen from your watery grave to—"

Nimshi did not finish the sentence. He flung himself out the tavern door as if he were being pursued by demons. In his haste he lost his balance and pitched headfirst to the ground.

Cotto, having heard the commotion, ran out into the street and tried to calm Nimshi, who was gasping for breath.

The stranger was at her heels. After kneeling beside the dancing girl, he explained, "I think this fellow has had too much to drink. He called me the ghost of a dead kinsman—someone named Theon. Believe me, I never saw your friend in my life. I am certainly not related to him."

The whites of Nimshi's eyes could be seen clearly as he frantically tried to drag himself away from the stranger.

Cotto stopped Nimshi and held him tightly as the stranger turned and walked back into the tavern.

"Cotto! It is him! It is Theon!" he said, gasping.

Cotto shook her head. "Relax, Nimshi. He's gone back inside now. Besides, I am growing very tired, and I have another show to do soon. Get control of yourself! If this is what the *shepenn* does to you, I may be forced to cut off your supply."

CHAPTER FIVE

Camp of the Harishaf Chariot Brigade
Red Sea, Egypt

The entire brigade—one hundred twenty chariots and two hundred forty men—was lined up on the low, rocky plain that fronted the Red Sea from the Egyptian shore. Each vehicle was manned by a driver and a warrior. The handpicked brigade was geared to speed and killing power. They were nicknamed "the locusts of death" by their enemies.

The charioteer stood deep inside the platform over the two-horse team, while the fighter stood at the rear, by the chariot step. Both men in each vehicle carried several stabbing spears with broad ivory heads. In addition, the warrior carried bow and arrows. The arrows' heads were painted red, identifying the bolts as belonging to this elite brigade. The fighters also carried a short-haft battle ax made of stone and iron and several bone daggers.

31

At the front of the formation, facing his chariots, was Brigade Commander Ma-Set. His lean, sunburned body stood erect on the chariot step. Two ugly scars made by thrusting spears during the last Libyan campaign, were visible over his right breast. He carried no shield and wore no body armor.

When Ma-Set determined that the chariots were properly in line, he held one fist high over his head. Immediately, the lead vehicle in each of the twelve rows of the formation unfurled the brigade banners— enormous red flags bearing the white and black symbols of the sacred ram.

Once the banners were flapping and snapping sharply in the wind, Ma-Set's charioteer turned his horses. Now the brigade commander was no longer facing his troops but was looking west. Ma-Set stared grimly ahead, searching the horizon. He was ill at ease, uncomfortable, confused. He was a field commander of the best chariot brigade in the Egyptian army, and he could not understand why Ramses III, pharaoh of all Egypt, divine successor to Horus and Seth, keeper of the keys to all the worlds beyond, was about to visit the base camp.

"Look there, sir! Southwest!" his charioteer called out.

Ma-Set turned and saw the cloud of dust grow in size. He nervously adjusted his leather helmet, making certain it was straight. He squinted at the royal spectacle: First came the pharaoh's bodyguards—Nubians on horseback, carrying their nine-foot-long spears upright in their stirrups. The spearheads gleamed in the blazing sunlight. And then came what seemed to be a great black tent on rollers, drawn across the ground by twenty-four matched black horses. Over the rolling tent flew the falcon pennant, signifying the presence of the cosmic god Horus.

Closer and closer they came. The immense dust cloud swirled higher, and the noise of the pounding horses' hooves sounded like rolling thunder.

When Ma-Set could make out the face of the lead Nubian, he raised his fist and pumped it twice in the air. His brigade raised its banners high and shouted its victory cry in honor of the pharaoh.

At last the massive black tent ceased rolling. Ma-Set could see that it was made of the most exquisite rubbed linen, the same cloth used for royal shrouds. The Nubian guard opened a path, and Ma-Set's chariot moved through. When his vehicle reached the front wooden rollers on which the tent was transported, the charioteer pulled the horses up sharply, and Ma-Set leaped lightly to the ground. He prostrated himself in front of the tent.

An imposing man emerged. A large gold medallion hung around his neck. A single dagger was stuck through his waistband. It was General Shakko, commander-in-chief of all Egyptian forces. When he held the tent flap open, Ma-Set raised himself from the ground and saluted. Beyond the general, Ma-Set could see the divine presence seated within the tent. The pharaoh stared straight ahead with benign dignity. His fine hands held a bejeweled drinking cup. His head was covered with resplendent scarves, which were gently sprinkled with water by his eunuchs to dispel the heat. Before Ma-Set could decide whether to go into the tent or drop prostrate on the ground, Shakko let the tent flap close.

"His Majesty," said the general, "is indisposed from the heat. But hear this message."

Ma-Set bowed.

"The empire is under attack. Those cursed barbarians, the Sea Peoples, are despoiling our coastline. Crete and Mycenae, our allies to the north, have been destroyed. And our enemies on the great plain between the Tigris and the Euphrates rivers are now supplying weapons to the violent sun-god sects on the Upper Nile who have sworn to overthrow our state."

The general paused and stared out over the brigade formations; his practiced eye evaluating, even from a distance, their morale, their equipment, their horses.

"I am fully aware, sir, of the dangers besetting us," Ma-Set promised him.

Shakko, ignoring this assurance, continued. "And most troubling to our pharaoh is a lunatic bandit called Blood. He and his men ravage all of south Canaan, destroying our caravans on Egypt's most important trading route. As a result, food, spices, ore, lumber, and many more necessary commodities are in dangerously short supply. His Majesty is so concerned over this development that he has traveled here at great discomfort to present you with his orders."

Ma-Set bowed again.

Shakko drew himself up, grasped the hilt of his dagger, and spoke loudly in the voice of officialdom. "Listen to the orders of Ramses the Third, beloved king and beloved god, pharaoh of Upper and Lower Egypt, wisest of the wise. You, Ma-Set, are to take the Hari-shaf Brigade across the Sinai into Canaan. With all possible speed, you are to hunt down and destroy the bandit called Blood and all his followers and beasts and possessions. Leave no one alive!"

General Shakko unexpectedly placed his hand on Ma-Set's shoulder. His voice became warm, fatherly. "Go quickly, my friend. The stakes are large. You must not fail in your mission. Be as ruthless as necessary to destroy Blood and his band."

"It will be done," Ma-Set replied confidently.

The general stared at him in silence for a long time, as if trying to measure his resolve. Then Shakko quickly turned, opened the tent flap, and vanished within.

Ma-Set walked back to his chariot, which moved back through the Nubian phalanx, toward the waiting brigade.

CHAPTER SIX

City of Ur/Kingdom of Babylon

Luti gazed down at her sleeping son. She had had a very beautiful and very expensive bed made specially for him, but this unique child chose to sleep on cushions on the floor, near the window. And she had bought him many expensive toys, but Drak still preferred the simple wooden playthings that Ossaf, the Hittite servant, had carved for him.

Although Drak was ten years old, he still slept with his favorite toy, a camel. It had had wheels on the legs and a rope through its nose so when Drak was younger, he could pull it behind him around the room. When it became his sleeping companion, the toy's rope and wheels had been removed.

She smiled at the sight of the ten-year-old boy fast asleep, one arm draped around the camel. He was such a handsome child! He had inherited her high cheekbones, but otherwise he favored his father. His hair was so black it had blue highlights, and a long, impossible-to-comb forelock kept falling into his wide-set eyes.

Drak was short for his age, but he was sturdily built. Because of Micah's height, Luti was confident that the boy would also be tall someday. And he was a very intelligent child, precocious in thought and behavior. But, like all boys of his age, he was, at times, alternately shy or boisterous.

Luti realized that she would be very content to stand there for hours and watch him. He stirred and muttered in his sleep, flung his other arm out, and turned. Luti caught a glimpse of her son's birthmark, the red-wine-colored lion's paw on the background of white skin.

As Luti watched her son dream, the tears began to roll down her cheeks. She remembered what Drak had done once. She had come upon him as he awkwardly attempted to scrub away the birthmark with soap and water. He had told her that he did not like to walk around "dirty" all the time, with strange blotches on his body.

She remembered that as a child she, too, had tried to wash off the mark from her own back—but that was before she had learned of the honor with which the paw print was held by those more worldly than she. Now she recalled the exact words she had said to her boy that day: "The mark on your body, Drak, cannot be washed away. It was formed while you were in my body and will be with you until the day you die. Nor is it dirty, Drak. It is a mark of great renown. It is a mark that sets you apart from other people. One day you will realize how very precious it is. One day you will be called upon to earn it."

He had not really understood a word she had said, but he had left the lion's-paw birthmark alone after that.

Luti tiptoed closer to his sleeping form. The moonlight slanted through the window, painting the room with calm and elegant beauty. She hesitated to wake Drak, but she had to. She had to tell him that she was going away for a while—but not to the north as originally planned.

She sat down on a cushion, leaned over, and lightly kissed his forehead. He stirred but did not wake. Smiling, she slid his toy camel from under his hand, and this woke him immediately.

The child sat up and rubbed his eyes. "Mommy?"

"Yes, dear. Were you dreaming, darling?" she asked him.

Still groggy, he shook his head. "I can't remember."

"I am going to have to leave you for a little while," she whispered.

His lower lip protruded in a pout. "You told me you might take me with you to the north . . . to see the people who ride on ponies. The men are like turtles, you said . . . they carry their houses on their backs. I want to see the turtles."

Turtles? She laughed and kissed him. His imagery was wonderful. "Not turtles, Drak, nomads. And they carry their tents wherever they go. But I have changed my mind. I am not going north. I am going south, to a land called Canaan. And it may be dangerous there for children. You must stay here.

"You watch my house for me. Ossaf will stay here to take care of you."

He retrieved his toy camel and hugged it. "If it is dangerous, then why are you going? I don't want you to go." His voice sounded tight, constricted.

She realized she had made a mistake telling the child that her journey was dangerous. Above all, she did not want him to worry.

"Well, Drak, it won't be dangerous for adults. And it's a long, long trip. You wouldn't enjoy it."

"Why are you going?" he demanded. "I don't want you to leave me."

"I am going to Canaan to find your father."

The child's eyes grew wide. "But you told me that my daddy was dead."

"Yes, I told you that, and I believed it at the time. Now I know I was mistaken—at least I think I was mistaken. I think he is alive and in need of my help. I am going to find him."

"Will you bring him back?" Drak asked.

"Yes," she replied.

"And we will all be together?" he asked.

"Yes."

"Will he like me?"

"Very, very much!"

"Will you still love me when he comes to live with us?"

"Of course, darling. You'll have twice as much love, with a mommy and a daddy."

His excitement was suddenly tempered. "But why was he not with us?"

"It is a long story, Drak. I will tell you when I bring him back."

"But if you don't come back, then I won't have a mommy or a daddy."

She pulled the child to her and kissed him. "Oh, I will be back, I assure you. I will never leave you for good, I promise!"

Her sudden explosion of intense emotion frightened the child. He pulled away from her, drew his knees up to his chin, and stared out the window.

"You must be a good boy when I am gone," she said. "Promise me you won't go down to the river alone."

"I promise."

"And that you will listen to Ossaf."

The little boy shouted back angrily, "He makes me bathe every day."

"Well then, bathe! And don't give your tutor any trouble."

"He's stupid," the boy retorted. "All he does is talk about numbers and stars and all kinds of stupid things."

"You will appreciate him one day," she replied. "He's one of the wisest men in Ur."

"But I don't care about the stars!" He leaped to his feet, retrieved a small wooden sword from among his toys, and sliced at imaginary demons. Then he asked, "Does my daddy have a sword?"

"Probably."

"Is he a great warrior?"

"I don't know, Drak. Let me find him first."

Then the child walked over to her and took her hand so gently that Luti began to weep. "I will be a good boy when you are gone," he promised.

"I know you will," she whispered, burying her face in his hair.

"And," he said suddenly, with great excitement, "I will give you my sword to take on your journey."

All she could do in response to his great gift was to hold him more tightly. She looked past him and saw that Ossaf was standing at the entrance to the room, his face showing concern at the noise that must have awakened him. She smiled wanly and motioned with her hand to the servant that all was well.

CHAPTER SEVEN

Al Mazar Oasis, Jordanian Desert

The night fires in the Bedouin camp had been banked, the camels hobbled. King Zalmunnah sat placidly in front of his tent and listened to the report of his warlords, Oreb and Zeeb. Other Midianites sat cross-legged in a circle around them. Their swords had been removed from their back scabbards and rested across their thighs. Wine was passed around the circle. The strong beverage, made from the fruit of desert succulents and enhanced by fermented camel's milk, was quaffed from ceremonial jugs fashioned out of the skulls of their victims.

Little distinguished Zalmunnah from the other Bedouins in dress or appearance—he alone wore gold earrings in both ears—but since the kingship of the Midianites was earned by feats of arms, not by heredity, Zalmunnah elicited total obedience. He was the fiercest warrior in that fierce tribe. More than three hundred souls had breathed their last at the point of his sword.

"So, our one-eyed Raven," Zalmunnah said to Oreb, "I hear that you played games today with some Israelites. I hear that you have become a lover of music." His words brought appreciative guffaws from the circle.

Oreb, helped by Zeeb, staggered to his feet and stood unsteadily in front of his king. "They were too poor and ugly to kill, my lord, but one of them had a trumpet around his scrawny neck."

"No one is too ugly to kill," Zalmunnah corrected, and for a moment no one knew whether he was joking or not. Then a wicked grin stole over his face.

"So he played for us, my lord," Oreb continued. "That naked, circumsized dog of an Israelite tooted his horn while his scrawny slave danced like a bitch in heat."

Zalmunnah began to laugh so hard that the tears rolled down his face. The other Bedouins in the circle hooted and thumped their palms against the ground in appreciation. The noise filled the desert night.

Then Zeeb shouted, "And the last we saw of them, my lord, their naked rumps were tied to their jackasses, which trotted to the south."

Again the Bedouin circle exploded in laughter.

Zalmunnah held up one hand, and he was rewarded by immediate silence. "This laughter is a good omen, my brothers, for the time has come to take the land we desire and bury all the dogs who now foul it. Hear me! In a short time we will all cross the Jordan—bringing our tents and our women and our livestock. The area of our raids must increase. The ferocity of our raids must increase. We must give the Israelites no rest. We must root them out. Since there is no rain, we shall drench the land with their blood."

An expectant silence settled over the gathering. This was the news for which they had been waiting! They would take the land they needed for their flocks and camels, and they would dip their swords in Israelite blood—again and again. And they would have the sweet Israelite women and children as slaves and the Israelites' hidden jewels for their own purses.

"We must celebrate," Zalmunnah proclaimed, and shouts of assent went up from the circle.

The Midianite king reached into a pouch, made from the cured skin of a slain enemy, at his side and pulled out a handful of the most beautiful golden earrings the Bedouins had ever seen. Zalmunnah held them up so they would sparkle in the light from the embers.

"A contest, my brothers," the king announced. "We shall have a contest, and those who are proven worthy shall win these."

A roar of happiness burst from the gathering.

"Bring the captives!" Zalmunnah ordered.

The circle of Bedouins dispersed. Within minutes, three wooden poles had been driven into the ground. Then three Israelites were dragged from the outer reaches of the encampment. Two were young men. The third was a middle-aged woman. Their hands had been bound behind their backs with leather thongs. Their faces were cut and bruised and their naked bodies covered with the most loathsome sores and welts.

The three unfortunates were quickly bound to the poles. They made no protest; they were too weak and too frightened to cry out. Their eyes were dull with despair. The woman's terror was so great that white flecks of spittle bubbled out from the sides of her mouth. After the Israelites were secured, Bedouin women and children ran up to spit in their faces and cut small chunks of flesh out of their bodies with bone knives.

"Enough!" Zalmunnah shouted. "Begin the contest!"

A long path was cleared. Zeeb was the first competitor in this familiar game. He mounted his white racing camel about one hundred yards from the captives. He gripped the reins in his teeth, drew the great sword from its back scabbard, and held it in one hand. He pressed his other hand, which was deformed, against the hilt for balance. Slowly he began to swing the sword around his head. The weapon flashed. The other Bedouins, now lined up along the path where camel and rider would make their run, cheered him enthusiastically.

Zeeb kicked the camel, sending it hurtling down the path. Faster and faster the beast went, and the warlord pressed his knees against its ribs. The onlookers were silent now; all that could be heard were the pounding feet of the magnificent white camel on the hard desert floor.

Just as beast and rider reached the first pole, Zeeb screamed out the ferocious war cry of the Midianites, and leaning forward in the saddle, he brought the sword down. The pole and the head of the woman captive were severed. A great torrent of blood spurted outward, splattering the closest onlookers.

Zeeb pulled the camel up as quickly as possible, turned it, and trotted back to inspect the carnage. Using the tip of the sword, he coolly picked up the severed head. Nearby, the Israelite men cringed against their poles and averted their eyes.

The Bedouins cheered him, raising their own swords high. The women chanted the piercing cry of victory, punctuated by rapid clicking noises as they moved their tongues against the roofs of their mouths.

Zeeb, meanwhile, guided his camel to where Zalmunnah stood. "A sweet fruit for the king of the Midianites," the warlord said, forcing the camel to its knees. He dismounted to make his tribute.

The king grinned. He grasped the woman's hair with one hand and yanked the head off the sword. With the other hand he retrieved one of the beautiful earrings and presented it to the Jackal.

Zeeb removed one of the bone daggers from his belt and with its sharp point pierced his left ear. Three earrings were already embedded in the flesh; this was the fourth. As he fastened his prize, the Bedouins called out his name for praises and blessed him and his progeny for generations to come.

When Zalmunnah made a swift motion with his hand, Zeeb mounted the camel and trotted off.

"Next contestant," the king called out. "There are earrings left and Israelites alive."

The two remaining captives now struggled desperately against the thongs that held them to the poles. But their efforts proved futile. The next camel and rider moved toward them—and toward the headless body of their sister captive, still fastened to the truncated wood.

CHAPTER EIGHT

Salt Sea, Southern Canaan

The bandit called Blood sat in the moonlight, staring east at the still waters of the Salt Sea. His raiders slept in the ravine behind him. They were exhausted after the long and grueling raid into Philistine Territory. He stared intently at the sky. Dawn was still two or three hours away. He, too, was weary; but he would not sleep this night.

The attack had been a debacle, yielding no gold or precious stones. The bandits found only hides, weapons, grain, and three women to be used for his raiders' pleasure and then ransomed.

Blood wore a loincloth made from the skins of hares. His hair was long and matted and hung loose down his back. He wore no sandals because his leathery feet were impervious to the heat and rocks of the Wilderness of Judea, which had been the site of his base camp for years. Six throwing daggers in leather scabbards hung around his powerful neck, and a thick rope around his waist held two iron battle axes.

A sound interrupted his reveries—someone or something had dislodged a pebble on the path behind him. His whole body tensed, and one hand circled the haft of a battle ax. Then he relaxed. He saw that it was the old Greek Anistos, his second-in-command, who had been with him almost from the beginning. The old Greek still wore the long robe of the mainland. He carried no blades, only a thick ash bow and an enormous quiver of bronze-tipped arrows.

"The moon will be full for one more night," the Greek remarked, squatting on the ground next to Blood. His limbs were remarkably resilient despite his age.

Anistos was invaluable. He was able to speak the language of practically everyone in the band—Turks and Bedouins and Greeks and Israelites and Egyptians . . . men drawn to Blood because he promised booty and because they were outlaws, wanted men, the scum of the earth.

Anistos was the glue that bound the band together, but it was fear of Blood that kept the raiders in line. They all knew that his real name was Micah. He was the famous Canaanite mercenary who had assassinated Eglon of Moab for the Israelites. After that feat of daring Micah had been spurned by the Israelites because he had abandoned their cause before the final battles against Hazor. Instead he had gone off on an ill-fated journey with his brother. Once those wars were over and Micah had returned to his adopted people, the Israelites had shunned him, having no use for a hired killer.

Yes, Blood's raiders knew all the stories about their vicious captain, and on raids they witnessed his passion for killing, his willingness to take any risks, his imperviousness to wounds and heat and thirst and exhaustion. To them, he was no longer human. He was a killing machine whose throwing knives and battle axes would make them wealthy one day.

"We will not raid again toward the coast," Blood said to the Greek. "We will return to the Egyptian caravan routes to the south."

"When?"

"In two days' time. Let the men rest." Blood stared down at the sleeping raiders, then asked, "How many casualties?"

"Two dead and ten wounded," Anistos answered.

The two men remained silent for a long time. At last Anistos said quietly, "One of the women captives is very beautiful."

"Good," replied Blood. "The men will enjoy her, and she will fetch more as ransom."

"I was thinking of saving her for you," Anistos explained.

Blood grinned. "I don't want a woman."

The old man looked sadly at his commander. "Sometimes a woman will help."

"My father is dead, old man," Blood snapped. "Are you trying to become my father?"

Anistos squirmed. "No, not your father. Maybe a friend."

"I have no friends."

"Then a loyal underling. No one, not even you, can live such a harsh existence without occasionally letting in one gleam of tenderness, of joy—even of love."

Blood spat on the ground. He pulled one of the sharpened battle axes from his belt and ran his thumb along the blade so that his blood spurted out.

The Greek turned his face away from the self-mutilation.

"Listen, old man," Blood said harshly. "I want none of what you offer. If you want to be a philosopher, go back to Greece. If you want to raid with me, learn to sheathe your tongue."

Without a word the old man stood up and wearily started to walk back down the path to where the other raiders slept.

"Anistos," Blood called out.

The old man stopped but did not turn around.

"You are a good fellow, but I am years beyond aid. My name is Death. My fate is violence. My love is the blade. My future is . . ."

When Blood did not finish his thought, the old man started down the path again.

After the Greek had vanished, Blood stood and

began to pace along the rocks. The stupid old fellow had irritated him. What did Anistos know, anyway? Blood stood still, erect, and let a slight breeze play about his face. His anger at the old man ebbed, and in its place came a memory so sweet and powerful that his limbs grew weak. He remembered that night of passion so many years before with Luti, the beautiful Babylonian girl. With her he had known tenderness, joy, and love. He remembered the silkiness of her flesh and the powerful intimacy as they had held each other. He remembered the softness of her voice and how her body had opened to him. From time to time over the years he had thought of her, but never had he experienced such a sudden rush of explicit memory. It was as though embers were being flung at him from the past.

Then, as quickly as the memories had engulfed him, they vanished. He squatted once again on the ground and pressed his still-bleeding thumb against a flat rock, to stanch the flow. He pivoted so that he was looking south and began to plan the route his raiders would take to hit the Egyptian caravan routes again.

CHAPTER NINE

West Bank, Jordan River

The Israelites—five men, three women, and two adolescents—walked slowly, searching for brush or driftwood that had been deposited by the river on the bank. Leather slings crossed their backs, in which to carry the wood home for fuel. Fatigue etched their faces and slowed their muttered curses at the barrenness of the land, for they had been on this particular search since dawn, and their leather slings were for the most part empty.

At noon they rested and shared a few pitiful dried fruits and a meager supply of barley, which had been softened in the river water.

"If this drought continues and more trees and bushes die, we shall have to revert to the ways of the Bedouins—using the dried dung of our flocks to heat our fires." The old man who spoke these words was named Abram. His body was bent almost double from decades of hard work.

49

"We don't have our flocks anymore," Dahlia reminded bitterly.

"As long as the land is sick, we shall be sick. It is a sign," Abram predicted.

The other Israelites laughed and hooted at the old man's attempt at prophecy.

"The next thing you will do," said a sturdy middle-aged man named Emmas, "is turn a staff into a serpent. Can you do that, old man? For all we know you're Moses and Aaron brought back to life and rolled into one brilliant scholar."

"Don't mock him," Dahlia said angrily, and Emmas shut up, making an ugly gesture with his hand signifying that the old man was no longer in possession of his faculties.

"Crazy, am I?" the old man shouted, taking a stick and heading toward the younger man.

His progress was interrupted by Dahlia's scream— a scream of such terror that it paralyzed the others.

Around them, on all sides, from all directions, was a circle of horror—Midianite Bedouins, seated on their camels. They had emerged so suddenly and surrounded the small group so completely, it seemed to the Israelites they were dealing with a force of nature—like a wind or a storm or a flood. The warriors' swords, unsheathed in the burning sun, caught the light on their blades and flung it toward the Israelites.

"Run! Run!" Dahlia screamed.

The Israelites dropped their leather slings and scattered. Their eyes were wide with fear as their bodies strained for speed. But it was too late to run. The circle was closed.

"Look there, sir, by the river," Purah called out to his master, who, like himself, was leading his donkey in the heat of the afternoon.

Gideon stopped and stared up at the circling buzzards and vultures. Both men had the same thought: Where there were corpses, there may be food, no matter how spoiled. Both men had spent the better part of two days searching for any kind of edibles to bring back home; but all they had found were some roots and about two buckets of green berries. Gideon's entire family—father, mother, sister, and wife along with their children—were, like other Israelites, in desperate straits. They were depending on Gideon to forage successfully for something, anything to eat.

They started to pull their donkeys at a quicker pace toward the river's edge. As they approached, a scene of a massacre became painfully apparent. Blackflies rose in dark swarms. Gideon quickly flung the trumpet around to the back of his neck as if to protect it from the onslaught.

The first body they came to was spread-eagled on the ground. The man's ears, nose, and genitals had been amputated.

"I think I know this one," said Gideon, fighting down the bitter bile at the back of his throat. "I think his name was Emmas."

There was no food by his body, so Gideon and Purah moved to the next mutilated corpse, then on to the next one. But the murderers had picked their victims clean of all possessions, just as the vultures were about to pick them clean of their flesh. The only items left were small, carved-stone Baal idols, which many Israelites carried for luck. These had been left contemptuously where they fell, and the attackers had urinated on some of them.

"Shall I roll them over, sir?" Purah asked, placing his toe tentatively against one of the corpses.

"Why?"

"Maybe there are some dates or some barley cakes under them."

Gideon shook his head sadly. "No. Let's get out of here."

Purah dropped the idea. As the men continued their walk, blackflies hovered around them. The stench was overwhelming, and Gideon wondered if it was permeating his skin, if he would smell the rotting corpses until he himself died.

One corpse was isolated from the others. It was an old man's, and he had been tortured severely. Virtually every part of his body had been charred by torches, and the killers had broken his ankles, obviously for their fiendish enjoyment.

Gideon and Purah stared at this particular corpse for a long time, as if this old man succinctly symbolized the plight of all Israelites.

"Should we bury him, sir, or say a prayer?" Purah asked.

"If we bury him, you fool," Gideon grated, "then we must bury them all. And if we say a prayer over her—" He pointed to Dahlia's corpse and shook his head vigorously, to show it was impossible.

Gideon pulled the trumpet around the front of his neck and grasped it lovingly with one hand. Purah cringed, but his master did not bring the horn to his lips.

"And whom can we pray to, anyway?" Gideon asked. Then his eye settled on something on the bloody ground beside the old man's corpse. He gestured, and they both approached cautiously, as if the pain and terror the old man suffered before he died would somehow be transmitted to them.

"What is it?" Purah asked, squinting down.

"Some kind of sign. The old man made some kind of sign before he died."

"A message?"

"Perhaps."

"Maybe it was the murderers who left the message?" Purah suggested.

"No, Purah. Look closely. It is done with a trembling hand—with a hand in pain."

Ignoring the heat and the flies and the blood and the stench, the men squatted beside the corpse. The old man had scratched out his message with a fingernail on the hard ground.

"I just can't make it out," Gideon admitted.

"It's a name," said Purah. "I've seen it before. But he didn't finish the last letter. That's why it's hard to read."

"The old man's name?" Gideon asked testily, angry that Purah seemed to be able to make sense out of it while he could not.

"The name is Yahweh, sir," replied Purah.

Disgusted, Gideon stood up quickly.

"The old man must have scratched it there while they were torturing him," Purah noted.

"The old fool," Gideon grated. "Get up, Purah. Why are you on the ground like some roach? Why did you bring me here?"

"But, sir—"

"Shut up and get moving!" Gideon yelled at his servant.

He made a sudden movement toward his sword hilt, threatening to draw it and smack the flat edge against Purah's rump. The servant scrambled toward his donkey.

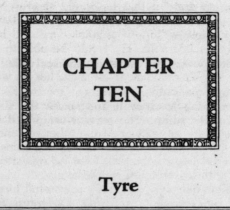

CHAPTER
TEN

Tyre

Even the severe pain in his leg stump could not prevent Nimshi from furiously pacing the floors of his home like a madman, for hour after hour. Everything in his life had gone wrong, that was certain. But he still had his mental integrity. He still knew the difference between reality and fantasy, and the stranger in the Safe Haven Tavern had been Theon! It had been his kinsman, assumed drowned in an abortive attempt to rescue Iri's widow and her son from Troy.

But Cotto had told him that it was probably a trick played by the drugs. Did she mean he was going crazy? Did she mean he could not recognize a close relative, a fellow Child of the Lion?

When Nimshi stumbled and almost fell, he leaned heavily against a wall. He was breathing hard. The ramifications of his discovery were important and could prove lucrative. If Khalkeus could reunite his beloved daughter with her husband, he would be most appreciative. Besides, Theon had been Khalkeus's most trusted emissary. No doubt Theon could turn the family business around and make it profitable once again.

Nimshi closed his eyes. He could imagine Khalkeus being so grateful that he would shower Nimshi with bonuses. He would pay off all his debts. He would obtain an unlimited supply of painkillers, and his life would become bearable. He would be able to afford good clothes and magnificent horses and take Cotto away from her life as a dancer and make her his woman, solely and permanently.

The pacing had made him thirsty. He stared across the room at the table near the window. On it rested two pitchers, one of water and the other of wine. But he could not get over there now; the leg pains were severe. He slid down the wall until he was sitting on the floor, with his crutches beside him.

He knew that only one thing prevented him from becoming the recipient of Khalkeus's largess for his having discovered that Theon was alive: Someone had to confirm that the stranger who called himself Zeno was actually Theon—someone who knew him well.

Nimshi grinned suddenly and leaned his head back against the wall. Of course! He knew someone who could make a positive identification . . . someone who had known Theon intimately—Tirzah, Theon's onetime lover, the woman who had been married to Nimshi's own half brother, Pepi. Tirzah now lived in Ramah, in the hill country of Canaan.

The messenger from Tyre found Tirzah at the simple grave of the prophetess Deborah. He delivered the message from Nimshi orally, then wheeled around his tired, dust-streaked mount and was gone.

Tirzah's legs began to shake so violently that she was forced to sink to the ground. Her weight crushed the flowers she had brought with her to beautify Deborah's grave. It was something she did at least once a week in honor of the woman who had changed her meaningless, loveless life. Deborah had given her the courage to face each day anew and had encouraged her to sell all her considerable commercial holdings and to dedicate herself to the poor people of the hill country, the same people whom Deborah had served.

Tirzah was not an Israelite, but the people had grown to love her and she, them. Now, with the drought, the invasion of the Midianites, and Yahweh's withdrawal of His protection, the Israelites needed her charity more than ever. As an angel of mercy to the hill people, she dispensed food and medicines bought with her own money and gave advice to whoever asked.

But this totally unexpected message had been disorienting. How could it possibly be true? Theon had been drowned at sea ten years before. His body had not been found, but many corpses from his ship's crew had washed up on shore. Supposedly, the ship had gone down with all hands aboard. Tirzah had mourned his loss deeply. Was Nimshi making up this story? Had he gone mad? His reputation, however, held him to be an honest man. . . .

Lying on the ground, trying to recover her strength, she stared at Deborah's grave and wondered what the kindly prophetess would have advised her to do. But memories of Theon began to push away all other thoughts. She and Theon had been commercial allies, then foes; but for a few glorious days they had been lovers. And in all her years as a brothel slave, chained to a bed in Damascus, and in all her years as a loving wife—first to a Canaanite farmer, next to Pepi, then to Ephai—no night of love had ever compared to the sexual excitement that had been shared by Theon and her.

Tirzah closed her eyes and allowed the erotic reminiscences to wash over her. She was still a handsome woman, even though her magnificent blond hair had turned silver. She wore simple tunics, and her broad shoulders stooped just a bit. Her pale, smooth skin was creased and bronzed by the sun. But men still turned to stare with appreciation at this tall, regal woman. They still desired her.

What would the blessed Deborah have suggested she do? Tirzah wondered again. Stay with the hill people and continue to help them when they needed her most? Or travel to Tyre and confirm or deny whether Theon was alive?

She smiled grimly. How odd it was that the two great loves of her life—Pepi and Theon—were both Children of the Lion, the legendary armorers to the Israelites in their glory days, when they could raise mighty armies, and well before, when they were a small band of nomads. And her only friend had been an Israelite woman who had contempt for all weapons unless they were controlled by Yahweh.

"Forgive me," she whispered to the woman in the grave. Then Tirzah stood and rearranged the crushed flowers on it. "I know full well that you would wish for me to stay." Then she blurted out a cry from her heart, "But I must go to Tyre. I must see Theon again if he is indeed alive."

"He is inside now," Nimshi said nervously. He grasped his crutches with such great force that his knuckles were white.

Nimshi and Tirzah were standing in front of the entrance to the Safe Haven Tavern. Night had just fallen, so the bar was not yet spilling its drunken sailors out onto the street.

"What do you know about him?" Tirzah asked.

"Only that he claims to be a ship's captain named Zeno. He is reported to have a wife and three children in one of the coastal cities of the Philistine League, just south of here."

Nimshi looked expectantly at his companion, but Tirzah made no move to enter.

"What are we waiting for?" he asked.

Tirzah did not answer. She was terrified. When she had arrived in Tyre she had been glad she had made the decision to come. But now she was truly frightened and confused. Was she hoping to transform the past? Was she chasing after a happiness that was never to be hers? She felt that she was doing something very dangerous.

Nimshi impatiently thumped one of his crutches

onto the ground. "Are we going or aren't we going?" he demanded.

"We're going," Tirzah replied in a calm voice after the benefit of a deep and steadying breath.

Together, the pain-ridden drug addict and the cool, regal woman entered the tavern. They had not been inside the place for more than a minute when Nimshi poked at her arm. "There! There he is, drinking at the bar."

Tirzah found herself staring at the back of a well-built middle-aged man wearing the blue tunic of a ship's captain and simple sailor's sandals. His thick hair, black and gray, curled down the back of his neck.

"I have to get closer," she whispered to Nimshi. "I have to see him full face."

Tirzah and Nimshi drifted nonchalantly to the bar, to stand alongside the stranger. But he, sensing other people invading his space, turned to face the woman and the man with crutches.

Tirzah cried out as if someone had clubbed her. Her hands flew to her mouth. She was astonished: his widow's peak, the wry smile, the hard eyes, the long aquiline nose, the powerful back . . . all were Theon's. It was Theon! She cried out his name, burst into tears, and flung her arms around the man's neck.

But he shoved her away, staring first at the woman and then at her companion, whom he clearly remembered. "When is this nonsense going to end?" he demanded, exasperated. "First it was him, and now you. Listen: My name is Zeno. I don't know anyone called Theon. I am not Theon. And you are starting to make me very angry."

When Nimshi started to respond, Tirzah turned, grasped him by the arm, and slowly led him out of the bar and onto the street. Once outside, she took a long moment to regain her composure.

Nimshi's dark eyes glistened with excitement, and he nearly hopped around on his crutches. "Well?" he demanded. "Well?"

"Of course it's Theon," she told him. "There can be no doubt."

"Ah ha!" Nimshi hooted an exuberant laugh. "I told you so!"

"It can only be loss of memory," Tirzah went on. "Maybe something cracked his skull during the shipwreck."

"Or he's faking his condition," Nimshi speculated, "and just wanted to assume a new identity for any number of reasons."

"I don't think so. He believes he is Zeno."

"Well, how do we bring him to his senses?"

"Tell me, Nimshi, does the tavern have cubicles in the back for lovemaking?"

"Many, available to all the drinkers if they give the owner a small gratuity for his kindness and don't stay in the room too long."

"Then go back to your house and wait for me. I am going to try a little seduction to jog Theon's memory."

Nimshi's eyes gleamed. The idea appealed to him. Whistling, he hobbled away.

Tirzah reentered the bar and quickly proceeded to the stranger.

"Don't you ever give up?" he asked.

She smiled and moved alongside him. "I want to apologize for bothering you," she said sincerely. "But you do bear an uncanny resemblance to this man we are seeking."

"Why are you looking for him?" he asked.

"Because he is dead," she replied, and the stranger who called himself Zeno burst into laughter.

When his mirth was controlled and he had ordered them both bowls of wine, he said, "I appreciate a woman who makes philosophical jokes." He patted Tirzah on the back gently.

The touch of his hand was like water on thirsty lips. She trembled but remained silent. Finally she said, "In spite of our little misunderstanding, Zeno, I think I can help you."

"Help me?" he asked, then laughed again. "I am in Tyre to find a fast ship with a good cargo in need of a captain. And then I'll need a strong wind. Can you help me with these?"

"No," said Tirzah, "but I can help you get what you really crave—wisdom."

"Are you sure I crave wisdom?" he asked sardonically.

"Quite sure. You have reached a point in your existence where you have to have some meaning in life—some kind of judgment on life and death."

Zeno appeared uncomfortable with the abrupt turn their banter had taken.

Tirzah pressed her advantage. "Can we go somewhere to talk in private?" she asked.

At first he refused, then he equivocated; but finally he stood up and followed her through the curtain at the rear of the bar and into one of the cubicles.

Once inside, he seemed extraordinarily nervous. "Wait a minute. I'm in this town to find work, not romance."

Tirzah did not answer. She kept her eyes downcast. Her hand reached out and touched his arm. He did not pull it away. She found a vein and kept a finger on it, feeling the dull throbbing of his life-force. It had been many years since she had engaged in any mind-control techniques, but just the feel of his pulse beneath her hand reassured her that the power was still hers.

"What do you really want of me?" he asked, his voice almost a whisper.

She did not answer. Instead she moved her fingers up his arm and could feel the blood in his veins and arteries rushing toward her fingers as they slid silently over his flesh.

Then she looked up. Her eyes found his. For a moment he tried to avert his gaze, but she fixed him with a stare and then began to project her strength onto him . . . to break down all his inhibitions . . . to shatter his morality. Her head swam from the strain of the technique. But it had worked, just as she desired.

His hands stripped the plain robes from her body, and he carried her to the small bed. He kissed her breasts and her belly. She could feel the explorations of his lips and teeth and tongue, as if they were flowers sucking up the very honey of her existence. *Theon, Theon, Theon* . . . she kept calling his name.

Then he was deep inside her, with his maleness and all the passion of a decade-old love. His hardness delved deep, deep, deep. Their bodies rose and fell in the age-old rhythm. Their limbs were like entwining vines. Their hearts beat in such close syncopation that they each could feel the other's love as if it had been grafted onto each body.

"Never stop, Theon. Never stop," she whispered in her love and longing.

"Well?" Nimshi asked. "Yes or no?"

"Yes, I seduced him. No, he didn't regain his memory."

"But you're still sure he's Theon."

"Of course he's Theon," Tirzah replied impatiently, "and he has the Child of the Lion birthmark on his rump to prove it."

"There must be a way to reawaken his memory," Nimshi said, then groaned piteously as he covered his stump with a wet cloth filled with medicinal herbs. It was what he was forced to use when he had no money to buy drugs and did not want to get any further in debt. Unfortunately, the application afforded little relief.

"I'm sure there is. But I don't know it." Tirzah was still dazed from the hours of lovemaking. She felt both elated and beaten. She knew she had in some way taken Theon back in time, but in another way he was less accessible than ever.

"If we could get him to Home," Nimshi proposed, "there is a good possibility the sight of the island, his wife, and children would restore his memory."

"But no one except Theon knows where Home is," Tirzah noted.

"I have an idea that may work," Nimshi said, chuckling as if he had thought of something wicked. "We hire Zeno to captain a ship through the Aegean. As the ship approaches one of the trade routes that leads to Home, his sailor's nautical memory will be

activated. He will intuitively remember how to sail to
Home even if he doesn't remember his name." Nimshi
cackled again. "He may, in fact, feel compelled to sail
there, like a migrating bird who flies in the exact same
direction at the exact same altitude at the exact same
time of the year."

Tirzah did not answer. It was, she realized, an
ingenious plan. Thank the gods that Nimshi still had
his wits about him in spite of the drugs and the dancing
girls and the wine. But what if it worked? It was too
cruel: After all these years . . . after having found her
lover again, Theon might choose to stay with Nuhara
and the twins. As suddenly as Tirzah had found him,
she would lose him. Nuhara would sink her claws into
him forever, and once again Tirzah would be alone with
her memories. And what about the wife and children
of Zeno? What would happen to them?

She was about to refuse to participate in the plan.
But then she remembered some advice passed along to
her by Deborah: "Tirzah, if you live only for yourself,
you will never feel alive."

She walked quickly to the window and stared out
at the port, which was just coming alive for a new day.
She was exhausted; she needed sleep. But her path was
now clear. She realized that she must take her chances.
Theon might ultimately choose her over Nuhara. As for
his new wife in the south, Tirzah would deal with her
if and when the time came.

She turned back to Nimshi. His complexion was
grayish from the pain. "Very well. I have some money
deposited in the Phoenician banks here. We'll use it to
hire a ship and our captain."

After Tirzah left to return to the large suite of
rooms she had rented a few blocks away, Nimshi fell
into a deep, wine-induced sleep. When he awoke, the
sun was high. He drank some watered wine, ate a small
piece of flat bread and some lentil stew, and then just
stared out the window at the ships. Many concerns
were bothering him. His plan was a good one, but what
if it did not work? What if Theon's memory was past

repair? And what if the plan did work, but Khalkeus decided not to reward him with anything other than a commendation?

"I have been a fool again," he berated himself. "If a wolf is circling a chicken coop, only a madman would cast his lot with the chickens. And surely Khalkeus is the chicken, Home the coop, and the circling wolf the Phoenicians."

Nimshi leaned thoughtfully on one of his crutches, his cheek on the wood. What, he wondered, would Navan the Phoenician and his friends pay, in hard shekels, for the delivery of the prize they had long sought— control of Home and the entire commercial empire of the Children of the Lion? A mountain of shekels, that was what they would pay. If they believed he could offer Home on a platter, they would open their coffers to him. A shiver went through his body. He would pay Navan the Phoenician a visit soon. But it must be a very secret visit.

CHAPTER ELEVEN

Canaan
Tribal Territory of Manasseh

Gideon saw his father, Joash the Abiezerite, waiting for him by the broken gate that was now fastened pathetically with a tent peg. Behind the old man stood Gideon's scowling wife, Shulamith, and his shy sister, Miriam.

Gideon slowed his pace. He knew what they were waiting for—food—and he had returned with almost nothing.

"They look very hungry, sir, particularly your father. He looks angry, also."

Gideon turned on his donkey and shouted at his servant; "Idiot, I have two eyes! I don't need you to tell me that." But the moment after he had yelled at Purah, Gideon was sorry. Sometimes Purah infuriated him. He knew Purah did not like his trumpet blowing, but Gideon did not really mind that—after all, not everyone could have an appreciation of music and beauty. What really annoyed him about Purah was his servant saying the obvious as if it were a profound discovery.

When Gideon and Purah rode through the gate and dismounted in the dusty courtyard, they set on a blanket what they had obtained in their foraging expedition: a few dates, the green berries, two marsh waterfowl, small amounts of five different grains, and ten wild onions. Then they stepped back, ashamed.

Joash stared at the food in consternation. Then he turned in a fury on his son. "How can this feed ten people? Don't you know that there are ten people you're responsible for, including the workers, who should have moved out a long time ago—and your stupid manservant, who doesn't know how to do anything except ride a donkey's wrong end."

"Think of our children, Gideon," complained his wife.

"I am going to have to sell the last valuable thing we own—the bull in the north pasture." Joash spoke these words as if someone were twisting a dagger in his innards. "We can take it to the market and get half its weight in grain."

Gideon winced with shame and was unable to look at his father.

"I think Gideon is brave and resourceful," Miriam said in a voice that was, for her, very loud. "I think he brought us enough for a good stew because I have found more mushrooms. And I think we should thank him from the bottom of our hearts instead of berating him."

No one said a word because Miriam was much loved. She had made it her business to know the valleys and the woods well, so this shy young woman had been able to find mushrooms that grew even when there had been no rain at all. It was a mystery, for everyone knew that mushrooms only appear after a rain.

Miriam gathered in the hem of her simple cloth robe all the food that Gideon had obtained and ran toward the house. The others followed slowly, silently, their bodies aching.

Only Gideon remained in the courtyard. He called out to his servant. But Purah was already out of earshot. Gideon wearily took off his weapons and laid them on the back of the donkey. He did not want to go into the house. He wanted to be alone for a while and play his trumpet. There was only one place to do that in peace and quiet—the now-abandoned shed, which used to contain a working winepress before the Midianites destroyed the vines.

On his way to the winepress he walked through the sacred grove his father had planted to the god Baal. A stone statue of the deity stood in the center of the grove. Before the drought the statue was almost hidden by the lovely, laden limbs of the surrounding fruit trees. Gideon stopped for a moment in front of the statue, bowed his head reverently, then walked quickly from the grove. It was considered very arrogant to linger there.

Once inside the shed, he leaned against an old wooden vat, removed the trumpet from the cord around his neck, and began to play a very soft and mournful melody. There were words to the tune, but Gideon had long forgotten them. The song told the story of an Israelite sold into slavery as an oarsman on the galleys, his memories of the hill country of Canaan, and his longing for the swift-flowing spring streams.

When Gideon finished, he wetted his lips and started to play another tune.

"Not bad, not bad at all," said a voice from behind him.

Gideon pulled the trumpet away from his mouth and stared at a stranger who had been listening from the shadows.

"Who are you? Step forward!" Gideon demanded.

A man dressed in blacksmith's garb, including leather apron and hat and thick sandals, stepped close to him. The stranger was a short, powerfully built fellow with a bald head and a bulbous nose.

"A little tinny," the stranger continued, "and you left out a few parts."

Gideon's voice was angry now. The man irritated

him. "What's your name? What are you doing here? We don't need a blacksmith. We don't have any livestock left except for one bull that is about to be sold."

"My name is Messenger. It used to be Angel. But that was a long, long time ago. I was the one sent down to tell Abraham that he had to slit his son's throat. You remember Isaac, don't you? It was well before your time, but I suppose you heard of that incident. And I was the one who told Moses that he wouldn't be able to enter the Promised Land of Canaan."

"Stop it!" Gideon shouted. "Talk sense!"

"Yahweh sent me to you, Gideon. I am His messenger."

Gideon stared wide-eyed at the stranger. "Yahweh? A messenger from Yahweh?" Gideon grinned. "But everyone knows, Master Messenger, that Yahweh doesn't live in Canaan anymore. No one knows where He is. He left this land after we destroyed the Hazorite armies, and we haven't seen Him since. All we've seen are drought and Midianites."

The messenger walked closer and condescendingly patted Gideon. "Calm down, young man. If you're going to bow your head before an idol like Baal, Gideon, you'll never see Yahweh around. Don't you remember what He told your people? 'Thou shalt have no other gods before Me.' And you'll never see Him around if you play music on the Sabbath instead of resting and praying. Because He also told you: 'Remember the Sabbath day and keep it holy.' " The stranger shrugged. "Anyway, that's all past now. I wasn't sent here by Yahweh to discuss that with you."

"Then what?" Gideon inquired, totally confused and more than a little frightened.

"First I need some food. Some meat and some barley cakes and a little wine would be nice."

"Food?" Gideon laughed harshly. "There is no food here. My whole family is starving."

The messenger ignored his words. "I'll wait here while you get the food, and then I'll give you the instructions after I've eaten. It has been a very long trip."

Gideon remembered that a small, secret cache of food was kept in the empty well behind the winepress. It had been placed there in a cool spot in case the Midianites raided the farm again and Gideon and his family were forced into a siege. No one was allowed to disturb it.

Now he felt torn. How could he jeopardize the safety of his family by opening the cache? But what if this stranger did have a message from Yahweh, the God of Abraham and Isaac and Jacob, the God of his forefathers who took the Israelites out of Egypt and into this land that was once filled with milk and honey? What if the stranger was telling the truth?

He went to the well and brought up a few pieces of dried meat, three barley cakes, and a single small jug of old wine.

The stranger grabbed the food and gobbled it in the manner of one who had not eaten in days. He crunched and slavered and swallowed it in the way of a wild animal. A messenger of God, Gideon thought in disgust, should have better manners!

He screamed out in rage. He had been played for a fool by a starving madman with a wild story. He had been tricked into feeding the man his own family's precious food.

"I'll kill you!" he cried, and swung his trumpet with all his strength at the man's head.

The stranger nimbly sidestepped the wild thrust and held out one hand to point at Gideon. "Be still," he said calmly. "Be quiet and listen."

His voice transfixed Gideon. He stood motionless, still breathing hard from the rage he felt.

"Yahweh has chosen you to destroy the Midianites and to bring His children—His chosen children, the Israelites—back to peace and prosperity and wisdom that can only come from the worship of Him."

Gideon covered his ears with his hands. What was this madman saying? How could he, Gideon, destroy the Midianites? He had already met the Midianites, and instead of acting bravely, he had begged for his life and ended up being humiliated.

"Did you hear me, Gideon?" the stranger asked.

"You're a lunatic," Gideon shouted. "Get out of here."

The stranger smiled gently, removed his small blacksmith's cap, and stretched his hand toward the remaining particles of food. A white-hot flame burst forth from the food. The radiating heat was so intense, it singed Gideon's eyebrows. He staggered back, raising his arms in protection.

A moment later the flames vanished. Gideon stared at the food. Miraculously, it had not been scorched. He fell to his knees in front of the stranger, and his whole body trembled in fear at this sign from Yahweh.

"Forgive me. Please forgive me," Gideon pleaded. But the stranger, too, had vanished.

CHAPTER TWELVE

The Syrian Desert

"The last of the food is being loaded now," said Ossaf, the elaborately dressed Hittite slave who functioned efficiently as Luti's main house servant. He was walking beside her carrying chair and felt miffed at having to accompany his mistress to the small market on the outskirts of Ur, where Luti's caravan waited. Ossaf had come from a good family that had fallen on hard times. He had not been bred to accept subservience lightly. "Your guide and chief drover is named Callisto. He comes from the north, and he supposedly knows the Syrian desert like the palm of his hand." Ossaf handed Luti, who was seated on a large cushion inside the litter, a sweet date.

She examined the fruit, then stuck it in a pouch to eat later. "Fine. As always, you've done well, Ossaf. I am depending upon you to keep my son safe and amused while I am gone."

"He will be the happiest little boy in Ur," Ossaf

70

guaranteed as he helped her climb down from the chair. He held on to her hand for a moment longer than was appropriate. It was no secret to Luti that Ossaf adored her and that if their situation had been different, he would have counted himself among her suitors.

"Off with you now," Luti said. "Take the servants and the litter."

The Hittite bowed, then moved away, stopping occasionally to turn back and wave.

After Luti smiled fondly, she devoted her full attention to the caravan. She had assembled it very quickly after that prophetic incident with the blue heron. No matter what the cost or sacrifice involved, she had to follow the signs, go to Canaan, and find and rescue Micah. Her old mentor, Drak, had once told her that the psychic component in her mind was the truest instinct and must always be given the first priority. But she did not have to be persuaded, for her reawakened love for Micah had been overwhelming. She could think only of him . . . of saving him . . . of introducing him to his son.

"Madam," said the tall guide named Callisto, "we are ready to depart."

Luti nodded. The caravan consisted of camels, donkeys, and several small, tough, desert horses. In addition to Callisto, there were five drovers, three packers, a cook, and seven armed retainers.

"Do you understand the route?" Luti asked. She herself had decided on the path they would take. The Syrian desert had changed in the ten years since she had traveled through it and almost been murdered there. In those terrible days it had been a place of terror, rife with bandits and warring tribes. Now it was safe, quiet, peaceful. That was why she had decided not to go due west to Damascus before turning south, but to cut south much sooner and enter Canaan through the mountains near the Golan Pass.

"Yes, there should be no problem," Callisto told her. "But tell me, do you wish to ride, or should we set up a carrying chair?"

"One of the camels would be fine," she replied.

Slowly, the caravan filed out of the market square and into the trackless sands. For Luti it was a time of memories. She recalled that fateful day she had started out on the desert ten years before, determined to carry out a secret military mission for the old man who had saved her from execution for sorcery at the hands of the priests of Astarte. Her pleasure and memories intensified as she began to recognize landmarks and particularly unusual rock formations. And always, as she rode, her eyes scanned the horizon for birds—ravens, crows, owls, hawks. But she saw none. The only signs of wildlife were the tracks of scurrying land lizards and sometimes the quick-moving shadow of a poisonous snake.

The first day was a lark for the caravan. But by the second day the group was approaching the hottest part of the desert. The travelers rationed their water and stopped often. Callisto frequently checked the route, using ground sticks that caught the angle of the sun by day and the moon by night. Luti was impressed by his knowledge and diligence.

At dusk, the caravan's tents were set up to prevent the cold, penetrating winds of the desert from chilling the travelers. Fresh meat was cooked over open fires, and sweet honey cakes were enjoyed afterward.

On the third night in camp, Callisto informed Luti that the caravan had turned south a few hours before, and she would soon notice the change in the terrain— the much more rocky ground would make for harder times on the camels and the horses.

Luti snuggled into her beautifully woven sleeping bag, which was lined with ibex fur. She looked up at a sky brilliant with stars. Her thoughts went to her son, young Drak, and then to Micah, somewhere to the south and in great and persistent danger. She felt as if she had embarked on a journey that would bring her the peace and joy and love that her wealth had been unable to provide. She closed her eyes tightly, trying to envision how it would be: Micah and her and their child in Ur, a family, walking together down by the river. She idly wondered if she would ever see that blue heron again.

She heard a strange sound in the night. It was like a *puff,* and then another and another. Some creatures were flying through the night air. Moths, perhaps, or . . .

Something heavy thudded to the ground beside her. She reached out, and her hand touched an arrow driven deep into the chest of one of her drovers.

The puffs she had heard were the passage of feathered arrows.

"*Amalekites!*" someone screamed.

Luti sat bolt upright. Amalekites were fierce Bedouins, part of the Midianite federation. She had heard of them, but they usually raided much farther south. She had no reports of their having been seen in the Syrian desert for years.

A moment later Callisto was at her side. He whispered, "We'll make a dash to where the horses are tethered. We'll have to run like the wind."

Holding on to her arm he started out, crouching and running low to the ground. Around them were the screams of the dying.

"Faster!" Callisto whispered. "We have to move faster."

Her chest pounding, Luti increased her speed. Callisto's grip was almost pulling her arm out of the shoulder socket.

Suddenly Callisto stopped and turned toward her. His smile was grotesque as he staggered and fell heavily against her. The warm innards of his body poured out onto her robe. The Bedouin sword that had impaled him gleamed wetly in the moonlight.

Towering over her now was a robed and masked Bedouin. He held a flaming torch in one hand. In the other dangled the severed head of the caravan's cook.

Luti could no longer run. She held up her hands in fear and supplication. The Bedouin ripped her robe from her body and raped her right there. She fought and screamed, but her protests were futile. The man was strong and brutal. After he had pleased himself, she felt him coming close again, something gleaming in his hand. She felt a sharp, intense pain on her face, and then all went black. . . .

The smell of smoke brought her to consciousness. It was morning. Her ankles were tied together, but her hands were free. The morning light revealed the carnage. Everyone of her caravan had been slaughtered. Their bodies had been scattered around the camp. Off to one side, the Bedouins sat around a fire. Some looked asleep, some looked as if they were praying.

She turned her head to the far side of the camp to see what had happened to the horses and camels, but the moment she turned, a horrible pain stabbed through her nose. Her hand tenderly explored the area and came away bloody. Again she tentatively touched the nostril. The realization of what had occurred made her sick to her stomach. The Bedouin who had raped her had also pierced one nostril and inserted a small iron ring. It was the sign of a slave.

CHAPTER THIRTEEN

Al Nazareth, Southern Tip of the Salt Sea

It was a moon-flooded night. Wrapped in a blanket, Blood lay on the ground and watched as three jackals fought over a dead snake. Blood had moved south with his men, out of the Wilderness of Judea to the southern end of the Salt Sea. From there he could mount swift, slashing raids south along the Egyptian caravan routes.

Two of the jackals were pulling at one end of the snake, and the third strained at the other end. They grappled silently, without yelping or snarling. The only sound was the scuffling of their paws and nails on the baked ground.

The struggle made Blood very sad, for it reminded him of his brother Nimshi, whom he hadn't seen in ten years. Like the jackals, Nimshi and he were always tugging at something from opposite ends. They were

75

brothers in flesh and Children of the Lion, but in their minds and hearts they were strangers.

As Blood watched, the snake suddenly gave way in the middle, and the two jackals who had been united against the third now found themselves fighting each other.

Blood turned in his blanket to stare up at the night sky. He wondered if Nimshi was still alive. From time to time rumors about his brother drifted down to the south. Blood had heard that he was living in Tyre . . . that his leg had been amputated . . . that he had fallen under the spell of an evil but beautiful dancer. But these were just rumors, and he had not heard anything new for a long time now.

During the raids into Philistine territory, Blood had heard that under Khalkeus of Gournia, the Children of the Lion were losing their grip on their commercial empire . . . that their enormous fleets were slowly being dismantled . . . that all their financial gambles had had disastrous results. But Blood could not care less about the trading empire. The only thing he treasured about his lineage was the armorer's trade, which had made the Children of the Lion famous and given them entrée to all the princely houses of the civilized world.

He rolled on his side again and sighed. It was going to be another long and sleepless night. Two of the jackals had vanished. Only one remained in sight, chewing contentedly on the flesh of the snake. Just beyond he could see night sentries walking the perimeter of the camp. Several new recruits, three of them Israelites, had joined the band recently. This was not surprising; more and more Israelites were forced into banditry simply to survive. Blood knew what was happening in the north—the Israelites had become so fragmented that marauding Bedouins had totally crushed their will and their ability to resist.

Sometimes Blood gloated over the Israelites' predicament. At other times he remembered the great love he had felt for this people and the love they had had for him, and he became sad.

"Blood! Are you awake?" a voice whispered from the darkness.

"Yes," Blood answered, releasing his grasp on his throwing daggers. He had been fighting for so long, had been in danger for so long, that any sound triggered an involuntary defense reflex.

Anistos, the old Greek who was his second-in-command, and a scout named Mahal, a tiny, gnarled dwarf of a man, came into view. Mahal was Blood's most trusted scout. He could range far and wide with little need for water and food. He could run for hours without stopping and, if cornered, would fight to the death. The powerful dwarf wore a camel's skin wrapped about him and carried a single iron-tipped lance. He looked exhausted.

"Sit, rest yourselves," Blood invited.

The scout and Anistos squatted on the ground. Blood reached under his blanket and pulled out a small skin. After setting it on the ground in front of Mahal, Blood unwrapped the skin and offered the scout one of several pieces of an aloe plant. The succulent, which grew on the northwestern side of the Salt Sea, was difficult to find. When dried and chewed, it provided a sudden but temporary rush of energy and courage and clarity.

"No, thank you," Mahal said. "Anistos has given me wine."

When the Greek also refused the offer, Blood nodded, rewrapped the cut plant, and replaced it under his blanket.

"Mahal has news of great importance," explained Anistos. "That is why I did not wait for morning."

"Speak, Mahal. Tell me everything."

The small man changed his position on the ground so that his legs would not cramp. Then he began his report. "I was searching out targets east of Gaza for you, Blood, when I heard that an Egyptian unit has crossed the Sinai and entered Canaan. They are camped in the village of Nahal Oz, just south of Gaza."

"Egyptians?" Blood exhaled and leaned forward.

"Yes. My informant tells me that the unit entered

Canaan and has plans to raid Gaza and two other cities of the Philistine League on the coast. This is to punish them for giving safe transit to the ships of the Sea Peoples, which have been raiding the coast of Egypt regularly."

"Sounds plausible," Blood remarked. "Did you go to Nahal Oz?"

"Yes, I went there and saw the Egyptian army unit myself. But it was not infantry nor mounted; it was the Harishaf Chariot Brigade."

Blood was astonished. The Harishaf Chariot Brigade was the most feared unit in the Egyptian army. Why, he wondered, would the pharaoh waste it on frightening the Philistines? It did not make sense. But Mahal was his most trusted scout. He had good eyes and faultless logic. "You're sure it was the Harishaf?"

Mahal nodded grimly. "I saw their chariots, their weapons, and their banners. And I even got a glimpse of their commander, Ma-Set."

"A man to be feared," Anistos added in a low voice.

Mahal shifted his weight again before speaking. "I learned something else at a local inn, from a Harishaf spearman who had drunk too much wine. The brigade had crossed the Sinai into Canaan on direct orders of Ramses the Third. This was no training or harassing operation."

"Then the story that they're going north to punish the Philistines is a cover," Blood said.

"Right," Mahal affirmed.

"Then what's their target?" Blood asked.

"You," Mahal said quietly.

Blood did not know, at first, whether Mahal was making a joke. But the scout was not smiling. "Why would the Harishaf Chariot Brigade come for me? We are just bandits."

"You have infuriated the pharaoh by stopping the free flow of goods across the southern desert. And, according to the spearman, they know you are guilty of looting the caravan route."

"When will they move, Mahal?" Blood wanted to know.

"They're on their way now. They left the village yesterday morning, feigned to the north, then headed due east. Their orders are to stay in the field for as long as it takes to hunt you down and kill you and all who ride with you."

The three men sat in silence for a long time. Blood carved into the ground with one of his throwing daggers. Mahal dozed off, and Anistos just sat there, his dark and serious eyes on Blood.

Finally, Blood replaced the dagger into his belt and seemed to have reached a decision. "Assemble the men now," he told Anistos.

"All of them?" Anistos asked.

"Every man who can walk," Blood replied.

Soon the entire band had been roused from their sleep and gathered in a semicircle around Blood and Anistos.

Blood looked from face to face. Some of the men had ridden with him for years; others were relatively new. They were for the most part, he knew, the scum of humanity—men whose only trade and appetite were for death. And yet Blood felt an odd affection for them. It was such a peculiar feeling that he was forced to turn away, so close was he to shedding tears.

They waited in silence for their leader to speak.

"Listen to me carefully," he began in a strong but emotionless monotone. "The Harishaf Chariot Brigade has crossed the Sinai and is now engaged in a search-and-destroy mission against each and every one of us. They have been ordered to do this by none other than the pharaoh of Egypt.

"This brigade, commanded by Ma-Set, is the finest fighting machine the Egyptian army possesses. It is comprised of more than one hundred chariots, each manned by two highly armed warriors. They are disciplined, they are fanatical, and they have never been defeated in battle.

"Listen to the truth: We are no match for them. Our only hope is to break camp immediately and move back into the Wilderness of Judea. From there we will conduct hit-and-run operations against the brigade. There is a slight chance that we can harass the Egyptians enough so that any further pursuit will not be worth their losses. It is the only hope of success we have.

"We must travel light. You will immediately bury all valuables and booty and immediately release our captives. Carry with you only weapons, food, and water. Is that clear?"

He waited. He saw his men nod in silent assent.

"Then do it now," he ordered, "and remember, you are not dead until the spear pierces you."

The men jumped up and ran to follow Blood's instructions. Meanwhile, the band's leader and his Greek lieutenant remained where they were, watching the activity.

"I have never seen you like this," Anistos said quietly.

"Like what?" Blood snapped at him.

"Frightened," Anistos said, knowing full well that if any other member of the band had questioned Blood's courage, he would have earned a quick dagger in the throat.

But Blood merely nodded and placed a hand on Anistos's back. "You are right, old friend. I am frightened. You must understand that in the days of Moses, my family, the Children of the Lion, helped the Israelites break the Egyptian yoke. Now, generations later, I have become the vehicle through which the Egyptian nation will exact its vengeance. I am not frightened of physical death; I am frightened because I seem to have lost control of my destiny. It is as if cosmic forces are playing a game of senet, and I am the prize."

Anistos started to reply, but Blood waved him away with an imperative sweep of the hand. When the old Greek had gone, Blood hunkered down on the ground and unfolded his blanket over his head, shutting out the sounds of men breaking camp. He might have been praying to the very forces determined to destroy him.

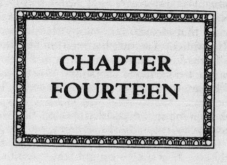

CHAPTER
FOURTEEN

The Aegean Sea

The *Cretan Queen*, a beautifully built vessel, was now five days out of Tyre. Captained by Zeno, it carried Nimshi, Tirzah, two slaves, and a six-man crew. Because there was no cargo, small cabins could be built in the hold for the passengers.

The weather had been magnificent, the wind brisk and predictable, keeping the white sails full and the rowers happy. And the ship was fast, cutting through the water like a marlin, her ribs rolling up and over and down into the gentle waves.

From the moment the ship left Tyre, Tirzah had stayed close to Zeno, utilizing all her techniques of mind control to help him retrieve his memory. Very slowly, very painfully, and with much befuddlement, he had begun to respond. He vaguely remembered incidents from the past. He seemed to realize that Tirzah had known him many years before, and as a result of that perception he became more friendly and more passionate toward her. Soon he was visiting her cabin every night. But the name Theon still meant nothing to him.

On the morning of the sixth day, the weather turned foul. Dark storm clouds raced across the sky, and a raging wind buffeted the voyagers. Zeno, however, remained unremittingly happy. He looked at Tirzah and Nimshi, who stood nearby. "I'm starting to like this assignment," he enthused. "At first I thought you were crazy. I never heard of people chartering a boat and then telling the captain to sail it wherever his heart desired."

As Zeno swung the rudder, taking the ship on a more easterly course, Nimshi, leaning on his crutches by the rail, looked quickly at Tirzah and grinned. She nodded. They had both caught the significance of Theon's actions: Not only was he beginning to remember certain events from the past, he was also starting to steer the *Cretan Queen* purposefully. Had something buried deep in his brain suddenly emerged and given him a map? There was no way to know with certainty, but the vessel was now obviously making a change of course to the northeast.

The storm passed over them quickly, and a breezeless calm followed. The rowers were set to their task. Nimshi had sat down so as not to lose his balance during the rough weather. But Tirzah chose to stand next to Zeno. Her hand gently touched his back from time to time, so the auras of their bodies remained in contact. In that way she could continue to trap his psychic shadow in turmoil. Only when the deep disturbances troubled his mind would the memories have a possibility of surfacing.

A slave brought them small bowls of heated juice, which they drank greedily.

"I only get seasick when the sea is calm like this," Nimshi said. "The storm waves didn't bother me at all."

"The wind will come up soon," Tirzah assured him.

"How do you know?" Zeno blurted out in an unexpectedly bitter voice. "How do you know the wind will ever come up again?"

Both Tirzah and Nimshi were startled by Zeno's angry outburst. Then Zeno looked away from them, embarrassed. Tirzah, undaunted, moved to face him. She saw an expression that she had never seen on Zeno's face—he looked frightened, drained of strength and resolve. Although Tirzah wanted to kiss him and hold him and soothe his fears, she did not. Free-floating anxiety was a necessary part of the recovery process. The very foundation of his false personality had to be shattered by fears and joys and mysteries from the past.

"Who are you people?" Zeno asked, looking with great sadness at Nimshi, then at Tirzah.

"We are your friends," Nimshi responded gently.

"Friends? *Friends?* No, I think not. You both are trying to confuse me, to satisfy motives I know nothing about."

Nimshi laughed; he was trying to make light of the accusation. "Why would you say that, Zeno? We merely rented a ship and hired you to sail wherever you wished to take us in the Aegean. A pleasure excursion, if you will. Why do you say we are confusing you?"

A shadow was over Zeno's face. Tirzah could see the veins in his neck. The jaw muscles were trembling. *Yes*, she thought, *this is the way it must happen—he will crumble, and then he will rebuild.*

Suddenly a cold wind crossed the bow, and for the first time in hours the sails filled. The moment of crisis passed as Zeno, consumed by the immediate concerns of supervising the crew, began yelling orders. Nimshi rolled himself up in a blanket and tried to sleep. Tirzah, wanting to be alone, walked slowly to her cabin.

"Are you asleep?" a voice whispered through the cabin door.

"I am always awake for you, my love," Tirzah answered huskily, and moved over on the bed so that there would be room for Zeno.

He closed the door, undressed quickly, letting his tunic fall to the floor, and slipped into the bed beside her.

Her hands roamed joyously over his strong, naked body. She pressed herself against him.

"Forgive me for talking so angrily earlier," Zeno apologized. "I have been feeling very odd."

"Physically ill?"

"No, not exactly. I have been plagued by strange images before my eyes. Suddenly, I envision things that I recognize but can't identify. Do you understand what I am saying?"

"Try to sleep, Zeno. You will feel better in the morning. It will be a good day tomorrow." She guided his weary head against her naked breast.

"I don't want to sleep," he whispered, kissing her deeply. She moaned with pleasure. She could feel his maleness growing hard and stiff against her leg.

"I love you, Theon," she said as he took her in the gently rolling cabin.

Nimshi wakened on the deck and stared out over the bow. He could not believe what he was sure he was seeing. At first he thought it was a dream, but then a shooting pain in his leg affirmed that he was awake and in reality. Besides, although he had never set foot on the island, he knew from Theon's descriptions many years before exactly what Home looked like.

It had worked! His plan had worked beyond his wildest dreams! Now he had but to give the signal. He struggled to stand, fell, and then fought his way back up. The crutches were unsteady under his clammy hands. His forehead was bathed with sweat.

He hurried off the deck and down the wooden ladder to his tiny cabin. From under the cot he removed a hidden object wrapped in a sheepskin. Pinning it precariously under his arm, he climbed to the deck again, moved to the railing, sat down, and extracted an oil-soaked torch from the sheepskin. Inside his belt were the flints.

With trembling hands he struck the stones again and again until finally the sparks caught the oil and the torch lighted. Next he leaned over the side of the ship and swung the blazing brand in a large arc five times.

Then he pulled the torch back and suffocated the flames with the sheepskin, which singed.

Exhausted, in great pain, and breathing heavily, he sank to the deck and closed his eyes. Everything would be good now. He would have Cotto all to himself. He would no longer be in debt. He would have all the drugs he needed.

His relief was short-lived, however. The most dreadful feelings he had ever experienced suddenly washed over him. They caused an emotional agony that dwarfed the throbbing, cutting pain in his leg. He felt as if his body weighed a thousand pounds. Every pore of his skin seemed to exude the poison of guilt.

His eyes grew wide with shock as he came to an awful realization: Home was, after all, his, too, although he had never been there. The inhabitants of the island were his family. They were all Children of the Lion.

The horror of his selfishness overwhelmed him. "What have I done? Oh, gods, what have I done?" he whispered.

Although the first light of dawn filtered into Tirzah's cabin, she was awakened not by the brightness but by Zeno's kisses. She clung to him, drinking in his love.

"I don't know if I'll ever be able to make love to my wife again after having known this pleasure with you," Zeno whispered.

Tirzah said nothing, for his words saddened her. She realized that the moment he regained his memory and became Theon again, he would forget his entire existence as Zeno. His new wife and children would be forgotten, and Nuhara and the twins would be the only family he would be able to recall. Would he forget her as well? Tirzah wondered. Or would he remember what had happened ten years before, when she was called Huldah and they had been combatants as well as lovers?

She forced all that out of her mind. This was real . . . now . . . being close to him . . . loving him in the dawn's light.

At last they dressed, and she preceded him up to the deck. Her eyes caught a shadow against the horizon. "Look!" she cried out.

There, in the distance, rising like a green emerald from the blue Aegean, was Home. She recognized it immediately. Often she had heard her late husband Pepi speak of it—how the island was shaped in the form of an undulating snake and ringed by steep cliffs covered with brilliant green foliage . . . how three identical harbors were carved out of the belly of this snake, each one capable of accommodating a dozen of the largest vessels.

"It's Home, Theon! The island Home!" she shouted. Then she called for Nimshi; but he did not answer and was nowhere to be seen.

She looked at Theon, who seemed utterly confused. He appeared to know the paradise on the horizon but was frightened by its sudden appearance.

"Captain Zeno! Captain Zeno!" A deckhand was shouting and gesticulating wildly toward the bow.

Tirzah looked out over the water on the other end of the ship, then froze in horror.

Not more than a thousand yards from the *Cretan Queen* she saw a line of twenty ships. They rode high in the water. On the red sails of each was painted the dreaded insignia of Poseidon, god of the oceans.

She realized immediately what she was seeing: Sea Peoples' fighting ships. Each vessel was known to carry eighty hard-muscled warriors who doubled as oarsmen when the wind was down. Their shields glinted in the morning light.

A sickening sinking feeling clenched her gut. Someone had betrayed them! Nimshi! Where was Nimshi? She balled her fists. Had the Sea Peoples been following the *Queen* all the while? Had Nimshi signaled them that Home had been located? It had to be he! The Sea Peoples were controlled by the Phoenicians, and everyone in Tyre knew that Nimshi was in debt to them. And it was Nimshi who had suggested the trip.

Tirzah burst into tears of frustration and anger. How could Nimshi have betrayed his own family? How could he have sentenced the island's men, women, and children to certain torture and death in exchange for Phoenician gold?

She ran off the deck and down into the hold.

The curtain to Nimshi's small cabin was pulled back. She stepped through and saw on the floor the burned-out torch lying in a singed sheepskin.

Then she looked up. She stepped back and staggered.

Nimshi hung by the neck from the beam of the cabin. His lifeless body swung gently with the ship's motion. His crutches lay on the floor.

And in the distance she could hear the battle horns of the Sea Peoples.

CHAPTER FIFTEEN

Canaan

Gideon woke suddenly and sat up in bed. It was still dark outside, and for a moment, he did not know where he was. Then he saw Shulamith, his wife, beside him, sleeping. He relaxed. He was in his own bed. From the corridor he could hear the cooing of the baby in his woven basket.

Gideon lay back, folded his arms behind his head, and grinned. He felt very good—rested and confident and happy. In fact, he could not remember feeling so well after waking up. He hummed a few bars of a sprightly tune before he realized that he might awaken everyone.

Why am I so happy? Gideon wondered. *Why do I feel like a carefree boy again?* It was very strange, for nothing in his miserable life had changed: His shrewish wife was still beside him; the children were still hungry; his father was at the point of disowning him for not being able to provide sustenance for the family; and his people, the Israelites, were still oppressed. What was there to feel happy about?

Gideon stared at the mud-and-wattle ceiling, which was badly in need of repair. But he continued to smile. At last he remembered why he was happy: That strange-looking man who claimed to be a messenger from Yahweh had told him that Yahweh had chosen none other than Gideon to crush the Midianites and free the children of Israel from their brutal yoke.

So why should he not be elated? One does not get chosen by Yahweh every day for such glorious deeds.

Lying there, giddy, chosen, he felt enormous strength and vitality flow through his limbs. He rolled out of bed, grabbed his sword and his trumpet, then ran naked from the house and into an adjoining field.

Brambles cut Gideon's feet, but he did not mind. Joyously he battled imaginary Midianites. He swung his sword in mighty sweeps as he decapitated and disemboweled. Never had he felt so powerful and free! Never had he felt such immense strength in his arms and legs and back. He was tireless. He was without fear.

Finally, the bizarre make-believe ended in exhaustion, and Gideon sank to the ground. He laid down the sword and gently stroked his trumpet.

"What do you think you are doing?" a voice asked from the darkness.

Gideon grabbed his sword and jumped to his feet, swinging the blade defensively. "Who's there? Who are you?"

"Relax," said the voice, "and put down your weapon."

It was the stranger, the messenger from Yahweh. The man, still dressed in his blacksmith's garb, stepped into view.

"I was practicing," Gideon explained, shamefaced. "Why shouldn't I? After all, you told me that I must destroy the Midianites."

"Who are you kidding, Gideon? You weren't practicing. You were fantasizing."

"Well, what does it matter?"

"Not much . . . unless you're ready to get down to some real salvation work."

"I'm ready," Gideon said fiercely.

"Good. The first step is to destroy the statue of Baal and the Baal altar."

Gideon looked at the messenger incredulously. "You mean my father's statue and altar?"

"Right," replied the angel matter-of-factly.

"I can't do that. It would cause my father great grief."

The messenger ignored his protests. "Your second task, Gideon, is to destroy the sacred grove in which the statue of Baal and the altar rest."

Gideon responded with anger. "My father planted those trees with his own hands. If I destroyed the grove, I would break his heart."

The angel contemptuously waved aside his objection. "Third, you will slaughter your father's bull."

"You're joking!"

"Slaughter him in the tradition of your forefathers."

"But that can't be done. No, never. Sorry. My father is going to sell the bull and purchase grain for our family. We are starving. You can't ask me to kill the bull."

"I am not asking. Yahweh is telling you."

"Everything has already been taken from us," Gideon whined pathetically. "Our gold, our grain, our vegetable crops, our clothes, our livestock. That beast is the only wealth we have left. That bull is the only way my father can ensure our survival."

"Everyone is suffering deprivation, Gideon. Now, after you slaughter the bull, you will sacrifice it to Yahweh."

Gideon's frustration boiled over. He swung his sword and beheaded a bush. "Don't you understand?" he shouted, then lowered his voice. "My father doesn't worship Yahweh anymore. And he certainly isn't going to approve of my sacrificing his bull to a diety he doesn't believe in."

Once again Messenger ignored his protestations. He looked distracted, in a hurry, as if he had another set of instructions to deliver elsewhere. "Well, Gideon, those are your duties. If I were you, I'd start moving on them and forget the child's games with your sword." He paused, then added: "And I'd advise you to put some clothes on before you wander the countryside."

"Maybe I don't want to wear clothes," Gideon said petulantly.

"Well, you could always cover your private parts with a fig leaf," the angel suggested, chuckling at his own joke.

"I thought Yahweh was going to make me into a great warrior," Gideon said. He was almost begging.

"He may do that, also."

"Let me explain to you why I can't—" Gideon broke off in midsentence because the messenger had vanished.

Gideon grew somber and frightened. The idea of rushing out into a field with his sword was no longer a happy joke. Any one of the four tasks the angel had told him to accomplish could mean his own death or, at the very least, a savage beating. His whole family would turn against him.

He needed time to think. He did not want to anger anyone, particularly Yahweh, who he remembered was a jealous god and did not like disobedient servants.

CHAPTER SIXTEEN

The Aegean Sea

The lead warship of the Sea Peoples' fleet entered the main harbor of Home without resistance. It seemed as if the entire populace of the island was still asleep.

Pelops, commander of the landing party from that lead ship, peered over the railing. Navan the Phoenician had briefed all the Sea Peoples' officers prior to sailing, but he had frankly admitted that all the intelligence that had been provided was just informed guesswork. No one had ever located the island, let alone invaded it. Pelops could see a group of squat buildings on the rise of the first hill. Those, he figured, must be the warehouses. Past them he could see a walled dwelling, much like a Cretan royal house. That, he guessed, must be where Khalkeus lived.

Pelops turned to his men, who crouched behind the rail. Each wore a visored helmet, a beaten iron breastplate, and bronze greaves. Most carried a shield and several throwing spears with wide cutting edges. A few of the men carried short teak bows, which sent their feathered shafts with the barbed points toward their target with enormous striking power.

"A few minutes more," he called out to his men, and watched with satisfaction as they grasped their weapons tightly. Pelops squinted toward the other ships following his ship in. He was confident that the remainder of the fleet was entering the two other harbors at precisely the same time.

"Visors down," he ordered, and the clank of visors snapped in place in unison reverberated through the ship. "Listen closely, men. You know the stakes here. We are about to pluck the richest plum in the Aegean. Our deal with the Phoenicians gives them half the take; but we keep fifty percent of all the booty—gold, silk, ivory, spices, everything. That'll still be plenty to keep you fat and sassy till the end of your days if you work quickly and mercilessly."

He could see their anxious eyes through the visors. All his men were true Sea Peoples, savage invaders from the north and east, mercenaries roaming the open water for the benefit of the highest bidder. This was their chance to change their lives—to buy a farm, to purchase a fishing vessel, or to become a land trader in Canaan or Lebanon or even on the great plain where the Tigris and the Euphrates meandered.

"When we hit the shore, men, we must move fast. Go first to the warehouses where the wealth is stored, then to the palace, which contains Khalkeus's private treasure. We are facing Children of the Lion, so they will be well armed. Kill everyone who resists. Do not waste time sparing lives. Our goal is booty, all we can find and all we can take. Anyone who does not deposit the booty in the common coffers to be shared later will be dealt with severely. I personally will chop off his greedy hands." He waited until the warning had sunk in, then shouted, "Are you ready, men?"

In response, they beat on their shields with their spears. That rhythmic noise continued until the ship anchored in shallow water and Pelops leaped over the rail. His men followed, crossing the beach and climbing the rise. There they stopped.

Standing not twenty feet from them were about five island residents, all unarmed, all very thin. They seemed startled but showed no inclination to resist the invaders.

The soldiers looked at Pelops. Why were the residents' clothes so poorly made? Why were their faces so haggard?

"Forget them!" Pelops shouted. "Remember why we're here. Remember what we're after."

The soldiers surged forward to the warehouses. They reached the first bolted door.

"Smash it down!" Pelops yelled.

Twenty troopers removed their breastplates, to be utilized to splinter the wood. Again and again they charged, to the cheers and encouragement of their comrades. There was a splintering sound as the door began to break apart. Finally the job was done and Pelops leaped through into the warehouse. His men followed.

The dank interior was absolutely empty except for a few crumpled, moldering skins, which lay in one corner.

The soldiers, dumbfounded, stood in the emptiness. They stared at one another, and then at Pelops. No one knew what to say.

They ran to the next warehouse and smashed down that door. But that room was empty, also. As were the next one and the next one—all empty.

When the soldiers emerged from the last empty warehouse, they found the island inhabitants watching them. The invaders vented their rage and disappointment. War cries split the air as they massacred the helpless residents. Men, women, and children were cut down, impaled, clubbed. Blood ran like spring-swollen rivulets along the ground.

Only Pelops did not participate. He ran among his men, beating them with the flat side of his spear, yelling at them to stop, ordering them to follow him to the palace because *that* was where the real treasure lay— the treasure of Khalkeus.

Finally his words took hold, and the soldiers put up their weapons and formed ranks. The air was already thick with flies feasting on the warm blood of the corpses that littered the ground. Pelops pointed to the royal house of Khalkeus, nestled in a series of beautifully terraced green hills above them. He started off at a trot, the soldiers at his heels.

Talus looked wildly around his hut. His heart was beating so fast he thought it would jump out of his chest. He had realized the moment he had seen the sails from the cliff that his chance to escape from Home had arrived. He knew whose ships they were. Phorbus, before he had died, had spoken often of the fearsome Sea Peoples with their Poseidon insignia.

Talus did not fear for his safety; the Sea Peoples had nothing against him. He himself had been repudiated by the rulers of Home. He, too, was an exile, just like the Sea Peoples. Surely they would give him safe passage anywhere. Or maybe he could even hire on as a mercenary.

He flung articles about the hut. What was worth keeping? What should he take with him when he left the island? Finally, he calmed down and sank onto his cot. There was, he admitted, nothing of value except a few fishhooks, which he wrapped carefully, a piece of jewelry that had been his mother's, Phorbus's knife, a few extra skins, and several pieces of dried meat. He rolled it all in a worn blanket, slung it over his shoulder, and started down the path. Only once did he look back at the hovel that had been the scene of so much misery and frustration.

Feeling truly optimistic for the first time in years, he loped effortlessly toward his goal—the main wharves where the first ships had landed. It was a long run down dozens of interlocking mountain trails and then through the warehouse district. It would be a hot day, and the bag slung over his shoulder would become heavy. The stones and brush would cut his feet and legs. But none of this mattered. He was going to be free! He was going to leave this cursed island, where he had buried the only people he had ever loved and been scorned by those who owed him acceptance.

After an hour's steady jog he reached a broad avenue lined with locust trees. He slowed to a walk and within minutes entered the low flat plain that contained the warehouses.

He stopped in horror. Covering the ground, as far as he could see, were twisted corpses. Men, women, and children had died in pain and terror, and their upturned, contorted faces mirrored their fear.

His joy, his plans, his exhilaration, all were swept away by the slaughter. He realized instantly that the Sea Peoples were here on a mission of death, and if given the opportunity, they would do to him exactly what they had done to these poor souls.

Weak, nauseated, he sat hard on the ground. Sweat dripped down his face. There were only two options now: He could go back to his hut high in the uninhabited area of the island and pray that the invaders never searched there. But that would doom him to a lifetime of loneliness and despair. He would be better off dead.

The second option was the cliff. Phorbus, in his madness, had not waited for the high tide. Phorbus had leaped from the cliff into the sea and died, but Talus decided that if he jumped into the sea and lived, at least he would have a chance of being picked up by a merchant ship.

The young man wearily rose, turned, and trudged back up the path. It had to be the cliff. He was too tired to be frightened and too miserable to care whether he lived or died.

Nuhara was staying, as she often did, at the Pink Villa, some distance from her usual suite of rooms in the palace. It was called the Pink Villa because it was built out of very expensive pink limestone. Khalkeus had given his daughter the dwelling as a gift after Theon was drowned at sea, as a way to ease her grief.

The inner courtyard of the villa contained a beautiful floating garden constructed over a series of artificial ponds. It was here that Nuhara spent most of her time.

Now she was waiting impatiently for that girl, Allomander, to come from the palace and paint her toe-nails. She lay on a large, elegantly covered lounge chair, which was situated beside one of the lushest areas of the floating garden. Her eyes lingered over a giant lotus, which sat serenely in the water. But Nuhara did not feel serene. Something was wrong. She did not know what because the Pink Villa was isolated. But something in the air and strange, echoing sounds in the distance unsettled her mood.

Suddenly there was a commotion in the hallway leading from the living area to the gardens.

"Mistress! Mistress! Come quick!" a servant cried shrilly.

Nuhara, annoyed, walked to the hallway. Two of her servants were holding up an exhausted and terrified Allomander. Blood streaked her legs, and an open wound bled over one eye.

"Bring her some watered wine and wash her wounds," Nuhara instructed.

The two servants rushed off and returned quickly. After several minutes of ministering, Allomander was reviving. Her cuts were severe, though, and would need the attention of a magus.

"The Sea Peoples have invaded," she rasped to Nuhara. "Their boats are in all the harbors, and their soldiers are all over the island. They are in the palace now."

Nuhara stepped back as if she had been hit with a club. Then she steadied herself and grasped Allomander's shoulders. "Are Gravis and Hela safe? Are my children safe?" Nuhara was now shaking the terrified young woman.

"I don't know! I don't know!"

Nuhara walked back to the garden to gather her thoughts. Rage, fear, bitterness, loss—the powerful feelings sapped her strength. Everything had been going so well. The secret alliances had been concluded. The treasure had been spirited away, and her father had gone with it. The groundwork had been set for the new life for her and her children and her father—a life away from this dying island and the shipping enterprise that had been so important to her husband and meaningless to her and her father. Now all that had been aborted.

She closed her eyes and swayed unsteadily. Someone must have betrayed them. Someone within the family, within the Children of the Lion. But who? And why? She would puzzle it out later, for she knew that only one thing was important now—her survival. How could she escape the wrath of the Sea Peoples?

An idea came to her. Her twins had once told her about treks they had taken into the uninhabited section of the island. She had never found out why they went there, but Gravis had once described a cliff overlooking the sea, where one could dive and safely reach the deep, open water. Her dear child had told her that if he were a bird, it was on that cliff he would nest, looking always toward the free and clear sea.

Maybe, she thought, full of hope, Gravis and Hela had managed to slip out of the palace. If so, perhaps they would head to the cliff and take their chance with the sea. If not, there was nothing she could do about it now. She had to save herself.

"Allomander!" she called out sharply. "Get up."

When Allomander did not stir, Nuhara kicked her. "Go to my rooms and pack some clothes. Then go into the kitchen and gather cakes and meats for our journey."

"Our journey?" the young woman asked.

"Our journey off this island. Do you want to stay here and die?"

"No! No!" Allomander moaned and climbed to her feet to do Nuhara's bidding.

The two woman left the Pink Villa within the hour. The villa's servants had already run away. Nuhara carried nothing but a gold-tipped cane. Allomander carried the small, hastily gathered bundles of clothes and food. Because of the servant's weakened condition, Nuhara was forced to stop often. She was not used to walking, however, and the trails always were steep, so she did not mind overly much. She had no idea which trails to follow, but she could see the cliffs to the north,

and she guessed that one of those opened out to the
sea passage.

Sounds of the invasion could be heard drifting up
from the island's settlements, and as the women gained
a vantage point, they could see the chaos and corpses
below.

Hour after torturous hour passed, and the sun sank
low on the horizon. Nuhara put more clothes on to
guard herself against the chill. Her body ached with
fatigue. Her limbs trembled, and her lungs felt as if
they were being crushed. But on she climbed, and the
young woman with the burdens followed at a distance.
Although Nuhara was used to having Allomander's services, the girl was proving detrimental to the escape
plan.

When dawn came, Nuhara could see the outline
of a massive cliff, shaped like a fishhook. Its sharp point
jutted out toward the north. She held up her hand and
stopped.

"We rest here," she said to Allomander. The two
women sank exhausted to the ground.

"Tell me, madam," Allomander asked. "How are
we to leave this island?"

"You will know shortly," Nuhara replied. "Sleep
now."

After the young woman had dozed off, Nuhara
removed a small linen packet from her robes. She
unwrapped the cloth and stared at the treasure she had
been smart enough to take from the Pink Villa: ten
long, thin daggers made of solid gold. It was rumored
that they had been fashioned by Shobai many generations before. Each was worth a fortune. If she managed
to escape the island and had need of quick wealth,
these daggers could easily be converted into coin.

She picked up one of the weapons and rolled it
between her palms. Moving silently, she knelt beside
the sleeping servant and drove the dagger point into
her head, behind the lobe of the ear. Allomander died
instantly.

Nuhara wiped the blade on the ground, replaced
it in the linen, rolled the packet up, and strapped it

securely to her ankle, so her treasure would not be lost
when she leaped into the sea.

She strode to the cliff, took a deep breath to
strengthen her resolve, then jumped, never to return
to Home again.

The palace servant's left arm had been brutally
impaled on a sword driven into a wooden door. Another
sword was poised to inflict the same cruel injury to the
right arm.

"Tell me now," Pelops whispered savagely into the
prisoner's ear.

The man shook his head. Sweat beads whipped
from his hair and face.

Pelops nodded. One of the Sea Peoples' soldiers
began to lunge with his blade.

"No! No more!" the servant suddenly screamed
just as the sword was about to pierce the arm.

Pelops stepped back and smiled grimly. "Where
are the treasure vaults of Khalkeus?"

"You enter beneath the west stairs. There is a
stone hinge. Pull it with all your strength, and the
stones will part."

They left the gasping servant impaled on the door
and ran to the stairway. So far they had found nothing
of value in the palace, and Khalkeus himself seemed to
have vanished with the wind.

Pelops and two of his soldiers grabbed hold of the
hinge and pulled. It gave way very slowly, but eventually a hidden passageway was revealed. The three
invaders moved down the darkened corridor. They
found torches fastened on the wall, which, when lit,
hastened their movements.

"Wait!" Pelops shouted, holding up his arm and
stopping dead in his tracks.

A gasp of astonishment rose from the soldiers.
They were staring at a massive wall painting. It was
very bizarre but very beautiful. The main figure was
half man, half goat. He was playing a flute. A garland
wreathed his head. His face was smiling but demonic.
His cloven hooves were sharp. Behind him were nine

women, following in single file. They were naked except for clusters of grapevines strewn over their bodies.

The painting had a powerful effect. The eyes of the women seemed crazed with fear and longing, and the soldiers forced their eyes away. They had to turn aside, for the impact was the same as it would have been had they been staring at the sun.

"Who is he?" a soldier whispered. "Is he a god?"

"How can a god be half man and half goat?" another soldier responded.

Whoever it was, it was obvious that this strange deity was from their homeland. The fauna in the painting was Greek. It filled the men with a sudden longing for home.

Pelops realized that this pause was wasting time. He moved on, calling on his men to double their pace.

Finally the passageway widened into a huge, high-domed vault. Massive chests, each with a strong lock, were stacked against the walls.

Pelops grinned. At last! Treasure! "Break the locks!" he ordered. "Break them off!" His men swarmed around the chests, smashing the locks with their swords and shields until the tops lay splintered on the chamber floor. They stepped back to give their leader the first honor of dipping his hands into the booty.

In the torchlight, the chest seemed filled with a glittering mix, perhaps diamonds and other precious stones. Pelops thrust his hands down into it. Then a shudder passed through his body as his hands sifted through the substance.

"Worthless!" he screamed, pulling his hands out and flinging the crushed stone about the chamber. "It's gravel! The chest is filled with gravel! Check the others."

Each chest was opened but yielded nothing except a mound of gravel where gold or jewels had once been stored.

Silence settled over the chamber. The soldiers, exhausted and bitter, dropped to their knees, leaving one chest unopened in the shadows. The dream of great wealth was dead. There was no treasure on Home.

After they had discovered that the warehouses were empty, they had vented their rage on the island's inhabitants. But now, in that subterranean chamber, they felt little anger—only weariness and profound disappointment.

Pelops was just about to rally his men for the march back through the passageway when he heard a strange sound. He motioned to one of his lieutenants, who ran to the last, locked chest. The lid was pried up after the lock was smashed.

More sounds came, and then a great turmoil erupted in the chest. Finally two figures pushed their way up through the gravel, gasping for air and shaking themselves. The soldiers' weapons were poised to run them through.

"Wait!" Pelops called out. The weapons stopped inches away from the two peoples' throats.

Pelops stared at the young man and woman. They looked nearly identical. They were incredibly beautiful, even though their clothes, hair, and faces were filthy.

Pelops remembered what the Phoenician had told him: Several of Khalkeus's family would probably fetch a nice price on the slave block, particularly Khalkeus's grandchildren, the young twins Gravis and Hela. The Phoenician had said they were quite handsome and reputed to have occult powers.

Pelops peered at them. They were, assuredly, Gravis and Hela. They could be no one else. Both looked calmly ahead, oblivious to the dangers. To his astonishment, he even could see the slight traces of smiles.

"Bind them! We'll take them back to the boat with us!" Pelops ordered. What they would fetch on the slave block, Pelops thought, would be enough to buy the wine necessary to drown the broken dreams of wealth among his men and himself.

Talus dived from the cliff at dawn when the tide was high. The shock of hitting the water knocked him cold, and only when he rose from the depths like a corked bottle did he regain his senses and begin spitting out the water. Finally he felt buoyant enough to start swimming—a slow stroke out toward the open sea.

The water was colder than he had anticipated, and he became very quickly fatigued. He abandoned the swimming stroke and settled on floating on his back and propelling himself by flutter kicks with his legs.

Soon that, too, became tiring. He began to search the water for driftwood or anything that he could hold on to. He noticed that the tide was slowly pulling him toward the central harbor of Home.

The sun was high and hot when Talus finally found a long piece of slimy wood that might once have been the rudder of a small fishing ship. Some signs were etched into the wood, but he could not decipher them. The wood could not support him totally, but it did give him extra buoyancy.

By midday his face began to blister painfully from the combination of sun and salt water. That part of his body that remained submerged became numb, so he floated on his back and kicked his legs to restore the circulation.

As the day wore on he slipped in and out of sleep. It was a troubled sleep—almost delirium—and he saw the faces of his mother and Phorbus and the horrors of the burning city of Troy. At dusk he could see the fires of Home, sacked by the Sea Peoples.

When nightfall came he held tightly on to the wood, fearful that he would not live through the night, that he would slip off and fall forever into the darkness beneath him. With the night came shivering cold and delusions and fear. He wept and prayed.

"Whooo . . . whooooo . . . whooooo . . ."

The strange sound broke the darkness. Talus opened his eyes. An owl? he wondered. But how could there be an owl at sea? *Perhaps it is the wind,* he thought. Then it came again, closer, and he knew in his heart that it was the voice of another human being. He concentrated, hopeful of determining the direction of the voice. It came again, louder. Gathering all his remaining strength, Talus painfully swam toward the sound. The moonlit water began to assume strange shapes, a jungle of dangerous creatures that bore down upon him with malice.

"Whooooo . . . whoooooo."

The sound came again, very close now, and definitely a human sound.

And then he saw the body of a woman not twenty feet from him. Her arms were flailing wildly, as if she had lost all strength and was about to go under.

The strange owllike sounds were coming from her lips. They were moans for help.

Talus sliced through the sea and grasped her hair just as the water gurgled over her mouth. Then he pulled her over the wood. She kept making the strange moaning sounds.

"You're safe," he kept whispering to her, trying to calm her. Then he realized what a fool he was to say those words. They were not safe. They were both about to become fish food. For the first time since he dived off the cliff, Talus lost hope.

"There! Look there!" The lookout on the *Cretan Queen* was pointing just off the bow. "Do you see them?"

Captain Zeno swung the ship slowly around in the brisk morning breeze and pointed her toward the spot.

Tirzah, wrapped in a shawl, stood on the deck and watched the maneuver. "Survivors from Home?" she asked Zeno.

"It appears that way. There should have been a lot more."

From where they had been anchored, everyone on the *Cretan Queen* knew what had happened. From a safe distance they had seen the signals that the Sea Peoples' patrols sent back to their ships, reporting that the treasure had vanished and the soldiers were wreaking their vengeance on the inhabitants.

Ropes were flung overboard, and then sailors climbed down to fasten the ropes to the people in the water. The two survivors were slowly hoisted on board, and then gently lowered onto a pile of skins that had been spread on the deck.

"Even from here I can tell they haven't been in the water too long—maybe a day," Zeno said.

"How can you tell?"

"Their skin. After three days in the water the skin is all washed out, like a corpse's." The captain then handed the wheel to an underling and headed toward the survivors. Tirzah followed.

"They'll come to soon, sir," said a sailor, stepping back to permit his captain a closer look.

"Get some broth," Captain Zeno called back as he stood directly over the nearer survivor, a middle-aged woman.

He stared down at her. Then his body stiffened so suddenly and so violently that Tirzah, who was by his side, was startled.

He started to say something. At first it was a whisper, and no one could make it out. Then it seemed to be a name, and it became louder and louder. "Nuhara! Nuhara!" he screamed. "It is I, Theon, your beloved husband." He looked around the ship wildly, as if trying to understand where he was. Then he picked up the unconscious woman in his arms and began to whirl and dash around the deck with her as if he had found the greatest treasure in the world.

Tirzah closed her eyes and tried to keep back the hot tears. The sudden recovery of Theon's memory meant she had lost him again. She sank to one knee, weak from the realization of her loss. Would there ever be a chance for them to be together? Would she ever be able to replace Nuhara? Would she ever again experience the joys of love she had reveled in during this voyage—the closeness, the conversation, the humor, the passion? And all this with a man who did not know who he was. But now he did know! Now would be the test.

As she started to rise, her hand brushed against the flesh of the other survivor—the young man.

On his backside was the Child of the Lion birthmark—the lion's paw. It could not be a mistake. Tirzah knew the mark well from Pepi and Theon.

She raised his head carefully. "Who are you, stranger?" she asked.

The young man struggled to answer, but the words made no sense. Tirzah wiped the water from his lips and the brine and the caked green scum from his eyelids.

Finally he was able to answer her: "Talus, son of Iri of Thebes."

Tirzah was astonished. Talus and his blind mother, Keturah, and Iri's adopted son, Phorbus, had vanished at the same time as Theon's supposed death at sea. If they had been on Home all those years, why had no one spoken of them or seen them?

She stroked his forehead gently. "Rest now, Talus. Soon you will be strong again. You have been a brave young man. And Theon will be eternally grateful to you for rescuing his Nuhara."

The young man's eyes widened in horror. He suddenly fought to get up.

Tirzah restrained him. "What is the matter, Talus? What have I said? Please, be calm. Rest."

Talus struggled some more, but then he collapsed. Tirzah did not understand the young man's horror.

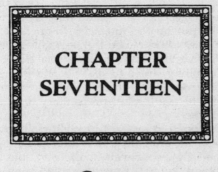

CHAPTER SEVENTEEN

Canaan

"Are you ill, master?" Purah asked Gideon. They were bypassing the outskirts of a godforsaken village called Hamidya on the southeastern end of the Valley of Jezreel. Never before had they been this far south on their food-foraging expeditions, but the family's unabating hunger made it necessary.

"Are you ill, sir?" Purah repeated when Gideon did not answer. All morning Gideon had been silent, sitting on his donkey without speaking, without playing his horn, without even dismounting when there was the possibility of some roots or fruit to be gathered. It was Purah who was doing all the work.

"I am not ill, Purah. I am frightened."

They had been spotting Midianite signs all morning—corpses of Israelites, camel dung, and abandoned Bedouin campfires—so Purah thought Gideon's fears stemmed from that. He replied, "If we are careful, sir, we need not run into any Midianites."

"It is not the Bedouins of whom I am frightened," Gideon said angrily. "It is what Yahweh demands of me to be a hero of my people."

Purah did not reply. He had spotted a stunted acacia tree in a hollow off the path. He dismounted quickly and jogged to it, brandishing a short cutting knife. He began to peel the bark from the middle of the tree, taking care to keep the peel unbroken. It was well-known that the bark of the acacia tree could be steeped in boiling water to make a nourishing liquid. Then the men continued their journey, swinging north, staying close to the Jordan, preparatory to making the final ride home.

They stopped to rest in an Israelite village that had been abandoned, probably as a result of a Bedouin raid. It had been stripped of every tool, every stick of furniture, and every animal. Everything had been taken or destroyed. Many of the huts had been burned, and the ones that had not were shredded by the swords and rendered uninhabitable.

There were no corpses. Gideon voiced the hope that the inhabitants had had prior warning, allowing them to escape into the hills or to the gullies by the river. Any other fate was too terrible to consider.

"Sir," Purah said distastefully, "this is a very depressing place. Perhaps we should go on."

"Good idea," Gideon said, and they quickly mounted their donkeys and made their way out of the village. If they moved steadily, they would be home at dusk.

It was Gideon who first noticed something lying in the road.

"I see it, sir," Purah said, reining in his donkey.

Very slowly and tentatively Gideon urged his mount forward again, with Purah following at the same speed.

Five feet from the object they stopped again.

"A child, sir," Purah said softly.

"No, Purah, not a child," Gideon corrected. "What once was a child." He turned his face away.

The Bedouins had apparently crushed the girl to

death with their camels. But the warriors had not been content with just killing her. It was obvious they had run their camels over her again and again until her flesh and bones were literally part of the ground.

Gideon guessed at what happened: One Israelite girl of about six years had not left the village with the others. Perhaps she had been playing nearby. And her parents had been so frightened that they had escaped without thought of her safety, leaving their daughter trapped in the village.

He forced himself to look again at the pathetic corpse. Tears rolled freely down his cheeks as he wept convulsively, his entire body heaving. As quickly as the tears came, they vanished, and in their place burned a rage so powerful that his hands began to shake.

"No more!" he vowed.

"What, sir?"

"I said no more. No more!"

Purah flinched at his master's anger.

"We must get home before dark, Purah. It is time for me to act. It is time for me to heed the messenger of Yahweh."

When Purah and he reached Gideon's family's village, the man said to his servant: "Bring what food we have found into the house, then water and get the donkeys settled down. I shall be in my father's sacred grove."

"To pray to Baal?" Purah asked, confused.

"No, not to pray. To deliver a message to Baal and to the Midianites—in fact, to all the enemies of Israel."

"Sir, shouldn't you rest first? You are distraught and exhausted. We have come a long way today."

"Do what I say, Purah, then join me, if you wish, in the sacred grove. But if you do, remain silent, for I have much to do in very little time and cannot afford the distraction of weary servants."

Purah shrugged, then obeyed. Gideon watched the man enter the house. It was the moment of truth for the Israelite. What would happen to him when he did the angel's bidding? He felt so alone, knowing he would be sacrificing both family and friends. In the house were his loved ones—his own flesh and blood—who would reject him entirely for what he was about to do. But it was time to act; he could not equivocate anymore.

The memory of the child ground into the dust flashed across his consciousness. It was, he knew, a sight that would haunt him for the rest of his life.

He removed the trumpet from around his neck and dangled it loosely from his left hand. He unsheathed his sword and held it gently in his right hand. Feeling a greater resolve and sense of centeredness than he had ever experienced in his life, the changed man strode purposefully toward the sacred grove of Baal.

The young man called Balak listened impatiently to the sounds of lovemaking coming from behind the tree—the gasping, the heavy breathing, the sharp little cries of pleasure.

"Finish up," he called loudly to the love makers, his friend Simeon and the girl Zela.

Balak felt a little uneasy in the pit of his stomach. He had drunk too much raw wine. Otherwise he would have wanted to have Zela, also. After all, she was willing, and he was one never to let opportunity pass by. But then, everyone had consumed too much wine tonight. His friends wanted a good time. As the night wore on, however, all his male companions, except for Simeon, had slowed down and gone home to sleep.

"Well, how was it?" he asked as the two disheveled figures emerged, rearranging their clothes.

"Too skinny," said Simeon.

"He's not experienced enough to give a woman pleasure," Zela replied contemptuously.

"Now maybe we can finish what we started?" Balak asked. The three young villagers walked swiftly across the road and crossed into Joash's property. Before they had begun to drink excessively, they had planned to steal Joash's bull, then walk for a day to a town where they would not be recognized and sell the beast. It would be a great feat and would put a lot of shekels in their pockets—enough to allow them to party for a month. Given the drought, the famine, and the Bedouin raids, only a fool took life seriously anymore.

"Where is the bull kept?" Simeon asked.

"In the far field," said Balak.

"We don't have any weapons," Zela noted.

"We won't need any," Balak told her. "Are you turning coward on us?"

"No . . . but what if the bull doesn't want to cooperate?" she asked.

"Then Simeon will bite his nose."

Both Zela and Simeon laughed drunkenly at Balak's ridiculous solution. They ran quickly across the near field, circled the village, and started past the sacred grove. Once beyond the grove they would reach the bull's pasture. Balak had already removed the coiled length of rope from his shirt.

"Wait!" Simeon hissed.

"What? What?" Balak asked angrily.

"There's someone in the sacred grove."

"I don't see anyone," Zela said, squinting as she peered around.

"Keep your voice down!" Balak whispered. "There, can you see him now?"

The three crouched in the shadows. They all knew the man; it was the son of Joash.

Simeon snorted contemptuously. "It's only Gideon, that fool who lives to play his trumpet. Keep going. He's no threat to us."

"No," Zela said. "Look! Look what he's doing!"

They watched in wide-eyed horror. All three made the sign against evil.

Gideon's sword slashed against the carefully cultivated vine that framed the entrance to the sacred grove. After he cut the vine to ribbons and the archway collapsed, he moved to the small fruit trees and methodically hacked their limbs to pieces.

Next he went to the meticulously groomed ornamental bushes that lined the borders of the sacred grove. These he crushed with both sword and feet.

Within minutes the ugly stone altar and statue of Baal stood alone, bereft of its decorative cloth.

He urinated on the statue of Baal and then kicked the stone altar down, one piece at a time. Finally Gideon stepped back and surveyed the enormous damage he had wreaked. He was happy. *Now*, he thought, *for my father's bull.*

He turned and jogged to the adjoining field. The bull was visible against the east fence. Gideon unlatched the gate and walked inside, closing it carefully behind him. This bull was alert and ugly and violent. As Gideon approached the beast, he whistled softly to calm it. Just as it seemed Gideon would be able to get close the bull would move away, snorting and pawing at the sod with his foot.

He knew he had to hurry things along. Time was fleeting, and someone might hear him and try to stop him before he fulfilled his obligation to Yahweh. The Israelite felt strong and confident now; but if his father came screaming out of the house, Gideon did not know if his resolve would falter.

Then he had an idea. He raised his trumpet to his lips and blew a series of soft, plaintive notes. The bull stared at him, disoriented, snorted, then stood quietly. Gideon continued to blow the notes and slowly come closer. It worked! The recalcitrant bull was completely entranced by the sound. Five feet away . . . three feet . . . Gideon slowly readied for the sword stroke . . . twelve inches . . . The bull's breath was like a hot wind on Gideon's face.

With the trumpet still at his lips, he plunged his sword deep into the bull's neck. Blood spurted into the night air. The beast fell to its knees. Gideon pulled the blade out and drove it through the bull's left eye with all the strength he could muster. He staggered back, trembling from the effort. The bull pitched on its side, twitched momentarily, then was dead.

Now all Gideon had to do was sacrifice the beast to Yahweh. But a hundred questions popped into his mind. What portion of the bull should he sacrifice? What were the necessary prayers? What was the ritual?

He did not know. His father was a follower of Baal. None of the old Israelite traditions pertaining to Yahweh existed in his family's life.

First, he guessed, he would need an altar, and that was easy enough to arrange. Having decided against using any materials from the sacred grove, Gideon moved quickly about the field, gathering rocks and stones and swiftly piling them up into a makeshift altar. On top of the stones he placed dried twigs and grass.

Which parts of the bull did Yahweh desire? Gideon decided upon the tongue and the heart. Using his sword, he slit the bull open and removed the heart, then severed the tongue, and laid them on the tinder. Lastly, using flint, he lighted the kindling. The flesh began to sputter as it burned.

He vaguely recalled having heard only one prayer, the Sh'ma. So he recited it aloud in the open field to the stars: "HEAR O ISRAEL, THE LORD OUR GOD, THE LORD IS ONE."

Reciting the prayer triggered a memory, which was startlingly clear. If the sacrifice was a guilt offering, the priest would do the following to the one desirous of being cleansed: Place the blood of the sacrifice on the tip of the right ear, on the thumb of the right hand, and on the great toe of the right foot. Gideon dipped his hand into the belly of the slain beast and performed the blood anointing.

Now the man's heart felt full. For one who had always been so agitated, Gideon felt amazingly at peace. He had satisfaction in knowing that he had done the right thing.

Aram the elder glared with contempt at the three young villagers standing before him. He spat on the ground, then turned to his companions, who were gathered in the parched village clearing.

"These three young drunkards," Aram announced, "say they have important news for us."

Everyone laughed.

"Their information is so important," Aram continued sarcastically, "that it could not wait till morning."

Again everyone laughed. "I know we do not have reputations for honesty or seriousness," Balak allowed, "but you won't keep laughing when you hear us."

"Then spit it out, you young fool."

Simeon straightened his back and puffed out his chest importantly. "Gideon has destroyed his father's sacred grove. And he dismantled the altar to Baal. And he pissed on the statue of the god."

His words were greeted with a gasp, then shocked silence. Suddenly one elder guffawed, and the others joined in.

When the hilarity subsided, Aram grabbed Simeon by the neck.

"Let him alone!" Zela screamed. "He is telling the truth. We all saw it. I swear to you."

Aram released his hold and shoved Simeon away. He stepped back and looked speculatively at the revelers. Behind him, murmurings had grown into an ugly roar. Other villagers, meanwhile, were drifting into the clearing.

Simeon said repeatedly, "He pissed on our lord Baal. He has brought shame and ill fortune to all of us!"

"Then we must kill Gideon!" a voice screamed.

"Kill him now!" another demanded. "Who knows how much of our misfortune is Gideon's fault!"

The crowd was growing hysterical. Many of the men ran to their huts to retrieve their weapons.

"Are we all agreed that Gideon must pay?" Aram shouted.

A roar of assent shook the night. The frustration born of poverty and oppression had found its scapegoat. Aram motioned to the three informants to lead the way. They started down the road, toward the house of Joash. Aram followed, and behind him came the armed and angry villagers, who vented their fury in threats and curses. Men began to circulate bladders of wine. Women removed daggers from their robes and pressed the weapons into the hands of the men as they passed.

Soon a hymn to Baal rose from the crowd. It sounded like a battle cry.

*   *   *

Gideon trembled in the face of his father's wrath.

"What have you done? What have you done?" Joash stared at the remains of his slaughtered bull, the bull whose sale he had counted on to rescue his family from starvation. "Purah told me I'd find you here, but he didn't say what you had planned to do. I'll kill him for keeping this secret."

"Purah didn't know," Gideon said.

Joash raised his fists above his head and brought them down with all his strength onto Gideon's face. The blow dropped Gideon to his knees. The old man pummeled his son, berating him for his stupidity, until Shulamith and young Miriam rushed to Joash and tried to pull him away. But the man flung them aside. Weeping and screaming he flailed at Gideon, who made no move to defend or protect himself.

"You have betrayed your own father! You have betrayed your wife and your sister and your children! You have—" Joash fell exhausted to the ground beside his son.

Miriam rushed between them, kissing them both again and again, trying to wipe the blood from Gideon's forehead and the tears from Joash's sunken cheeks. "Please," she begged, "no more violence between you. Please, Father."

"Look! Look!" Shulamith shouted.

All eyes turned toward the edge of the field. In the darkness an army of bobbing torches was approaching. And then the angry shouts of the villagers came to them on the wind.

"Kill Gideon!"

"Murder the blasphemer!"

"Run, Gideon, run!" Miriam cried, helping him to his feet.

But he fell back, still dizzy from his father's blows. He rose again with his sister's aid, stumbled, and finally began to run awkwardly toward the sacred grove. He could see the villagers gaining on him. Their torches gave the illusion of streaming tails of fire as the men quickly approached.

Although he ran as fast as he could, a quick glance over his shoulder showed Balak separating from the others and closing the distance. The young man tackled Gideon just as he reached the outskirts of the grove. The men landed with a grunt, then Balak leaped up and landed a well-aimed kick to Gideon's groin. Pain exploded before his eyes, and he rolled in agony on the ground. Dozens of villagers pounced upon him, kicking, punching, spitting, tearing his garments.

Miriam came running up and pulled at the attackers' robes as she shrieked at them to stop before they killed her brother. Finally, after the first-blood frenzy was over, the mob stepped back, their chests heaving. Gideon lay curled on his side on the ground, barely moving. The blood was soaking his robes.

Aram and all the elders stalked off into the grove to inspect the damage. The others waited just outside the destroyed archway entrance. When the elders emerged, their faces were dark with anger.

"Tie him to that tree," Aram ordered through clenched jaws.

Rough hands hauled a semiconscious Gideon off the ground and, using belts from their robes, strapped his legs and arms around the trunk. He slowly moved loosened teeth toward the front of his mouth with his tongue and allowed them to escape through his lips to the ground.

Aram turned to the crowd and described in detail how Gideon had destroyed the sacred grove . . . had broken the altar of Baal . . . had so foully dishonored the likeness of the god.

"Flay him! Flay him!" came the dread cry from the crowd.

Balak and Simeon and the other younger villagers quickly gathered whiplike branches from the ground. They tested them in the night air, swinging them back and forth, creating whistling sounds. They were satisfied; the branches would easily slice through flesh.

Gideon opened his swollen eyes as much as he could, but they were mere slits. He had no will to live. When the piteous sobs of his mother and wife and

Miriam reached his ears, he had the desire to die. Every part of his body ached; his mouth was full of blood. Something sharp struck him on his face. Someone was slamming his trumpet against the tree trunk, destroying the instrument with each stroke until it was a mangled piece of junk.

Through the confusion and the smoke Gideon could hazily make out the forms of many people he knew—fellows he had played with as a child and fought with as an adolescent, men whose families had been friends with his own for generations. He knew they had drunk too much wine, but that did not explain the pure hatred in their eyes.

"I did it for you," he rasped. "For all of you . . . and for your children." He wanted them to understand, so his kin would not be disgraced after his death.

"Shut him up!" Aram seethed.

A dozen fists crashed into Gideon's face, sending his head bouncing off the tree trunk.

"Flay him now! Flay him!"

The demands became more insistent. Someone flung a torch at Gideon. It struck his body, and Gideon screamed from the pain and fear before the brand fell to the ground and extinguished itself.

Simeon danced out in front of Gideon and swung a makeshift whip. It whistled through the air and struck Gideon's naked chest, opening a thin cut from shoulder to crotch. The pain forced Gideon's head back against the tree trunk. Then the girl Zela jumped out and struck with her branch, but lower, across his thighs.

Gideon's family watched helplessly from the perimeter of the crowd.

"You must help him, Father," Miriam pleaded, pulling at his arm in desperation.

The old man did not reply. He watched his son writhing on the tree as the blows rained upon him.

Miriam collapsed at her father's feet. She had been the love child of his middle age. Her tears broke his heart, but the old man's shame and anger would not allow him to intervene.

"I beg you, Father. You know that you have not been well lately, that you may not live to see another year. Please, do not go to your death with your son's blood on your conscience."

"He dishonored all of us," Joash said, touching his beloved Miriam on the forehead.

"No, Father! He could never do that. There must be some explanation, if we would but take the time to hear what it is. Look at him—he is in agony. I beg you, have mercy on Gideon."

Joash tried to shut his ears to his daughter's pleas, but they burned into his soul.

Then she asked quietly, "Would you watch me die, too? Would you also watch me be tortured to death?"

Joash could no longer ignore her. He pushed through the crowd and stood between his son and the attackers. He raised his hands to signal that the flaying must cease.

"Get out of our way, Joash," Aram warned. "You don't want to get killed for something you didn't have a part in."

"No more, Aram. I say no more to all of you." Joash scanned the crowd defiantly. "I will not tolerate my son's execution. What he did was to *my* bull, to *my* grove, on *my* land. What gives you the right to—"

Shouts of anger from the crowd overrode his words. An empty wineskin sailed through the air and struck Joash on the side of his head. He staggered but did not fall.

"Your son has brought dishonor and bad fortune on all of us, Joash. How can you defend him?"

"I am not defending him," Joash shrewdly said. "I am imploring you to stop and let the punishment be carried out by someone else."

"Who?" the crowd shouted.

"By the great Baal himself," Joash replied.

His answer pitched the crowd into silence. They did not know how to respond.

"Your words confuse us, Joash," Aram said.

"There should be no confusion. If he has indeed blasphemed against Baal, then it is Baal who must punish my son."

For the first time, murmurs of assent circulated among the crowd, responding to the logic of his words.

Joash, seeing Miriam's eyes glowing with approval, pressed his advantage. "And if my son is truly guilty, then I assure you that Baal's vengeance will be a thousand times more ferocious than anything we mortals can muster."

Aram, also responding to the change in the villagers' mood, nodded vigorously, then waved his arms to signal the crowd that the game was all over. The mob quickly dissolved into small groups and began to wend their way out of the fields and off Joash's property.

When the family was alone, Joash drew his knife and cut the bonds that held Gideon to the tree.

"Thank you, Father," Gideon whispered.

"Don't thank me," Gideon snapped. "Miriam persuaded me to save you. But it shall never happen again. From this day to the end of time, you are no longer my son, and I am no longer your father. You will leave my house immediately and never step foot upon my land again."

Then Joash turned and, pulling a weeping Miriam along with him, stalked back to the house. Gideon's mother and wife were nowhere to be seen. They had already left with the villagers.

Gideon awakened at noon. He was lying on a small hillock a few miles from his father's house. A sheepskin covered his horribly bruised body. He was exhausted and confused. Blood had caked in the wounds, and there was not a part of him that did not throb with pain. The sun was hot. He rolled slowly over, longing for a sip of cool water.

No sooner had the desire been expressed than he felt cool liquid against his mouth. He opened his swollen eyes a bit and saw a man standing directly in front of him, holding a small water basin. Gideon drank the water slowly through his damaged mouth, and only when he lay back did he realize that his benefactor was none other than the messenger of Yahweh.

"You have done well, Gideon," the angel complimented. "You have followed Yahweh's instructions."

"Done well?" he retorted sardonically. "Yes, look at me. See how very well I have done."

"Now you must crush the Midianites."

Gideon laughed, then clutched his ribs to ease the agony. "Crush the Midianites? The only thing I have been able to do is shame my family and lose them forever. What kind of God is this Yahweh who makes me break one of His own commandments—who forces me to dishonor my father?"

Messenger clucked his tongue. "Are you losing heart again, Gideon? Are you acting like a little boy because that crowd destroyed your horn? Because a few rascals cut you a little? Is that it, Gideon?"

"Why don't you answer my question first?"

"Very well. Yahweh is your real father. Joash is just a substitute."

Gideon glared in disgust at the angel. "You talk riddles, always riddles."

"The Midianites are not riddles. They are well-armed, ruthless fighting men. Now that you have passed your first few tests, you will spread the word of insurrection, of resistance, among all the Israelite tribes. Understand? You will bring them your new-found power. You will destroy all vestiges of Baal in their villages and show them how to sacrifice to Yahweh. You will tell the tribesmen that Yahweh is about to break the back of the Midianite army and all its allies."

Gideon did not reply for a long time. He stared at Messenger and finally said, "I want another sign that Yahweh is with me."

"You have had enough signs, Gideon."

"No—I need one more. I must have some indication that I have done the right thing. I need assurance that I will never be deserted . . . so that if I am hung on another tree, I will be brave."

"Very well. Stand up."

Gideon did so with assistance from the angel. "Follow me," the blacksmith requested.

Gideon followed the angel for about a hundred yards.

"Do you see that spot of grass?" he asked Gideon.
"Yes."

"Well, tonight you shall sleep there in your sheep-skin. And when you awake in the morning, the grass will be drenched with dew, while your sheepskin shall remain as dry as the tinder you used to sacrifice to Yahweh." The moment he spoke those words, he was gone.

Gideon rested on the small grassy spot for the entire day and fell asleep early. When he opened his eyes again, it was dawn. He reached out hurriedly with his hand. It came back from the grass drenched with a thick dew. Then he stood up and inspected the sheep-skin. Inside and out it was totally dry. But even more miraculous, he was free of pain. His eyes were clear, their swelling gone. He had every tooth in his mouth. His flayed skin had been restored, the bruises healed, and his movements were easy.

He had not gone twenty feet when he heard, "Master!" Gideon turned to the sound. On the path was Purah, leading two donkeys and carrying a sword in a scabbard, a bow, and a quiver of arrows.

"What are you doing here?" he asked his servant.

"I wish to accompany you, sir," Purah said.

"Your loyalty is commendable, but I am not going on a food-foraging expedition this time. Now I am going to preach insurrection and violence. I am going to destroy a god named Baal and the murderous Midianite horde."

"But it is my duty to accompany you, sir."

Purah spoke with such trusting resoluteness that tears came to Gideon's eyes.

"Then follow me," he consented.

CHAPTER EIGHTEEN

Mediterranean Sea

There were not enough accommodations for the newcomers on the *Cretan Queen*. The long, cavernous hold had been temporarily partitioned into cubicles for Tirzah and Nimshi. Nuhara was assigned Nimshi's old cabin, now that that unfortunate life had ended. Talus made do with a small hammock given privacy by woven straw mats, which were hung from overhead beams.

Now Talus lay on his hammock. It swung with the movement of the ship as the vessel cut swiftly through the waves, heading toward Tyre. He was exhausted but could not sleep. The motion of the ship in the strong wind was like potent wine; it made him giddy.

His thoughts went to that other ship's voyage he had taken as a boy. That vessel had been a much smaller boat, fleeing from the burning city of Troy; his childish fears had been allayed by the soothing words of his mother and the confident professionalism of Phorbus. Now his body felt peculiar from his long immersion in the cold seawater; the skin felt tender and tingly.

Dim candlelight crossed his eyes and then vanished. He heard the creak of footsteps on wood. Someone had entered his cubicle.

"Who's there?" he asked, swinging up into a sitting position.

He heard a sardonic laugh. The visitor was Nuhara.

"What are you doing?" she asked nastily. "Brooding, perhaps? Are you berating yourself for having been stupid enough to save the life of the very woman who denied you your rightful place on Home?" She laughed again. "Are you agonizing over the blind fate that caused you to rescue the daughter of Khalkeus, the witch who condemned you to ten years of pain and hunger and poverty?"

"Leave me alone," Talus said tiredly, and lay down again. He did not want to speak to her or look at her.

She moved closer. Her expression was hard, and she spoke in a low, dangerous tone. "Are you plotting against me, Talus? Are you planning to slip a knife into my heart because I am to blame for your mother's and stepbrother's deaths? That's what I'd expect of you—that's all vagabonds like you know—knives in the dead of night."

"All I want to do is sleep, Nuhara," he replied. "Go away." Her presence frightened him. He did not know how to deal with any woman, much less someone like this Nuhara.

She yanked hard at the middle of the hammock, sending it spinning around so quickly that Talus was thrown from it. He landed hard on the planks.

When he looked up, she was bent over him, glowering. "Maybe," she hissed, "you are going to enlist Theon in your vengeance plot. Perhaps you believe he can rectify all the wrongs done to you. Like the other Children of the Lion you probably believe that Theon is brave, wise, and good. Well, let me tell you a little secret: Theon is a fool. And now he is powerless. He continues to exist only at my pleasure, and when it pleases me, he will die."

"Theon is just a name to me," Talus replied, too frightened to move off the floor. "Just a name I heard from my mother and my stepbrother."

"Make sure he remains only that," she warned. "Just a name. Otherwise you will be dealt with in the same way I am going to dispose of his other wife and children—the ones who know him as Zeno, when he supposedly lost his memory. The bastard."

She drew her finger across her throat.

Talus rose. He was taller than she, but her burning energy and hatred made her seem larger than life.

"Don't threaten me, Nuhara," he said. "My life has been garbage because of you. And, yes, I do blame you for the deaths of my mother and Phorbus. Just feel fortunate that I'm too tired right now to do anything about it. You'd be smart to leave me alone."

She threw back her head and laughed. "Ah, Talus, Talus . . . Don't you understand? I will kill you if you interfere with me."

It was difficult for the young man to believe that this violent, scheming, incredibly bold woman in front of him was the mother of Gravis and Hela—the gentle twins who had brought him food all those years.

Suddenly, Nuhara smiled sweetly. "We have shared a great adventure—and great danger, haven't we? There is no reason either of us should step on the other's toes. You have a long life ahead of you, Talus. Why should it not be a pleasant life?"

She was beginning to confuse him now. First she threatened him with death; now she was wishing him a long and happy life. He started to climb back into his hammock. She turned and smiled at him over her shoulder as she pulled back the hanging straw mat. "I do hope they give us some fresh fruit tomorrow, don't you?"

And then she was gone, and he was alone, swaying in the hammock to the movement of the ship. The world outside the mountain where he had lived for so many years was a very strange and frightening place. The people were too complex for him to understand. Nuhara was entirely beyond his comprehension. But he did sense fully the danger she represented, and intuitively he felt that she was playing a game with very high stakes—a game where the winners became wealthy and the losers died. He sighed deeply, closed his eyes, and tried to sleep.

CHAPTER NINETEEN

The Syrian Desert

Shortly before noon the Amalekite war party stopped, and the slaves, including Luti, set up long rows of black tents. The warriors quickly crawled beneath the shelters to wait out the hottest time of the day.

Luti, who had lost all sense of time, lay chained to a tent peg, her body half in and half out of the shade. Had it been two days or four since she was captured and her caravan destroyed? She could not remember. All she knew for a certainty was that the Amalekites were traveling southward.

The sun had parched and broken her skin. Her lips festered and oozed, and her body was bruised and sore. Every muscle ached from the sexual violations visited upon her; the warriors had used her like a beast. Her once smooth and manicured hands were swollen from the constant chores—grinding meal, making fires, feeding the camels.

Her eyes burned and teared, but from where she was tethered she could see Bedouins inside a tent across the way enjoying their midday meal. They chewed on small pieces of dried mutton, fillets that each of them carried in a small pouch around the neck. They dipped wooden bowls into a caldron of hastily prepared hot herb tea. This they drank greedily, straining the small leaves through their brown-stained teeth, then spitting the soggy herbs onto the ground. The warriors remained silent as they ate and drank.

Luti kept shifting her weight from side to side. She no longer cared about her nakedness but hoped to prevent the sun's rays from burning into any one part of her with a prolonged intensity. She was like a chicken cooking on a spit, turning constantly.

The sun became hotter and hotter. After the meal inside the tent, the Bedouins dozed. During these few precious moments of peace, Luti thought of her beloved son. She tried to imagine his being safe and sound in Ur, being taken by Ossaf for a cool stroll by the river. All her images were interrupted, however, by overriding mental pictures of sand and blood and heat and terror.

Luti shook her head to cast away the violent tableaux, and in so doing she noticed that one of the Bedouins inside the tent rose and stretched.

Luti immediately stopped moving. She wanted to disappear, to dissolve into nothingness. *Please, please,* she thought, *no more, not again.*

Her eyes followed the nomad as he moved slowly across the tent floor and toward her. He was one of the worst of the Amalekites—a tall, rawboned man with powerful hands. Like the others of the band, he wore no jewelry, nor were his robes ornamented. On his face, however, a ferocious design had been applied permanently with blue dye.

He bent to step outside the tent, then placed his foot on her breast. The sole of his foot was hardened from years of desert travel. It cut into her nipple.

"Please leave me alone," she whispered through cracked lips.

He glared down at her. She squirmed to escape the pain, but he kept her pinned. She could not look away from his cruel, lusting eyes.

"On all fours," he commanded.

"Not again, I beg you!" She squirmed with all her might and finally escaped from the foot. It did her no good; she was tethered. Fear and loathing shook her body in a series of tremors. All the rapes had been like this—the Bedouins wanted their women to be like dogs. How many times had it happened? How many more times could she stand?

He kicked her over onto her stomach. Her tongue tasted the burning desert floor. He squatted and sank his teeth into her buttocks. She cried out again and again until her voice was barely audible. Then, like the cowed, beaten terrified slave she had become, she rose to all fours and endured the brutal and sudden penetration. Blood trickled down her thighs and onto the desert floor, like petals falling from a short-lived spring flower.

And then it was over. He pulled out, straightened his robes, and strode away. She lay there, without moving, beyond weeping.

Blessed night—at night there were no beatings and no rapes. Luti had been moved and was tethered near the camels now. Wide awake, she shivered from the cold as her eyes searched the camp.

She had decided to kill herself, to find something sharp and cut her own throat. Death was a pleasant, inviting alternative to what she had been enduring, even if she would never see her son again. Unfortunately, except for the swords and daggers carried by the Bedouins, the desert seemed cleared of lethal objects.

In despair, Luti hugged herself against the cold and closed her eyes.

A low whirring sound awakened her. She sat up, wide-eyed and frightened. Two bright specks peered back at her in the night. They were the eyes of a bird of prey, a hawk, only two feet away from her. Its eyes were like golden orbs, which turned silver, then red in the cold moonlight. Its talons grasped a small pack rat, and its beak savagely ripped chunks of flesh from the prey.

She stared at the hawk's beautiful feathers—black and brown with small bursts of iridescent colors on the tips.

As she stared at the nighthawk, memories of her old benefactor, Drak, flooded her consciousness. He had saved her life by activating her occult powers when the priests of the goddess Astarte had charged her with blasphemy. The way he had done so was simply by wearing a coat made of the feathers of the nighthawk. Luti had always been fascinated by birds and felt a special affinity for them, but she had never suspected that these proud and beautiful creatures could bring out a mystical power within her. Drak, however, had seemed aware of her gift from their first meeting. Luti tried desperately to recall his explanation of the "miracle" he had unleashed, but she could not. It had something to do, however, with the zodiacal configurations of the feathers and her own zodiacal sign.

For the first time since she had been captured she felt a surge of hope. What if she could activate her own occult powers? What if this hawk could locate Micah and guide him to her, saving them both?

I must stay calm, she told herself. *I must clear my mind of all fear and pain.* She closed her eyes and relaxed. She tried to empty herself of memories and exist in the desert as if she were a natural force, just like a tree or a stone.

A strange lightness flowed up her spine. It reached her neck, eyes, and head, then radiated to her hands. She felt totally at ease and powerful. She laughed joyously, as if she were watching something beautiful and playful, as if she were watching a child.

She held out an arm toward the hawk. The bird did not move.

"Come, my lovely," she whispered.

Slowly, tentatively, the hawk dropped the prey on which it had been feasting and climbed onto her wrist. She felt the talons bite into her hand, but the pain was pleasurable.

"Micah . . ." she whispered. "Bring me Micah."

In her mind she formed a picture of his face and his body and transmitted it through her hand to the hawk. It was as though a living thing were passing between them—a force so powerful and so mysterious that it could never be named.

A second later, with an enormous beating of its beautiful wings, the hawk flew off into the darkness.

She turned and, smiling, settled down to go back to sleep. Instead she found herself staring into the eyes of a Bedouin. He was not more than six feet away, and his hands held a long, curved sword in front of him. He had seen everything.

"What were you doing?" he demanded, his eyes wide with horror and fear.

Luti cringed away from him. She did not answer.

"Who are you? What magic is this?" he asked.

Luti steadied herself. She realized he was one of the younger Bedouins, called Umas, and one of the few who had not raped her.

"Are you a witch?" he asked, still terrified.

Luti studied the man. Once again a feeling of hope rippled through her. *If the nighthawk does not perform,* she thought, *perhaps I can use my wits to break my chains.*

She finally replied in a low, dramatic whisper, "I am Luti of Ur. I am a great sorceress. I can turn the tides of battle. I stop the rivers. I can bring fruit from the ear of a camel."

The young Bedouin seemed mesmerized by her calm demeanor. She could see sweat rolling down his face. Then he began to pace. Finally, he bent close to her.

"Will you come with me to the Midianite camp and display your powers?"

"For what purpose?" she asked slyly.

"If you are a true sorceress, the warlords Oreb and Zeeb will reward me for bringing you to them. The fools in this camp will realize that I could be a great leader. And you will be given your freedom and a mountain of gold earrings in exchange for your assistance."

She bowed her head to hide her smile. "I will go where you take me," she agreed.

CHAPTER TWENTY

Tyre

They were all bathed, fed, rested, and clothed. It was late morning in the spacious apartment Tirzah had rented when she had first arrived in Tyre in response to Nimshi's message. Talus sat cross-legged on a cushion in the corner of the large reception hall. Tirzah rested on a hammock. Theon sat erect on a wooden chair that was carved with griffins. Only Nuhara was agitated. She had been pacing the hall for most of the morning. A noontime repast—bowls of warm milk, fruit, and sweet cakes—set on a low, long table, was ignored by all.

It had been a tense several days. Talus's years-old anger toward Nuhara had not abated. If anything, it had been exacerbated by the woman's ingratitude and threats toward him after he had saved her life.

Tirzah, meanwhile, was still numb from the tragedy of the massacre on Home, Nimshi's betrayal, and his subsequent suicide. She silently thanked the gods that her husband Pepi had not lived to witness the violent downfall of the Children of the Lion. It was almost inconceivable that the entire financial empire of the once-proud clan had been destroyed.

She looked over at Theon for a moment and hoped to catch his eye. At least he was alive and his memory recovered. Theon, however, did not return her look; he was watching his wife.

Nuhara suddenly stopped, raised her arms, and cried out: "Where are my children? Where is my father?" With a violent gesture she knocked two of the bowls of milk off the table and onto the floor. White rivulets crept between the baked clay floor tiles.

"It is too early to have word of them, Nuhara," Tirzah reminded gently. She hated Nuhara and was jealous of her, but now, she knew, was not the time to attempt to recapture Theon for her own. As a result she had resolved not to let her feelings for Theon's wife show. Any display of hostility on her part, Tirzah reasoned, would only alienate Theon.

Nuhara wheeled to face her husband. "This is all your fault. None of this would have happened if you hadn't abandoned us."

Theon started to speak, but Nuhara picked up another bowl and flung it at him. The bowl landed with a sickening thud against Theon's cheekbone. Tirzah started to get up to go to him, but Theon raised a hand, stopping her. He merely sat still, accepting the pain as if he deserved it. His handsome face was almost expressionless.

"Do you think I believe your story?" Nuhara shouted.

"It is true," Theon replied softly.

"No! Lies! All lies! You abandoned me and the twins. For what? For a barmaid? For money? To be free?"

"I lost my memory, Nuhara."

"No! Not your memory! Your responsibility!"

"Please, Nuhara. After I saw you, I remembered a fierce storm at sea and a blow to my head. I remember trying desperately to keep afloat but sinking. I remember the screams of drowning men all around me."

Her voice was thick with bitterness. "Betrayer! Lout! Murderer!"

Theon did not reply.

Tirzah, both pleased and embarrassed by Nuhara's outburst, fought back the desire to go to him and console him and give him strength against his wife's cruel words. She glanced at Talus. The young man's face was blank, although he could not have helped but hear the venomous outburst.

Finally Theon spoke. "I thought, Nuhara, that all this was past us. I thought that after our reconciliation on the ship, we would be together like we were in the old days when we met. I thought you had forgiven me."

"You thought wrong."

"I cannot bring back those ten lost years," he said.

"Nor can you bring back Hela and Gravis. Nor can you bring back my father. Just what *can* you do, Theon?"

"I swear that I will look for our children until they are found."

"You swear? What good are your promises? What good were your marriage vows, for example?"

Theon stood and moved toward her. "Things are never as bad as they seem, Nuhara. Remember, when Demetrios was alive, I increased the value of the family's business by manyfold, and I can do it again. All is not lost."

She smiled at him, but her eyes remained hard. For the first time Tirzah realized that Nuhara was much more dangerous than she seemed. In fact, Tirzah had the sudden revelation that Nuhara's rage and grief were manufactured in an attempt to manipulate Theon. The woman was working him like a puppet.

"How little you know, my dear husband," Nuhara said contemptuously.

Theon touched her gently on the shoulder, but she knocked his hand away.

"I will make up for all those years, Nuhara. I will

be a good husband. I will find our children and your father. Please believe me. Let me dedicate myself to you. Remember how we loved each other. . . ."

Tirzah stole another glance at Talus. A look of pure hatred clouded his face. *Strange*, Tirzah thought. *What clues to Nuhara's dark side might Talus have from his years of living on the island?*

Tirzah turned back to Nuhara. She had allowed Theon to touch her, and they were speaking in lowered tones.

"It will be good again, Nuhara," Theon promised.

"No. It's too late for a lasting reconciliation. You have been away too long."

"Why too late? We are still young enough to dream."

"My only dream is that my children and my father will be restored to me."

Theon buried his face in his wife's hair and clung to her. They stood together for a long time like that.

It was getting painful for Tirzah to watch and listen, but Nuhara's performance was fascinating.

"Come with me upstairs now," Theon urged. "I want to be alone with you."

Nuhara smiled. "Can't it wait?" she asked ingenuously.

"We have waited too long already."

Hand in hand and oblivious to everyone else in the room, the couple walked slowly toward the bedroom suites.

Tirzah lay sleeping on a couch in her bedroom. The afternoon sun was kept out of the room by a heavy, dark cloth pulled across the windows. The room was dank and musty. Tirzah was suffering one of her recurring nightmares. Her eyelids fluttered, her feet and hands twitched, and she moaned piteously.

In the dream she was back in the brothel in Damascus, where she had been enslaved many years before. She was chained naked to the bed as a man entered the room. He was huge, dressed in some foreigner's costume that she could not identify, and speaking in a language she could not comprehend. His eyes bespoke the potential for horrible cruelty. She tried to crawl beneath the bed, but the chain was not long enough.

When the man undressed in front of her, she saw that he had a strange tattoo on his chest—an image of the sun, with a horse and rider in its center. He demanded by gesture that she touch the design. Terrified, she obeyed, and miraculously the design began to change, first into a moon, then into a plant, and finally into a picture of herself so terrible—

Tirzah awakened with a scream. Her body was drenched with sweat, and her heart beat wildly. For a moment she did not know where or who she was.

Someone was knocking softly at her door.

"Come in," she said, panting.

Talus entered quickly and closed the door behind him.

"May I speak to you for a moment?" he asked.

"Of course," she said, trying to compose herself as rapidly as possible. She swung her feet over the side of the bed and pointed him to a small chair.

"Are you recovering from your experiences?" she asked.

"Yes, thanks to your hospitality."

"Well, you are young and strong." She wanted to ask about his hatred for Nuhara, but she decided against it. The young man was obviously troubled enough, and she did not want to bring up a painful topic.

"I want to know—" Talus paused uncomfortably and looked around the room. Then after a deep breath he continued. "I want to know why Nimshi betrayed Home."

"I think," Tirzah said slowly, "we should try to understand that poor man. He suffered greatly."

"But why? By allowing Home to be destroyed, Nimshi took all hope from my life. All my dreams of gaining what was *mine*, truly and rightfully mine, were lost!" Talus showed anger for the first time, and Tirzah was taken aback by its obvious depth. She realized that

Talus was after something. He had some kind of secret agenda. To whoever betrayed him, he would be a formidable foe. He had his father's strength and resolve. As for brains? Well, that she could not discern just yet. She decided to tell the young man exactly what she knew about Nimshi, although that was not very much. She had not been in Tyre long enough to obtain complete information.

"Nimshi was constantly in pain, and to get relief, he bought drugs. He needed money and fell into debt with the Phoenicians, particularly a moneylender named Navan, who also owns the Safe Haven Tavern. That is where Nimshi spent most of his time. It has also come to my attention that he was desperately in love with one of Navan's dancing girls—a whore named Cotto. She supplied the drugs to him. That's all I know."

Talus said nothing for a long time. He seemed to be searching for words, to be trying to tell her something about himself and his own feelings.

"I know that Nimshi's betrayal was responsible for death and misery," Tirzah sympathized. "But he was a very sad man, a person who, even in death, cries out for compassion."

"Thank you," was all Talus said. Then he rose and left as quickly and as quietly as he had entered.

Tirzah leaned back onto the bed, closed her eyes, and tried to go to sleep.

Just as she was drifting off, a sound came through the wall from the adjoining room. And then another sound filtered through, but louder this time, and rhythmic, like gusts of wind blowing hard through a field.

Tirzah sat up. What was it? she wondered. And then she understood. These were the sounds of passion. Theon was making love to Nuhara.

Tirzah felt the bottom dropping out of her world and experienced the most excruciating pain to her spirit. She remembered how Theon's strong hands felt upon her own body; she remembered his passionate caresses. She sat on her bed, fists clenched, heart burning with jealousy and longing. At that moment she came to terms with the fact that she would go to any lengths to get Theon back.

The sounds became louder and louder. Each moan, each exhalation of breath, seemed to pierce her like a knife. Her misery was so great that she prayed to Deborah's God, Yahweh, for help. And then she tightly covered her ears with her hands so she would no longer hear the sounds of love.

Talus softly closed the door of his room and walked to the window, where the light was strongest. He pulled out the long knife he had taken from Tirzah's kitchen. It had a good blade—iron. But the handle was of a maggoty sandalwood and too loosely fitted the blade.

He went to a small chest and carefully removed the fine piece of leather he had purchased the day before. He cut the skin into very narrow strips and proceeded to rebind the handle, covering the wood tightly with layer upon layer of skin to stabilize the grip and ensure the driving power.

When he was finished, he slashed the air, then hefted the weapon from hand to hand. It was good now, balanced and tight. It would do the work. Let these middle-aged fools play out their games of reconciliation and love, he thought. He was after bigger quarry. He was going to avenge that massacre on Home. First he was going to kill the dancing girl who had lured Nimshi into betrayal, and then he would take care of the Phoenician who pulled the strings.

As for Theon and Tirzah—well, they were good people, and he was grateful to them for their kindness; but their brains were addled. From their ship they had not seen all that had happened on Home. They had not witnessed the extent of the holocaust. Besides, Tirzah could not be expected to seek justice; she was not a Child of the Lion by blood. Theon was, but after ten years of amnesia, he probably no longer cared about his proud lineage.

Talus had thought of confiding his plan to Theon. The older man inspired trust and affection. Talus felt close to Theon, even though they had not said much to each other since he had been plucked from the water. Talus decided his instant affinity with Theon was due to their blood kinship. Above all, he would never blame Theon for Nuhara's perfidy.

Ah, Nuhara! Talus thought. How could Theon love her above Tirzah? How could a woman so beautiful have such a rotten core? Talus's grip on his blade hilt tightened.

He stared out the window. Dusk was still a few hours away. Then he would go to the Safe Haven Tavern. He squatted against a wall and waited. The idea of resting on the soft, canopied bed was alien to him after so many years of rough living in the mountains of Home. He placed the knife on the floor in front of him, the point facing away.

It was odd, he reflected, that for ten years, ever since he, his mother, and Phorbus had arrived at the island from Troy, he had never given a damn for that birthmark on his back or what it represented. But now it seemed to be the most important thing in the world, the very core of his existence. He leaned forward, picked up the knife, and touched the blade's point with his finger. He gritted his teeth and pressed down hard on the point. It broke the skin, and the blood trickled out. He smiled grimly; the pain felt good.

He leaned back and savored the pain. It molded to his mood. He thought about his mother, and her gentle face appeared to him: The deeply etched lines of woe made his heart ache. What would she say of his mission? he wondered.

Just as the last rays of sunlight filtered through the window, Talus slipped out of the apartment and to the street. He did not know Tyre at all and was forced to stop often and ask directions to the tavern.

Once inside the already crowded inn he used one of the coins Tirzah had so generously given him. He purchased the cheapest bowl of wine available, then sipped it, grimacing, as he studied the crowd. This was his first time inside a tavern, and the cursing and yelling and pushing made him realize how little he knew of the world. The second bowl of wine put him more at ease, and he poked at the arm of a grizzled old sailor who sat slumped over the bar next to him.

"What do you want, boy?" the man growled.

Talus's eyes widened when the man turned toward him. One of the sailor's ears was missing, giving him the appearance of a demon animal, like those painted on the rocks of Home.

"Sir, can you tell me when Cotto dances?"

The old sailor leered as if Talus had made a dirty joke.

"It'll cost you a bowl o' wine to get an answer," the sailor said.

Talus flipped another coin on the bar, and the old man snatched it up with amazing speed. Within a minute his bowl was refilled then drained. The sailor answered, "Not tonight, boy. Not here."

"But I thought she dances here."

"She does most of the time. But tonight she dances for her lord and master."

Talus remembered what Tirzah had told him. "Would that be Navan?" he asked.

"Aye, Navan the Phoenician—the ugliest bloodsucker that ever crawled out of a hole. Aye, she dances for Navan tonight at his grand house by the north port."

Talus's face fell. This was a bitter disappointment. He leaned forward against the bar, and the knife concealed in his garment made a dull metallic noise. Talus withdrew it, to better secure the weapon in his clothes.

"What are you up to, boy," the old man asked, "with a weapon like that in your tunic?"

"Nothing," Talus muttered.

The sailor clapped him on the back. "If you're up to nothing, then my name is Khalkeus of Gournia. Come close, lad, and I'll tell you something."

Talus hesitated, then moved closer.

"You're a nice boy, and you took care of me," the sailor whispered conspiratorially, "so now I'll take care o' you. You can't miss Navan's house. It's right on the water. Behind its low wall are all kinds o' fancy trees and plants from across the sea. Now, the Phoenicians hire Sea Peoples to guard their houses, and the Sea Peoples are hungry for money. All they got for their pains at the island Home was blood. So if you have one of those coins left, just give it to the guard at the gate, and he'll let you in. He won't care; a lot of people come to Navan's when Cotto dances there. You'll just be another ugly face." He laughed at his own joke.

Talus did not wait any longer. He thanked the man, pushed his own bowl of leftover wine within the sailor's easy reach, and walked out.

Talus knew his way back to the port—it was near Tirzah's apartment—and he found Navan's house quickly. It was just as the sailor had described: the low wall, beautiful plants illuminated by the port fires, which were kept burning all night as a navigational aid, and Sea Peoples guards stationed around the perimeter. But so many people were walking in through the main gate, the guards seemed barely to be checking.

Maybe, Talus thought, *I can sneak in.* But he decided to follow the old sailor's instructions, after all. His simple garments were nothing to be ashamed of, but he was not dressed in finery, as were the guests. He feared he would be immediately stopped by the guards if they caught even the slightest glimpse of him. Quickly he devised a simple plan.

After presenting himself to a guard at one of the smaller side gates, he said deferentially, "My master wishes me to fetch a woman within. Her name is Aiisha. She is a friend of Cotto's. She knows that I am coming."

The guard screwed his face up and stared malevolently at Talus.

"It must be done discreetly," Talus went on, trying to sound confident, "and my master asked me to give this to you, as a guarantee for your silence." He shook the last two coins out of his pouch and dropped them into the guard's hand.

Not another word was exchanged. The guard simply turned away, and Talus, his heart beating hard, walked inside. He passed through elaborate gardens and entered the main courtyard, which was set off from the rest of the house by twenty-four marble pillars. In the center of the courtyard were pools with fountains that sent enormous spurts of water high into the air.

Talus was both dazzled and repulsed by the lavish surroundings and the sophisticated, beautiful people. Slaves circulated with trays of succulent tidbits. The Phoenicians with their high hats and pointed beards glided about, their intricately embroidered robes rustling silkily. The women wore form-fitting gowns with overdresses of the sheerest materials. Gold shone around their necks and ankles and wrists. Gems glittered in their earlobes and on their toes and fingers. This was a wonderland of wealth, something he had never experienced before. And yet it had been earned through ruthless betrayal, drug dependency, and death. Many of the non-Phoenician guests were exotic. They wore garments and fine, strappy sandals the likes of which Talus had never seen. And their languages were totally incomprehensible to him. Some words sounded similar to the language he had heard in Troy as a young boy. *Are there Trojans in the courtyard?* he wondered. There was no way to know.

No one bothered with Talus. He felt oddly invisible. The slaves passed him by without offering him food or drink. The guests did not even glance at him. He did not belong to their world, and apparently he emanated no threat at all. Talus grinned nastily. Little did they know. . The knife inside his tunic was soothing to him.

As he strolled through the gathering, his attention was captured by one Phoenician in particular. The man seemed to be hovering around the festivities without participating. He gave occasional orders to one slave who seemed to be a supervisor of the others, greeted new guests, smoothed any difficulties, brought people together. This, Talus decided, must be Navan. He studied the host's face carefully so that when the time came there would be no mistake—his knife must be buried in the chest of the correct man. But first he must deal with Cotto.

Two very young slaves with beautiful faces materialized from nowhere in the center of the courtyard and began to ring tiny silver bells. Their peals were so pure that virtually all conversation among the guests ceased as they looked up toward the bell ringers. The children rang the bells three more times, and then the man Navan called out to the assembled: "It is time, my friends, for Cotto!"

Immediately there was much cheering and applause, and the guests standing in one area of the courtyard were gently ushered away to provide space for a stage. The guests waited in expectant silence.

First a drummer emerged from the hallway to the courtyard, bowed elegantly, and settled himself on a raised cushion. Then a tambourine player entered and sat opposite the drummer. When a woman with a lyre joined them, they began to play what struck Talus as a very sad melody.

Murmurs rippled through the gathering as Cotto appeared from the hallway and stepped into the center of the courtyard. She was exceedingly beautiful, the most lovely creature Talus had ever set eyes upon. She had luxurious dark hair, sparkling golden eyes, and the whitest, smoothest skin. She was small boned, but her breasts were large and her feet delicate and narrow. She wore a single diaphanous garment of snowy white.

To Talus, she had an otherworldly quality. He could not look away as she began to move sinuously to the music. Her garment swirled about, first revealing, then hiding, giving the odd impression that she was naked, then clothed.

Talus watched, his body tense, his eyes fixed on the dancer. He had never seen a professional erotic dancer. At first he was ashamed to look, but then he drank her in. Every movement of her limbs became grist for his fantasies. He wanted to edge closer to her, but there were no openings to accommodate him. Sometimes she would dance out of view for a moment, and his whole body would twist to avoid losing sight of her. Not watching her every step or nuance would be a tragedy for him.

He narrowed his eyes and stared at her with a burning intensity that, he prayed, would cause her to meet his gaze.

As the dance progressed from restraint to abandon,

Cotto began to mime the act of love in all its graphic manifestations. The audience, caught up in the music and the passion, began to move with her. It was as if the entire crowd were making passionate love to one dancing girl, as she, in turn, made love to them.

Talus's knees began to tremble. His neck and his chest were wet with sweat. His mouth was dry. Never in his life had he wanted so much to touch someone . . . to sway with her . . . to make love to her. . . .

Cotto mimicked one last shudder of erotic ecstasy, and then she crumpled to the floor in a heap. The performance was over. The crowd burst into applause and cries of acclaim. They begged for an encore.

Talus came to his senses. He was not there as a spectator, he was there to administer justice, to kill her. It was obvious that the crowd's reaction would prompt Cotto to give an encore, and Talus realized that his resolve would falter if he watched her dance again. His eyes located the passageway from which she had first emerged. There might be a room off that hall, where she had changed into her costume. That was where he would wait for her. Slowly, elbowing and pushing, he worked his way through the still frenzied crowd and into the passageway.

Talus found only one room with a latch. He opened it, slipped inside, and noted with satisfaction that it was a jumble of dancer's veils and cosmetics and sandals and gowns. He stationed himself next to the closed door so that the moment she passed into the room he could drive his long knife into her treacherous heart.

The darkened room was cool and quiet. He faintly heard the sound of music, so he relaxed, knowing he had the time. He pulled out the knife and held it by his side. He was ready. He was ready to avenge Home and his family. His mind began to race, replaying the slaughter he had seen.

The horror of his reverie ceased when the music stopped and he heard more wild applause, more shouts. Then all was silent.

He pressed his back against the wall. His palms

were sweating. It would be soon. She would be coming back to the dressing room soon. Talus stood rigid, not breathing. Suddenly the door swung open.

Cotto entered, closed the door behind her, and stood for a moment, exhausted. Then she walked to the low pile of cushions at the far end of the room.

Talus stepped out, savagely grabbed her shoulder, and flung her hard to the floor. He stood over her, the knife's point pressed at her heart. The dancing gown was open; her breasts and nipples were naked near the knife. He stared down at her. Her lovely face was contorted with terror.

"Who are you? What do you want?" she whispered, her voice quaking with fear.

"I am Talus, a Child of the Lion."

Her eyes seemed to glitter with recognition. "Like Nimshi."

"Like those who were murdered on Home by Nimshi's betrayal of his own blood."

"Please . . . you have no quarrel with me."

"Don't lie to me—I know everything. I know you gave drugs to Nimshi. I know you work for Navan. I know that you led Nimshi to the betrayal."

Talus raised the knife with both hands and held it aloft as he stared at her trembling body. All he had to do was bring the blade down and drive it home, tearing the living heart from this dangerous creature.

"Please don't! You have misjudged me. Have mercy on me. I have done nothing wrong. I tried to help your kinsman."

Talus listened to her pleas. Her voice was beautiful, like a song. Why could he not kill her? He shut his eyes and tried to envision the carnage she had caused.

"I saw you watching me," she whispered. Her voice was low, seductive. "I know that you like me. Put your knife away and stay with me. I will show you love. I will make you happier than you have ever been in your life."

Her body gleamed with perspiration. Her eyes were like pools of liquid gold. He felt himself growing weak. He felt the knife slipping from his hands.

"Come lie with me," she intoned. "Put your knife down. Come with me."

He staggered backward and dropped the knife. She rose quickly and went to him, placing her hands behind his neck and pulling his face down to her breasts. He kissed them slowly at first, and then with a desperation that seemed to drain the will for violence from his body.

How many times had they made love? He did not know. But in the few short hours he had shared with her, he experienced a joy and a release that he had never thought possible. Their first coupling was fired by his rage at what Nimshi and Navan had wrought, and Talus's climax was at once painful and ecstatic. After that catharsis, their lovemaking changed to pure pleasure. Her lips were like sweet water. Her movements were like a wild animal's. Her body was like a sword and then a feather and then a narcotic. He could not get enough of her.

Now he gazed at her sleeping face. Her hand was open, and he kissed the palm. She stirred but did not awaken.

He rolled over, on to his back, and stared at the ceiling. Where was his knife? He did not care. The weapon and his dark intent seemed a thousand miles away. He closed his eyes and fell into a deep peaceful sleep. . . .

"Talus, wake up."

He sat up quickly. The first rays of dawn were slanting into the room. He turned to her. A smile graced her beautiful face. She reached out and stroked his cheek.

"I think I love you, Cotto," he said suddenly and with great passion.

She chuckled and moved closer to him.

"And I think you are just a young man who has never had a woman before. You don't love me—you are pleased with me. That's all."

He squeezed her hand with such fervor that she

winced from the pain. Realizing what he had done, he kissed her hand repeatedly. "I swear that I love you. I love you more than life itself."

She kissed his eyes, then asked seriously, "Do you love me enough to help me escape from Navan?"

He did not understand her question. Was she a prisoner in Tyre?

"If you truly love me," she pressed in an urgent voice, "then you will help me steal Navan's gold coins—no less than I deserve, after all my services for him—and come with me away from here, far away, to a new life."

Talus kissed her passionately, and she pushed him away playfully. *Why shouldn't I go away with her?* he thought. *My home is gone, my people are gone, my past and future are gone.* But stealing gold coins?

"I am not a thief," he told her.

Cotto smiled craftily. "It is the same gold that hired the Sea Peoples to attack the lair of the Children of the Lion."

Talus's face brightened. He understood what she was saying—that if he wanted vengeance on the real betrayers, the Phoenicians, the way to do it was to take their gold.

"Yes, yes! I'll do it, Cotto. When?"

"Right now," she replied.

"Now?" he responded, astonished. "You mean we steal the gold today and then escape?"

"Yes! Are you frightened?" she taunted. "Or do you have to say good-bye to people?"

"I am afraid of nothing. And there is no one who gives a damn about me," Talus replied.

"Except me," Cotto corrected.

He moved off the cushions, retrieved his clothing and his knife, and dressed. As he watched her dress and comb her hair, he realized with great joy that he would be with her for night after night, morning after morning, into the future. Maybe he could be with her forever.

They closed the door softly behind them and walked through the courtyard where Cotto had danced.

She held his hand gently. Dozens of revelers from the night before were sleeping off their drunkenness, stretched out on stone benches. Cotto ultimately led him to a passageway behind the opulent kitchen and down a flight of steep, slippery stone stairs. She stopped in front of a large wooden door reinforced with metal straps and motioned for him to open it. It was difficult, but finally the door swung open.

"You see," Cotto said as they stepped into a high-ceilinged vault, "the Phoenicians collect beauty."

The room was indeed filled with wondrous objects: magnificent woven rugs, delicately painted vases, urns, and tiles, and large jars filled with jewels and ornaments.

"There! In the corner!" Cotto said excitedly. "That's the chest!"

It was an old, ugly, wooden chest.

"Open it quickly, Talus," she urged.

He knelt in front of the chest, broke the latch with the handle of his knife, and eased back the lid. The sight inside was dazzling. The chest was filled with thousands of small gold balls, none larger than a grape.

Cotto sank to the floor beside him and thrust her hand into the wealth. "Egyptian beads," she whispered. "Each one is pure gold." She picked one up and held it in front of Talus's eyes. "Look, dear. What do you see?"

Talus squinted. He could discern a design, but he had no idea what it meant. He shrugged.

She smiled and kissed him. "The Egyptians use these as royal coinage. The design on each bead is that of Horus, their feared falcon god. But we must go quickly now." She produced six small leather bags. "Fill these. They'll be all we'll be able to carry on our trip, but they'll be enough."

Talus dug his hands into the chest, scooped out handfuls of beads, and filled the bags.

"Quickly, quickly!" Cotto urged.

The bags held more than he had estimated, but finally they were filled almost to the top. He tied the pouches around his waist, to the belt under his outer robe, using the thongs that held the six bags closed. Then he stood, staggering a bit under the unexpected weight.

"Can you manage?" Cotto asked, taking his elbow.

"For you I could carry triple this weight," Talus replied.

She led him slowly down another long passageway and finally out into the bright morning. Talus turned around but could see no sign of the Phoenician's house. This was bewildering. They were right at the water's edge, in front of what seemed to be a private wharf. Several small boats were tied to the pier. The passageway, he realized, must have gone for a long way under the street.

"The Phoenicians," Cotto explained, seeing his disorientation, "always make sure they have an escape route." She walked along the wharf, and Talus followed. "We'll use that boat." She pointed to a small vessel with the oars lashed to the sides.

Talus nodded, then started to climb down into the boat.

Cotto stopped him. "No, just cut the rope so the boat will drift away. We're not going by water, but we want them to think we are."

He nodded, aware of the value of the ruse, and severed the rope that held the boat to the pier. It began to drift slowly out to sea with the tide.

Then Cotto started to walk swiftly along the water's edge. Talus struggled to keep pace—it felt as if the bags were growing heavier by the minute. The young lovers finally exited the city at one of the small southern gates. Merchants were already setting up their stalls for vegetables, fruits, garments, and tableware. Cotto walked around them, to the pens where traders displayed their beasts of burden.

"Look at these," she said to Talus, pointing out two sturdy young donkeys. "They're the best kind— from the south, surefooted and tough. Give me a gold bead."

As the toothless Bedouin donkey trader watched, Talus walked a short distance away, turned his back, and rummaged under his outer robe. When he returned to Cotto's side, he handed her a bead. She held it up to the trader and gestured that it was intended as payment for both beasts.

"If I wanted to haggle," she whispered to Talus, "I could get five donkeys for the single gold piece."

The trader grabbed it eagerly and called his brethren over to show them the remarkable exchange he had made. Meanwhile Talus and Cotto climbed onto their donkeys and rode off.

"Where are we going?" asked Talus.

"My home. Megiddo."

"Where is that?"

"In Canaan. Didn't you know that I am an Israelite?"

Talus was astonished, but he did not reply. It had never dawned on him that this dancing girl was a member of that religious sect with whom generations of Children of the Lion had been so close. He realized that she would probably disclose many more surprises.

"Yes," she added happily, her smile brighter than the sunny day, "thanks to you I am going home."

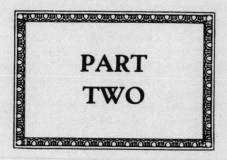

PART
TWO

PART
TWO

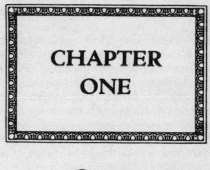

CHAPTER ONE

Canaan

"That is a high mountain, sir," Purah remarked as he and Gideon reined in their donkeys on the slopes of Mount Tabor. "I'm not sure we'll be able to—"

"Nonsense, Purah," Gideon retorted confidently. "We are now beloved of Yahweh. We each have the strength of ten—nay, twenty; nay, a *hundred* men! Can't you feel the strength and virility inside you?"

"Actually, sir, I'm hungry, thirsty, and exhausted."

Gideon waved away his servant's complaint, then he stared up at the trail leading to the mountain summit. The lack of rain had created a brown patchwork landscape. "I have never prayed to Yahweh," Gideon said quietly, "but at the summit I will. Yahweh has always manifested Himself from the mountaintops. The Law, if you recall, was given on Mount Sinai. We must go to the top to offer our prayers."

"As you wish, sir," Purah said, sighing.

The men kicked the donkeys and began the ascent.

153

The path was not steep, but its configuration quickly wearied riders and their mounts. Soon Gideon was drenched with sweat, and his muscles ached like fire. But the higher he climbed and the more tired he felt, the clearer and more resolute his thoughts became.

"Look!" Purah suddenly shouted. "There, sir, off to the left!"

Gideon looked. Just off the path sat a low, thorny bush with oddly curling leaves. But nestled within the bush were three magnificent clusters of red ripe ground berries. The Israelite blinked.

"It is a mirage, Purah. Our fatigue, hunger, and thirst have played tricks with our eyes. Don't bother to dismount."

But Purah had already slid down from his donkey and was hurrying across the path. "This is no mirage, sir. Come quickly!"

Gideon dismounted and joined his servant. They stared at the lowly bush.

"Have you ever seen anything so beautiful?" Gideon asked Purah.

But the servant did not answer. He was already stuffing the berries into his mouth. Gideon happily followed Purah's example, and within seconds every berry had been consumed. The sweetness of the fruit dizzied the men, and they stood for a moment staring stupidly at each other.

"Think they were poisonous?" Purah asked as he pressed his fingertips to his temples.

"You fool, this bush was a gift from Yahweh to give us strength and hope. But like all of Yahweh's gifts, they are too powerful for mere mortals."

The men sat down. Gradually their dizziness abated, and they felt refreshed. They continued on their journey until they reached the small plateau on the top of Mount Tabor.

"That is where I will pray," Gideon said to Purah, pointing to a small area bordered by a clump of stunted trees and a line of chipped rocks, which seemed to form a kind of natural room.

He handed his weapons to Purah, then walked proudly to his destination. Once there, he raised his arms skyward and called out in a loud, clear voice: "I am Gideon, Your servant. I have heard the words of the God of Abraham and Isaac and Jacob. I will do Your bidding. I beg You to give me the courage I will need. I ask You to lend me Your strong right arm so that Your people—the Children of Israel—may once again live in peace and prosperity in the land You set aside for them. Make me brave, Lord. Enable me to endure pain. Watch over me so that this land may become as You had intended: a kingdom of priests and a holy people." He fell to his knees and prayed silently: *Hear O Israel, the Lord God Yahweh, the Lord is one.*

Gideon rose and turned to walk back to where Purah stood beside the donkeys. A metallic glint sparkled from the ground well to the left and caught Gideon's attention. He blinked and moved closer to investigate. He found an object with a bronze finish.

Strange, he thought. *It wasn't there before.* His eyes widened, and he took another step. The breath caught in his throat when the object became recognizable. Gideon yelped with joy and ran to the spot. He snatched a brilliant trumpet off the ground and held it high in triumph.

"Look!" he shouted. "Yahweh has restored my trumpet." He clutched it to his chest and nearly wept with happiness.

"It surely is a trumpet, sir," Purah agreed, "but it is not yours. The markings and the mouthpiece are totally different."

Purah's logic could not stem the joy in Gideon's heart. This was the day's third miracle. First the trip to Mount Tabor to pray, next the luscious berries to sustain him, and now the trumpet! Gideon raised the horn to his lips to prepare to play. But at the last moment, he lowered the instrument.

"I shall never blow this horn frivolously," he vowed quietly, "until the enemy has been destroyed. Yahweh has given it to me for my mission."

"You may have your first opportunity to play it soon, sir. Look down there."

Gideon stared at where Purah was pointing. Just

north of Teacher's Hill in the Jezreel Valley were more
Midianites than he had ever seen in his life . . . more
Midianites than he ever believed existed on earth.

"They must have crossed over the Jordan, sir,"
Purah whispered, frightened, as if their presence could
be revealed by speech even at that distance. "It looks
like their entire army."

Gideon could see the hundreds of tents, topped
by fluttering demonic banners, neatly arranged in rows.
He could see the nomads' tethered racing camels mill-
ing in the distance like huge flocks of sheep. Gideon
strapped on his weapons. This, he realized, was yet
another miracle. Yahweh had preordained everything:
By exposing the whereabouts of the Midianite camp,
Yahweh had aided Gideon in planning the Bedouins'
destruction. He straightened his back and let his eyes
roam in all directions. He looked past the camp and
saw the sparkling Spring of Harod. He suddenly realized that from a camp beside the spring's fresh, clear
waters, the Israelites would strike at their oppressors.
The Spring of Harod was the place Yahweh had
selected for the Israelites' gathering.

"We must ride quickly now, Purah," he said.

"Where to, sir?"

"North, to the Sea of Chinnereth, to the tribe of
Dan. They will be the first to learn the news."

It had been a long ride, but at last Gideon could
see the campfires along the edge of the water. "A small
settlement," he remarked to his servant, "but this is
where we will begin. Let's leave everything but our
weapons here."

A few moments later Gideon strode off. Purah hurried at his heels. As they reached the small group of
huts, Gideon raised his trumpet and blew a long, strong
blast. Immediately, men, women, and children ran
from their hovels and scurried about the settlement to
discover the source of the sound.

Gideon strode to the center of the village. The
confused villagers surrounded him. Their dark eyes
were fearful, and their weapons remained half-drawn.

The flickering campfires threw bizarre shadows across their faces.

When Gideon stared at them angrily, their murmurings ceased.

"Tribesmen of Dan, I am Gideon, servant of Yahweh," he called out.

Some laughter erupted from the villagers, who thought they were in the presence of a madman.

"Listen to Yahweh's commands!" Gideon shouted.

"The only thing Yahweh commands is drought," a voice called out from the rank of villagers.

Gideon drew his weapon, located the heckler, and ran toward the man. He drove his sword point into the fellow's ankle and sent him screaming to the ground. Although a roar of protest rose from the gathering, no one stepped forward to challenge the newcomer. Gideon strode about the circle, glaring into everyone's eyes, daring anyone to step forward. In the flickering light he looked like the fiercest of men; he looked like a warrior who could not be vanquished.

"On your knees before Yahweh!" he yelled.

Slowly, one by one, the villagers sank to their knees.

"Now listen to the voice of your Lord. First, you will destroy all idols to Baal. Second, you will slaughter your finest sheep—one for each family—and offer it up to the God of Abraham, Isaac, and Jacob. And finally, in three days' time, you will all march to the Spring of Harod and prepare to do battle with the Midianite army camped near there."

The tribesmen of Dan were silent. Gideon stood still, letting his words sink in.

Finally he said, "Now rise, all of you. Remember, you are the beloved of Yahweh—His chosen people. Listen to His words and be free again. Ignore His words, and your poverty and pain will be increased tenfold."

Then he lifted his horn and blew a melody that seemed to enter the soul of every living being in earshot. It was a melody so beautiful and so powerful that many of the villagers began to weep.

Gideon then strode out of the village and into the black night, followed by Purah.

"Where to now, sir?" his servant asked with new respect.

"To Megiddo," Gideon answered. Sounds came from behind him. He wheeled with drawn sword.

Three young villagers had followed him. "We wish to go with you," one of them said.

"Then come. Yahweh is pleased."

CHAPTER TWO

Wilderness of Judea

The renegade called Blood crawled very slowly along the hard ground. The first rays of dawn were beginning to pierce the darkness over the eastern horizon. He stopped and glanced back. His lieutenant, Anistos, was about twenty feet to his rear and next to the Greek, the scout Mahal. Behind them he could see the heads of six of his men. He paused for about a minute to give them a chance to catch up, and then began to crawl again.

At last Micah reached the top of the rise. He peered down into the gulley. Six Egyptian chariots from the infamous Harishaf Brigade were arranged in their nighttime defensive formation, positioned like the spokes of a wheel. He nodded to himself, satisfied. He and his men would prevail over those who hunted them.

Quietly, carefully, Micah removed his throwing daggers from the scabbards slung around his neck.

Again he turned back to look; his men were in place, and he gave them the signal. Micah jumped up, leaped over the rise, and trotted down the embankment. He moved faster and faster until he was running with all his strength, pumping his well-muscled legs and screaming his war cry. Behind him, the men echoed his call for battle and Egyptian lives.

He reached the encampment and vaulted lightly over the first chariot. Daggers ready, he turned inside the circle and leaped past a chariot to begin the slaughter. His men were at his heels. But the area within the chariots' circle was empty. He turned a full circle, and a feeling of dread coiled in his stomach as his men, breathing heavily from the run, joined him in the center of the formation.

Suddenly one of his men grunted and, clutching the feathered shaft that had impaled itself in his breastbone, fell to his knees.

"Ambush!" Micah yelled.

A rain of arrows hissed through the air. Crouching low, Micah ran past the chariots. Once he was in the open, he ran until he reached the rocky embankment and scrambled up the steep slope. He felt a stabbing pain in his lower back. Sharp outcroppings and loose stones cut his flesh. Thorns fastened themselves to his legs as he climbed. Finally he collapsed. He could run no more.

He slid into a crevice, confident the shadows would conceal him. There he would be protected from the blistering sun. There he would wait for the rest of his men. He knew that they would be coming soon, he told himself, and then they would regroup and attack again.

Another sudden pain in his lower back caused him to cry out. He reached back with questing fingers, and warm, sticky blood soaked his fingers. An arrow, he realized, must have gouged out his flesh. Hours passed. He turned on his stomach and moved out of the shade so that the sun would help to clot and dry the oozing wound in his back. His muscles cramped, but he could not risk movement. He passed the time by berating himself. His hit-and-run strategy had been a disaster. All his tactics had failed. Finally he admitted to himself that most of his men were dead, and he held little hope for those he had left below. The Egyptians were too powerful, too fast, too well armed.

As morning became midday, then late afternoon, his confidence dwindled further. Micah's failure created a collapse of his self-assurance. He believed that the gods themselves had ordained his downfall the moment the Egyptians had crossed the Sinai. No less than the tide of history had overwhelmed him, allowing the Egyptians to wreak their vengeance on a Child of the Lion, the clan that had been so integral to the Israelites' escape from bondage to the pharaoh generations before. No force on earth could break the power of the past. What god had doomed him? Micah wondered miserably. There was no way to know. What terrible act in his lawless, nearly loveless life had caused the gods to choose him as the target for the Egyptians' revenge?

"Blood! Blood!"

Micah tightly grasped his last remaining throwing dagger and readied himself for an attack. If the enemy found him, Micah knew he would not live to see another day.

"Blood! It's me! Anistos! Where are you?"

"Here, up here," Micah cried out hoarsely, thankfully, and struggled to his feet.

Then the old soldier staggered into sight. An arrow was embedded in his right side, and blood trickled from a wound in his neck. He collapsed beside his friend.

"Mahal is dead," the Greek rasped bitterly, "and many others. The Egyptian bastards shot our comrades' corpses full of arrows for target practice."

"How many got away?"

"I don't know." The old trooper's face was twisted with pain.

Micah studied the embedded arrow. It would be best not to remove it now . . . Anistos's face already had an unhealthy pallor, and he could not survive much more blood loss. The wound in his neck was still bleeding. Micah stanched it with a piece of skin cut from his garment.

"Rest for a minute, Anistos. Don't talk," Micah said.

The lieutenant nodded and closed his eyes. Soon he began to rant. The sun and the pain and the loss of blood had obviously deranged him. Nothing he said made sense. Finally, he slipped into an exhausted sleep.

Micah let the old man sleep for an hour, then shook him gently. "Anistos, can you get up? We must go."

"Where?" the old man asked weakly.

"Deeper into the Wilderness of Judea. To the Khareitun Caves. We will be safe there. And our men who survive will surely head there, also, to meet up with us."

Anistos nodded and struggled to rise. Micah helped him, and soon the two wounded bandits, each helping the other, hobbled toward the north.

They walked for the rest of the night and then spent the next day hidden under a nest Micah constructed of cracked juniper branches. Once, as they tried to sleep in that stifling space, they heard the whir of chariot wheels. From the sound Micah knew there were at least six chariots—the normal contingent for an Egyptian patrol. There was no doubt that the Harishaf Brigade would not rest until Blood and Anistos were dead.

When it was dark, the pair started off again. Their pace was slow, but they were making progress. In the moonlight they could see changes in the terrain. As they moved deeper into the Wilderness of Judea, trees vanished. Strange rock configurations jutted up from the earth. Unseen lizards and snakes made sounds at the men's feet.

"Let me rest," Anistos begged.

Micah stopped and helped the old bandit settle on the ground. After carefully positioning Anistos on his side, Micah hunkered down near the old man and kept watch for the enemy while waiting for his friend to recover his strength.

Suddenly the old man shuddered and cried out a name: "Pia! Pia!" Then he slumped forward.

Micah raised Anistos's head. "It's going to be fine, old friend. We'll be fine. Don't worry."

But the old man did not hear. Anistos was dead.

Micah closed Anistos's eyes and laid him gently on his back. Tears fell freely down Micah's face. Who was Pia? he wondered. Was she a wife? a daughter? a girlfriend? a secret love left in some distant village when a young Anistos had to flee for his life for some crime? In his grief and loneliness, the question of the woman's identity took on great importance. He had soldiered with Anistos for years! They had fought together up and down Canaan. They had drunk together and killed together and looted together—but the name Pia had never been mentioned before.

Why not? he agonized.

Micah calmed at last. "Rest in peace, dear friend," he said, and continued his solitary journey north.

Micah lay in the mouth of the cave. His field of vision covered a wide expanse of wilderness. He had sighted no chariots, but he sensed they were close, very close. None of his men had shown up, and there were no signs of them—neither bloodstains nor broken bushes, nor scuffs in the rocky soil. Were they all dead?

Slumped in pain, thirsty and fearful, he watched the sun reach the zenith. He had an eerie feeling that all this had happened before. It was such a strong and bizarre sensation that Micah heaved himself up and, leaning on the rock wall for support, walked ten paces deeper into the cave before collapsing. He stared up at the walls of the cave. They seemed to lengthen as he went deeper. Then Micah realized that indeed he had been here before—this was the very cave in which he had made love to the Babylonian girl Luti.

Why had he not recognized it immediately? Because all the forges and chariots and metalworkers had long since departed. What had once been a secret installation of forges and armorers turning out superior war chariots had now become wilderness again, as if nothing important had ever happened. But it *had* happened. He remembered with bittersweet pain the shape and feel and taste and touch of Luti's nakedness. He had never desired a woman more. He remembered his passion and how it was reciprocated.

And he remembered her betrayal of him in order to take back to her people the chariot they needed to be safe. He had tried to forgive her for that; Luti had been a soldier, just as he had also been. But often he had wished circumstances could have been different.

He closed his eyes and thought of Luti. He let the memories wash over him like clear, cool water. He let her body resurrect itself on his . . . he let her breasts once again be pressed against his mouth . . . and then he drifted into the deep, dreamless sleep of exhaustion.

It was dark when he awoke. A slight movement had brought stabs of pain from his back wound, rousing him from sleep. His thirst felt like a spear in his throat and chest, and his dry lips were so scabbed and blistered, he could barely open his mouth.

He crawled toward the mouth of the cave. If he was going to survive, he knew he had to find water and food. Slowly, laboriously, he crawled out of the cave. A cool breeze blew from the west, but the baked ground of the wilderness still radiated heat from the sun, which had set hours before. He crawled and rested . . . crawled and rested. His fingers searched the ground for anything edible, for anything moist to slake his thirst, for any hidden pool of strength.

By dawn he had found and consumed only two small green berries. They were so acidic that they burned his parched mouth. It was then that he turned and realized that he had crawled too far from the cave. He would never have the strength to get back to its sheltering protection. He would die where he was, in the broiling sun, a remnant of a man. It was the wrong time, the wrong place, the wrong way to die. He was Micah! He was Blood! He should die in battle, with a weapon in his hand! But as the sun climbed in the sky, he was like a twitching lizard being broiled to death.

"Soon," he whispered to himself, "soon."

Sometimes, when the agony was too great, he weakly called out, "Help! Help!"

But no one heard. He was alone. Then he lost consciousness. . . .

It was pitch dark. *I am dead,* Micah thought. But there were stars above, and the night wind played against his cheeks. He blinked. *No, I am alive.*

But why? he wondered. To suffer another scorching day of agony? *"Take your revenge!"* he cried to the gods. "Take me, if that will sate your blood lust!"

Suddenly he heard a whirring, as if the wind had grown in ferocity. Had Death come to whisk him away? But it was not the wind or death, he decided. Something, some creature, was near him. Again that strange sound flickered across his brain.

He squinted into the night. Yes, he could make something out. It was very close; but he was too weak to defend himself, even if it was a carrion eater, come to consume him while he still lived. He narrowed his eyes. A hawk was five feet from him, on the ground, its wings mantled. In its mouth was a small limp object . . . a baby rabbit.

The hawk's baleful eyes fastened on him. Micah felt a sudden rush of comradeship. He, too, had lived his life as a hunter.

"Brother Hawk," he whispered, "do what you will. Pluck my eyes out. Eat my brains. I understand."

The hawk hopped swiftly toward him, dropped the prey in front of his face, and then hopped out of reach and glared at Micah.

The dying man stared wide-eyed at the fresh kill. Then, gathering his strength, he leaned forward and sank his teeth into the life-giving flesh and blood.

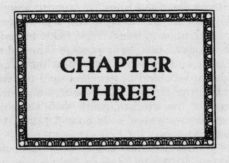

CHAPTER THREE

Camp of the Midianites

Umas, the young Amalekite, whispered to Luti, "Remain kneeling until I address you." Then he turned to speak to the semicircle of fierce Midianites who had gathered at his request.

Luti shuddered as she watched the Midianite warlords. They were the most ferocious men she had ever seen. As badly as she had been treated by the Amalekites, she realized that her situation would have been far worse if she had been captured by Midianites. Their scowls . . . their arrogance . . . their dark, glittering eyes . . . their weapons—all bespoke a cruelty and a brutality that shook her to the core. But she had to seem calm and confident, for this was her only chance to survive.

"My lords," Umas began in the customary flowery tone of oratory, "all the tribes of the confederation pay homage to you for your bravery. We honor your king, Zalmunnah, and your great warlords, Oreb and Zeeb, who have kindly permitted this audience with them. I am proud to bring you a great gift. This filthy slave with a pierced nose who kneels before you was once a great and influential woman. She was stolen from a caravan that had set out from the wondrous Babylonian city of Ur. In her native land she was a sorceress of renown. She can be of inestimable value to you in your conquest of Canaan and beyond. She can read the stars and the birds and the secret hearts of men."

Umas paused, waiting for his words to take effect. And they did; a great muttering rose from the Midianites.

"I myself saw her charm a wild hawk into her hands. I myself saw her create magic." Umas then half turned and gestured at Luti. He wanted her to rise. She did so and stood quietly before the barbarian tribunal.

"Is this so, bitch?" Oreb asked her angrily, leaning over to accentuate his threat. "Can you create magic? Can you foresee the future?"

"I can, my lord," Luti responded. "Even as a child I was able to read the secrets of birds and their journeys across the heavens."

"Birds?" Zeeb exclaimed, then barked a laugh. "We *eat* birds."

There were guffaws among the gathering, but the laughter quickly faded. The Midianites, like all desert Bedouins, believed very strongly in magical properties, unseen powers, and sorceresses. This was no light matter. Only those with magical powers could uncover hidden wells. Only those with magical powers could put a child into the belly of a barren woman. Only those with magical powers could guarantee victory in battle.

"If you were such a great sorceress in Ur, how is it you were captured? How is it you are now a slave whose only function in life is to perform lowly chores and satisfy men?"

"I cannot perform magic for myself, lord. Only for others."

"What kinds of magic?"

"I can find water," Luti replied. Now there was much restlessness among the council. Water was valued above gold. That a miserable slave with a pierced nose could find water at will was both frightening and appealing to them.

"And can you find pear trees?" Zeeb asked sarcastically.

Luti did not respond immediately. She desperately tried to think of the words to ease their suspicion and increase her credibility. "I can speak to the spirits of the dead and relay their words," she lied.

"How?"

"Through trance, lord."

"Can you speak with the spirits of all the Midianites who fell in battle?"

"Yes, all of them."

Luti knew for the first time that she had touched these cruel men. They were taking her seriously.

A Midianite warrior dashed out of the circle and ran toward her, drawing his weapon as he ran. He stopped a few inches from her face and screamed, "Then speak with the spirit of my brother, Ehud, who fell in battle last year. Speak to him and tell me his thoughts. Does he still have anger toward me?"

Luti closed her eyes. She needed time to think. She had never been able to contact the spirit of her dead master, Drak, no matter how many times she had tried. Her occult powers, as vast as they were, simply did not include the spirit world of the human dead. As she stood there, eyes closed, feeling the threatening presence of the Midianite, she fought to construct a logical scenario in her head from the little information the warrior had provided. But there was no time. She had to act fast. "I am in contact with Ehud," she said simply, staring with unfocused eyes, hoping she appeared to be on the edge of a trance.

Her comment deflated him completely. "Tell me what he says," he begged.

"First bring me some water," Luti commanded.

The Midianite rushed back to the circle, picked up a bowl of water, and ran to her with it, offering it to her as if she were a queen.

As Luti slowly drank from the bowl, her eyes surreptitiously surveyed the Midianite onlookers. They all seemed rapt, almost mesmerized by her supposed powers—all except the warlord Zeeb, who stared with suspicion and hate at her. She must be careful of him, she realized. She finished the water. It was time to play the game out. She had no alternative.

She threw the bowl down. Then she intoned, "Your brother, Ehud, forgives you for the camel incident. He says he is no longer angry. He says he has great love for you."

The eyes of the Midianite gleamed, then filled with tears. Brandishing his sword, he leaped joyously around Luti as if he were a delirious child.

She exhaled slowly. The ruse had worked. She had just said the most likely of all possibilities. She had guessed that there must have been some feud about camels, for all Bedouins fought about camels. It had been easy.

She saw Umas the Amalekite gloating that his protégée had performed so well. Obviously he was thinking of the honors that would be heaped upon him.

How ironic it was, she thought, that ten years before, she had saved her life by persuading the priests of Astarte that she was not a sorceress but a Child of the Lion with hereditary powers of craftsmanship and artistry. Now the only way to survive was to prove that she was a sorceress.

Suddenly, Zeeb leaped from the circle of Midianites and cried out, "Fakery! All fakery and a lucky guess. How can you listen to this slut? I'll give her a real test. Bring that Israelite captive from my tent. Cover the captive with a blanket from head to toe."

An underling ran to carry out Zeeb's orders. Luti was confused. What did the barbarian have in mind?

Soon the underling returned half carrying, half pushing a human being who was completely swathed in a filthy bloodstained blanket.

"Listen to me, slut," Zeeb said. "A spear will be run through the captive's body. The moment the captive is dead, you will speak to its spirit. You will learn the captive's name, sex, and age and tell us what they are. If you are truly a sorceress, this task will be easy for you. And then many good things will fall at your feet."

As Umas's eyes widened in trepidation, a murmur of agreement circulated among the Midianites. By their expression, Luti could tell that the nomads perceived this as a fair test. She began to tremble. This Zeeb was a monster. She would have to assent to the cold-blooded murder of the captive or die herself. She stared frantically at the figure. Who was beneath it? What could she do?

"Seka, bring your spear!" Zeeb shouted.

A huge Bedouin carrying a long spear stepped out of the shadows of the tent. He approached the covered captive, raised his weapon, and remained frozen in that position.

"Do you agree to this test?" Zeeb challenged. He looked unnaturally amused. "Do you agree to prove to us that you are indeed a great sorceress from Ur?"

She continued to stare at the blanketed figure. It was obvious that the captive was quaking; that could be seen. Luti knew she had a chance to guess correctly after the captive was slain. She had always been intuitive. She had always guessed right. But how could she stake her own life against the life of a stranger?

"Well, sorceress?" Zeeb demanded. "Just raise your right hand when you're ready, and Seka will drive the spear home."

Luti's legs felt weak. Her shoulders slumped in despair. "I cannot do it," she whispered.

Zeeb turned to Umas the Amalekite. "Fools deserve to die," he told him, then nodded to Seka, who drove the spear through the Amalekite's heart.

"As for our 'sorceress,'" Zeeb said contemptuously, "give her to the men in the tents. Let them have their way with her."

A soldier dragged Luti off by the hair. She never did see the face of the Israelite captive.

CHAPTER FOUR

City of Ur/Kingdom of Babylon

The cooks, maids, gardeners, and all the other servants gathered in the hallway of Luti's grand home and whispered to one another. Their faces were pale and frightened. The dreadful news had swept like fire through their ranks.

The moment Ossaf entered the hallway, they fell silent. Ossaf, they knew, would be able to confirm or deny what they had heard. He was the head servant, and they were used to taking their instructions from him. Their mistress, Luti, rarely spoke to them directly.

The man looked terrible, as if grief had gripped his heart. He was wearing one of his elegant robes—a garment that would usually inspire them to joke about his pretensions. But no jokes were made now, and no contemptuous stares were cast his way.

Ossaf addressed them. "The worst has happened. Our mistress's caravan was attacked by marauders. Apparently there were no survivors. Word was brought

171

into Ur this morning by three linen traders who stumbled onto the mutilated remains. It is a very sad day."

Many servants burst into tears. Several began to pull out their hair and rip their clothes. One woman began the eerie mourning wails.

"What will happen to us?" a voice cried out.

Another asked, "Where shall we go?"

Ossaf raised his arms. "Our mistress knew she was embarking on a dangerous journey. She made provisions in case of her death. Her son, Drak, is the sole heir to her property, and the estate will be administered by a well-respected banker until the child comes of age. None of us have anything to fear. We will not be sold. The household will function as it always has."

There were more shouts, more questions. Ossaf barked back, "Shut up! I don't want to hear any whining. I have to inform the child now. Go back to work—all of you." He turned on his heel and slowly climbed the marble stairs to the upper chambers of the opulent home.

He closed his eyes. In spite of his bravado, he knew that the other servants had been right—their future and his were now precarious. The banker who would administer the estate until Drak reached legal age could, on a whim, sweep away the entire household staff. Ossaf could end his days on a galley ship or in one of the linen sweatshops—or, the gods forbid, in the fields as a fruit picker.

Ossaf knocked and waited deferentially just outside the room to be asked to enter. The child either did not hear him or did not want to see him. There was no response. A sudden fury rose in Ossaf's heart. He knew Drak was in his room, probably staring dreamily out the window at the river.

Now was not the time to continue the master-slave relationship. Yes, he was an indentured servant, but he was also the child's protector. Besides, Drak had never seemed to take into account that in Ossaf's native land, before the reversal of his fortunes, the servant himself had been a man of property, a man who demanded respect. It was only the unforeseen impact of war on his country's economy that had brought him to this present disgrace. He knocked louder and did not wait for Drak to answer. He just walked into the room.

Drak turned and said, "I promised my mother to be a good boy. But I really hate my tutor. Today he talked about farming. I don't want to be a farmer, Ossaf."

The servant stared at his young charge. Sometimes Drak infuriated him. And sometimes, like at this moment, he felt a deep affection for the child.

"I have been a good boy, haven't I, Ossaf?"

"Yes, you have," the servant agreed.

"Then tell my mother so when she gets back. She won't believe me if I am the only one who tells her."

"Your mother is not coming back," Ossaf said flatly.

"Of course she is," the boy said angrily. "And she is bringing my father with her."

Ossaf moved closer. He did not want to cause pain to his charge. He was silent for a long time, but he realized that there was no gentle way to accomplish his grim purpose.

"Your mother is dead, Drak. Her caravan was ambushed in the desert. There were no survivors."

The child looked as if he had been struck across the face. He staggered away from the window. Ossaf reached out to catch him. But Drak, in a fury, pushed the helping hands away.

Very slowly, woodenly, hollowly, he said, "I think I will go to the river to play." He took two or three rigid steps, then stopped. He said in that same strange voice, "I can't go to the river to play. I told Mommy I wouldn't."

And then the bravado collapsed, and the child fell to the floor in a heap, sobbing wildly.

The sobs triggered Ossaf's own grief. For years Luti had been the partner of his nighttime fantasies. No servant had ever loved a mistress so totally or so futilely. He stared down at the child. What could he do? Nothing, nothing at all.

He covered the boy's heaving frame with a soft

robe and drew him into his lap, where he stroked Drak's forehead and whispered consolation until the lad fell asleep. After carrying Drak to the bed, Ossaf left the room to begin his chores. But halfway to the stairs he stopped and leaned heavily against the wall.

Why was he so concerned about a sobbing child? Why did he not worry about himself? No doubt he was about to be discarded onto some dung heap in some forsaken province. Ossaf shook his head. When he had fallen into slavery, he never thought he would survive the indignities. Yet, he had adjusted. To allow himself to suffer a worse situation, however, was beyond all comprehension. He would do whatever was necessary to prevent that from happening.

Beads of sweat appeared on his forehead. No half-hearted measures would help him now. The moment he had heard of Luti's death, he had thought of a plan so bold, so radical, so all encompassing, that it would turn the world—his world—upside down. The slave would become the master. But a moment after he had thought of the scheme, he had pushed it out of his mind. It seemed to him to be one of his Hittite fantasies . . . just as he had imagined over the years making love to his mistress.

He wiped the sweat away with the sleeve of his robe. Now he realized that the audacious plan was his only hope for salvation. If it worked, he would achieve what he deserved. If it did not work, what did it matter?

He looked both ways along the wall, suddenly frightened that somehow his thoughts had been heard. He would have to work quickly. He would have to set the plan into motion in the morning. He rushed down the stairs and out to the shed in the garden, where his wood-carving tools were stored.

Early the next morning Ossaf arrived at the administrative offices of the Temple of Astarte. It was the center of the cult of the goddess in southern Babylon, and the opulent artwork and furniture attested to the power and wealth of the priests.

He waited for hours, holding a large bag gently between his legs. It was past noon when he was finally ushered in to see Lokka, the personal secretary to the most feared man in Ur, the high priest of Astarte.

"I don't have much time," Lokka said the moment Ossaf entered the room. "Be brief and to the point."

"I am here concerning the death of Luti of Ur, sir, and the disposition of her sizable estate."

"You were a servant of the deceased?"

"Yes, head servant for many years, although I am a Hittite by birth."

Lokka grinned nastily at Ossaf's comment, as it was already evident by the cut of his beard and style of dress that he was a despised Hittite.

"My mistress was very wealthy and controversial," Ossaf said, "and—"

"Yes, yes, everyone in Ur knows of the wealth of your late mistress. And many remember that ten years ago she was brought up on charges of blasphemy against the goddess, only to be acquitted through the wiles of a magician." The man turned slightly as he spoke and for the first time since he entered the room Ossaf noticed that he had the small blue Morning Star tattoo of the cult on his left cheek.

Ossaf's confidence grew. This man was a believer, not just a functionary.

"My mistress left her entire estate to her young son."

"Well," replied Lokka with great sarcasm, "I didn't think she left any of her wealth to the goddess."

Ossaf grinned. The man had a sense of humor. "Sir, can a legitimate will be set aside if the writer of the will was guilty of capital crimes against the state and the goddess?"

Suddenly Lokka became interested. "What are you getting at?"

Ossaf chose his words very carefully. "Would Luti's will become invalid if it was proved that the original charges of blasphemy against her were correct? And if it was proved that until her death she continued to blaspheme against the goddess Astarte?"

"A special tribunal would have to be called, but there are precedents. There is no doubt that her will would become invalid. Her citizenship in Ur would be revoked, and that revocation would be retroactive. In other words, all the wealth she accrued would have been acquired as part of a criminal conspiracy."

Ossaf felt his palms sweating. His heart was pounding in his chest. Lokka's analysis had been exciting. His plan was working. "If, sir, the will is declared invalid, who would inherit the wealth?"

"Well," Lokka said, "the child would have to be taken care of with a small annual stipend until his majority. That would be the compassionate thing to do. But the bulk of the estate would be assigned to the goddess, who protects Ur with her mercy."

"As it should be," Ossaf agreed with intensity.

Lokka picked up a quill and twirled it in his hands. Then he said, "This is a most enjoyable conversation of hypotheticals. But I'm a very busy man. . . ."

Ossaf knew that the crucial moment had come. Lokka had given him the opening; he had signaled that he was interested. "Sir, I have evidence that my mistress, Luti of Ur, was a blasphemer of the goddess and that she acted in a criminal fashion until the day of her death. She conspired to induce others to blaspheme."

"What evidence?"

"Sir, if you will forgive me, I am understandably reluctant to provide that evidence until I have a guarantee from you."

"What guarantee?"

"That when the will is set aside, I will receive one-third of my mistress's estate, including her home and her riverfront property. The remaining two-thirds can go the Temple of Astarte."

Lokka set the quill down and circled the room. Finally he said, "This evidence, my dear Hittite, must be very strong. It must prove the charges beyond any doubt. There must be physical evidence—not mere hearsay."

Ossaf smiled. "I performed many tasks for my mistress; among them was the carving of wooden toys for her son and her son's friends."

"What does that have to do with anything?" Lokka snapped.

For the first time Ossaf's voice dropped its respectful inflection. "I will show you after you give me your assurance that we have a deal."

"You fool!" Lokka replied contemptuously. "Of course we have a deal if you have the evidence."

Ossaf opened the sack he had brought with him and dumped the contents onto Lokka's desktop. The dozen wooden toys spilled out. Ossaf picked one up and held it high so that Lokka could clearly see its contours. The personal secretary of the high priest of Astarte grew pale as he stared wide-eyed at the object.

It was a toy with wheels for the child to pull. The carving was a hideous caricature of the goddess Astarte, with bulging eyes, a fat body, and deformed limbs. And the goddess was being mounted from behind by a loathsome jackal.

One after another, Ossaf held up the hard evidence for the explicit and horrendous blasphemy. These objects proved that over the years Luti of Ur had ordered her wood-carver to create loathsome likenesses of the blessed goddess and distribute these objects to children.

Cold fury tightened Lokka's voice. "Not one blade of grass that she acquired will remain in her family. Not one piece of bread that she earned will be bequeathed to anyone of that witch's blood. And if we could find her grave, we would strip the shards of decayed flesh from her bones."

Ossaf trembled. He had succeeded! This particular fantasy had become a reality.

CHAPTER FIVE

Tyre

Tirzah did not wait for her servants to open the door when the knock sounded. Relieved, she went to the door herself. It had to be Talus, safe. She had been worried sick when he had not returned to the house.

But it was not Talus. Instead, a tall, somber Phoenician stood in the doorway. Behind him was a bodyguard wearing full armor in the fashion of the Sea Peoples. The Phoenician, clothed in the usual long gown and high cap and sporting a well-manicured square beard, bowed slightly.

"It is an honor to meet you finally, madam. Your business prowess is legendary, even in Tyre."

Tirzah looked at him blankly.

"I am Navan," he continued smoothly. "You have been making inquiries about me, so I decided to pay you a visit and impart any information you require. I hope I have not called at a bad time."

"Navan, the moneylender to drug addicts," she said with contempt.

"Ah, you are referring to poor Nimshi, I presume. But surely you understand someone else would have provided him with the drugs if I had not. His craving was constant, his pain intolerable." He smiled sadly. "May I come in?"

Tirzah stepped aside and ushered Navan and the bodyguard into the sitting room. She silently resolved to keep her temper.

"Madam, I am afraid I have some bad news for you concerning the young man whom you befriended."

"His name is Talus," she replied.

"Ah, yes, Talus. Well, it seems that he had a dalliance of a sexual nature with Cotto, one of my dancing girls. The passion and the wine must have gone to their heads, for they slipped away from my estate in the early morning hours after stealing a great deal of gold from my coffers. They were last seen purchasing mounts outside the city gates."

Tirzah did not reply. She stared coldly at Navan. The Phoenicians, she knew, were famous for their cunning and perfidy. Navan must have an ulterior motive for making up such a ridiculous story. What was it?

But then she remembered that brief visit Talus had made to her room. He had acted very strangely. And she had told him about Cotto and Navan. But why would he have sought them out? Had he wanted vengeance? Was it blood for blood? Had he intended to kill the girl who betrayed Nimshi and the Children of the Lion?

"I am afraid," she said, "that I find your story difficult to believe."

"Nevertheless," the Phoenician responded calmly, "I am telling you the truth."

"The truth is a delicate thing."

"Ah, a philosophical woman. So rare in our time. And so appreciated." He inclined his head.

She marveled at the arrogance of the man. Navan was calmly standing in her foyer less than a month after he and his colleagues had organized a horrendous massacre on Home. Maybe his conscience was clean, she thought, because the purpose of the raid was not slaughter but booty. Perhaps he did not feel responsible for the fact that his Sea Peoples underlings had gone berserk after no booty was found.

"I have some other news for you," Navan said. "The grandchildren of Khalkeus of Gournia—the twins— are most likely on their way to one of the cities in the Philistine League, to be sold as slaves."

"Have they been harmed?"

"Not that I know of. Twins rarely are. Blemishes diminish their especially high price."

"And Khalkeus?"

"I have no idea of his fate. He vanished."

"And the fabled wealth of Home?"

"It vanished with him." Navan clucked his tongue. "The whole affair was very sad."

The moment he called the slaughter "sad," her fury erupted out of control. "You butcher!" she screamed.

The bodyguard quickly stepped in between them.

Navan said quietly, "I think, madam, I have worn out my welcome. But please remember that should you ever grow tired of good deeds and wish to return to the world of finance, I'd like you to contact me."

The visitors left quickly. Exhausted, Tirzah sprawled out on a sofa. She fell into a troubled sleep filled with macabre images of young Talus. When she awoke she called for some fruit and milk. After consuming the refreshments she felt much better and waited for Theon and Nuhara to emerge from their room.

Finally, they came into the sitting area. They were holding hands like newlyweds. The sight sickened Tirzah.

"Ah, finally," she said. "I have very good news for you."

They sat down next to each other, their thighs touching.

"Your children are alive and well. They are on their way to one of the coastal cities of the Philistine League to be sold as slaves."

"Gaza?" Theon asked.

"I don't know which city."

Theon and Nuhara embraced. "At least Gravis and Hela are alive!" Nuhara said. "At least they escaped death on that island."

She and Theon laughed and cried. It was the best of news and the worst of news. The horrors of slavery were muted by the gift of life.

Theon stood and looked at Tirzah. "Under the circumstances, Nuhara and I must leave. We must look for the twins." Then he held out his hands in a gesture of futility. "But we have no money, no resources. We have nothing."

Tirzah closed her eyes. She could not bear to watch her beloved's anguish. She knew he had to go; but she could not bear the thought of parting again, even if Nuhara had replaced her in his heart. There was a way to help him and be with him at the same time, she realized.

"Listen to me, Theon," she said. "I have more money than I know what to do with. Let me finance your trip. I'll give you all the gold you need to buy passage, mounts, weapons, and retainers. And I give it to you as a gift. All I ask is that you allow me to accompany you."

"You are so kind, Tirzah. How can we refuse such a generous and loving offer?" Theon replied.

"I can refuse it," Nuhara interjected angrily. "I don't want this woman accompanying us anywhere. Gravis and Hela aren't her children."

"But Nuhara," Theon pleaded.

"You heard me, Theon. No. Never."

Tirzah studied Nuhara and tried to keep her anger in check. It was becoming painfully clear that this charade could not continue. If she wanted to take Theon away from Nuhara, it had to be now or never.

Why was she hesitating? Why did she continue to hope everything would work out for the best? Tirzah realized at that moment that she was afraid of Nuhara. But that was ridiculous! She had never been afraid of another woman in her life. There was, however, something deadly about Nuhara—she was lethal and shrewd, perhaps the most complex woman Tirzah had ever faced. It was as if Nuhara incorporated layers upon layers of subtlety, and if one peeled away the skin as one might peel an onion, each new exposure would reveal something more dangerous.

What is the matter with me? she asked herself. *I have to make my move now!*

"Theon," Tirzah said in as steady a voice as she could manage, "there is a small black leather pouch in the chest in my bedroom. It is fastened with a rawhide thong. Please take it out and count how many gold coins are in it. Check it carefully."

Theon hesitated. He seemed to be evaluating his options and where each might lead. For the first time Tirzah noted the lines on his strong, handsome face. Then he stared guiltily at his wife and walked quickly and silently up the stairs.

The two women waited patiently until they heard him close the bedroom door behind him.

"It is a mistake to confront me," Nuhara warned.

"How do you know that is my intention?" Tirzah retorted.

Nuhara raised her chin. "Because you are so obvious. Because you are so pathetic."

Tirzah did not respond to the insult. This woman, she realized, was eager for a battle. Tirzah wished she understood Nuhara's motives in holding on to Theon. The woman was a spider in a vast web of intrigue, and Theon was just one thin strand. But Tirzah could not intuit the parameters of the web.

"Yes, pathetic," Nuhara continued, "the most pathetic woman I know." Her wicked smile grew, then changed into a leer. "Look how smugly you sit. Except for possessing Theon, the world is your oyster now, isn't it? You bask in the adulation; you love to hear people whisper about how you clawed your way out of the brothel in Damascus to become the most adept merchant princess of the Great Sea. And then to even greater accolades you threw it all away to become a veritable model of altruism. You love to hear people talk about how you became a disciple of that dumpy

Israelite prophetess, Deborah, and how you now spend all your time and money helping the poor and wretched of the earth." She spat contemptuously onto the floor.

Tirzah listened to the withering attack. She was startled at how much this vindictive woman knew about her.

Nuhara lowered her voice. "Even my father spoke highly of you—both as a trading rival of the Children of the Lion and afterward, as a great legend of charity." Then Nuhara closed the distance between them and stabbed her finger at Tirzah's face. "But *I* know the truth. Weakness, not strength, turned you into a bene-factor. Weakness and fear and age. A dried-up old whore is no good to anyone, and you couldn't trust your business judgment once the Trojan War changed the rules of shipping. You could no longer control your own destiny, so you crawled away to the hills of Canaan to hide."

"I have done what my conscience told me to do," Tirzah answered.

Nuhara snorted. "Conscience is the last gasp of a coward."

Tirzah was beginning to understand the source of this woman's power. One moment she spoke like high-born royalty; the next moment she spat on the floor like a common sailor. Then she sounded like a philoso-pher. It was almost impossible to take aim at her—she slithered out of all descriptions.

"You are arrogant as well as pathetic, Tirzah. What gives you the right to think that Theon would be better off with you than with me? I am the only one who can provide Theon with what he needs."

Tirzah turned on Nuhara viciously. "Don't make me laugh, Nuhara. You love no one so much as your-self. Listen, you bitch, you never loved anyone in your life. Money and power are all that matter to you. Greed oozes out of you like mud."

"At least I'm not a whore."

"Of course not. Who would pay to sleep with you?"

"Theon would."

"Only because he knows his duty as a husband. It's me he really wants, Nuhara. We have been lovers, then and now. Our love has endured over time. What we feel for each other is genuine, mature. Your marriage disintegrated a long time ago—even before he lost his memory. Let him go! Give him his freedom!"

"A slut like you doesn't know what the word *freedom* means," Nuhara retorted.

Tirzah slapped Nuhara hard across the face. Nuhara stifled a scream and then reached out with a hand to claw Tirzah's cheek, from temple to jaw.

A moment later the two women were at each other's throats, kicking and biting and swinging their arms in wide arcs to inflict as much pain as possible. Tirzah had never felt such fury in her life. She wanted to destroy this creature.

They fell onto the divan. Tirzah's hand found one of the pillows. She pushed the cushion against Nuhara's face and drove her down into the fabric. Tirzah put all her weight onto the pillow. Nuhara lashed out with her hands, but Tirzah kept the pressure steady, and soon Nuhara stopped struggling.

Tirzah released the pillow. The enormity of what she had done suddenly struck her. Her heart beat wildly, and her body trembled. She closed her eyes as if it were a bad dream.

"A present for you," she suddenly heard Nuhara whisper.

Tirzah realized too late that the woman had been feigning death. She opened her eyes and found herself staring at a slim, elegant gold knife blade. The point was next to her throat.

Nuhara was grinning. "Now let me see you use your vaunted powers of the mind to keep my hand from driving this blade through your neck. Come now, Tirzah, see if you can stop it."

The bedroom door upstairs opened. Nuhara quickly slid the blade back into her garment. The two women separated and stood up.

"Why don't we let Theon choose?" Nuhara suggested lightly, as if their violent confrontation had never taken place.

The question was like a sudden thrust in Tirzah's heart. For a second, it made her wish that Nuhara's blade had found her throat. She began to weep. No matter how much Theon loved her, he would never abandon the mother of his children.

He ran down the stairs, holding the leather bag in his hand. He was so excited at the coming journey in search of the twins he did not notice that the two women were totally disheveled—or noticed but discreetly said nothing.

"There's a great deal of gold here, Tirzah," he said.

"Take it all," she whispered. "But please, leave now with your wife. There is no time to waste. As for me, I will not accompany you."

She sat motionless on the divan while Theon and Nuhara quickly packed their few belongings. When the couple came back downstairs, Nuhara and Tirzah avoided looking at each other.

"Will you go back to Canaan or remain in Tyre?" Theon asked Tirzah as he stood by the door, ready to leave.

"I don't know, Theon."

"How can I ever repay you?" he whispered.

She thought, *You have repaid me a million times over. You have given me your love and accepted mine.* But all she could say was, "Move quickly! Be alert! May all the gods help you to recover your children!"

Nuhara finally turned to look triumphantly at Tirzah. Then she moved away while Theon kissed Tirzah gently on the cheek. Finally he and Nuhara walked out the door. Tirzah watched them from the doorway until they were lost to sight. She felt weak, as if all the muscles had been sucked out of her body. She had the horrible feeling that she would never see her beloved again.

PART THREE

CHAPTER ONE

Canaan

I

Talus watched as Cotto bargained with a grain trader on the Plain of Esdralon. The peddler sat high on his wagon, and precious cargo-filled, bulging sacks were piled up behind him. The negotiations had started peacefully but now degenerated into a shouting match. The seller accused Cotto of being a bloodsucker; she accused him of being a thief. But the man's eyes were wide with fascination as he watched her jiggle several gold Egyptian beads in her hand. Gold was a commodity he saw rarely.

Talus smiled in wonder at his lover's persistence. Bewildered, he had no idea why she wanted to buy the grain or why, since leaving Tyre, she had purchased everything she could get her hands on. Cotto and he had escaped from the city after purchasing two donkeys and several goats. Now they owned literally a caravan of donkeys. Each pack animal carried a variety of food, fabric, utensils, and trussed-up fowl. If it could be bought, Cotto had bought it. Where was this crazy acquisitiveness going to end? he wondered.

He was, however, too much in love to protest or question her motives. The nights redeemed all the extra work necessitated by these purchases. At night he held her in his arms, and they made love until exhaustion carried them into sleep. No one and nothing else mattered to him. He would die for Cotto; he would kill for her. He would lead the longest donkey caravan in the world for her. If she had gone crazy, so what?

Finally the bargain was struck. Talus hefted three bags of grain onto his shoulder, secured them to a donkey, and then he and Cotto started off again, heading southeast over the Plain of Esdralon. She took the lead, with Talus at her heels, managing the long train of beasts and newly acquired products.

As they rode, the land and climate began to change. The soil became more barren, the sun hotter, and the area less populated. According to Cotto, this was supposed to be one of the most settled Israelite lands, so Talus wondered where all the people were and why he saw no crops, tilled fields, or grazing flocks.

When the sun was high the travelers rested.

"Are you happy that you came with me, Talus?" Cotto asked, handing him three ripe figs and a bowl of warm goat's milk.

Talus gulped the milk before answering. "I have never even known what the word *happiness* meant until I loved you," he replied.

Cotto stroked his face gently and then kissed him on the mouth. He pulled her against him, but she twisted free, laughing. "No time for lovemaking now, Talus. We must cover more miles today."

After eating the fruit, they started off again. They had ridden about an hour when Cotto asked, "Do you know where we are headed?"

"No," Talus admitted, "but I trust you."

"To Megiddo," she told him. "And if we keep going, we shall reach it by dawn."

Suddenly the air was split by the hysterical braying of donkeys. Talus turned and saw that a single donkey halfway down the line had gone beserk. It bucked and threw off its pack, then swung its legs, striking the other beasts and sending them into a panic.

Both Talus and Cotto dismounted and ran back along the line. Talus reached the errant beast first, grabbed the harness, and sank his teeth into the animal's left ear. The donkey screamed with pain and then stood silent, trembling.

"Easy, easy," Talus whispered to the beast, stroking it gently. "Calm down, boy."

The crisis over, Talus started to take Cotto's arm and walk back to the front of the line. But the woman wrenched away from him, and her eyes shone with anger.

"It's all right, now," he said.

She pointed at the produce that littered the ground.

"No, it's not all right," she said, mocking him. She walked to the offending donkey, picked up a switch, and began to slash at the beast, landing strong, powerful strokes that bit into the donkey's soft muzzle. Cotto's beautiful face was a contorted mask of hatred.

Talus was astonished. He had never seen her behave like that. He did not know what to do. The donkey's plaintive cries filled the air. Talus stepped forward and grabbed her arm. "Cotto, please, no more! You are hurting the poor animal. There is no need—"

She savagely shook his arm off and swung the switch at him. It cut deeply into the side of his face, and the pain was intense. He brought his hand to his cheek and felt blood.

"You stupid fool, don't ever tell me what to do!" she screamed.

He staggered backward from her sudden transformation as much as from her assault and sank to his knees. A second later Cotto was beside him, pleading for forgiveness and trying to stanch the blood.

Talus sat dazed and disillusioned. What had come over his angelic darling? he wondered. But as her sweet kisses covered his face and as her gentle ministrations soothed his body and spirit, all misgivings faded. Soon they were on the trail again. The lovers camped for the night when the foothills loomed up before them. Cotto was pleased by the progress and said that they were only a few hours from Megiddo.

That night, the beautiful dancer made love to him with greater passion than ever before, as if she wanted to compensate for the violent incident with the donkey by using her most intimate charms. After she had brought Talus to satisfaction, she fell fast asleep.

But he remained awake, still troubled and confused by that new persona his beloved had assumed. What did it mean? Who was she really? What did he truly know about her?

They entered the village of Megiddo. It was deserted. They saw no human, no animal.

"Where is everyone?" Talus asked.

"In the hills. In caves. In burrows. Didn't you know that the Israelites are forced to live like rodents?"

"No. Why?"

"The Bedouin raiders hit Megiddo a dozen times, killing and looting, so the inhabitants finally abandoned the village."

They rode through the cracking mud buildings and the few courtyards that fronted empty stone dwellings. Many houses were in such bad condition that their original shape could no longer be ascertained.

After they had passed through Megiddo, Cotto and Talus entered a landscape of inclines that brought them higher and higher. The terrain became forbidding, difficult to traverse. Tangled vines and rocks along the ground tripped them, and sudden thrusts of granite shelves covered by yellowing vines with hideous thorns tore at their limbs and clothes.

"We stop here," Cotto said.

Talus stared around. "Why here, Cotto? It's a wasteland."

"Are you sure?" Cotto asked, her eyes twinkling.

"I'm sure," Talus said disgustedly.

The sun was blazingly hot now, and Talus found

breathing difficult. Shading his eyes, he squinted down
the line of donkeys burdened by all of Cotto's purchases. The beasts seemed as miserable as he was.

"Cotto! Cotto!" A voice began to scream the girl's
name.

Talus was genuinely frightened. Whence were the
calls coming? He stared at his lover. She was smiling
delightedly.

A figure emerged abruptly from behind a bush. It
was a middle-aged woman dressed in skins. Her hair
was long and wild, and her eyes looked like a hunted
animal's. Next a man appeared not twenty feet from
her. He carried a long, pointed stick. Then Talus saw
others who seemed to pop up like mushrooms from the
ground—five, ten, twenty, fifty. And with each appearance, Cotto's smile deepened.

The newcomers ran out of their hiding places, surrounded the donkeys, then stripped the beasts of the
packs. They fell like crazed people upon the fruit. Juice
ran down their faces and arms as they devoured the
food and loudly smacked their lips. They wrapped dozens of new garments around their thin bodies and
danced. They guzzled the wine and the milk and the
porridge as if they had not eaten in weeks. They gorged
themselves on all the produce that the girl had so generously purchased.

Once again Talus stared at Cotto, who was still
grinning. *Is she mad?* Talus thought. *These half-
human, half-animal lunatics are looting the caravan.*

Talus was infuriated. He had risked his neck to
steal the gold. He had drained his energy to load the
donkeys and lead them to this place. And for whom?
Strangers? He flailed at the looters, driving them from
the donkeys.

"Talus! Stop it!" He whirled when Cotto called his
name. "Put away the stick, Talus, and meet my
mother." Walking toward him, arm in arm with his
beloved dancer, was the wild-haired woman.

"Your mother?" he spluttered. Astonished and embarrassed, he immediately dropped the stick.

"Yes," Cotto confirmed. "All this food and clothing

is for my family and friends. Let them have their fun, Talus. Life is harsh for them."

At that moment all Talus knew for a certainty was that when he was imprisoned and isolated on the island Home, he had never imagined the real world could be so strange.

II

"What is your name, son?"
"Josiah."
"And your tribe?"
"Ephraim."

Gideon squinted up at the young man he was questioning. The sun was high, and he was dog tired. He should be sleeping. Since they raided by night, daytime provided the only opportunity for rest. But this young man had to be interviewed; he had traveled a long way to find Gideon. The tribe of Ephraim held the land to the south, between Jerusalem and the coast.

In the last few days, many young recruits had presented themselves for service. Gideon had already allowed twenty to join his force. This fellow, like the others, was a zealot, caught up in the romantic stories that had begun to circulate about Gideon. People were beginning to call the meager, makeshift army Yahweh's Commandos because they appeared only at night and demanded sacrifice to God. Songs were composed about them. Children who did not obey were being threatened by their parents with punishment from the Commandos.

A spark had been lit, and Gideon's small band was the flint. Sometimes they would raid up to ten Israelite settlements in a single night. The attacks had become routine for Gideon: first the sounding of the trumpet, the defacing of the Baal altars with words scrawled in blood, the short speech demanding that the villagers sacrifice to Yahweh, and then exhorting the tribesmen to journey to the Spring of Harod for the final battle against the Midianites.

These raids were anything but routine for the Israelite villagers. Gideon's band seemed to explode out of the darkness and then vanish as quickly. Gideon's assaults filled them with terror and hope. The Israelites were being reawakened to the viable power of Yahweh, even if they no longer remembered the rituals associated with Him. After a visit from Gideon's posse, the ground in most of the villages ran red with blood as many sacrifices to Yahweh were prepared.

"And what are they saying about me in the south?" Gideon asked the young man from Ephraim.

The fellow was about to answer when Gideon noticed his servant about twenty feet away, cleaning a bridle. He held up his hand to the recruit to wait, then called out, "Purah, stop wasting your time shining leather. Come here and listen to this young man with me."

Purah laid the object down, hurried over to Gideon, and squatted by his side. Gideon now motioned for the recruit to continue. But the young fellow, looking extremely uncomfortable, was silent.

"Do you have anything to say in response to my question?" Gideon asked sharply.

"I do, sir, but I would prefer to speak to you privately." And then he nodded slightly toward Purah.

"Purah is my oldest and truest friend as well as my valet," Gideon said coldly. "I have no secrets from him."

The recruit flushed, causing Gideon to wonder if it was possible that some people did not like Purah. Did they not trust him? What nonsense! Of course Purah was a bit strange, but so what? He was an Israelite patriot!

The young man cleared his throat. He glanced once at Purah, but the servant ignored him. "Among the tribe of Ephraim, sir, it is rumored that you are another Joshua."

Gideon stared in wide-eyed astonishment at the young man. "Another Joshua?"

"Yes. That Yahweh has created a duplicate. That he has poured the great Joshua's body and soul and passion into a man called Gideon."

"A great honor, my lord," Purah remarked.

Gideon fingered the stops on his trumpet. "But an absurd one. Joshua was the general of a mighty army of conquest assembled under the banner of Yahweh."

"And you will have your army, also," Purah replied.

"Why do the southern tribesmen think I am Joshua reborn?" Gideon asked the young stranger.

"Just as the horns brought down the walls of Jericho, so does your horn bring down the altars of Baal."

"Many people say that it was an earthquake, not music, that brought down the walls of Jericho," Gideon pointed out.

Josiah the Ephraimite seemed undeterred. "And, sir, just as Joshua mercilessly destroyed those who prevented the Children of Israel from entering this land of milk and honey, so, it is said, will you totally destroy the Midianite hordes."

Gideon laughed out loud. These people did not understand the power of the Midianites. The Bedouins were not at all like the irregular tribal armies Joshua had fought; the Midianites were an intensely trained, well-mounted, daring force. And every last one of them was required to fight to the death. In fact, they welcomed death in battle as a high honor.

The young man continued, his excitement mounting. "And many people believe that after the land has been restored to us and we are living in safety, you will become king of Israel."

"Yahweh is King," Gideon said quietly.

But the young man forged ahead. "And you will choose a beautiful queen from out of Jerusalem, and this queen shall—"

"I am already married," Gideon interrupted. "I have no need for another queen."

Purah chuckled at his master's joke. Gideon's wife was no queen by any stretch of the imagination. Josiah started to speak again, but Gideon stopped him with a wave of the hand. The moment the conversation had turned to his family, he had grown sad. He missed his mother and his sister, Miriam, very much and prayed fervently that they were well. He even missed his wife.

As for his father—well, their parting had been too painful to deal with. All that remained was the ache in his heart and the echoing of his father's words that he, Gideon, had betrayed his family.

"Leave me for a while," Gideon said to the recruit. "I will make my decision shortly."

The young man moved off, and Gideon was left alone with Purah. "You should sleep now," the servant advised.

Gideon shook his head. He suddenly felt very awake. "Tell me, Purah, in all honesty—do you believe I am the new Joshua?"

"I honestly don't know, sir."

"I didn't ask you what you *knew*. What do you believe?"

"Well, sir, what I believe is this: that you are Yahweh's messenger and that you have grown in power, stature, and resolve since you accepted the mission. You have always been a high-strung fellow, but you seem to be dealing with the pressures well, and I pray that you do not eventually fly apart from your burdens. You now stand ten cubits over all other men. But as to whether you are the new Joshua . . . that I cannot even begin to think about."

"Do you think we should let young Josiah join us?"

"Why not? Other zealots have, with nothing to recommend them but their unbridled enthusiasm."

Gideon nodded. "I hope thousands of others just like them will join us before the battle against the Midianites."

"Your message has been powerful, sir. I don't know of anything you've left undone."

Gideon nodded again, then drew into himself. He had been feeling very strange in the weeks since he had started to deliver the instructions from Yahweh. He no longer felt he was Gideon, husband and father, brother and son. Nor did he believe that he was Joshua reborn. But he had begun to experience spurts of immense strength and clairvoyance. And he, like Purah, prayed that he could hold himself together for as long as Yahweh wanted to use him.

He closed his eyes in the sunlight. As for becoming king of Israel, that was ridiculous. The Israelites had never had a king; Yahweh was a jealous God. But, Gideon knew, he was no longer a mere Israelite. Yahweh had exalted him beyond the priests. Yahweh had chosen him from among the chosen people. Perhaps, he thought, he was no longer a mere human being at all. Perhaps Yahweh had elevated him to the status of a future patriarch, like Abraham, Isaac, and Jacob. Perhaps he would leave this earth on a bejeweled chariot with golden wings and be swept into the clouds.

His speculations became so heady that he lost his balance and almost fell. Embarrassed, he opened his eyes wide. He was alone. Purah had returned to cleaning leather.

III

Micah lay in a shallow trench on the barren ground. He had piled some large flat stones over himself as shields against the brutal sun. Flies were feeding on his back wound. He squinted at the sky. It was just past noon, he reckoned. There were many hours to endure before blessed darkness, before he could move again, before he could find and follow. . . .

But what if that strange hawk did not appear to guide and to feed him? What then? There would be no small creatures given to him so that he might subsist on their warm blood and flesh, minimal though it was. He would die a miserable death in this ditch.

Micah shifted his position slightly. The acute pain sharpened his sense of reality. *Perhaps,* he thought, *I am mad and imagining all of this.*

His situation was unreal, he decided. For example, how did the hawk locate him each evening? How could a hawk feed a man? How could a hawk lead a man? Where was the hawk leading him? And why should a hawk be doing this in the first place? *Yes,* he thought, *I am mad from sun and thirst and hunger. Only a*

madman would believe that a magical hawk would
appear at sunset and . . .

Confused, exhausted, he buried his face in his
hands. He was made more desperate because the glaring sun seemed to bake the very stones he had hoped
would provide him with some shelter.

Micah slipped into one of his delusional states. He
called out to his men to be careful; next he issued
orders to Anistos, planning hit-and-run attacks against
the Egyptian chariot forces. At last he fell asleep and
dreamed he was a child in Jerusalem. He clearly saw
his parents and their beautiful home. He could hear
the cool water in their courtyard's fountain. Then, as
an adolescent, he was speaking to the mighty Joshua
and asking to bear arms for the Israelites. The moment
Joshua assented in the dream, the great leader transformed into the hateful Eglon of Moab, and Micah, an
assassin for the Israelites, was plunging the knife again
and again into Eglon's fat belly. . . .

He pushed the stones off his back and sat up; his
body was drenched with the acrid sweat of fear from
the dream. A cool breeze played against his face. He
was thankful when he saw that the sun was almost
down. He had slept for hours. It was time!

He fought to rise, stumbled, fell, then rose again
to steady himself finally on his feet. He waited, breathing hard. The sun vanished ever so slowly, and in its
place came a dull, queer darkness that was not quite
night.

What am I waiting for? he asked himself, feeling
ashamed. *Why am I waiting for a mirage . . . a dream?*
I am Blood, the most feared bandit in all of Canaan.
Why am I waiting for a bird to feed me? If only, he
thought, he had kept one of the throwing daggers. He
could draw it across his throat and end this lunacy.

Darkness settled across the wasteland. There were
few stars, and the moon was obscured by wispy clouds.
He could not survive much longer, he realized. He did
not have his daggers, but he would find some instrument of death somewhere.

Even as he considered suicide, an anticipatory tingling thrilled him. Again he wondered what he was waiting for. Suddenly he heard and recognized it: a sound in the night! Off in the distance but coming closer, from his right, a whirring. And then the sweet smell of warm blood.

Food! The smell of blood made him weaker. But it also made him stronger. The scent acted like the flat of a sword beating him on the head.

He saw two dots of light—the eyes of the hawk hovering in the air near him.

The hawk settled lightly onto the ground very close to him and shook a dead rodent loose from a talon.

Micah cried out incoherently, fell to his knees, and crawled toward the prey. As he had the night before, he picked it up and savagely bit into the still warm creature. His teeth ripped the flesh and skin. He devoured it in the manner of an animal.

Micah staggered about. The hawk was behind him, then in front of him. The bird climbed into the air on strongly beating wings, then suddenly swooped down. Its two pinpointed eyes were always visible.

Micah started to walk slowly, very slowly, and doggedly, as if he were a cripple learning to walk again.

He did not know where he was going, but he followed the sound of wings. Was the hawk leading him, or was he leading the hawk? Was this a bizarre dream? He knew he was moving to the northeast, but why in that direction?

Then the whirring vanished, and he was lost again. He could not move without the frightening but comforting sound. He waited in the darkness for a long time.

Without warning the hawk dived at him out of the darkness. Micah ducked and pivoted to escape its savage swoop. Something slammed him hard on the chest. It was a large lizard, still living. He plucked the writhing reptile from his chest and bit off its head. Then he consumed it entirely while the hawk hovered ten feet away.

At last the bird flew off, and Micah followed. The

painful, confusing desert trek continued. When the first
rays of dawn began to lift the darkness, Micah could
see the hawk more clearly. He fixed his eyes on its
diving, soaring flight.

The morning light shone fully, and Micah, dazzled
by the sun's harsh rays, began to hallucinate. The
hawk's body assumed a strange shape, as if the creature
were transforming itself. First the shape was amor-
phous, undefinable. Then it took form very clearly. He
was following a woman, a very beautiful woman. He
knew that as a certainty, even though he could not see
her face. The hawk's wings became her arms, and she
was wearing a brown and white billowing garment with
black sunburst markings across the shoulders.

The apparition became so real that he reached
toward her, crying out his need. Then he staggered
and fell. He lay there and wept with disappointment
and fatigue. Finally he looked up. The hawk was gone.
It was morning. He had to sleep. But first he needed
to crawl into a place where he would be safe from the
killing sun.

IV

Talus awoke surrounded by near darkness. For a
moment he did not remember where he was. The hut
he was lying in was even more primitive than his cabin
on Home, and the sleeping mat under him was made
of broken and tattered reeds sewn haphazardly together. Then he noticed Cotto sleeping beside him,
and he was disoriented no more—he was in the small
hill village just outside the deserted town of Megiddo.

Her family had celebrated her return for hours.
And then the festivities had faded and died, as if the
villagers realized that Cotto and her gifts would be gone
soon, and once again the family would be overwhelmed
by poverty and despair.

He lay back down and stared at his darling's beautiful face. This was the first night since they had been

together that they did not make love. Cotto had been too tired and too excited by the reunion with her family. Talus's eyes roamed over the contours of her body. Would he ever get enough of her? How had he survived before he met her? What would happen to him if they were parted? He moved closer to her on the mat so he could hear her breathing.

Suddenly a powerful sound rent the air. Cotto sat up, wide-eyed, and stared around. Talus had clutched his long knife and was ready to protect her. The frightening blast repeated, and Talus could hear people running and shouting.

"A trumpet! It's a trumpet," Cotto said, then started to laugh.

She jumped up, took Talus's hand, and dragged him to his feet. They left the hut quickly. Outside, the night was lighted by torches.

"It's Gideon and his commandos," the hill dwellers muttered among themselves.

Talus stared at the stern-faced young men who had suddenly appeared out of the night. There were about twenty of them, each one armed and carrying a torch. Standing in front was the man they called Gideon. A trumpet hung on a long cord around his neck. He was not large, but in the glare of the torches he seemed a giant. The sturdy bow on his back seemed to offer testimony of enormous strength and daring.

"Who is Gideon?" Talus asked Cotto. "What does he want?"

"Some say he is a prophet," she answered, "while some believe he is a madman."

Whatever these Israelites thought about Gideon, Talus saw that they listened respectfully to him. Their poor hovels behind them, the people had drawn up in a semicircle on the hillside.

"Hear me!" Gideon began, his eyes surveying the audience. "Time is short! I bring the word of Yahweh to a wicked and stubborn people. I bring you hope. I bring you a chance of redemption. Listen to me."

Talus could feel the excitement spreading through the people as they hung on Gideon's every word. Their glittering eyes reflected the torchlight. He felt himself being swept up into rapt participation, and his heart beat fast.

"Look at you!" Gideon's accusations seem to pierce the hearts of the listeners. "You deserted Megiddo out of fear, and now you live like stray dogs in this garbage heap. Where is your honor? Where is your worth? Isn't it time that you stood on your feet again? Isn't it time that you fed your wives and your children and kept them safe? Isn't it time you picked up the sword?"

"Yes!" the audience chanted. "Yes! Yes!"

"You are Israelites, the conquerors of Canaan!" Gideon cried out. "You are the people who broke the power of the pharaohs. You are the people beloved by Yahweh."

At this mention of Yahweh, many of the people fell to their knees and beat their chests.

"Yes, atone for your failures! Rend your garments! For you have truly offended your Lord with the worship of Baal. I say to you that every charm, every medallion, every statue and talisman and altar to the false god must be destroyed. You must slaughter the most comely of your flock and offer it up immediately as sacrifice to your Lord God, Yahweh, the Lord of Hosts."

People began to cry out Yahweh's name. Some prayed in a language that Talus could not understand. All around him a frenzy of religious fervor broke loose.

"After you have sacrificed," Gideon ordered, "leave these wretched huts and go to the Spring of Harod. There, all the people of Israel are assembling, and there, we will crush the Midianites."

Cotto gripped Talus's arm. *Who are these Midianites?* he wondered. *Why do Cotto and her family and friends seem so happy that the Midianites might be crushed?* Then he remembered that she had told him that the Israelites lived in fear of the Bedouin armies. The Midianites, he decided, must be Bedouins.

"Do you hear me?" Gideon cried out, and the torches of his men were raised high in the night. "We will crush them. We will destroy their armies, their camels, and their tents. Yahweh will wipe them off the face of the earth."

A mighty roar went up from the people. But quickly the enthusiasm was replaced by uncertainty. Heads turned away from Gideon as Dakoon, a priest of Baal, strode regally toward the front of the gathering. The crowd parted for him, and he stopped not more than three feet from Gideon.

Talus had never seen a man dressed as grandly as the priest. He was wearing a magnificent long robe of deep blue silk. The garment, obviously brought out for this occasion, was embroidered with many of the symbols of the god Baal—the sacred tree, the owl, the phallus, the woman with three breasts, the lion with two heads. The priest's huge headdress made him look like some large vulture.

Three of Gideon's men, weapons drawn, rushed toward him.

"Stop!" Gideon ordered. "Let him speak."

Dakoon planted his staff emphatically on the ground and stared at the crowd; then he spoke in a powerful voice. "Listen to me, my children. This man bewitches you with his horn. He will lead you to doom. Yahweh is no longer your Lord, and you will never triumph over the mighty armies of Midian. Stay where you are, here and safe. Give thanks to *Baal* for your survival. Sing the songs of Baal. Gideon is a false prophet."

He spoke with such surety and authority that many in the audience began to assent and to curl their lips at the man with the horn.

Then Gideon stepped forward again. "Purah," he called out, "bring one of the torches."

The servant moved near him, carrying one of the flaming brands.

Gideon addressed the people. "Let us see who is telling the truth. Let us see who represents the false god. I challenge this priest of Baal to a trial by fire. I challenge him to place his hand in the fire and let Baal heal him."

Talus watched with growing astonishment. Cotto's

grip on his arm tightened, and he pulled her closer to his side. These people, the Israelites, were violent to the extreme in all their imagery and actions. He stared down at Cotto, who was totally caught up in the drama. Did she share the same beliefs as Gideon? Was she violent and fanatical beneath her beauty?

"I am not here to play games," the priest of Baal scoffed.

"Afraid?" Gideon inquired.

When the priest did not answer, Gideon grinned wickedly to the crowd as if pointing out that Dakoon could not trust the power of his own god. The crowd cheered Gideon and called out insults to Dakoon.

"Is he really going to do it?" Talus whispered to Cotto.

"What do you think?" she asked.

"I don't think either of them will go through with it."

"Then you have led a very sheltered life on your island," Cotto replied.

Gideon raised his right hand high and called out to the crowd: "Yahweh is King. Yahweh is Lord. Yahweh destroys, and Yahweh heals."

Then, as the crowd gasped in horror, Gideon placed his right forearm directly into the dancing flames of the torch and held it there.

A woman screamed. Men began to curse under their breath. Gideon's followers averted their gaze. Talus could not pull his eyes away from the sight of that flesh in that fire. It was the most bizarre display he had ever watched. He knew he was witnessing something he could not completely comprehend. The stench of searing flesh fouled the air.

Gideon pulled his arm out of the flames and held it up. The arm was on fire. The flames changed colors, from glowing red to black and back again. Then Gideon lifted his trumpet with the unburned hand and blew one long, steady note. At the sound, a watery mist issued from the instrument and enveloped Gideon, causing the fearful assemblage to fall to their knees.

When the mist cleared, Gideon waved his charred

arm. The limb was healed. It was as if it had never been placed in the fire.

Gideon wavered and seemed about to fall. Several men rushed to his side to steady him; but he shook them off and remained standing unassisted.

A voice cried out from the crowd, "A miracle! Yahweh's miracle, like the burning bush in Moses's time." Gideon offered the torch to Dakoon so the priest might have a try. But the man shook his head and slunk away.

Shouts of triumph and hosannas rose from the Israelites. Then Gideon and his band vanished into the darkness.

Immediately after Gideon's departure, the Israelites stripped themselves of all charms and amulets pertaining to Baal. Then they ran back to their huts to select a sacrifice to Yahweh. They moved like people possessed, and their voices demanded the blood of the Midianites. They prayed for forgiveness from Yahweh, then expressed gratitude to Gideon, who had shown them the power of the God of their Fathers, of Abraham, Isaac, and Jacob.

Talus and Cotto walked slowly and silently back to their hut, moved the privacy curtain across the opening, and lay down on their sleeping mat. Talus was bemused and exhausted by the wonders he had seen. Cotto nestled close to him.

"It will be dawn soon," she whispered.

Although he did not answer in words, he pulled her close, and his hands found her breasts.

"Do you still love me, Talus?"

"More than ever."

"Even now, when you are weary and horrified and perplexed?"

"Yes."

"And do you trust me?"

"Why shouldn't I?"

"Well, we Israelites can be a strange and difficult people."

He kissed her into silence. His tongue sought the inside of her mouth. He wanted to enter her, but she pulled away.

"Come back with me to Tyre," she said. "Now."

He sat abruptly, unable to believe what he had heard. "Are you mad, Cotto?" he finally sputtered.

"Why do you ask that?"

"We are criminals. We stole the Phoenician's gold. If we go back, Navan will kill us."

"Ah, Talus," she said, smiling sadly, "you do not understand the Phoenicians. True, they are great traders who dearly love their gold. And Navan will surely be very angry with us. But Phoenicians can get all the gold they want. More than gold, they love their pleasures, and they will do anything—even forgive a theft— to get back a favorite dancing girl."

Talus did not know whether or not what she said was true. It did sound persuasive, and he knew that he himself would forgive Cotto of any crime. But he did not understand why she would care to take the risk. "Cotto, there is no reason to go back. Why take the chance?"

"Because I want to provide for my family, and I can do that only by returning to Tyre."

"But this poverty is going to be over soon for your family and all the Israelites. At least that is what Gideon says."

Cotto suddenly hissed and spat at him, as if she were a cornered cat. The shock caused Talus to turn away, repulsed. He wiped his cheek clean of spittle.

"So, then," she snarled, "hear the truth, you naive fool. Look at my body. You love it, don't you? You want it all the time, don't you? But in ten years my hair will be stringy and my breasts sagging. Then what? Don't you understand? Right now you and I are worth nothing. We are penniless and without power. Sooner or later we will be crushed to death." She paused and glared at him.

Talus could not respond. Had another woman emerged from the body of his beloved Cotto? Had a witch possessed her, body and soul?

"I am going back to Tyre, Talus, to rob the Phoenicians on a scale they have never imagined possible. I am going to steal their cargoes and their ships. I am going to counterfeit bank drafts. I am going to take over their prostitution rings. I am going to become powerful and wealthy. Do you understand me?"

"But Cotto, have you forgotten about us? About our love?"

Her sardonic laugh cut him to the heart. "Love?" she screamed. "Look around, you fool. Look at this hovel, at the threadbare mat. You call this love? Love takes place in a golden villa. The man is clean and perfumed with the most expensive scents, and the woman's skin has been made soft by the most precious oils. Musicians play for true lovers, and sweetmeats are pressed onto their tongues by willing eunuchs. *That* is love." She paused, panting, her eyes accusing him of being insufferably stupid.

He hid his face behind his hands. He felt ill.

"Make your choice, Talus. Now! If you love me, come back to Tyre with me. I will show you a world to conquer, and we will never have to part."

He kept his face buried in his hands. Then he felt her fingers run through his hair. Just her touch sent tremors through his body. He realized that he would follow her anywhere and for any reason. Nothing on earth meant anything unless he and Cotto were together. He grabbed her wrist and pressed his lips to her palm. She smiled.

V

"Please, don't hurt me any more," Luti begged in a desperate whisper as she felt a hand slide beneath her head and raise it a bit off the ground.

"Quiet! I'm not going to hurt you. I've brought you water."

Luti felt the blessed fluid pass through her parched lips. Her eyes focused, and she saw a thin, haggard woman of indeterminate age kneeling beside her, holding a small water gourd. Her nose was pierced with a slave ring.

"Where am I?" Luti asked after she could drink no more.

"In an Amalekite camp. They brought you back last night. We heard what happened. I'm sorry for you."

Memories flooded back, and Luti began to tremble uncontrollably. For punishment, the Midianites had staked her out onto the ground in the tent area, and any passing Bedouin man could violate her. How many had there been? Ten? Twenty? Fifty? She had lost consciousness when the pain and degradation had become too much to bear.

"What is your name?" she asked her angel of mercy.

"Slaves like us no longer have names," the woman answered bitterly as she helped Luti to sit up. "I have been in this camp and others like it for more than two years. I was captured near Hamidya. I am an Israelite."

The women held on to each other in comforting silence. And then the Israelite admonished, "Why would you attempt such a scheme? Didn't you know that the Midianite warlords Oreb and Zeeb could not be fooled?"

"I had to try something," Luti replied. "I could not give up hope."

"Hope?" The woman snorted. "What is that?"

Luti closed her eyes. She could not fault the woman for her cynicism. The notion of being a Bedouin slave for two years was almost incomprehensible.

"Is there no way to escape?" Luti asked. "Is there no way to be free again?"

"When we stop breathing, we will be free. And you may well wish for an early death—the Amalekites are very angry at you. They blame you for the murder of the young Bedouin who believed your sorceress story and took you to the Midianite camp. I am afraid the Amalekites will make things very hard for you."

Shouting erupted from the main part of the camp, and the two women froze with fear. Then the noise died down.

"Something has been going on all day," the Israelite woman said ominously. "Something about a great battle that may take place on the other side of the Jordan."

"Who will fight?"

"The Midianites and their auxiliaries against an Israelite prophet who is gathering people to oppose them. The Bedouins call this prophet a madman and say they will crush his forces like gnats."

"Do you know him?"

"No," the Israelite woman answered, "and I don't believe a word of it anyway. My people are too weak." She heaved a long sigh, then asked, "Tell me, where are you from?"

"Ur, a city in Babylon."

"That is a long way from here."

"A lifetime away."

"How did you get here?"

"My caravan was ambushed. I was traveling to Canaan to find an old lover."

The Israelite grinned. "What fools we woman are," she said. "As if any man is worth jeopardizing our freedom."

"This one was."

"Where is he now?"

"I don't know. It all came to me in a vision."

The woman's eyes widened. "Then you *are* a sorceress?"

"I don't know what I am. But it is true I have certain gifts."

"Slavery makes all gifts worthless."

Luti nodded her head grimly. The woman was right.

"Tell me about Babylon."

"It is a beautiful country. I lived near a river and the greenest fields and marshes where birds flock. Every morning and evening I would take my son to the river's edge, and I would point out the birds to him." She started to weep. "And he would laugh."

What would become of her son now? she agonized for the millionth time. She had been so stupid to leave him! What had possessed her?

"I, too, had a son, and a daughter," the Israelite woman said.

The women became lost in their private worlds of grief and memory, of children abandoned through violence. Then, suddenly, the Israelite woman laughed wildly and asked, "Do you have fruit in your country? Fresh fruit? I would kill for something juicy and sweet—anything to break the monotony of that horrid millet dampened by rancid milk."

"My land is very fertile," Luti answered. "Along the river are fields of peppers and vineyards and groves of pear trees."

"It has been a long time since I tasted a pear," the Israelite said wistfully.

"The pears of Ur are small and well shaped with a thick stem. They are both sweet and tart, and the cores are used to make jelly." Luti closed her eyes. The memory of the pear taste came upon her with such clarity and definition that she felt she could chew it, that it had actually entered her mouth. For a moment the memory was a precious treasure . . . and then the absurdity of it made her weep again. "What will happen to our memories? Will they keep us sane, or will they drive us mad from the wanting?"

"They will vanish. You cannot survive here on the strength of your memories. You must make your mind a blank if you wish to survive."

"No!" Luti cried out. "I refuse to do that. I want to remember what was good. I want to wake up remembering and fall asleep remembering."

The Israelite retorted bitterly, "And do you plan to concentrate upon your child or your parents or your beloved while you are being raped by a filthy, crazed nomad?"

Luti's misery prevented her from answering. She and the woman stared grimly toward the main camp and waited to be summoned.

VI

Micah stood in the darkness and waited for a long time, but the hawk did not return. There was no prey with which to sate his hunger or quench his thirst. He heard no comforting sound of whirring wings.

At last he shrugged his shoulders and gave up. He was thankful for the hawk's miraculous visits and what he had gained therefrom. The back wound no longer bothered him much, and his legs were no longer rubbery. Best of all, for the first time in a very long time, his head was clear. He remembered accurately what had happened to him, the death of Anistos and many other of his men, and the futile battles with the Egyptian chariot brigade.

I am the great bandit, Blood, he thought, and then, right there in the darkness, he began to chuckle at his pretensions. He was naked, alone, without weapons. And he was waiting for a hawk to lead him somewhere. Where? He did not know. He sat down and, at a loss for what else to do, laughed uproariously at his predicament. Now he was going to have to find his own way. Now he was going to have to feed himself. No more lizards, bats, or rabbits would be dropped at his feet by that hawk.

His hands felt his legs. They seemed quite thin, but he believed that his strength was returning to him. He reached around to touch the wound on his back. It had scabbed over and caused him no pain. He stood quickly, testing his body. He started to walk, then increased the pace until he moved at a long, loping gait.

He traveled all night, enveloped in a profound sense of well-being. At dawn he knew exactly where he was—Wadi Al Harir, a small fertile oasis east of the Jordan.

He was so self-absorbed, pleased by the ease and strength with which he had moved and the fact that he could recognize the terrain, that he did not notice the tents until they were fewer than a hundred yards away. He froze the moment he saw them, then cursing himself for being so nonobservant, scurried to the nearest gully and flung himself over the top. Safely concealed, Micah waited, pressed against the gully walls. All was silent. He blew out a deep, shuddering breath. The tents he had seen were obviously part of a Bedouin encampment—and those unpredictable nomads might either be welcoming or happy to slit an intruder's throat. He had no desire to try his luck with them, but there was no alternative; he needed food, weapons, and clothing.

He glanced at the sky. It would be morning soon. He raised his head above the gully and peered at the large encampment. He counted at least twenty tents. But the area was quiet, and Micah assumed that the Bedouins were still asleep. If there was a supply tent, he could be in and out of it before anyone knew.

Micah decided to enter the camp from the east, with the sun directly behind him. The eastern edge of the wadi was on higher ground, and his vantage point would enable him to see the layout of the entire area. He climbed slowly out of the gully and crawled toward the encampment. He utilized every rock and bush as cover for his progress.

Lying between him and the camp was a fast-running stream, which vanished underground every few feet. Directly past the stream were the tethered camels and then the tents. Bedouin raiding parties, Micah knew, usually placed the supply tent near the camels, so immediate access to weapons and flight were assured. He scanned the tents but could not determine whether or not one was set aside to hold supplies.

Suddenly a jangling sound reached his ears. Frightened, he immediately crouched down and longed for the knives he no longer had. The noise drew his eyes downstream, where three women walked along the stream bank. Behind them was a Bedouin warrior. Micah could see by the man's robe that he was an Amalekite.

So, Micah thought, it was an Amalekite camp. As the women came closer, the sound grew louder. It was, he realized, the clanking of the women's chains. They were slaves.

The Bedouin shouted at the captives, then lay down on the stream bank. The women, evidently following the man's orders, waded into the water to bathe.

Micah could not move until the slaves finished their bath, for the only way into the camp from the east was across the stream. He waited. The morning sun felt strong on his back and neck.

The slaves washed slowly and thoroughly. They appeared weak and morose, and their thin bodies were covered with ugly sores. The sun had burned them a deep copper, and even from where he watched, Micah could see the small tremors shaking their bodies, a quivering that bespoke a lack of good food.

Micah curled his lip in contempt. The Amalekites and their brothers were known to beat and starve slaves to death. They never understood that slaves should be treated as valuable property; it was beyond the nomads' comprehension. In their mind slaves existed only to be abused. Micah, as the bandit Blood, had never taken slaves—hostages, yes, but slaves, never. Something in the stream glinted. At first Micah thought that one of the slaves had hidden a knife. Then he realized it was a reflection of the sun from the slave rings in the women's noses.

Finally the slaves finished bathing and slowly walked out of the stream to re-join the guard. The small group headed back toward the tents.

Micah kept his eyes fastened on the women. Something about one of them attracted and held his gaze. He stared hard, blinking away the sweat and his sudden fatigue. Something on the slave's lower back caused Micah's heart to lurch. A wound? Was it a wound? No. He narrowed his eyes intently, as if the mark's identification was extremely important.

Then he realized what he was looking at. He spun around, and his legs collapsed beneath him. As he fell to the ground, his hands were trembling and his right eye began to twitch.

He had seen the lion's-paw birthmark. She was a Child of the Lion.

"*Luti*," he whispered.

CHAPTER
TWO

Coastal Road, Philistine League

"What is the matter with you, Theon?" Nuhara asked angrily. "Why do you keep stopping and starting?"

Theon looked at his wife but made no move to urge his mount forward and placate Nuhara's demands. "It is strange, but I keep recalling things, they seem to bubble up now that my memory has been restored."

"Well, let them bubble as you ride," she replied tartly.

Theon still did not move. "For example, I was in Tirzah's apartment for three days with Talus, and yet it is only just now that I realized he is the same Talus I went to rescue from Troy ten years ago, before I was shipwrecked. The young man is Iri's boy—a Child of the Lion."

"So what?"

"Well, I should have talked to him. I wonder how he escaped from Troy and what happened to his mother and adopted brother. A fortune was being held for them on Home. It was Iri's legacy."

"Keep your mind on your children," Nuhara said sharply.

Sighing, Theon finally applied his heels to the mount's flank. He and Nuhara rode in silence, leading two more pack animals, purchased with Tirzah's coins, to hold supplies for the long journey.

Theon felt tired and pessimistic. They had found nothing in Ashdod. The main slave market, they were told, had been moved to Ashkelon, another city of the Philistine League. They were headed there now. Nuhara's behavior in Ashdod had been odd. She had vanished for hours at a time, and he once found her speaking to unsavory-looking strangers.

"Nuhara, who were those men?" he asked.

Her head snapped around. "Which men?"

"The ones in Ashdod. That old man with the shawl you were speaking with in the port. And the one you met near the abandoned slave market."

"Sources of information, Theon, that's all." She smiled ingenuously. "Are you jealous?"

"No," Theon replied quickly.

"You had better not be jealous, my dear. After all, it was you who carried on with that cow of a woman on board ship before you rescued me," Nuhara accused, her voice becoming shrill. "And it was you who married another woman and had children by her."

"I did many things that I regret, Nuhara." Theon lapsed into a moody silence. The mention of Tirzah brought back confused, conflicting memories of the past . . . of the present . . . of a passion that he could not extirpate even though he had pledged his love once again to his lawful wife.

On they rode in search of their children. Imagined rescues and reunions consumed Theon's thoughts. For him, however, this journey meant much more than saving the beloved twins. If Hela and Gravis could be found safe, it would, he hoped, somehow resurrect the love he once bore for Nuhara. Now he was merely going through the motions, pretending to feel obligations and uphold his honor . . . but the possibility existed that the tenderness, deep love, and passion he had felt for Nuhara the bride would once again beat true in his heart. How he longed for that.

Her harsh voice brought him out of his reveries. "Bear right, Theon. We are going down the path to the shore."

Her announcement startled him. Why not just continue along the shore road? Why take a detour—a difficult one—to the water's edge? He looked at the steep path that led down to the sea.

"Are you sure that's your preference?" he asked gently.

She shot him a savage look, then spurred her mount past him and down the path. He had no choice but to follow. The donkeys slipped and slid but managed to get safely to the rocky shore.

"Look!" she said, her dark eyes glowing.

Theon followed the line of her gaze. Anchored just off the shore was a ship. The black pitch that covered the sides at first led him to believe he was staring at a Phoenician merchant vessel; all the Phoenicians' ships had that black protective covering.

But Theon knew ships. He looked closer and realized that the pitch covering was being used as a disguise—an attempt to confuse other vessels at sea. He realized he was actually looking at one of the newest and most formidable fighting ships that had ever been built—an Egyptian battering warship. He could make out the massive metal-shod battering ram on the bow. One powerful steering oar protruded at the vessel's rear.

Theon narrowed his eyes and counted thirteen rowers on the near side, all of them armed and protected by high-planked bulwarks. He knew that number would be doubled on the ship's far side. In the center of the sleek, powerful vessel rose a single mast with an innovative fighting sail, which could be furled and unfurled at a moment's notice. The old-fashioned sail required that the entire mast be pulled down to effect any changes. The Egyptian ship was magnificent.

"You like it?" Nuhara asked.

"Of course. I am a ship's captain and learned ship-building in my youth. I recognize a beautiful fighting ship when I see one."

"It's ours," Nuhara said simply.

"Ours?" Theon was astonished.

"That's the business I was conducting in Ashdod."

"You bought this ship?"

"Yes."

"With what, Nuhara? Where did you get the money to purchase a ship like this?"

"I did not leave Home without taking with me several golden blades from the collection of your ancestors. I sold several made by Shobai."

Theon kept a tight rein on his temper. She had had no right to sell irreplaceable family treasures, but now was not a good time to discuss it. Everything was too confusing right now. What was done could not be undone.

Theon stared again at the ship. He could see that the crew was on deck and ready to sail. A small raft had been launched toward the shore.

"But why do we need a ship?" he asked.

"To get to Ashkelon."

"But the city is only a day's journey away. And why do we need a fighting ship?"

"To rescue our children."

Was his wife mad? he wondered. What did she think they would do—enter the port and demand the twins' release? That was romantic nonsense. No single ship could execute such blackmail; there would be dozens of Philistine fighting ships in Ashkelon's harbor.

"We'll leave the mounts and the supplies here," Nuhara said. "Everything we'll need is on board."

The small raft carried them out to the ship. Again Theon decided not to challenge Nuhara; nothing would dissuade her now that she had made up her mind.

Once aboard, Theon marveled at the efficiency of the crew, made up of men from many races. They went about their business quickly, silently. Theon noticed that the ship was indeed primed for battle. Large stones were piled on the deck for use in the slings. There were shields, spears, and bows stacked neatly within easy reach of each rower and crewman. The captain, a small wiry man, bowed to Nuhara and brought her two full wineskins, then left to resume his duties.

Nuhara handed one to Theon. "Drink, Husband, and let us celebrate the coming freedom of our children."

As Theon drank, the sail was unfurled and the ship moved out to sea. The rowers supplemented the wind with their efforts.

"Drink more, Theon. It is the finest wine that gold can buy."

It was good wine, Theon had to admit. He took another deep swallow and closed his eyes. The pleasure at being on a ship at sea consumed him. He reveled in the sensation of sea breezes playing about his face. He finished the wineskin, and Nuhara handed him the other.

"Are you trying to get me drunk?" he asked, laughing. He grabbed the wineskin and let his free hand caress her breast. She did not object. Then he walked toward the wooden bulwark that protected the oarsmen. Clutching the railing, he stared over the side at the flashing oars. Suddenly, he stood up straight and sniffed the air.

"Wait a minute," he said quietly. Then he shouted, "Wait a minute!"

"Drink your wine, Theon."

"No! We are moving north, Nuhara—not south to Ashkelon! What is going on?"

He strode toward her in a threatening manner. A second later two heavily armed oarsmen were upon him, pressing their ugly spears against his chest.

"What have you done, Nuhara?" he screamed in despair. "What about our children?"

She moved to him quickly, her eyes hard.

"Listen to me, you poor excuse for a husband and a man, I'm doing this my own way. Only a god can save our children, a god whose favor is assured by the wealth of the Children of the Lion. And I have been introduced to such a god. He lives in the north, in Thrace, and his power is beyond anything you could ever imagine. I know that, and the Thracians know that. Most importantly, my father knows that. Yes, Theon, my father is alive. He is in Thrace, safe. And with him is the vast treasure of the Children of the Lion. We started to remove it years ago, quietly, secretly. That's why the Phoenicians couldn't find even a copper coin in their raids."

"Stop this madness," Theon whispered. "Order these men to release me."

"Madness? Is the wealth of Home madness? Is my father, the great Khalkeus, mad? Is the god Dionysus, the most beautiful creature ever to tread the face of the earth, mad?"

Nuhara hovered over him as the oarsmen wrestled him to the deck and bound his wrists. Her breasts were heaving, her body tensed. "Do you hear me, Theon? Your family's fortune is mine now—mine and my father's. You're ruined. The Children of the Lion will never crawl out of poverty again! Only Dionysus can save Gravis and Hela. And we sail now to Dionysus."

She turned and left him lying there, terrified and confused, on the deck.

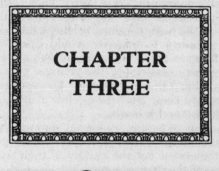

CHAPTER
THREE

Canaan

Every hour more Israelites came from the north, south, east, and west to the Spring of Harod. Men, women, and children arrived singly, in families, and as whole villages. They brought their pots and pans and weapons. Some came carrying their aged parents. Some came laughing, as if they were attending a party. Some came somberly, as if they were attending a funeral.

Soon all the tribes were represented. Every piece of ground was staked out by newcomers from every social class and profession. The encampment grew to encompass the entire area of the spring and then expanded into the foothills. And still the people came.

A city had been created in a few days' time. There were no buildings, squares, or marketplaces. But a giant beehive of undirected activity, of commerce and life and death and sex popped up like a mushroom in the oasis by the spring. People died, and people were born. The ground was trampled into dust. The air was

221

thick with the stench of living. A dozen Israelite dialects were heard in a constant cacophony.

The smell of smoke rode the air as many of those assembled began to sacrifice to Yahweh. The young people danced, and several of the revelers reached such a fevered pitch of ecstasy that they claimed they were possessed by a Spirit of Yahweh. They babbled incoherently or preached to whoever would listen. Old men with gentle eyes held classes in the fields, where they imparted their memories to the younger generations of how to worship Yahweh correctly. The young men and women turned their fresh faces, full of hope, to their elders and listened intently.

Hundreds of people wandered through the crowd, selling fruit, bread, water, and cloth. Their voices were shrill as they cried out the quality of their wares.

Many of the Israelite men sat cross-legged upon the ground for hour after hour, day after day, sharpening their swords and daggers, making certain their arrows were straight and well feathered, restringing their bows, and polishing whatever body armor they possessed. They had no interest in the peddlers' wares, the fanatics' preaching, or the elders' instruction in religious ritual. Their thoughts were only for the hated Midianites and winning the war that Gideon had promised.

It was just past dawn when Gideon and his exhausted band of commandos arrived at the outskirts of this miraculous and seething assemblage. The raiders could not believe their eyes.

Gideon was the first to dismount. His body was newly hard and taut, and the grime and sweat from his raids made his muscles stand out like knotted ropes. As he stared out over the masses his eyes went wide and seemed to penetrate deeply within whatever object or person they focused on.

Purah climbed down from his mount and joined his master. "It is beyond your wildest dreams," he whispered.

Behind them, the twenty young commandos chattered excitedly. Gideon raised his hand, and all talking immediately ceased. Leading his mount, beckoning that his men should follow, Gideon walked slowly into the first circle of people.

Very quickly he was recognized. The people shouted his name. Women threw flowers at him. Many rushed up to kiss his feet or the hem of his garment.

"It's Gideon! Gideon has come!"

"Honor and glory to Gideon! Glory to Yahweh and Gideon! Glory to the sword and the trumpet!"

Little children ran after him and begged him to play his horn. Dark-eyed women threw themselves upon his men, only to be shaken off.

No matter how thick the crowd or how hysterical the adulation, Gideon did not respond in either word or deed. The noise became deafening, but he just kept walking slowly forward, serious and dignified. Many of the Israelite young men—those who had weapons—beat their spears on their iron visors and raised a terrible din. But still Gideon pushed on through the encampment.

It seemed as if he and his commandos had walked for hours, but finally the crowds of people thinned. They had reached the beginning of no-man's-land, the flat plain that lay between the new Israelite gathering in the south and the Bedouin army north of Teacher's Hill. To the east, in the distance, they could see the sloping banks of the Jordan River.

At last Gideon stopped. He motioned to Purah not to allow his men to approach him. He closed his eyes and stood still. No matter how hard he tried, he could not stem the tears that coursed down his face. At first they were an expression of the joy he felt at the enormous response of the Israelites to Yahweh's message. But a deeper and more profound cause for his tears soon surfaced: He realized that in spite of the Israelites' astounding enthusiasm, they could never defeat the Midianite army.

Purah rushed to his side. "My lord, are you ill?"

"No, Purah. I am weak and frightened."

"Why? A short time ago fire could not burn your flesh. You were invincible!"

Gideon snorted derisively. "Ironic, isn't it? I was the strongest man in the world. I was immortal, and no force on earth could resist me because Yahweh was with me."

"Yes, my lord, and that is still so."

"No, Purah, unfortunately you are wrong. Look to the north, to the Bedouin army. Do you really believe our well-meaning rabble can defeat them? Perhaps I misunderstood Yahweh's instructions when we were on Mount Tabor together. Perhaps it was only my fervent desire to end the oppression that caused me to call the Israelites here!" He turned toward Purah, and the anguish was so deeply etched in his face, the servant averted his eyes. "There was no messenger from Yahweh! There was no sacred dream! I had no revelation during the act of sacrifice! Don't you remember, Purah? It came from within me, but I thought it came from Yahweh. Oh, Lord, forgive this fool!"

Gideon fell to his knees and clenched his fists in impotent fury. His confidence was gone. He felt like a man with a wasting disease.

"Please, sir!" Purah implored. "Think of what you're doing. Consider the effect this is having on your soldiers! Come now, you must get up!"

"How can I send this untrained throng against the Midianites, Purah? It will be a certain and horrible death for them. They have no hope of victory."

"Sir," Purah said, taking Gideon's arm and raising him to his feet, "I am merely a servant. I cannot advise you on this. But our success against the Bedouins rests, I believe, upon your inner strength."

"Right now, Purah, I have no inner strength." He smiled humorlessly. "And no outer strength, either. No surety, no . . ." He could not speak. He turned to stare at the Israelite throngs. Those farthest from him were still dancing, still singing hymns to Yahweh and Gideon. The ones nearby, however, stood solemnly in a half-circle facing him. Why had he not played the trumpet as they had begged? Why could he not maintain an outward appearance of confidence? He did not know.

"You are just tired, sir," Purah said softly. "It would be best if we pitch our tents here and all of us got some sleep. We cannot predict what will happen next. But we do need to recover our strength."

Gideon nodded at his servant's good sense. Purah went back to the pack animals, and soon all the raiders were busy putting up the tents.

When the sun had reached the noon hour, the shelters were ready. Gideon, without another word, walked into his tent and lay down on the soft mat that Purah always provided. He set his trumpet and weapons beside him and immediately fell asleep.

CHAPTER FOUR

Port of Ashkelon/Philistine League

When they heard the shouts, Pelops and three of his Sea Peoples marines were about to climb into the small rowboat that would take them back to their mother ship. They turned and stared at the boy running down the long pier toward them. He was yelling as if he were being chased by wild boars.

When the boy reached Pelops, he collapsed, too winded to speak. Pelops picked him up and shook him like a dog shakes a rat. "Spit it out, boy. The tide is going out, and I don't have time." Pelops was tired and irritable. It had been a long day delivering the twins, Gravis and Hela, to the Philistine slave trader Hindus.

"My master, Hindus, says you must come now!" the boy croaked.

"You tell him I'll be back tomorrow for the auction."

"My master says it can't wait," the boy said gasping. "He says a terrible thing has happened."

226

"Are the slaves hurt?" Pelops was very concerned. If the goods had been damaged, their price would drop considerably.

"Sir, all I know is that my master says you must return now."

Pelops cursed and savagely kicked the side of the rowboat. Ever since he had carried those twins onto the ship, there had been nothing but trouble. It was not that the twins had been violent prisoners; on the contrary, they followed all orders. But they were weird . . . eerie . . . strange. Their very presence had adversely affected his men, who had taken to displaying their own unusual behavior. Some of his sailors had sneaked the prisoners fresh fruit; others had cleaned up the muddy, rat-infested hold where the twins had been chained. And one of his men had even had the gall to petition his captain to allow the twins above deck for fresh air and exercise. Many of his men had clamored for guard duty, just to be near the pair. Oh, no doubt there was something very bizarre about them. They were so damned gentle and quiet, and they seemed to know the future.

He cursed, realizing that he had no choice but to return to the slave pens. It would be very bad business to irritate Hindus.

"Wait for me here," he told his marines, then following the boy, started off down the long pier.

As he walked, Pelops grew more angry. If anything happened to this particular transaction, if the twins could not be sold for a good price, then the entire adventure would have been a total bust. The whole bloody slaughter . . . the invasion, all the planning . . . everything . . . would not yield one copper coin.

Hindus, pacing back and forth, was waiting for him near the holding pens. His scowling face was red. He wore body armor as a precaution because he was constantly handling slaves, and he grasped a curved cattle prod in one hand.

"What kind of stock did you give me, Pelops?" he demanded.

"I gave you a pair of healthy, good-looking twins

who happen to be the grandchildren of Khalkeus of Gournia. Maybe they were too rich for your Philistine blood? Maybe I should have given you a couple of one-legged pimps kidnapped from Ashdod."

"Come with me," Hindus said urgently.

They approached the slave pens, which were two large wooden cages on wheels. Each pen had a single door fastened with strong ropes. Long wooden planks had been placed overhead. From these planks Hindus's workers poured down water from buckets to clean the pens.

A crowd had gathered around one of the pens. The people were shouting and cursing and flinging stones and other debris through the spaces in the cage. Hindus elbowed his way right through the rabble. He cursed and pushed until he reached the door of the pen. The crowd quieted down. Hindus, followed by Pelops, climbed up and into the cage.

An astonishing sight greeted Pelops. The twins were standing calmly at one end of the cage. Around them were heaps of stones and garbage that had been flung by the crowd.

The girl's tunic had been ripped away, and her breasts were exposed. Hela showed no shame, nor did she attempt to cover herself. Once again, Pelops felt entranced by the twins' beauty and calmness. They looked at him with recognition, as if he were an old friend rather than their captor.

"Look," Hindus said, pulling roughly at Pelops's arm.

On the filthy, straw-covered floor lay a Philistine. Pelops could tell by his clothes that he was an employee of Hindus.

"This fool," Hindus continued, kicking the man contemptuously with his foot, "ripped her tunic and tried to rape her. He didn't get far. Look at him!"

Pelops stared down at the man. He was lying on his back, his eyes wide open. He was breathing calmly. There was something very odd about him.

"Don't you see? He's paralyzed, totally paralyzed. He can't even close his eyelids."

Pelops knelt beside the man. Hindus was right. He looked up at the trader. "Maybe he became overexcited. Maybe he never saw such beautiful breasts."

"No!" Hindus shouted. Then, realizing his loud shout would inflame the crowd again, he moved closer and whispered: "She paralyzed him! She's a witch, Pelops! That's why the crowd wants to kill her. They saw it all."

Pelops stood. His palms were sweating. The girl, a sorceress with strange and deadly powers? That was absurd!

He strode over to Hela and stopped very close to her. The sight of her breasts was beginning to excite him. He moved back and averted his eyes. "Listen to me: You and your brother are in grave danger. I know this pig tried to rape you, and he no doubt got what he had coming; but the crowd believes you bewitched him, that you stole his strength with magic."

She stared at him steadily. A gentle smile played at the corners of her mouth.

Pelops, giving up on Hela, turned to her brother. "Do you know what happened?"

Gravis said nothing. He looked kindly at the soldier.

"Don't you understand? The mob is going to try to kill you now, right in this cage."

"Give me your hand," Hela said so quietly that Pelops thought at first that he was imagining it. "Your hand?" she repeated.

He reached out with his left hand.

"The other hand," she said.

He pulled back his left and reached out with his right.

She kissed his palm. "Go to that man," she said, "and touch his right foot."

He did not question the request. The whole episode was inexplicable. Pelops walked to the paralyzed man and placed his right hand against the man's paralyzed right foot. Then he stepped back.

The man blinked, shivered once, and then jumped up as if nothing had happened.

The crowd cheered enthusiastically. The man leaped out of the cage, and the crowd carried him off with good-natured taunts.

Pelops turned to Hela. "Who are you?" he whispered, thoroughly frightened. "*What* are you?"

She did not answer. She reached down and pulled her torn tunic upward, covering her breasts.

"We have to talk," Hindus said urgently, tugging on Pelops's arm.

When they were alone, far from the pens, Hindus grated, "I want them out of here, Pelops. I won't put them on the slave block. They're trouble—nothing but trouble."

"I need the money, Hindus. You can't back out on me now."

"Get them out of here, Pelops! Or you'll never deliver another slave to me."

Pelops shook his head sadly. It was no use. The slaver was adamant.

Hindus lowered his voice. "Listen to me, Pelops. You've been a good supplier over the years, so I'll tell you something that I overheard—something you may be very interested in."

"You mean how to get a good meal in this lousy town?"

"No, I mean a way to get rid of those twins for twenty times the money I could have gotten for them."

Pelops suddenly became interested.

"I have heard," Hindus said, "that an Egyptian contacted several slave traders in Gaza. He was looking for slaves—a certain kind of slave."

"What kind?"

"Twins, specifically a male and female."

"Why?"

"How should I know? But he told one of the slavers that he was acting for Shakko."

Pelops shook his head incredulously. "General Shakko? Commander-in-chief of the Egyptian army?"

Hindus nodded.

Why, Pelops wondered, would the finest, most famous general in the Egyptian army want a set of twins as slaves? Shakko was not a young man anymore. Had his sexual tastes become perverse in a pathetic attempt to regain his virility? Pelops shook his head. He could speculate for days on such a bizarre need. "But Shakko's forces take about one hundred thousand slaves a year. Why would he send his emissary into Gaza?"

"I don't know. But Shakko's agent said that the price he's offering for such a set of twins is silver ingots, piled to match the height and breadth of ten men standing shoulder to shoulder."

Pelops breathed deeply. How much credence could he put in the story? He did not know. Could he afford not to believe it? "I'll take the twins back shortly, Hindus, but as for now, I have to think."

"Think hard and fast, my friend," Hindus urged, then walked off toward the pens.

Pelops was exhausted. Those twins were a thorn in his flesh. If he wanted to remove that thorn and fill it with silver ingots, he would have to journey to Gaza—an ugly, hot town. He closed his eyes so as to concentrate better, but what flooded his mind was the vision of Hela's perfect breasts.

CHAPTER FIVE

North of Teacher's Hill

The warlords of the Midianites walked through the camp, followed by their surly, heavily armed aides. Their bodies were scarred from a thousand battles in the desert, their souls were warped and made cruel by the constant fight for survival. They passed Bedouin troopers, hunkered down in front of their tents, sharpening the blades of their swords. From time to time one of them offered up a song— a sad, wild song of the desert fighter. As soon as he finished a verse, he lapsed into a moody silence.

The men saluted the warlords with a wave of the swords, or sometimes they raised their bone daggers by the tip so that the hilt pointed toward Oreb and Zeeb, who acknowledged the respectful gesture with a nod.

The two warlords entered the area where the racing camels were kept. These camels were true wonders of the desert. Most stood six feet tall at the shoulders. All were various shades of white or buff, and some had dun markings on rump and neck and muzzle. A small

232

brush wall had been constructed to make sure the
beasts did not stray. Outside the barricade lay the saddles and bridles. Each one had been elaborately and
laboriously festooned by its Bedouin owner.

Inside the enclosure the camel grooms were busy.
One man was assigned to only three camels. These men
were usually well past their fighting years or had been
severely wounded in battle. No slaves were allowed to
touch the Midianite camels, to whom the fierce nomads
owed much of their success against their enemies.

Over a long stretch the camels proved faster than
horses. They were tougher and hardier than the desert
burro, and their ability to go without water or forage
for extended periods was legendary. Their disposition
was warlike; they spat and kicked at those who came
near. But once a Bedouin had negotiated the saddle
and was using the long whip gently, the camel became
the model of obedience.

Zeeb and Oreb moved through the enclosure and
checked the camels' feet for rot. The warlords stopped
to offer encouragement to the grooms, who were cursing a particularly fractious beast that was trying to splat-
ter them with evil-smelling yellow saliva.

Once the camel was under control, Oreb and Zeeb
left the enclosure and walked swiftly to the rise at the edge
of the camp where a meal was waiting for them. They sat
cross-legged on the ground and dipped their left hands into
the bowls of crushed millet and roasted lamb chunks. After
the food was taken from the bowl it was dipped into a dish
of salt before being brought to the mouth.

The warlords ate slowly, their eyes straight ahead.
Their retainers stood behind them at a respectful dis-
tance. From this rise they could keep an eye on the
Israelite masses who continued to gather near the
Spring of Harod.

"Look at the fools, camping in their own excrement," Oreb said.

Zeeb boomed a deep, nasty laugh that seemed to
spiral up from his bowels. "The sheep have come crawling, their throats upturned, to the wolves."

Oreb nodded. Fat from the lamb chunks gave a

sheen to the sides of his mouth, and he stroked his golden earring with one grease-stained hand.

Zeeb laughed again, and his face lighted up with a demonic glee. "We crossed the Jordan," he said, cackling, "to conquer Canaan. We thought the conquest would take months. But for our convenience the fools have delivered themselves to us. Now we will destroy them in a single day. We will turn their nation into a vanquished race and steal their armor, their jewels, and their women. They will be our slaves for generations to come."

"If only King Zalmunnah could see this . . ." Oreb said.

"We'll give him something better than battle: Before he crosses the Jordan with his retinue, we will have destroyed the Israelite nation. We will line the king's path with the heads and genitals of their warriors."

"They say a prophet has arisen among them," Oreb remarked, sneering.

"Some prophet! He blows his horn, and they come here to feed our swords."

"These Israelites must like music. Remember that fool with the trumpet we ran into not long ago?" Oreb snorted. "We made him and his companion strip, then made them play and dance."

They both laughed at the memory and kicked their now-empty wooden bowls across the ground. Their aides laughed, too.

Then Zeeb became serious, and a dangerous light shone in his eyes. "The more I look across at those fools, the more I want to see an Israelite bleed." He stood up and, with Oreb at his heels, walked purposefully to the slaves' compound.

The moment the warlords passed into that area, the emaciated, beaten captives began to cringe and scatter. A few trembled violently and began to whimper. It was obvious that the harsh treatment to which they had been subjected had unhinged their minds.

Zeeb stopped in the center of the slaves' compound and glared around. "Listen to me, dogs," he said loudly. "I am going to throw one of you a bone. I am going to free one of you to cross the plain and reunite with your fellow Israelite dogs, who now lift their legs against one another near the Spring of Harod."

A murmur rippled around the compound. The captives could not believe what they had heard. Free a captive? Such a thing had never happened.

Many of the slaves had been captive for years. The idea of being reunited with their families, from whom they had been separated for so long, was beyond their comprehension. They stood slack jawed and stared stupidly at the nomad warrior.

"Do you hear me?" Zeeb demanded, not liking the lack of response. "I said I will set one of you free. And then, maybe, I will set another one free."

Oreb motioned to his bodyguards, who charged the cowering prisoners and beat them with the flats of their swords because they apparently did not believe the warlord's declaration.

Zeeb held up his hand, and the assault stopped. "Now listen closely. I will free any one of you who can play a trumpet, the same instrument played by that ass of a so-called prophet who summons your brethren to their painful death. Well?"

An Israelite called Tikkum crouched low against the ground on the far end of the slaves' enclosure. He had been captured a little less than a year before near the Sea of Chinnereth. He, his brothers, his father, and his grandfather had been fishermen, plying the waters with mesh linen nets for the small but succulent bottom fish. Tikkum heard the warlord's fantastic offer. He could not play the trumpet, but he could play the flute—his father had given him a beautiful ash flute when he was very young, and he used to play it on the boat as his father and brothers had laid out the nets. Everyone in the tribe of Dan knew about Tikkum's gift for the flute.

If I can play the flute, he thought, *I might be able to play the trumpet also*. It was, he decided, worth the chance. He had no other option. He would not live much longer. He was near starvation, and his legs were covered with running sores. Constant pain shot through his stomach, and each day was a new torment. The Bedouin guards became more and more brutal to the Israelite captives now that people were gathering for battle by the spring.

Summoning all his strength and courage, Tikkum stood and made a sound that was not really coherent; it was a sort of grunt from deep inside his starving stomach. Slowly, he walked toward the center of the enclosure, where the warlord stood.

"You see?" Zeeb shouted. "A man has emerged at last! A man willing to play for his life."

Tikkum stopped before the warriors. His legs trembled as Oreb and Zeeb circled him, staring. There were low murmurs from the slaves.

"You can play the trumpet?" Zeeb shouted.

Tikkum nodded. His throat was so constricted by fear, he could not speak.

Zeeb turned to the assembled slaves and yelled: "You heard your brother. He can play the trumpet." Then he turned back to Tikkum and ordered, "Then play, dog!"

Confused, Tikkum held out his hands. "But I cannot play the trumpet unless I have one," he croaked.

"Listen to this dog!" Zeeb shouted. "Not only does he claim to play the trumpet, but he demands I give him one."

The warlords' bodyguards guffawed.

"Very well," Zeeb yelled. "Then I will give you a trumpet."

In a flash he drew the dagger from his belt and drove the blade through Tikkum's throat. "Here is your trumpet. Play it!"

Tikkum opened his mouth to scream, but all that came out was a torrent of blood. He brought his hands to his impaled throat and tried to pull the dagger out. His efforts were futile. He fell to his knees, then pitched forward so that he died on all fours like a dog digging for bones.

CHAPTER
SIX

Wadi Al Harir

Micah crouched just outside the Amalekite camp
and cursed the sun, which was setting too slowly for
him. His hunger to see the slave woman was worse
than the hunger from which the hawk had rescued him.
As he crouched there waiting for darkness, he was
assailed by doubt and confusion. Had his eyes played
a trick on him? Was the Child of the Lion birthmark
he thought he had seen actually something else? What
if the birthmark was real but on the lower back of a
different woman, not the beautiful and mysterious Babylonian girl, Luti, he had loved so wildly in the caves
and missed so terribly since then? Other women had
caught his eyes since that night in the cave, but none
had captured his heart and soul. Even before he had
seen her birthmark for the first time, he had known
that an important missing piece to the puzzle of his
miserable, violent life was Luti's to give him. Only
through her would he find inner peace.

No, he could not wait any longer. He was going into the camp, at any risk, at any cost. It was as if his life—the very possibility of continued existence—were waiting for him there. She held, he knew, a truth that would transform him. He had to know why she had left him behind so many years before. Why had she not even given him the chance to accompany her to Ur? Why!

As night enveloped her, Luti, chained to a stake about twenty yards from an Amalekite tent, began to shiver. Next to her was a small bowl of water, and next to that was a small round of flat bread.

The Midianites, she had heard, kept their slaves together in compounds. How nice it would be, she thought, to have someone to speak to. But Amalekites isolated their slaves from one another at night. There was no one to give comfort to . . . no one with whom to share the horror.

She folded her arms across her chest for warmth and thought about her son. She tried to envision Drak's brave but sad little face, as he looked when she started off on her journey. But the image was blurred, as if she were peering through a silken mesh. Her inability to conjure a clear picture of her beloved boy terrified her. It was a sign, she knew, that it was over for her.

There was no more hope. The hawk had failed her, and the future held only a lingering death far from home, far from her child. All her wealth and property and happiness in Ur were now ashes in her mouth because she had presumed to find a lost love. Luti wept bitterly and howled her anguish to the night. Why could she not have been satisfied with what she had? How could she have left her son to go on such a wild and futile adventure? She picked up the small pottery bowl and tipped out the water. If she could break the bowl, a sharp piece of pottery would serve well as a knife. Did she have the courage to take her own life? she wondered.

Luti rocked back and forth and struck her forehead repeatedly on the ground. She clutched the slave ring in her nose. The shame of her plight was a living death. Her broken and violated body had become a rag. She would find the courage for suicide, she knew, because living as a slave required even more fortitude than did dying.

Luti grasped the slave ring with her finger and gritted her teeth. She would yank the cursed thing from her nose, then kill herself.

Suddenly a powerful hand clamped tightly over her mouth. An arm pinned her arms and made it impossible to move. The attack was unexpected and overwhelming. She struggled with all her might against her assailant. But the man's grip was too great.

Her will faded. She wept silently and prayed to unknown gods. These men would never let her be. They would rape and beat her until she was broken.

But the grip relaxed just as she closed her eyes in resigned acceptance of the coming assault. She waited. Then she felt something strange. The encircling arms were not hostile. Yes, they were holding her tightly, but they were loving, protective. They were embracing rather than restraining her.

And then she felt something warm on the nape of her neck. Blood? Her own blood! No, not blood . . . She heard the sound of weeping and then realized the person who was holding her was crying, wetting her neck with his tears.

The grip relaxed completely, and Luti slowly turned and stared. She saw a black-haired man, naked except for a cloth around his middle. Even in the darkness she could see the ravages of sun and heat and starvation on his finely chiseled face.

"So long . . . it has been so long, so many years," he said, his voice cracking.

"Micah?" she whispered, incredulous. "Is that you, Micah? Can it really be you?"

Her body was trembling fiercely, but she managed to reach out and touch him gently on the face. He leaned forward and kissed her reverently, tenderly, gently. But his lips felt like a burning spear on her skin. His kisses felt like the gift of life itself.

"I came to Canaan to find you, Micah," she whispered, still not entirely believing what was happening. "I came to apologize for what happened on that terrible night in the caves when I betrayed you. I came to find you and be with you."

His fingers stopped her speech. "Hush, my darling. There is no need for apologies. That all happened a long time ago. Tonight the gods have given us both a gift. I was a dead man. A hawk brought me to you. It was a miracle, Luti, a miracle of love."

"We have a child, Micah, a son. In Ur. His name is Drak."

She heard him gasp, and tears coursed freely down his cheeks. He kissed her palms, her feet, the places where her skin had been rubbed raw by the chains.

"What have they done to you, my beloved? What have they done?" The anguish in his voice was terrible. She wondered if his suffering was worse than anything she had experienced among the Bedouins. She could not bear his pain.

"Nothing I have endured here, Micah, equaled the misery I felt at your absence. With each passing year, your memory became more beautiful and true. At last I knew I had to find you. We had to be reunited." She was whispering her love in his ear now. They were close, so very close. "You will meet your boy. We will be a family."

"I have led an ugly, violent existence without you," he confessed.

"And I have led a wasteful one."

Their arms wrapped around each other, they lay down together on the hard and dark desert floor. They both wept with joy and regret, and their tears mingled.

"Do you remember how it was with us, Micah?" she asked, gently bringing his face down to her breasts. She could feel the love of his mouth on them.

They both were starved, but their food now was love. They were weak, but their strength now was memory. They were in danger, but their courage now was their togetherness.

Nothing on earth could stop them from joining,

from flinging all the hurt and the betrayal and the fear from their minds and bodies. They held each other and made love until the night itself seemed to become a perfumed silken bed. Finally, their hands and lips locked, they slept, oblivious to the universe.

CHAPTER SEVEN

Spring of Harod

Gideon woke from his nap feeling refreshed and hungry. He chewed on a barley cake that Purah had left for him in his tent. A thin film of honey over the cake made it very palatable. As he washed the snack down with a bowl of clear water, a voice came to him from out of nowhere.

"Poor little Gideon. I hear you are having a crisis of confidence again."

Gideon was so astonished by the voice that he dropped the bowl. He had neither seen nor heard anyone entering his tent.

The sarcastic voice spoke again. "Yes, poor little Gideon is confused again. Just put a little pressure on him, and he gets confused."

Then Gideon saw Yahweh's messenger, wearing the same ludicrous blacksmith's clothes and standing in the corner of the tent.

"And you were doing so well, Gideon. We had all

heard about that burned-arm trick with the priest of Baal."

"It wasn't a trick," Gideon shot back angrily. The sarcasm stung him.

"Oh? Not a trick? A miracle, then? Is Gideon performing miracles?"

"Don't make fun of me!" Gideon clasped the hilt of his sword.

"Are you threatening me? Me? A messenger from the Lord of Hosts? Why, you poor pathetic idiot. With one flick of my small finger I could fry you alive."

Then the messenger began to pace angrily in the small tent and kicked aside everything that was not nailed down. "I am getting tired of you, Gideon. I am sick of all your so-called prophets and saviors who can't keep your head screwed on tight."

"But look at us," Gideon pleaded. "And look at them!"

"Oh, shut up. I know what you're frightened of. Every time you see the Midianite army you wet your pants and lose your faith. I just don't know which you do first."

"Half the people assembled here are Israelite women and children. How can I send them against the Midianite butchers? How—"

"Shut up, Gideon," the messenger interrupted. "I know exactly what you want—you want another sign. Right? Poor little insecure Gideon needs another sign that Yahweh is with him, or he can't go on. Isn't that right, Gideon?"

"Yes, but—"

"How many signs have you already received? Yahweh is losing patience with you. I myself think you are worthless."

"Please try to understand. My faith in Yahweh is total. It is just that—"

The angel had folded his leather cloak around his face and stood motionless in the center of the tent. "I will give you one last sign, Gideon. Yahweh has, in His mercy, given you the gift now to see what you desire most. Look outside your tent flap."

Gideon walked swiftly to the flap and swept it aside. At first he saw the familiar landscape. Then his vision began to blur. When his eyes focused again, the landscape had changed utterly. He saw a soft hillside, which the drought had not scarred. And there were lush trees and curling vines with lovely, heart-shaped leaves and a profusion of small blue wildflowers around the bases of the tree trunks.

Then he saw a figure of a graceful young woman walking effortlessly across the landscape. She seemed to be studying the ground as she moved. From her hand dangled a small basket, and from time to time she bent down, picked something off the ground, and placed it in the basket.

His heart lurched with joy. It was his beloved sister, Miriam, searching for food for the family. Tears flooded his eyes. She had been on his mind constantly since he was driven from their village. He had been worried that she might leave home and come to the Spring of Harod to fight the Midianites. He was terrified that she might be killed or maimed. Gentle, kind, lovely Miriam . . . who had saved his life from the Baal crowd—he could not bear the thought of her being in danger. And now, because of this vision, he knew for a certainty that she was safe and well.

He called out, his voice thick from his tears, "Miriam!"

But the moment he said her name, his vision blurred again, and she was gone. The verdant landscape was also gone, and he was staring at hard, baked ground.

Confused, frightened, he staggered backward and turned toward the messenger.

"Well?" the angel demanded. "You received the sign, didn't you?"

Gideon understood. He nodded, trying to compose himself.

"Now listen closely to Yahweh's instructions. Are you listening, Gideon?"

"Yes," he finally managed to whisper.

"First, you will immediately call a general assembly and address the Israelites. Explain to them in graphic detail exactly what horrors they will be facing in the coming battle. Tell the women that they are facing rape and slavery and every known abomination when they are captured—and many of them will be. Then tell the men what is facing them—torture and castration and worse."

"But—"

The messenger silenced Gideon before he could protest. "Be quiet and listen. Time is short. After you have painted a true picture of what faces the Israelites in battle against the Midianite army, you will ask for a show of hands as to who is frightened. Anyone who raises his or her hand will be sent home. Have I made myself clear?"

Gideon nodded. It was futile, he realized, to make any response.

"After you have weeded out the frightened ones, you will march the remainder to the spring and order everyone to drink. Send home immediately all those who kneel to drink. Only those who remain standing, who drink by reaching down, scooping up water into a cupped hand, then lapping it with their tongue—only those will you keep as your soldiers in the coming battle."

"I don't understand."

"Of course you don't, you halfhearted prophet. You see, those who naturally remain alert and drink like wary dogs are the only warriors you can trust. Is that too difficult a concept for you to comprehend?"

There was a logic in what the angel said, Gideon admitted.

"Now get out of here and start acting like an Israelite called to glory by Yahweh."

Shamed, Gideon strode from the tent to call Purah. He did not look back. The die was cast now, he knew. He could not waver again.

CHAPTER EIGHT

Wadi Al Harir

Micah awoke, his arms still wrapped around Luti. He was startled by the brightness of the desert morning. A bolt of pain suddenly shot through his skull. He blinked and realized it was not the sun that was causing the brightness or the pain—an Amalekite spear was pressed against his temple.

"Move and you die!" the Bedouin shouted.

Micah could feel Luti's body tense with fear. The spear point was digging into his scalp. The Amalekite had pinned him to the ground as if he were a snake. His sweat mingled with his blood.

The encampment came alive with shouts and the pounding of running feet, and soon a circle of Amalekites surrounded the two lovers. A few nomads pointed and laughed in derision. Some kicked Luti and Micah, while still others exhorted the spearman to drive the spear home.

Micah heard Luti whisper desperately in his ear,

246

"I love you, darling. If we die, at least we will die together."

A large, swarthy Bedouin with a jagged scar across his face pushed his way into the center of the circle and stared down at Micah. When the spearman started to press the weapon harder and deeper into Micah's flesh, the newcomer shouted, "Wait! Put the spear up!"

The spearman did not obey, and the scarred nomad forcefully yanked the spear away, sending the soldier sprawling.

"You are Blood, aren't you?" the scarred Bedouin asked.

Micah did not answer. He could hear the murmurs from the onlookers.

"You are Blood the bandit, aren't you?" the Bedouin repeated in a harsher tone.

"Yes," Micah said. "Yes, you foul-smelling pig of an Amalekite."

The Bedouin grinned broadly at the insult and showed strong square teeth. "Watch him," he ordered, then ran off. He came back shortly, leading a tall, haggard-looking, middle-aged Bedouin.

"Oh, gods, that is Adab, chief of the Amalekites," Luti whispered to Micah.

Adab walked around Micah and Luti several times, as if he were observing two very strange creatures in a foreign marketplace.

"So," he finally said, "the *great* bandit Blood has run his course. He sneaks naked and starving and wounded into my camp, to sleep with a slave." He paused and leered wickedly. "Not just any slave, of course."

Without warning Adab lashed out with his sandaled foot and kicked Luti hard on the side of the face. She cried out. Enraged, Micah leaped up and launched himself against the Amalekite chief. His fingers closed around the Bedouin's throat, but a dozen arms pulled Micah off and restrained him.

"This slave woman you tried to protect," Adab said, rubbing his neck, "deserves nothing. She has brought grief to my people. She led the young Amalekite Umas to an untimely and horrible end. And her lies have turned the great Midianites against us.

"And you, Blood," Adab continued, "have earned the death penalty for sneaking into my camp and using this slave without my permission. You have lived in the desert too long not to know its laws."

In response, Micah spat at the Bedouin chief. A dozen fists battered him to the ground. His head began to swim. Everything became dark. . . .

When Micah regained consciousness, he was in the same place. Luti was still chained. One side of her face was swollen and discolored. In front of each of them was a small bowl of milk. Nearby, Adab sat cross-legged on the ground, flanked by two of his advisers. The Bedouin gestured to Micah to drink the milk.

After Micah had done so, Adab asked, "Tell me, Blood, do you wish to live?"

"Yes."

"If you follow my instructions, I may allow you to do so. I know of your past—I know that you soldiered for many years with the Israelites, that you assassinated the hated Eglon of Moab and sparked the Israelites' Great Revolt. I know that the Israelites still revere you as a national hero."

"So what?" Micah responded bitterly. He saw Luti's eyes widen at this information. She had not known the particulars of his violent past.

"You can move among them unchallenged. You know their customs. You know the way they think."

"I used to. That was all a long time ago, my living with them."

Adab stroked his chin and smiled. "Some things one never forgets. My people have fallen out of favor with the Midianites, and that will hurt us when the Midianites conquer Canaan. I wish to get back in their good graces; otherwise they will not give us the land and water we need and deserve. I can do this only by destroying the new prophet who has risen from among the Israelites and is exhorting them to make war. His name is Gideon. If you kill him, Blood, your death sentence will be reversed. But if you agree to this plan and leave our camp, only to run away from your task, we will hunt you down and kill you. And I'm sure I don't need to elaborate on what will happen to this slave woman should you not return."

"How can one man alone perform such a task?" Micah asked.

"You assassinated Eglon of Moab without assistance, didn't you?"

"I was a zealot then and much younger," Micah replied.

"Then you'd best become a zealot again if you wish to survive. Despite your boniness you are still a vigorous man. I'm sure your life as a thief has kept you strong. We will give you Bedouin robes so you may pass safely through the Midianite camp. Once you are among the Israelites, you can fend for yourself. Just find and kill that lunatic with the horn around his neck."

"Horn? A shofar?"

"No, a trumpet. He aspires to be a great musician as well as a warrior," Adab said, laughing. His advisers echoed his merriment.

Micah knew the code of the desert. If he agreed to the pact, he would have to make a serious attempt to carry out the assassination. For his safety and Luti's, he could not simply escape and return south, to see if any of his men were still alive. The Amalekites would murder his beloved and ceaselessly hunt him down. He would have to look over his shoulder and guard his back for as long as he lived. But he was also weak and used up. He doubted that he still had the tenacity for such a task. But he had no choice. If he refused, Adab would kill him now.

He looked past Adab and his advisers to where Luti lay chained, one hand grasping the now-empty milk bowl. He shut his eyes in anguish at the sight of her captivity and evidence of brutal mistreatment. Oh, how he wanted her with him forever and to meet their son.

"All right. I will kill the Israelite with the horn. But I want more than just my life in payment."

"How can you be paid with more than your life?" Adab retorted angrily. "You are hardly in a position to bargain."

"I want her life, also," Micah answered.

"You must be joking. That slave woman is worth at least seven hundred shekels. She's young and strong and handsome—"

Micah interrupted boldly. "She must be part of the deal. I will kill this Israelite trumpet player for you. Then I will return a free man and take the slave away with me."

Adab thought for a moment. "You drive a very hard bargain," he said at last. "But I want Gideon dead, and you're the man to do it. All right, the slave, too. But kill this Gideon as quickly as you can. I want him dead before the battle even begins."

Micah nodded, and the deal was struck. He moved closer to Luti. At night, while they had made love, he could not see the condition of her body. Now, in the morning's light, he could see that beatings and rapes had taken their toll on her. He sat next to her, gathered her into his embrace, and pressed her head to his shoulder. "I will be back shortly for you, my love, and then we will go away together. Believe me, all this will be over soon." He buried his face in her hair.

"What if something happens to you?" Luti whispered. "I am so afraid, Micah."

"There's no reason for you to worry. I have done these kinds of things all my life. I'll be back soon. I promise."

She began to cry. "Be careful, Micah," she said in a strained voice. "I could not stand to lose you again."

Micah nodded, stood up, and started to move away. But Luti clutched at him and whispered desperately, "If you cannot succeed, escape without a thought of me. Go to Ur. Find our son and take care of him. Then I shall die happy." She released his hand.

He straightened. He had to think positively. He had to act swiftly and well. He had to destroy the Israelite prophet.

He bent to kiss Luti's cheek and jaw where Adab's foot had struck. He knew that he had been right: This woman did hold the key to his life. He knew that if he had the strength, he would kill anyone to bring her peace.

CHAPTER NINE

Spring of Harod

It was already dark when Gideon returned to his tent after having addressed the Israelites in assembly. He was startled to find Messenger on his mat, sound asleep. Gideon left the flap of the tent open so that the torch on the outside would send its light within. He felt exhausted, disgusted, and disillusioned.

"Well? What happened?" the angel asked, sitting up as if he had never been asleep at all.

"I did what you told me to do," Gideon replied.

"Then why do you sound so sad?"

"Because after I followed your instructions, I am left with only three hundred fighting men. The rest I sent back to their homes."

The angel stroked his chin thoughtfully. "Three hundred is a nice round number."

"How can you joke about this?" Gideon snapped. "Have you seen the size of the Bedouin army? They have thousands of warriors, perhaps tens of thousands."

"Don't you dare tell me you want more reassurance," the messenger said savagely.

"Of course not. I will fight to the death, even if I have only Purah at my side. But you must not ignore the reality of the situation."

"Ah, Gideon, it is *you* who have never understood the reality of the situation. That is why I was sent to you."

"I'm not going to argue. Just tell me what to do next."

"Attack the Midianite army in the morning."

"With only three hundred men?"

"Yes."

"What strategy should I use?"

"Each Israelite must carry a horn and a pitcher. Within each pitcher must be a torch, head down. When you reach the Midianite camp, each man will break his pitcher, revealing the bright torch. Then begin to blow the horns. Make a terrible ruckus. The sudden light and sound will send the Midianites into utter confusion from which they will not recover, and the battle will be yours."

Gideon stared wide-eyed at the angel. He was beginning to loathe this emissary from God. Did he really believe that three hundred men with horns and torches could destroy the powerful Midianite war machine?

"The Bedouins of Midian," Gideon responded as calmly as he could through clenched jaws, "are battle tested, fierce, and intelligent. They don't become afraid or confused easily."

"Ah, Gideon, Gideon . . ." He shook his head indulgently. "All humans are subject to confusion. All human power is worthless because it's limited. Can't you understand that?"

"I am trying."

"Then try harder."

"It is just that what I see before my eyes does not reconcile with the faith in my heart."

In an unexpected display of kindness, the messenger gently laid an arm on Gideon's shoulder. "Yes, that is always a problem. But you must remain strong. Put all your faith in Yahweh, for He is the Lord of inside and outside, of the earth and heavens. He will reconcile everything."

"I know that!" Gideon said loudly. "I know the power of Lord Yahweh. He healed my burned arm. I have witnessed miracle after miracle. My faith is powerful now. But always there is the gnawing doubt as to my own strength. It waxes and wanes. Sometimes I feel that no arrow or spear can pierce my flesh, and at other times I feel that a clod of dirt thrown by a child can destroy me."

"You are talking about the human condition, my friend," the messenger said, and his face softened into a smile that was so assuring that Gideon wished to embrace him. "Tomorrow, Gideon, at dawn, you must strike."

Gideon nodded at the angel's repetition of the command.

"I must go now," the angel said.

"No, wait! Have some food and drink. Let me show you our hospitality."

But the messenger only smiled, raised his arm in good-bye, and vanished. Gideon looked around wildly, but the tent was empty. Where had he gone? Why had he gone so quickly?

"Purah!" he shouted. There was no reply. "Purah! Purah! Get in here."

Breathlessly, Purah entered the tent. "I am sorry, my lord. I was eating."

"There is no time to eat. We strike at dawn."

"But, sir, we have only three hundred fighters. Can't we wait until more men arrive?"

Gideon ignored his servant's suggestion. "Each man, Purah, is to attack with a horn and a pitcher. Within each pitcher, a lighted torch, head down. I am depending upon you to make sure all of our men are equipped in this manner—in addition to their weapons, of course."

Purah looked at Gideon as if he was mad, but Gideon expected that. "Sir, is this some kind of joke?"

"It's no joke, Purah."

"Where am I to find horns and pitchers for every soldier?"

"I don't care where or how. Steal them. Or beg for them. Or simply requisition them from the merchants who have been plying their trade in the camp."

"I will do as you wish, sir," Purah replied, resigned. But he did not leave the tent. Instead he remained, starting to leave a dozen times and then turning back.

"What is the matter, Purah? Why are you so agitated?" Gideon asked his faithful servant.

"Can I be honest with you, sir?"

"Have I ever allowed less than honesty from you?" Gideon demanded, out of patience.

"Well, sir, it seems to me that this is a suicide mission. And a crazy one at that. Horns and pitchers and torches . . . What will the men think?"

Gideon did not reply. He could understand his servant's fears. The Israelite soldiers would no doubt be petrified when they learned that they, and they alone, would confront the Midianite army. And surely their confidence would suffer when they were handed pitchers and horns. Gideon realized that they would benefit from seeing a sign, just as he had. But it would be necessary for the sign to come from him, for he was the man who had spread Yahweh's word.

"Assure them that our victory is guaranteed. Our strategy has been carefully planned. I myself will reconnoiter the Midianite camp tonight."

"Oh, no, sir! Please! It is too dangerous!" Purah exclaimed.

"I will be very careful. And the men will be confident when they realize that I am making the final preparations myself, based on firsthand information."

"Let me go with you, sir."

"No, Purah. It is best I go alone. I will memorize the approaches and scout out the weaknesses in the Midianites' perimeter."

"May Yahweh go with you, sir."

"He does, Purah. I truly believe that He does."

Purah left the tent quickly to requisition the supplies.

Gideon, alone, removed his weapons. He knew he must travel fast and light. Only his trumpet remained fastened around his neck. He mixed some dirt from the ground with water and applied it to his face to darken his skin. He wore no metal that would betray him by glinting in the moonlight. Last of all, he removed his sandals. It would be best to travel barefooted.

Then he knelt and prayed for strength, courage, and wisdom from Yahweh. A moment later he slipped out of the tent and disappeared in the darkness.

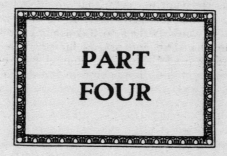

**PART
FOUR**

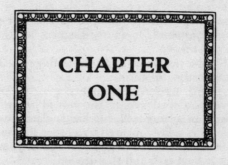

CHAPTER ONE

Teacher's Hill

Micah, entering the Midianite camp, strolled un-
molested past the sentries. The Amalekite robe and
headdress given to him by Adab were enough to identify him as an ally. Besides, no intruder was expected;
everyone knew that the Amalekites were on the move,
crossing the Jordan on the way to Teacher's Hill, where
they would join forces with King Zalmunnah's legions.
It was in this camp, Micah realized, where he would
redeem Luti after he had accomplished his mission.

Once inside the camp Micah looked around with
a practiced military eye. The moon was obscured by
clouds, but the camp was brightly lighted by hundreds
of cooking fires, which burned in front of the tents. He
was uncomfortable in the robe and headdress, but the
might of the Midianite army made him quickly forget
his discomfort and instead feel grateful for the security
they afforded.

What he saw startled him. Bedouins were famous

259

for their fighting ability, their courage, and their brilliance on the battlefield. But they had never been noted for their discipline. They had never been known to field a well-trained, well-equipped army on the Egyptian model. Yet he was in the midst of such an army now. Everything pointed to an iron discipline, to a chain of command, to the willingness to take orders and execute them.

The Israelites are utter fools, he thought. *The Midianites will crush them.*

He heard a sudden commotion in the otherwise placid, well-ordered camp. He moved toward it. He saw a Bedouin sitting with his hands clamped over his eyes in front of a fire. Around him other Bedouins were yelling, many in an insulting tone, "Tell us your dream. How can it hurt us? Tell the dream!"

They jumped around and tormented the sitting figure. Finally, much annoyed, he pulled his hands away from his face, stood, and raised his arms for quiet.

"Very well," he assented. "I will recount it to all of you. But you will be sorry. In the dream I had a sense of great danger, so I rushed from my tent and searched the sky—I don't know exactly for what. Maybe for a shooting star. Anyway, as I was staring at one part of the heavens, I heard a powerful sound, as if a mighty bird was shrieking nearby. I turned my head, only to see a giant barley cake flying through the air. It went by me at great speed and crushed my tent. Then I woke up."

"That's the whole dream?" one of the onlookers asked, incredulous at its brevity and simplicity.

"Yes."

The onlookers began to chuckle, then their amusement grew to heaving guffaws. Soldiers were bent double from the hilarity. Some wiped tears of laughter from their cheeks. Others picked up small stones and flung them at him, calling out: "Watch out for the flying barley cake!"

"Stop!" a strong voice called out.

Micah turned to see a Bedouin pushing his way

through the onlookers and stopping by the dreamer's side.

Micah could see that the newcomer was some kind of magician, for his robe bore symbols that none of the other Midianites had. Small, highly stylized designs were tattooed on his cheeks and across his brow. His earrings were much smaller than the usual Midianite warriors' jewelry. Micah listened carefully as the man addressed the gathering.

"Our brother has told us his dream. Why do you mock his fear? Our brother is right; this dream portends tragedy. We Bedouins eat millet. We do not make barley cakes—only the Israelites carry barley cakes with them. In the dream the cake destroyed a tent. I say to you that this dream portends that the Israelites will destroy all the tents of Midian."

His words were met with stunned silence. It was as if the speaker were using a new language that had to be translated. Then the laughter began again. The Bedouin warriors were amused at the absurd notion that the Israelite men, women, and children—that ludicrous army of cooks, servants, and herdsmen now gathered across from them on the plain—could destroy the Midianite force. Why, they could not even destroy the fleas that had overrun their camp.

Micah moved off, heading toward the far perimeter of the camp. He sauntered slowly, nonchalantly, and passed the enclosure that held the Midianites' white racing camels. Next he passed the supply tents and the well-dug latrines. The moment he was outside the camp and beyond the last Midianite sentry, he withdrew from his robes two daggers with which the Amalekites had supplied him, then discarded the garments and headdress with relief.

Now, alone, almost naked, carrying the daggers, he was in his element. He moved quickly in a crouch, headed across the broken floor of the valley and toward the Israelite camp. He was Blood again, the feared bandit, the man who could move like a wolf, the man who struck fear in all of southern Canaan.

He had not gone half a mile when he heard the

crackling of a dry plant. He froze. The sound could have been made by a lizard or a rabbit, or an old branch could be cracking under the pressure of a dry wind. He squinted into the darkness.

A man, naked and weaponless, was crawling across the ground. If he continued on a constant track, he would cross Micah's path. Micah could see that the stranger had a trumpet tied with a rope around his neck. The Amalekites had told him that Gideon was a madman and a trumpet player. Staring at this stranger in the night, he realized it must be Gideon. Only a madman would crawl out here unarmed and with a trumpet to spy on the enemy camp.

When the man was only a few feet away from him, Micah repositioned the daggers for a killing thrust. Sweat blinded his eyes. He wiped it away as he tensed for the attack. Then he lowered the daggers. He had to make certain he was killing the right man. Luti's life depended on it.

Micah stood so he could be seen. He whispered, "Gideon?"

The stranger turned toward the sound, and Micah could tell by the man's astonished expression that he had whispered the correct name. Luck be praised, he was face to face with his target! Micah sprang like a crazed lion onto the man and knocked him to the ground.

Then he straddled him and pressed the twin daggers against his throat. Micah could see the fear in the man's eyes as he fought to free himself. Then, realizing there was no hope, Gideon lay still.

"I know you," Gideon said, gasping. "I know you. I saw you many years ago, near the Jordan. My father and I shook your hand. You are the great Micah, the assassin who freed us from Eglon of Moab."

Micah did not respond. It was incredible that this man on the ground remembered all this. He did not want to listen.

"Please, let me get up. I am Gideon, a servant of Yahweh's."

"I know who you are, you fool. I came here to kill you."

"Me? But why, Micah? You have always helped my people. The Children of the Lion have always brought support to the Israelites."

I can't listen to this man, Micah thought. *For Luti's sake and our son's future, I have to kill him now. I have to drive the blades into his throat.*

"If you kill me, Yahweh's curse will be upon you forever," Gideon warned.

"And if I don't kill you," Micah whispered hoarsely, "the only woman I have ever loved will die a slow and horrible death."

Gideon did not speak again.

Time stood still for Micah as he stared down into his victim's eyes. The palms of his hands began to cramp, so tightly did he grasp the daggers. He knew he could not betray Luti. Besides, what did the Israelite mean to him? Nothing. He had paid his dues to the Israelites a long time before. He owed them nothing.

Kill him. Kill him. Kill him, Micah kept whispering to himself. He raised the daggers high so that the plunge into Gideon's throat would rip through the jugular and kill him instantly.

But just as he started to bring the daggers down, the face of Joshua appeared in his consciousness. The famous commander who had won Canaan for his people stared uncomprehending at Micah, as if shocked by the deed.

Micah lost his will and dropped the daggers from fingers devoid of all strength. The weapons clattered harmlessly to the baked ground. He rolled off Gideon and stood, trembling and exhausted, hating himself for his weakness. What of Luti? he agonized. What of his beloved Luti?

Gideon quietly led an unresisting Micah back to the Israelite camp and installed him in his own tent, then had a servant bring him water and food. When Micah had recovered a bit, Gideon asked for his help in the coming battle.

Micah looked up as if Gideon was mad. "But all your people have vanished. When we came into camp, I saw no soldiers to speak of. I assumed there would be no battle. The Midianites believe that thousands of

Israelites are still camped here because the huts have not been razed."

"We attack at dawn, Micah, with three hundred men."

"Three hundred men? Gideon, the Midianites have an army!"

"And so do I. My three hundred men were picked by Yahweh," Gideon replied.

When the Israelites decided to fight, Micah remembered, they were the bravest soldiers in the world. Enormous odds meant nothing to them, and they nearly always prevailed in battle. Micah remembered the strange incident in the Midianite camp—the dream of the flying barley cake and the Midianite wizard who had interpreted the dream to mean that the Israelites would destroy Midian. Maybe a miracle would happen. They had occurred time and time again in the past. And if there was a miracle, if the Midianites could be routed, then there was still a chance that Luti could be saved. Yes, there was still hope!

"Tell me your plan, Gideon."

Gideon described in great detail the attack strategy that Yahweh's messenger had outlined. After the Israelite finished talking, Micah remained silent.

"Well?" Gideon pressed. "What do you think?"

"It would be stupid of me to judge a military plan constructed, as you say, by Yahweh. But may I make a suggestion?"

"Of course," Gideon urged.

"The best way to sow discord in the Bedouin army is to frighten their camels. If we can get the camels to break out of their enclosure and stampede through the camp, the Bedouins will ignore all else to recapture them."

"But the camels are penned deep inside the camp."

"True. They can, however, be reached by fireballs flung from catapults."

Micah and Gideon were interrupted by a man whom the Israelite introduced as his loyal servant, Purah. He entered the tent carrying several trumpets.

These he showed to his master and remarked that the requisitioning process was yielding all kinds of odd-looking horns. Gideon, too excited about Micah's idea, paid little attention.

"How many catapults do you think we would need?"

"No more than ten."

"We can build those in a few hours."

When Micah glanced at the collection of horns that Purah brought in, another idea came to him. He did not have to wait for the Israelite attack to try to rescue Luti. He could return to the Midianites' camp now and claim to have assassinated Gideon. He could bring along one of the horns, stained with blood, as proof of the deed. And he could tell the Bedouins that the Israelites had all gone home, that there would be no war.

Micah described the plan to Gideon, who greeted it enthusiastically. He hustled Micah and Purah from the tent and, within minutes, with his own hand slaughtered a goat to spill blood over one of Purah's requisitioned horns.

"Here, Micah," Gideon said, holding out the instrument. "It's ready to take with you. No one will believe it is not my trumpet. And if the enemy is skeptical, why, just blow it." He, along with Purah, laughed uproariously at the joke.

Micah waited impatiently until the laughter had subsided. Then he took a twig and began to draw upon the ground in the light of a torch. He drew a diagram for Gideon, which outlined the Midianite camp, and showed him where the camels were kept.

"I suggest you organize your army into three columns for your attack," Micah said, "because their camp is so large and you are so few."

Gideon nodded his agreement.

Then Micah continued drawing on the ground and beckoned Gideon closer. "Here is a design for a very simple catapult. All it requires is a plank, a drum, and some stout rope. The plank is lashed to the drum. The rope is made wet and tightened until the plank becomes like a bowstring. Place the missile on the plank, cut the rope, and the mechanism fires. As for the missile itself, the Egyptians use small pieces of brushwood wrapped in rags that are allowed to burn for a while before being placed on the catapult."

"Thank you, Micah, for everything," Gideon said earnestly, clasping the newcomer about the shoulder.

Tears came to Micah's eyes. It was like old times again—an Israelite general depending upon him . . . a small but zealous Israelite army going out to fight a much larger foe, counting on their courage and the benevolence of a God they seldom worshiped.

There were a thousand things he wanted to say to Gideon, but he said nothing. There was not enough time. Luti was waiting for him. He picked up the bloody horn and hurriedly left the Israelite camp.

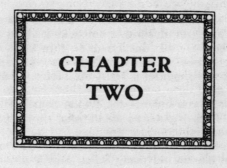

CHAPTER TWO

Tyre

It was a dark, moonless night, but from where the naked lovers lay, they could see the gates of Tyre because speckles of light from the city reflected off the cloudy sky. Cotto and Talus lay on a blanket that had been spread on a thick sheepskin. Behind them, snorting restlessly from time to time, their donkeys stood tethered.

Talus stared into Cotto's lovely face, framed by night shadows. Her eyes were closed, but Talus knew she was not sleeping. He gently kissed her ear. She stirred and smiled but did not open her eyes. His right arm circled her waist. The mere touch of her made him tremble, as it always did. He looked down and away, toward the gates of Tyre, as a grim foreboding overwhelmed him. Cotto was making a mistake; he knew that. She was going to be hurt by the Phoenicians, and even his devoted love would not be able to help her. He could not share her optimism, her belief that she was in control of her own destiny, her certainty that she understood the Phoenician mind.

"There's still time," he whispered to her.

"Yes," she said, smiling and reaching for him. "We have all night."

He chuckled mirthlessly. "I am not talking about making love, my darling. I am talking about entering Tyre. There is still time for us to turn back."

She turned so that her face was nestled between his neck and shoulder. "Trust me, Talus. I know what I am doing."

"I trust you but not the Phoenicians," he said fervently. "I am frightened about what they might do to you. I am frightened for our love."

She sat up abruptly and pouted. "You are starting to sound like an old man, Talus. Maybe you are tired of being my lover."

"Don't say such stupid things," he protested, and pulled her to him. She settled into his embrace and stroked his back. "Sometimes, Cotto, I feel that I don't know you at all."

"You know all there is to know," she whispered, taking his hand and pressing it to her breast.

He did not want to speak anymore. He wanted to taste her honeyed sweetness and touch her plush softness. His mouth lowered to her body, and she moaned and entwined her fingers in his hair.

"Cotto . . . Cotto . . . Cotto . . ." he whispered as she became more and more excited under his fingertips. Soon she opened herself to him. He entered her, and his body hummed with love and excitement. This was worth everything. This was the moment that obliterated all confusion and fears. The lovers moved together like one, each thrust bringing them deeper into the lovers' pact until, with a great shudder, Cotto cried out.

They lay together quietly, side by side, staring up at the night sky.

"I have had many lovers, Talus, but none to equal you."

"You are just being kind. I am inexperienced."

"It is not experience that determines whether a man is a good lover. It is imagination and daring."

"And I am daring?"

"Yes," Cotto said, smiling. "And you are gloriously imaginative."

"And Nimshi? What kind of lover was he?"

The moment the words escaped his lips, he regretted them. It was such a stupid thing to say. Why had he said it? Frightened that he had offended her, he waited in agony for her response.

"Are you so sure, then, that Nimshi and I were lovers?" she asked in a light, teasing tone.

"It is none of my business. I'm sorry I asked."

"No, it is your business, Talus. But Nimshi was a drug addict and in constant pain. He could hardly be a lover in the sense that you are."

"But he *was* your lover," he persisted, emboldened by her nonaggressive response.

"One day I will tell you all about poor Nimshi."

A noise that rode the quiet night breeze from the direction of the city gates interrupted the conversation.

"The grave diggers," Cotto said as a wagon drawn by four oxen left Tyre.

Talus, squinting, could make out heaps of corpses piled haphazardly on the wagon. The cart moved slowly, ponderously, on large wooden wheels.

"The Phoenicians value cleanliness," Cotto explained. "Each night wagons go through the city to remove the bodies of those who died in their beds from old age or in the streets from starvation or in some isolated alleyway from a knife wound."

"Where are the bodies buried?" he asked.

"Not buried, dumped in the sewerage pits near the water. They are eventually washed out to sea, and the gulls and the sharks pick them clean."

"That's horrible."

"Yes, but it is the lot of the poor. We shall not be poor much longer, Talus. I promise you that when it is our turn to die, we will have the wealth to be clothed in beautiful garments and carried out to the Great Sea in a ship with golden sails. Statues will be built to memorialize our names and our power."

Talus could not respond to her vision of opulence. His eyes were riveted on the cart until it vanished from sight.

"On Home," he said, "the bodies were burned. I remember sitting on the mountainside and watching the pyres. They were oddly beautiful. When my mother and adopted brother died, I had to bury them. If I ignited a pyre, the guards would come to investigate. I wasn't supposed to be living there."

"Poor Talus," Cotto murmured.

For an instant Talus thought he heard sarcasm in her tone, but he ignored it. He was tired, very tired. He knew he needed sleep to fortify him for whatever tomorrow would bring.

After Talus's breathing deepened into a slow sibilance, Cotto stood up and stretched. She walked to where the donkeys were tethered, rummaged through one of the packs, and took out some dried fruit. She stood, chewing thoughtfully, as she stared down at the city. From time to time her eyes wandered to the naked, sleeping body of her lover. She could dimly see the lion's-paw birthmark. Nimshi had had one just like it. She wondered why these Children of the Lion were feared and respected by so many people. From what she had seen of them—Nimshi and Talus—they were idealistic fools, as naive as children. They seemed never to grow up.

Talus stirred in his sleep and groaned as if he was having a horrible dream and then threw out one arm to the sky. Then he sank back into sleep.

She smiled, amused by his innocence. She remembered how she used to fear men. No longer. They were, she now knew, more vulnerable and weaker than she. She had learned how to use them, just as they had once used her—like a garment to be tossed away when it became worn.

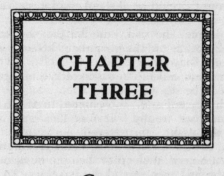

CHAPTER THREE

Canaan

The musical instrument, its sides streaked with blood, lay on a small rug as if it were some kind of rare jewel on display. The Amalekite king Adab stood proudly beside it. Facing Adab sat the warlords of the Midianites, Oreb and Zeeb, along with their retainers. The light from the torches danced on their golden earrings. Behind him stood Micah. An Amalekite robe was draped casually over his shoulders, and his whole attitude conveyed confidence.

Adab spoke in a loud but deferential voice. Although he was a king of the Amalekites, his rank meant nothing to the Midianites. The Amalekites and the Midianites were allies, yes; but Midian was the beast that drove and controlled the entire federation, whereas the Amalekites were just one of the many little gnats hovering about the beast's ears. Midianite warlords considered Amalekite kings to be no better than donkey washers, and Adab knew this. But he also knew that he had to appear as their equal.

"It is a night that will be long remembered," Adab began, "for on this rug is the horn of the Israelite Gideon. The trumpet was wrenched from his dying body by a man in the employ of the Amalekites. We present you with this horn as a gift to ease the strains between our two peoples and as a reminder that the Amalekites are faithful to the Midianite cause." He stopped and waited for a response.

There was none. Oreb snorted, then spat. Zeeb appeared to be dozing.

Adab stepped aside and pointed to Micah as if displaying another trophy. "It was this man who performed the task. He entered our camp, foolishly intending to steal a slave. After being captured he confessed that he was none other than the notorious bandit Blood, who had once served the Israelites. To help the Midianite cause, we offered him his freedom if he killed the trumpet-playing fool, Gideon. He has performed well. Here is Gideon's horn, with blood still on it."

"Where is the body?" Oreb asked. "How do we know it is Gideon's blood?"

It was Micah who spoke. "If you will send your scouts across the plain, you will see that the Israelites are abandoning their encampment. By morning only a few hundred will remain. They are leaving because their hero is dead. And it was I who drove the knife into his throat."

"Next time produce a head," Zeeb muttered, suddenly coming to life. "Or maybe the head would be too much for you to carry? . . ."

Micah did not respond.

Adab said, "My lords, I am proud that it was the Amalekites who removed the threat."

"What threat?" Oreb retorted. "Do you really believe that Israelites are a threat to us?"

"The Israelites can be dangerous," Micah answered, suddenly angered by the Midianite boasts.

"About as dangerous as you," Zeeb remarked contemptuously.

Micah turned in disgust to Adab. "I have done what you asked. I wish to leave now. Where is the slave woman you promised me?"

"I will take you to her shortly. The word of the Amalekites is sacred. The woman is yours."

"Why is the bandit so impatient?" Oreb inquired.

Adab laughed lightly. "He is much enamored of this slave. That is why I knew we could depend upon him."

"Perhaps, but he looks agitated," Zeeb said. "Maybe he should play Gideon's horn to calm himself."

Oreb chuckled. "A good idea, my friend. Let the assassin play the horn of the hero he killed."

"Pick it up and play, fool," Zeeb ordered.

"Play it yourself," Micah shot back.

Zeeb's retainers had drawn their swords and were on Micah before he realized what was happening. The warlord motioned that Micah should not be hurt, and the swords were sheathed as the retainers moved back. Then Zeeb looked at Adab. "Because your hireling has been disrespectful, he forfeits the slave woman."

"I cannot do that," Adab objected. "I have given him my tribal word."

"This is the camp of the Midianites. The tribal word of the Amalekites or of any other tribe is meaningless here."

Micah stepped forward. His face was grim but dangerous. He pulled aside the robe to reveal his daggers and to make plain his resolve. He faced the warlords and said boldly, "The woman is mine. I have earned her, and I will take her."

Again the retainers drew their weapons and positioned themselves between Micah and their masters.

"Disarm him!" Zeeb ordered.

Three Bedouins leaped toward him, but in one smooth motion Micah drew two daggers.

"Please put your knives away," Adab entreated. "You have no chance. They will kill you. Look there— at the entrance to the tent."

Micah looked and saw three archers ready to attack. Their bowstrings were drawn taut, and the points of their nocked arrows pointed at his chest.

"Drop your weapons, Blood. It is of no use. I am sorry." Adab lowered his head.

Micah trembled with rage. "You cannot do this to

me! I've earned the woman. I killed Gideon for her. These Midianite savages are breaking every law and tradition of the desert."

Adab spread his hands, palms up. "It is futile. Don't sacrifice your own life unnecessarily." He smiled wanly. "She is only a slave. You will find another woman to please your loins."

Micah dropped the daggers onto the ground.

Oreb and Zeeb, their dark eyes glittering with hatred, approached him. They moved like malevolent crabs, their shoulders hunched, their swords gleaming in their scabbards.

Zeeb picked up the bloody trumpet and dangled it distastefully from one finger.

"Now play it," he demanded.

Micah spat into his face. Zeeb cursed and slammed the trumpet hard against the side of Micah's jaw. Micah reeled, then lunged to attack his tormentor. But Oreb kicked out, and his foot caught Micah full in the chest. He dropped like a sack of flour. His body writhed with pain and from nausea. He heard Zeeb's instructions as if they came through a long tunnel.

"Beat him. And then throw him into the latrine pits with the rest of the excrement. If he can crawl out, he can live."

The Bedouins laughed heartily at the punishment.

"Forgive me, Blood," the Amalekite king whispered as the first blow struck against Micah's back.

And then a rain of blows assailed him. But he felt no physical pain—only the deep void in his heart because Luti would not be freed.

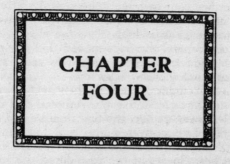

CHAPTER FOUR

Tyre

"This city hardly changes," Cotto said as Talus and she rode toward the estate of Navan the Phoenician.

"Was it the same before the Phoenicians took control?"

"No, it was a bit dirtier, a bit wilder, a bit poorer. The Phoenicians are very smart. They know what to change and what to leave alone. Near the port, for example, they built new homes but left the old taverns and the fish stalls alone."

"I don't understand your relationship to the Phoenicians, Cotto. Sometimes you sound as if you hate them, but sometimes you seem to love them."

"Well, let's just say that I admire them."

The two rode on in silence. The morning sun was not yet up. For the first time since they had headed back toward Tyre, Talus enjoyed a sense of well-being. He moved his donkey closer to Cotto's, so he could reach out from time to time and touch his beloved as they rode. His happiness with her was so great that sometimes he had to assure himself physically that she was truly there, that she was not a gorgeous mirage.

"Why did you come to Tyre in the first place?" he asked.

"I had to eat," she said simply. "I have been a dancer since I was a child. Tyre was always known as a port city whose taverns featured dancing girls. My family thought I was very wicked to come here. Do you think I am wicked, Talus?"

She was teasing him, he realized. "Beyond redemption," he agreed. He remembered that first time he had laid eyes on her, the first time he had seen her dance. She had captivated him with her beauty, and she had inflamed the passions of every man who watched her. No doubt she considered the concept of wickedness a joke; to Cotto, passion could never be wicked—it was natural to humans, like eating and sleeping. But she could have no idea what her movements did to a young man. He stared at her body now as she rode. She was so graceful. Her long neck was lovely. Her back was straight, and her elegant hands held the reins with a gentle kind of strength. The mount knew exactly where she wanted to go. Unlike Talus, she could transmit her orders to the donkey through the reins alone, without using her knees and feet.

"Look there, Talus! Melons!"

Indeed it was a vendor setting up for the day's business, removing one melon at a time from the crate, wiping it, and then placing it as artistically as possible on the stall. The man seemed to be working in slow motion, as if waiting for the dawn to bring more light. But there was already enough light to see the shape and color of each melon.

"Oh, get us some melons, Talus, so we can breakfast by the water."

Talus purchased two melons, and Cotto and he ate them by the sea. The flesh of the small, sweet Syrian fruit was bright red, and the seeds were pink. From where the lovers sat, they could watch the ships just outside the port area, waiting for the tide to bring them in.

Cotto pointed. "An Egyptian ship."

Talus studied the impressive square-sailed vessel. It was so much larger and so much more ungainly than the ships he used to see in the harbor of Home.

Cotto and Talus finished the melons and flung the rinds into the sea. The setting was so calm and peaceful along the shore. It was as if they were newlyweds on a honeymoon, rather than two thieves returning to the scene of the crime to beg forgiveness. The realization struck Talus as being funny, and he started to laugh.

"A private joke?" Cotto asked.

"Not really. I was just thinking about how calm we are, when actually we may be in great danger."

"There is nothing to worry about, Talus. During the next few weeks, I will show you the city. I will take you to the restaurants and the taverns and the grand houses. We will make love on the beach. Everything will be wonderful."

"All that you plan will cost a lot of money," Talus noted. Then he remembered the gold. He had forgotten all about it. What had happened to the rest of the gold they had stolen from the Phoenician? Cotto had spent quite a bit of it on food, clothing, and gifts for her extended family; but surely there must have been a great deal left.

"Cotto, is the rest of the gold safe? Are you going to give it back to Navan?"

"What gold?" she asked.

"What we didn't spend."

"It is all gone."

"How is that possible?"

"Oh, don't even ask, Talus. It will just confuse you. Forget the gold."

He smiled indulgently. This girl lived with abandon. What she had, she spent. What she felt, she expressed. Few of her desires were masked or delayed.

He leaned back and remembered how Phorbus used to speak about Myrrha, the Amazon woman he had loved in Troy. Was this wonderful, brave, and often foolhardy woman beside him like Phorbus's beloved? No, she was not a well-disciplined, battle-hardened soldier like the Amazon; she was a dancer. But Cotto possessed the same kind of determination that Phorbus often had talked about when describing Myrrha. Like the heroes and heroines of Troy, Cotto could live in the moment.

He gazed out to sea again. There was more light on the water now, so he could make out the various ships clearly: the Egyptian cargo vessel; the black sails and hulls of the Phoenicians; the Sea Peoples' ships with their ferocious carvings of Poseidon on the prows; the small barks of the northern traders with their produce clearly visible, stacked in high bales. What a fabulous, vital city this was! The Phoenicians had made it the commercial center of the world. All peoples yearned to trade with them, to buy from them, to sell to them.

"I have learned a lot from you, Cotto. You have opened up the world to me. And I thank you for it." His voice was gentle. His hand stroked her face and then her hair.

She took that hand and pressed her lips to the palm. "You will be my lord and master," she promised.

He laughed. Again he had the feeling that she was making fun of him, but he played the game. "Then, when we have our own house, I will order you to do many wicked things."

"My pleasure," she whispered seductively, and leaned over so that he felt her breasts against his hand.

"How many children shall we have?" he asked.

"Twenty-three," she answered without hesitation. "Nine boys, nine girls, and five eunuchs to keep the peace."

"And what gods will our children worship?" Talus asked her.

"Well, they will be the children of an Israelite mother and a Child of the Lion father, so perhaps Yahweh. Or perhaps the Egyptian gods. A Greek god, maybe, or one of those monsters from Babylon that eats humans twice a year. What does it matter, Talus? Do you have a preference?"

He did not know how to answer. His mother and Phorbus had spoken little to him about the history or religious affiliations of the Children of the Lion. The birthmark on his body marked him as someone special; but he did not know why, except that his people were great metalworkers and on that basis had risen to power in many countries of the world. As for gods, the whole idea confused him. But he would always remember what he had seen in Megiddo—how the Israelite Gideon had thrust his hand fearlessly into the flames and how it had been miraculously healed. Perhaps faith in the gods was needed for a man to survive.

"It is time to go," Cotto said when he gave no answer to her question.

Talus nodded. They mounted their donkeys, turned away from the sea, and rode toward the house of Navan.

CHAPTER FIVE

Canaan

The Israelite force of three hundred had left the Spring of Harod under the cover of darkness. Now, as dawn approached, they crouched in a gully fewer than one hundred yards from the first Midianite picket.

Gideon looked with enormous pride and love at his men. They had asked him for nothing but the opportunity to fight, the chance to die and offer their strong arms and stronger wills to the God of their fathers. Their faces looked beatific, serene in the half light.

He moved closer to them. Purah stayed at his side. The three columns of one hundred men each had already been formed. Every man carried a horn and a pitcher. In each pitcher was a torch, already lighted. Although the pitcher hid the torchlight from being seen, it could not stop the thick black smoke. The air was acrid and burned the eyes.

Five men in each column were responsible for carrying and operating small makeshift catapults. On their backs, like arrows in a quiver, they carried the brush torches that would be flung into the midst of the camel herds.

"Listen to me carefully," Gideon said to his men.

He waited while they broke ranks and gathered around him. The air felt heavy, as if the smoke from the muffled torches had fouled the good air and sapped the men of their optimism. Dread weighted the planes and angles of their faces.

"We will enter the camp very soon," he continued, "the moment the first rays of light break the darkness. Total darkness is no good for us. We'll need the shadows and forms. Only then will our enemies know beyond a doubt that Yahweh is upon them. They will fear for their souls as well as for their lives."

Gideon paused and stared around the circle of men to make certain they understood. It was astonishing how the faces of all these men seemed familiar to him. But of course he could not know them all; they had come from all over Canaan, members of different tribes, raised under varying circumstances.

Then his feeling of kinship deepened miraculously. He experienced an intense and enduring intimacy with each and every soldier. It was as though he knew the contours of their faces and their hearts. They had become his blessed brothers. Perhaps they would all be martyred, but no one would die alone—they were together under Yahweh. They had Yahweh's blessings.

"Oh, my brothers," he cried out with love, and then he was too overwhelmed by his tears to continue. He dropped to his knees as if he had been struck by a spear, and he covered his face with his hands.

Purah knelt beside him, frightened. "What is the matter, sir?" he asked urgently.

"Just a moment of love for these men—a moment so strong I could not bear it."

He blinked away the tears and stood, then spoke in a soft voice full of conviction. "Let us bow our heads and worship the King of Kings, the Holy One, Blessed be He."

The men silently obeyed as Gideon prayed.

"My God and God of My Fathers, give us the courage this hour to plant Thy standards in the hearts of the enemy. Give us the strength to be victors but the wisdom not to be cruel. Give us the stamina to pursue but the mercy not to be beasts. Make us different from our enemies. By Your blessings set us apart from all other peoples of the earth. O, Thou Who hast created the heavens and the earth and all the creatures upon it—give us the power to turn Canaan once again into Your garden. Then grant us peace when this sword is sheathed."

He turned and faced the Midianite camp. In only a few moments the destiny of his people would be decided. He was filled with a sense of awe. In the camp of the enemy were thousands of warriors. And behind him were three hundred Israelite souls.

For a moment he thought he saw the face of Yahweh's messenger in the darkened air. But then the vision was gone.

He raised his fist high. Two of the columns moved out, heading swiftly for their jump-off points. He waited tensely. Next to him was Purah, and behind him were the hundred men of his own column. A slight breeze came up, cooling the sweat on his face and body. He grasped his trumpet in one hand and the pitcher with the torch in the other. His grip was so tight, his knuckles turned white. He forced himself to relax a bit.

Gideon started to walk slowly forward. Then he picked up his pace. The fires of the Midianite camp appeared closer. He broke into a trot and heard the hundred men behind him following closely.

The first Midianite picket they reached flung his spear, then ran screaming back into the camp. Gideon slowed, raised his trumpet to his lips, and blew a long, powerful riff. The hundred men behind him followed suit. Gideon could hear the trumpets of the other columns. They sounded like a million demons.

Gideon smashed his pitcher and exposed the lighted torch. Holding the flaming brand high, he and his men ran into the Midianite encampment. Overhead, the burning missiles from the catapults whistled through the air, to land among the screaming camel herds.

The Midianites rushed from their tents, their weapons drawn. The light from the torches played havoc with their eyes in the predawn dimness. Huge shadows were cast on the tents and the ground. Panicked camels, having broken out of their enclosure, stampeded through the camp, trampling the Bedouin warriors. In their confusion, Bedouins mistook the beasts for enemies and slashed at them with their swords. Other Bedouins speared one another.

When Gideon and his tightly packed column reached the far end of the camp, they flung down their pitchers, torches, and horns and drew their swords. They emerged like wraiths of the netherworld from a swirling miasma of dust. Screams assaulted their ears. No one knew who was killing whom. It was as if the whole camp had gone mad, embarked on a frenzy of killing and maiming without knowledge or reason. The Midianites were looking for an enemy, and all they found were one another and their own dearly loved beasts. The sounds of wounded and dying men and camels rent the air like pathetic war cries.

Grim-faced, the Israelite soldiers marched into the center of the camp. This time their goal was not to sow confusion among the Midianites, but to sow death.

"For Yahweh and Gideon!" they cried out, and for the first time the Bedouins knew who the enemy was. But it was too late for that knowledge to save them.

CHAPTER
SIX

Tyre

Cotto and Talus, leaving the animals tethered outside, entered the main gate of Navan's estate. They
walked slowly, casually, and carried no weapons or
peace offerings. The guards at the gate stared in
astonishment at Cotto's boldness. When both Cotto and
Talus had entered the courtyard and the gate had been
swung shut, the guards surrounded the couple and
brandished weapons. They cursed the girl and described
the dire consequences she now faced for her betrayal
of the powerful Phoenician.

Talus stood helpless, grimly listening to the insults
of the guards. He felt the pressure of Cotto's hand on
his arm, reassuring him that this would soon pass, that
everything would be resolved.

"Please inform Navan that I am here to see him,"
Cotto told the guards. Her voice was authoritative.

The guards stepped back. Their fun was over.

"Did you hear me?" she shouted. "Get me Navan."

The guards retreated. Two returned to the gate, one ran to fetch the master. Cotto led Talus to the courtyard with translucent pools. A small, dead goldfish had floated up to the surface at the edge of the pool. It was a bad omen, and he shivered. He remembered that she had danced in this very area the first time he had set eyes on her. As the girl led him now into a receiving hall, he glanced back to find that one guard followed at a discreet distance.

Cotto and Talus sat side by side on a large divan and waited. He sat quietly, while Cotto seemed lost in private memories. He looked at her and took her hand. Cotto's lovely face softened with a reassuring smile. She bent to kiss him. He relaxed and lay back on the divan.

Then Navan swept into the hall. He was wearing a sleeping robe—a magnificent white garment that was embroidered with threads of gold along the wide sleeves. He appeared taller than Talus remembered, and his carefully trimmed beard was speckled with gray.

Behind him strode two Sea Peoples guards. Unlike the guards at the gate, these bore themselves in the manner of trained soldiers. They wore breastplates, and their eyes were hooded, like a cobra's. Their hands rested on the hilts of their short swords. They wore leather bands over their long golden hair to keep it from their eyes. Navan and the soldiers stopped five feet from his former dancing girl.

Cotto rose and bowed with graceful elegance. Talus stood up beside her. When Navan stared at them for a long time without speaking, Talus began to fidget under the scrutiny. His mouth went dry, and his hands trembled. The knife inside his belt reassured him, however. Ironically, it was the knife he had stolen from Tirzah's kitchen to murder Cotto—the knife with the makeshift handle. Everything had come full circle, but now he might have to use the knife to protect his beloved—not to murder her.

"And how was the weather around Megiddo?" Navan asked in a conversational tone.

Talus did not know whether to laugh or cry. It was the most ludicrous of questions given the circumstances.

"Hot, Navan," Cotto calmly replied. "But it always is at this time of year."

"Did you dance for your people, Cotto?"

"No. The Israelites, as you must be well aware, do not like my kind of exhibition with the human body," Cotto replied boldly.

"A strange people, very difficult to understand— and therefore very difficult to deal with."

Cotto did not respond to this comment. For the first time, Talus could sense that she was afraid.

Navan's dark eyes suddenly glittered with violent hatred. "Only an Israelite like you, Cotto, would have had the arrogance to return here after you have betrayed my trust and kindness. You have acted like a common thief. Did you really think that anything other than death would await you in my house?" His words were cold, biting.

Talus gripped Cotto's arm and held it tightly. His other hand moved toward the hidden dagger.

"And I had thought," Navan continued in a softer tone, "that you were the rarest of women—combining wisdom with beauty." He moved his head slightly to one side, enough to signal his bodyguards. The brawny soldiers withdrew their ugly blades half out of the scabbards.

"The reward for stupidity, Cotto, is death," Navan said flatly.

"No!" Cotto screamed. "I am innocent, Navan!" And then she shook loose from Talus's grasp and ran to Navan's side. She stabbed an accusing finger at Talus. "It was this animal who raped me and forced me to steal the gold! I swear to you on all that is sacred that I was kidnapped and violated at the point of a knife! That is why I have returned to you. I had to let you know the truth!"

Talus stared dumbly at his beloved, his accuser. He tried to whisper her name, but he could not. It was as if every bit of meaning and goodness had been sucked violently from his world.

CHAPTER
SEVEN

Canaan

Micah clung precariously to the side of the latrine pit and waited for a lull in the battle. He intended to climb out and find Luti. His eyes peered over the rim of the pit. In all the years he had been fighting—both as a soldier and as an outlaw—he had never seen such total panic prevail over a fighting force. And these nomads were trained men! The Bedouins were killing their own comrades and slaying their own camels. They slashed at their burning tents as if the shelters were enemies posing some threat. They were running chaotically back and forth, screaming with rage or weeping in frustration. And through the dust and confusion Micah could see small groups of Israelites, working in teams of five, moving methodically through the pandemonium and exacting terrible vengeance for years of torment.

The latrine pit itself was filling with the corpses of men and beasts, which were either slipping or being thrown over the sides. Several wounded camels had fallen in and were bleating pathetically in a tangle of broken limbs.

As the morning wore on, the heat of the battle-ground became intense. Many Bedouins ripped off their robes and fought naked. But this created more problems, for without their robes, the nomads were not easily distinguishable from the Israelites. While fighting, one had to peer through the swirling dust to look for the gold earrings that marked one's opponent as friend or foe.

Even more confusing was the fact that the majority of the Midianite auxiliaries, such as the Amalekites, wore no earrings at all. As a result, a huge number of Bedouins died at their comrades' hands. Others perished under the hooves of crazed camels, while still others suffocated or were burned to death by the tent fires.

The Israelite teams attacked again and again with great discipline, searching out one small, isolated Bedouin group after another, annihilating them, then moving on through the camp. Micah could see that hundreds of nomads were fleeing the area, to begin a march east and seek the safety of the Jordan River and beyond.

Battle cries rang in his ears: "Zalmunnah! Zalmunnah and Midian!" or "For Yahweh and Gideon!"

The war cries of the Israelites sent a shiver of joy through Micah. It had been a long time since he had seen Israelites fight. Once again they had miraculously transformed themselves from the meek and oppressed into a potent fighting force. Having been inside Gideon's camp, Micah was well aware that those three hundred fighters had been dedicated but without experience or knowledge of one another. Now, in all this confusion, they were falling upon their enemies like a finely honed fighting machine. They were outnumbered at least ten to one, but their grit and the confusion they had wrought had neutralized all odds.

Micah felt a sudden impulse to join them in battle, to fight alongside them once again. But his overriding concern was for Luti. He had to find and rescue her. Micah inched closer to the lip of the latrine pit. His hands and feet bled from the effort of climbing the hard dirt walls. Beneath the ooze that covered his body were bruises and cuts from the beating he had suffered before being thrown into the trench. He hoped he would not die from an infected wound after being exposed to all the filth.

An earsplitting scream burst over the top of the pit, and Micah quickly dropped below sight. He cautiously rose again to see, directly in front of him, a grief-maddened Bedouin cradling the head of his dying camel. The white coat of the beast was covered with blood and gore. The nomad's head was thrown back in anguish, and he was bellowing with hatred and shame at having lost that which was most precious to him.

Another Bedouin ran by and accidently kicked the dying camel. The beast's owner leaped up and, holding his long sword with both hands, slashed at the erring man. The blade cut deeply into the man's chest, and he toppled over, staring incomprehensibly at his fellow Bedouin. The swordsman, seemingly in shock, dropped his weapon and fell back to his knees beside his once-magnificent camel. It was insanity; all was insanity.

An Israelite phalanx appeared out of the smoke. Without a sound the soldiers drove their daggers into the kneeling Bedouin, then ripped the gold earrings from him. A second later the Bedouin's corpse and that of his camel came hurtling over the edge and into the pit. As the dead man plunged to the trench floor his hands slapped Micah across the face.

Then the Israelites vanished into the roiling smoke. For the moment the area around the pit was clear of fighters. Gathering all his strength, Micah pulled himself up and over. He crouched, took a deep breath, then ran close to the ground toward where the Amalekites had pitched their tents.

He was in the center of the maelstrom as he ran to the northeast quadrant of the encampment. Bedouins swung their long swords at him. Crazed camels blocked his path and spat gobs of their disgusting-smelling saliva. Israelites strung their bows and fired volleys of death all around him. Still he ran, dodging and rolling and sidestepping the missiles and the bodies and the weapons.

At last he found the Amalekite tents, clustered like grapes on the vine and set off from the main body of tents. None of the Amalekite shelters was on fire. For this Micah was thankful. He stopped for a moment, panting. Then he sprinted forward and entered the first tent. He looked around. It was empty. The second was empty, too. In the third tent, he found his beloved, along with five other trembling slaves, huddled together and terrified but safe. Exhausted, he dropped to his knees beside her.

"Micah! Oh, Micah, I knew you would come," she whispered. She held him close to her, in spite of the blood and excrement and sweat that covered his body.

"Where are the Amalekites?" he asked when he had regained his breath.

"They fled when the Israelites attacked," she answered.

Micah looked at the other captives. "If any of you are Israelites," he said, "you have every right to feel proud. Yahweh and Gideon are crushing the life out of the Midian beast."

A murmur of hope escaped the lips of several of the slaves.

Then Luti moved back and looked carefully into his face. "Your eyes look wild, Micah. And your body is so tense. Rest, darling. Stay with me. When the battle is over we—"

He kissed her passionately. Finding her safe was a miracle, but he wanted more now—he wanted to fight alongside the Israelites as they routed Midian. He wanted to pay back those warlords who had brutalized Luti and betrayed him. He held her close and asked, "Will you be safe here, darling? I must leave you again, but for only a little while. I want to fight with my brothers the Israelites as I fought with them in the past. There is a tie between them and me, between my people and their God. It's a tie that—"

She placed her fingers on his lips. "You do not have to explain. Go. I will wait for you here. Just be careful. I love you."

Micah kissed her once more, then slipped out of the tent and headed back toward the central area of the Midianite camp, where the fighting was still fierce. He could see that more Israelites had entered the fray. They were obviously irregulars, newcomers who had been waiting on the sidelines to see which way the wind would blow. Now they swarmed down onto the Bedouin army.

Thick black smoke from the burning tents had settled like a low blanket over the battlefield. It was difficult to see more than two feet ahead. Micah's eyes teared, and his throat and lungs burned.

While passing a Bedouin corpse, he bent down and removed the sword still clasped in the man's fingers. It was a typical Bedouin weapon, large and heavy and curved, and he was unfamiliar with its feel and balance—but there was no other.

He had to use it immediately. A wounded Midianite tripped him up, then came at him screaming. Micah caught his balance and parried the blow with the curved sword, then danced out of range. The Bedouin charged at him again, still screaming, holding his own sword over his head in a two-handed grip, and slashing the air with it again and again, as if he were cutting wheat.

With grim satisfaction Micah noticed that the wound in the nomad's neck was pumping blood. Micah was forced to give ground; while the man used the blade scythelike his reach was too long for Micah to venture closer. But it was obvious that the Bedouin was growing weaker. Soon the swings of his sword were like a child's, and then he sank to his knees in front of Micah and waited for the end. Micah finished him quickly, driving the curved sword up beneath the rib cage, then hooking it outward so that its wicked point pierced the heart.

Micah pulled out the sword, wiped the blade on the Bedouin's robes, and turned to continue his quest for the warlords. Suddenly something struck him across the top of the head. He staggered, then took the impact of another blow. He fell to his knees, his head swimming, his vision blurred.

"Look what crawled out of the pit," a seemingly distant voice jeered.

His eyes focused, and he found himself staring up at the scarred face of the crablike warlord called Oreb. Standing between them was one of the warlord's bodyguards, holding a thick staff. Micah recognized it as one that had been used to beat him.

Micah tried to rise but could not. As he attempted to crawl away, the staff crashed down on the back of his head and knocked him flat.

"Mix his blood into the dirt! Make him pay!" he heard Oreb order his bodyguard.

The bodyguard raised the massive wooden club for the final blow. Micah rolled onto his back and held up his palms in a futile gesture to ward off the death stroke.

But the blow never came. An arrow thumped into his attacker's stomach with a sickening sound. The bodyguard screamed and stood transfixed, staring down in disbelief at the barbed arrow point embedded in his stomach.

An Israelite archer stepped out of the smoke. Another arrow was already notched in his bow. He aimed it toward the warlord.

But Micah had a debt to pay. Quickly, in spite of his wounds, he retrieved his sword and lunged toward Oreb with all his remaining strength. The sword sang in a wide arc.

Oreb turned to run, but the blade caught him on the side of the neck and sliced through bone and muscle and cartilage. Grotesquely Oreb kept running, but his head was gone, rolling on the ground toward the archer.

Micah, panting, stopped and lowered his arms. He looked down at his sword. As he thanked the archer for having saved his life, he noticed that another Israelite had stepped out of the smoke screen. Micah called out in gladness. It was Gideon! The Israelite leader picked up the head on his own sword point and saluted Micah.

Micah took a few unsteady steps toward Gideon; but the ground began to tilt, and his vision blurred once again. Gideon caught Micah before he fell.

"Rest, my friend," he said. "The children of Israel still need you."

Micah managed a wan smile and held on tightly to his ally's arm. Yes, and Luti was waiting. But these were his comrades, and they needed him now.

CHAPTER EIGHT

Tyre

Cotto, sobbing piteously, clung to Navan's arm. She stabbed a finger at Talus and accused him of kidnap and rape and theft. She had had no choice, she wailed. She had acted to save her own life, she said.

Finally, disgusted by her increasingly frenzied behavior, Navan pushed the girl down onto a divan. She wept into her hands. Then her fingers parted, and her eyes slyly sought out Talus's. Her expression seemed to say that she hoped he understood—that she had no alternative but to betray him and that she was sorry.

He realized what a lovesick fool he had been and knew that she had played with him, had, in fact, set him up from the very beginning. For the first time he accepted that his own passions had destroyed whatever intelligence and common sense he had once possessed. But even as he stood there in shock at her betrayal, something even more bizarre occurred to him: He realized that he wanted to rush to Cotto's side and tell her not to worry. He wanted to hold her and kiss away her tears and make sure she was all right.

"Take him," Navan ordered the burly guards.

Their swords fully drawn, the two soldiers advanced on Talus. A cruel smile curled their lips.

Talus pulled his kitchen knife. It would be useless against the two soldiers, he knew. It would never penetrate their breastplates. For an instant he felt an urge to throw the knife at Cotto and impale her for her perfidy. But the idea shocked him. No, she must not be hurt. He still loved her. Two soldiers were preparing to murder him, and yet he still wanted to protect her.

If I were a real man, he thought, *I would throw the knife and split her lying, traitorous heart. No,* he decided, *it can't end like this.*

He could not die in this place, in front of the woman who had made a fool out of him, who had stolen his love. He refused to die at the hands of a Phoenician whose gold-trimmed robe was paid for by the coins of desperate drug users, such as Nimshi. *No! I am a Child of the Lion! I must fight for my life!*

"Take him!" Navan shouted again.

A feeling of power welled up in Talus's chest. He stared at Cotto. She might have condemned him to death, and she had clearly influenced the Sea Peoples and Phoenicians. But she had never seen him run, and she had no idea that he had already saved his life by racing up and down the mountain slopes of Home and leaping courageously off a high cliff and into the sea. If he was going to die today, first they would have to catch him.

He exploded into action, bursting between the two startled soldiers, who stood flat-footed and gaping as he plunged between them. Then he was out of the hall and running along the path in the courtyard. He remembered from his first visit the small side gates of Navan's house. Only one guard was at each of these entrances. The nearest gate was his goal. His heart pounded; his strong legs pumped; he clutched the knife tightly in one hand. Within seconds he caught sight of the closest side gate. It was half-open, and beside it stood a bewildered guard, listening to the shouts from within the house.

Faster! Faster! Talus leaped over a series of shrubs and drove his knife into the guard's groin. As the man screamed and fell thrashing to the ground, Talus had already kicked the gate open and gone through it, leaving his weapon behind.

He did not stop running until he reached the maze of alleys in the warehouse district. There he rested. Around him were hundreds of laborers pushing carts piled high with goods. No one would find him here. He leaned heavily against the alley wall and smiled grimly. He knew that Phorbus would have been proud of him. Then he burst into bitter tears. Cotto's betrayal would fester in his heart for as long as he drew breath on this earth.

CHAPTER NINE

Canaan

The battle was over. The Midianite camp was quiet except for the moans of wounded men and beasts and the crackle of dying fires. Israelite troopers, exhausted from the killing, sprawled on the ground. Many were wounded. Several wore Bedouin robes draped over their shoulders. Nearby were piles of earrings, human heads, and hands severed from the hated enemy.

Gideon, Purah, and Micah sat together on Bedouin saddles.

"What were our casualties?" Gideon asked Purah.

"Heavy, sir, very heavy. One hundred and ten dead. Forty-five seriously wounded. Twenty missing."

More than half the original attacking force. Gideon winced and closed his eyes. Virtually everyone carried minor wounds. He had expected terrible casualties, but now that it was a reality he found it difficult to accept.

"It was a great victory, Gideon," Micah said. "There must be two thousand Bedouin corpses scattered through this camp. It was a miracle. Your three hundred men broke the back of the most powerful army in Canaan."

Gideon opened his eyes and nodded sadly. "Come, let's visit the badly wounded."

The three men climbed to their feet and walked slowly to where the Israelites struggling to survive were laid out on blankets. Several, Gideon saw, had already bled to death. The men went from row to row, knelt beside those who were conscious, and spoke reassuringly to them.

One young soldier was thrashing wildly from pain. Gideon gripped the man's arm and tried to quiet him. An enormous wound in his stomach was beginning to stink, and blackflies were crawling the makeshift bandage.

"What is your name, son?" Gideon asked.

"Aaron," the man whispered. The pain had exhausted him. He could barely speak.

"Your name will be honored forever among the Israelites, and your bravery will always be remembered," Gideon said, speaking directly into the dying man's ear.

The man's lips started to move, but Gideon could not hear any words. He bent closer to the man's parched lips.

This soldier, Aaron, was praying! Gideon could now make out the prayer. "Blessed art Thou, O Lord our God, King of the universe, Who has created the fruit of the vine."

Tears filled Gideon's eyes. This brave young warrior was giving his thanks to Yahweh for the victory with what had to be the only prayer he knew—the ancient blessing recited before the drinking of sacramental wine. How little the Israelites knew of the God who had given them victory and freedom! How few of the prayers and the ceremonies they remembered!

Aaron went into convulsions. His eyes grew wide in pain and terror. Pathetic whimpers escaped his lips. Spittle and blood dripped out the corner of his mouth. His hands clenched and unclenched from the waves of agony that coursed through his mutilated body.

I must stop his pain, Gideon thought. *I must end his suffering.* His hand went to his sword, but he could not draw it. He could not put this valiant young man out of his misery. Gideon tightly squeezed his eyelids shut and blocked his ears with his hands so as not to hear the soldier's agony.

Aaron abruptly stopped convulsing. Gideon opened his eyes. Kneeling on the other side of the dying man was Yahweh's messenger. His hand rested lightly on the soldier's forehead. Aaron's body was relaxed now. On his face was a beatific smile. The messenger began to stroke the fevered brow, and then, a moment later, the soldier died.

"His suffering is over," the angel said, closing Aaron's eyes.

"Thank you," Gideon said.

"You have done well, Commander."

"Well?" Gideon said bitterly. "More than half of my men are on the verge of death."

Messenger ignored his comment. "Now you must destroy the head of the snake. He still lives, and his fangs are sharp. If you do not kill him, another body may grow."

"Look around you!" Gideon protested. "The Midianites are crushed."

"King Zalmunnah of Midian is on the far side of the Jordan, at Quargor. Go there now, Gideon, and destroy him."

Gideon flung up his hands in despair. "All the Midian stores were destroyed by fire. My men have no food or water. They are exhausted. I can't ask or expect them to do any more."

The angel straightened his leather apron. Some of the blood from the soldier's stomach wound had splattered it. He seemed to study the patterns the blood had created. Then he said to Gideon, "I understand your weariness and your grief. But now, my friend, is not the time to falter. Go now and destroy King Zalmunnah of Midian."

Messenger smoothed back the dusty, sweat-drenched hair of the dead man. Then he raised his hands and said, "Yahweh blesses this soldier and all who struggled with him. Yahweh is pleased."

The force and intensity of his words and the bliss on Aaron's face filled Gideon's heart with resolve. Although he had given all that he had thought possible and more, he knew he would have to do what the angel asked . . . even if it meant sacrificing himself in the process. He turned and walked to where Purah and Micah were waiting for him.

"We cross the Jordan now," Gideon told them. "Call the men."

He turned to wave to the angel, to assure him that his command would be carried out, but he had vanished. And Aaron was covered with a beautiful prayer shawl, so white that it seemed to gleam.

CHAPTER TEN

Tyre

Heat shimmers were beginning to rise from the city streets. Talus had not moved for hours. He just stood against the wall of the alley because he did not know what else to do. He knew he should probably run and hide because the Phoenician would have men out, searching for him. But he did not know where to go.

He had no weapon, and he was penniless. He thought about doubling back to where the donkeys were tethered and getting some of the food; but he decided it was too late—Cotto would have already disclosed where the animals had been left. Navan most likely had guards waiting there to ambush him.

Worse than the lack of food and weapons was his utter loneliness. He had no one. Cotto was gone, and their love was ashes. It had all happened so fast, so brutally. He closed his eyes and tried to remove the face and body of his betrayer from his thoughts. But she was not easily exorcised. Her beauty, the way she talked, her hands moving over his face and body all remained stubbornly fixed in his mind.

A low moan escaped him as he thought about his mother, father, and Phorbus. Everyone he had ever loved or who had loved him were gone, all gone. Was he doomed, he agonized, to a life of miserable solitude?

Tirzah! What about Tirzah? He had forgotten all about her! Did he dare show himself at her apartment again? After all, after accepting her hospitality, he had vanished without a good-bye or word of explanation. Could he presume to ask for her help? She seemed to be a kindly and understanding woman, and she seemed genuinely fond of him. And she had obviously loved Theon. Theon and he were both Children of the Lion. Would that be enough to gain her help?

He stepped away from the wall and tried to get his bearings. Yes, he remembered where she lived; he knew how to find the house.

Talus's eagerness prompted him to run. Then he forced himself to walk; it would be best not to attract any undue attention.

Talus located the street quickly. The window shades on the second floor helped him to identify Tirzah's apartment. He hesitated for a moment, ashamed of returning as a beggar with a price on his head.

When he overcame his reluctance, he walked to the door and banged loudly with a closed fist. No one answered. He banged again, harder and with both hands.

He heard scuffling within, and then the door opened just enough to allow an eye to peer out. Talus recognized it as belonging to one of the servants. He remembered her name. "Seka! It's me, Talus. May I come in?"

She opened the door wider and stared at him blankly.

"I don't know you," she replied, and blocked the door.

"Yes you do! Talus. I stayed here for a few days."

"I know no one called Talus," she said loudly.

"Then call Tirzah, your mistress. She knows who I am."

"No one lives here by that name."

"What are you talking about? This is Tirzah's house. She rented it. Now call her, please!"

"There is no Tirzah. Go away!" And she slammed the door with a bang.

Talus wandered off, dazed. Had he picked the wrong house? Was that servant not Seka after all, but really someone else? Where was he? What was going on?

Morose, he wandered to the piers and watched the ships. What could he do now? Steal? Hide in the alleys until some cutthroat, having heard that the Phoenicians wanted him, slipped a knife between his ribs in the hope of a reward?

"Talus! Talus!" He heard his name being whispered. He froze. Was he imagining it? But again he heard, "Talus! Talus!"

It came from behind a large wooden shipping crate—one of hundreds stacked along the pier. He walked there quickly, and even before he reached the crate, a woman peeked out from behind it. It was the servant from Tirzah's house. It was Seka.

"Please forgive me, Talus," she said, "but what I did was necessary. Three men came searching for you only a few minutes before you arrived. I was afraid they would come back."

"But what about Tirzah?"

"She is gone. She fell sick with a very bad fever a few days ago. The physician told her she must leave the city and go north, where the air is drier and cooler. She was taken to the village of Abbasiyah, north of here on the coast. It is a very lovely village, and I pray that the poor woman will recover there. She is kind and generous and deserves to live." Seka then handed him a skin bag and ran off.

Talus called out after her, but it made no difference. The woman was determined to say no more. He had no doubt that she had told the truth, but she must still be frightened.

He emptied the contents of the bag on the ground. Seka had provided him with several coins, some raisins, a few pieces of flat bread, a chunk of cheese, and a small knife. He smiled, grateful. Seka was a good woman. He replaced the goods.

Tyre was obviously no longer safe for him. There was only one place he would be secure. He decided he would visit Tirzah. If she were not too ill, she would help and advise him. He turned toward the north and started off at a trot.

PART
FIVE

CHAPTER ONE

Transjordan

After the rout of the Midianites, only eighty Israelites were able-bodied enough to cross the Jordan with Gideon. They pointed their mounts south along the riverbank, heading toward Succoth. Their plans were to obtain much needed food and water from the many Israelites who lived there.

They were a grim-faced, silent contingent. Gideon rode in the lead. Behind him were Micah and Purah, and then the troopers were strung out in random fashion. Many men dozed on their horses and donkeys. Some were so exhausted, they fell off their mounts, to suffer the good-natured but raucous jeers of their companions. Because so many of the Israelites suffered from superficial wounds, they left a trail of blood along the riverbank.

It was nearly dark when they reached Succoth—a collection of six villages around a central marketplace. Men, women, and children appeared at the sides of the road. They stared silently, suspiciously at the Israelite newcomers.

"What is the matter with these people?" Gideon asked. "Why don't they say something? Why don't they cheer? Why don't they speak to us?"

"They looked confused," Micah remarked.

As the troopers rode through the villages, more and more inhabitants lined up. But still the strange silence prevailed. Finally they reached the market square, where the headmen of Succoth had gathered. Only Gideon, Micah, and Purah dismounted; the others remained astride their mounts.

Gideon approached slowly, showing he was unarmed and meant no harm. After he had introduced himself, he said, "My men and I have come from the Valley of Jezreel, where we defeated the Midianite army. Now we are going to Quargor to take the head of King Zalmunnah. My men are hungry and thirsty. Please give us sustenance."

For a moment there was no response to his request. And then one of the younger headmen, a herder who introduced himself as Eleazer, burst out laughing. Gideon glared at him.

"Forgive me, Gideon," he said, still chuckling, "but how can you expect me to believe that the ragged men behind you on beaten asses have destroyed the Bedouin army?"

An older headman spoke quickly, in an attempt to calm the waters. His name was Likud.

"Forgive Eleazer, Gideon. He is young and has not mastered self-control. We have heard rumors about the battle and its outcome. But as you yourself will have to admit, it is very difficult to believe."

A murmur of assent came from all the headmen.

Gideon snapped, "Do you doubt the power of the One Living God?"

The headmen uncomfortably shuffled their feet and looked at one another.

"We need water, and we need food—*now!*" Gideon demanded.

"My good friend Gideon," Likud responded gently, "it is possible that what you say is true. And, if true, all of us are extremely grateful to you. Indeed, all the Israelites from the desert to the sea are deeply in your debt. On the other hand, perhaps you are exhausted from fighting, and your eyes and ears are playing tricks on you. Is it possible that you did not destroy the Midianite army? If that is the case and we give you food and water, the Midianites may learn of it and will swoop down upon Succoth and slaughter us all."

Likud paused, and his colleagues nodded in agreement. "Therefore," he continued, "as much as we would like to help you, it would not be prudent. As headmen responsible for the welfare of our people, we cannot supply you with food or water. I am sorry."

Micah screamed with rage and frustration and charged Likud, knocking the headman to the ground. He jumped to straddle the man, then pressed his dagger against Likud's throat. They all stared at the long-haired wild man who seemed intent on slitting the headman's neck.

Gideon was the first to react. He strode toward the pair and laid a gentle hand on Micah's back. "Don't kill him, my friend. Put your knife away."

Micah's burning eyes fixed on his victim's face and his knife was poised at Likud's flesh. "He is betraying you, Gideon, and your God! Let me kill this traitorous fool!"

"No! It is our task to kill Midianites," Gideon seethed from between clenched teeth. "Let Yahweh deal with His own."

Micah stared up into Gideon's face for a long moment, then relaxed. It was obvious that the commander held tenuous control on his own emotions. Not wanting to be the man who caused Gideon to snap, Micah stood and moved back, away from Likud. The headman scrambled to his feet, and the other elders helped him brush off his clothing.

Gideon, meanwhile, turned to the large crowd that had assembled. "You have still not learned the lessons of faith. You are still not aware of the power of Yahweh.

When you love Him, you will no longer fear any Bedouin. For your refusal to give us aid, I call a curse down upon you, your children, and your children's children."

Then, in disgust, he mounted and gestured for his troopers to follow. They rode silently and slowly out of Succoth.

They headed west, deeper into the desert, and then turned north. Micah took charge of their very survival. The men's thirst was at a life-threatening intensity. But even in the dark night he found desert thorn and thistle plants, which could be cut and sucked for fluids. He made snares and caught lizards and rats, which the men ate greedily without cooking. He dug for roots under the stars, and the soldiers wolfed down the bitter but succulent tubers.

When, due to Micah's effort, the edge was off their hunger and thirst, they fell onto the ground and slept like the dead.

Just before dawn Gideon woke them. Many exhausted soldiers were so deeply asleep that he had to kick them to rouse them. But finally all were awake and assembled and ready to begin the last part of their march to Quargor, a small, mud-baked oasis that had been a Bedouin stronghold for generations.

They reached Quargor just before noon. The sun was high and hot in the sky. The black tents of Zalmunnah and his royal guard lay just east of the oasis ridge. A few palm trees dotted the area, and one small, bubbling spring snaked out of the ground and then disappeared into a man-made rock basin.

"Yahweh is still with you, Gideon," Micah said, smiling foxily. "The Bedouins are in their tents, as they always are when the sun is overhead. And look! No guards! But why should there be? This is Bedouin territory. No one poses a threat to them here." Micah broke into laughter at the joke. He was beginning to enjoy the game of war again.

"How many?" Gideon asked.

"Six tents?" Micah said. "Not more than a hundred fifty men."

"Are the odds ever going to be in our favor?"

"Probably not, Gideon. Worse than the numbers, Zalmunnah's royal guard are likely to be handpicked, fierce warriors. They won't fall for any horn-and-torch nonsense. And your men are weak and tired, and most of them are wounded."

Gideon could see in Micah's eyes that a strategy was forming. The ex-bandit was just pretending to follow a chain of command.

"What do you suggest, Micah?" Gideon asked, inviting his ally to overcome any reluctance.

"Our timing is good. The Midianites will be sluggish from eating and taking their noon naps." Micah opened his saddlebag and pulled out a garment, which he handed to Gideon. "It's an Amalekite robe," he explained. "Now, you and your men work your way around to that rise by the trees on the east side of the oasis. I'll put on the robe and come running into camp from the west, shouting that Oreb and Zeeb are coming, bringing Zalmunnah the head of Gideon and hundreds of choice captives. When the Midianites run unarmed from their tents to await the triumphant procession, you and your men will sweep down and cut them off from their weapons, their tents, and their mounts."

It was a simple but ingenious plan, Gideon decided, but would the Bedouins believe the "Amalekite" messenger? He stared thoughtfully at Micah while making his decision.

"We'll do it, my courageous friend," he finally said. "Thank you."

Micah flashed a grin and flung the robes around himself. As the others watched, he took a stake from his bag and drove it into the hard ground. "When the sun's shadow touches the far side of this stake, assume your positions," he told Gideon. Then the two men clasped arms, and Micah was off.

When it was time, Gideon and his soldiers tethered their mounts securely and circled the camp to take up their positions on the eastern rise. There they waited. Gideon stared across the oasis, in the direction from which Micah would appear. He saw nothing at first, but then a black dot materialized and grew steadily larger. It was a man running. His robes flowed out behind him, and he was gesturing wildly and yelling. When the runner came closer, Gideon could make out words.

"Zalmunnah and Midian! A triumph, O, King! Oreb and Zeeb come! They bring the head of the Israelite leader! They bring gold! They bring captives!"

The tents seemed to spew out the Bedouins. Zalmunnah in his finery started to hurry toward the messenger. Around him, his Midianites began to cheer and prance about.

"They come, O King!" Micah screamed, jumping up and down and pointing frantically behind him.

It was time. Gideon rose silently and unsheathed his sword. Behind him, his men tensed, then stood. He started to run, closing the ground quickly, while the Midianites were still intent upon the western horizon, waiting for their nonexistent brothers. They did not hear the charging Israelites until they were twenty feet away.

Instinctively the nomads reached for their weapons, only to find that they had left their curved swords, removed for the noon meal, inside their tents.

Thirty Midianites died in the first charge. Dozens more scattered in every direction after they saw that the path back to their tents was blocked. In the confusion, Micah had disappeared. Gideon could not see him anywhere.

Zalmunnah survived the first charge. Ten of his elite bodyguards surrounded him and repeatedly warded off the Israelite attacks. When one guard fell, the others moved together. The circle grew smaller; but still Zalmunnah could not be reached.

Then Gideon noticed a rider approaching. It was Micah on a magnificent white camel. Evidently he had circled the camp after the raid had started, and saddled and bridled the beast. The camel was moving fast, in long, ground-eating strides as Micah leaned over its side and whipped it hard on its flanks.

Beast and man crashed through the king's protective circle and crushed two of the Midianites. As the camel and rider fell, Gideon found an opening. He leaped forward through the gap in the defensive ring.

Zalmunnah turned to run, but Gideon drove his sword between the king's shoulder blades. The king of the Midianites pitched heavily to the ground. His screams were terrible to hear. His fingers tore like talons at the hard ground as he tried to pull himself along, as if there were still a possibility of escape, as if the blade in his back did not mean death.

Gideon brought his foot down hard on Zalmunnah's head, arresting his movement. The king's head turned. His eye was dark with hatred, and although only one side of his face could be seen, his expression retained its arrogant, regal cast.

Gideon crouched beside him. "Listen to the sound of Yahweh, you butcher," he whispered to the dying monarch.

And then, right there, in that charnel oasis, Gideon played a tune on his trumpet. It was the sound of freedom. Zalmunnah gathered his strength and lunged upward, in an effort to knock the horn aside. Gideon easily sidestepped the swing. Then he dropped the trumpet and drove a dagger through Zalmunnah's eye and into the brain. The king lay still.

Gideon's legs began to wobble, and he would have fallen had Micah not rushed to his side and held him up. The two comrades stared down at the head of the snake. The battle was finally over.

The Israelites rested at Quargor for the remainder of the day and through the night. The next morning they rode west. Purah, who carried the head of Zalmunnah on a staff, led the column. As they approached the Jordan, thousands of local Israelites began to run alongside them, offering food and drink, tossing flowers, cheering them.

"We seem to have a slightly different reaction now than we had at Succoth," Micah remarked wryly. "Everyone must know of our victories and believe them."

Gideon nodded angrily. In a very short time he

had learned to be wary of and skeptical about any public acclaim.

They crossed the river just south of Beth-shean, and when they entered that small city, they found themselves surrounded by thousands of Israelites from all the tribes, celebrating the downfall of the Midianites. And many of the Israelites were wearing Bedouin gold. The soldiers were led to the farmer's market, where an enormous banquet had been prepared for them.

After the Israelite troopers had eaten their fill and quenched their thirst, they lay down on soft, stuffed hides and accepted the continuing praise of the populace.

One after another, visitors approached Gideon and proclaimed him the rightful king of Israel. Little girls and boys ran around the soldiers, singing ditties about King Gideon and the reign of peace and wealth he would bring to Canaan.

"How they yearn for a king," Micah observed.

"They have a king," Gideon replied bitterly. "But the moment after the victory, my people seem to have forgotten Yahweh. And you know, Micah, I think I can understand why. The mind and the body can only absorb so much. What you can't see, you can't give your whole allegiance to."

"But *you* see Yahweh, don't you, Gideon?" Micah inquired.

Gideon laughed. "My friend, don't confuse me with Moses. I am not Moses, and I never was Moses. I am only a fool who can play the trumpet."

People streamed out of the crowd and set gifts in front of the troopers. They left lambs, garments, weapons, and jewelry. Children with great bunches of fruit staggered toward their saviors and placed the offerings at their feet. And each gift delivered was accompanied by cheers from the crowd.

At last Gideon had had enough. He stood and held his hands outstretched. The crowd quieted immediately.

"Listen to me, my friends: We don't intend to rule over you. We plan to return to our homes and commence with our lives now that the victory is won. And we don't want your fruit, your clothes, or your weapons. But while we were dealing with the Midianite king, you went to the battlefield to take the earrings of the dead. We—my men and I—want only what is due us: the gold earrings of the Midianites."

The crowd was silent, apparently stunned by Gideon's request. He had become larger than life in their eyes—a prophet, a warrior, a king. That was why they had brought the gifts and covered him and his warriors with flowers and praise. But it jarred them to hear him ask for gold. They did not want to give it away.

Gideon remained standing but said nothing more. Expressions of dissent rippled through the crowd. It surged forward and backward as those gathered expressed their conflicting opinions.

Suddenly a small object was hurled from the crush of people and landed on the ground not more than ten feet from Gideon—and then another object, and another, until the air seemed to be full of flying birds or insects. The assemblage was tossing the gold earrings that they had taken from the battle site. Some still had the severed ear attached.

The pile grew in front of Gideon and his men. Gideon watched. He felt very tired. He suffered no guilt for asking for the gold, but he had no sense of joy, either. This was simply his due.

CHAPTER TWO

Tyre

The rough sailors in the bar had begun their chant: "Cotto, Cotto, Cotto." Often they added several lewd variations. She did not mind their enthusiasm. In fact, she often preferred to dance in the tavern for the sailors than for Navan's haughty acquaintances. The sailors were more open about their erotic responses, and that flattered her.

Cotto wondered if she was fit enough to dance, after the long trip to Megiddo and back and all the other adventures and hardships she had experienced. She felt fine; but if anything was lacking, it would show in her ability to interpret the dance, in subtleties.

Carefully she mixed red powder with water until it constituted a sticky paste. Then she daubed her nipples with the paste and drew thin red lines up along her breasts.

The door behind her swung open. A gust of air and noise blew in. Thinking it was the bartender, she did not turn around. "I'll be out shortly. Tell them to calm down."

"Take your time," she heard. It was not the bartender; it was Navan. He closed the door softly behind him and stood quietly in the center of the tiny room. She turned around in the chair. This was the first time Navan had ever visited her at the tavern

"We have not been able to locate that boy who kidnapped you," he said.

"Did you try the house of Nimshi's friend—the woman who came to Tyre to see him?"

"Yes. A servant told us they were no longer there. The woman was sick and left Tyre. The boy had not been seen. I have many people looking for him. I'll find him."

Cotto nodded, affirming the confidence in Navan's voice. But she knew there was a good chance Talus would have escaped. He had been a brave and resourceful young man. She frowned. It would be best for everyone if they found him and killed him fast. Idealists and romantics like Talus were not to be trusted. They wore their hearts on their sleeve and were too naive to live.

Navan crossed the room in one long stride and dropped a bundle in front of her.

She sat back, astonished, staring at the beautiful soft cloth.

"What is this?" she asked.

"A present for you," he said, and caressed her neck. It was a gesture both gentle and threatening. "Unwrap it."

She opened the cloth and sat back. Inside was the most beautiful tortoiseshell comb she had ever seen. It had a white bone handle with delicate carvings of young gazelles sprinting across the top. Each animal was in a different elevation of leap each more beautiful and elegant than the last.

"Thank you," she breathed. She turned again and faced him. Why had he given her a present? Did he want her to sleep with him? But she had always been available to him. After all, he was powerful and rich, and she would have done whatever he desired as often as he wanted. Navan was her employer. She knew on which side her bread was buttered.

She looked at him for some clue as to why he had given her the gift, but he was as impassive as usual.

Then the thought occurred to her that he might be rewarding her for her machinations—that he knew Talus had not kidnapped her as she claimed . . . that he knew she had lied to get back in his good graces and was rewarding her for being ruthless and evil. It was the kind of thing a Phoenician might do. They loved unscrupulous people. They appreciated clever crimes.

But there was no way to be certain. Navan was too enigmatic. As she stared at him, he smiled. Were they now in a combat of wills? Were they now in a contest? Did he know that she planned to exploit every one of her charms to achieve the wealth and power she craved?

"Thank you. I shall use it every day," was all she said.

"And every night, too, I hope," he replied, and then left the small room without another word.

The clamor from outside grew stronger. It was time for her to dance.

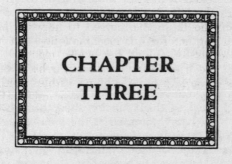

CHAPTER THREE

Canaan

Micah slipped away from the victory celebration after a brief but intense farewell to Gideon. Gideon had pressed upon him a large pouch filled with gold earrings and, as a special thanks, his own sword. Gideon had also offered Micah his choice of mounts; but Micah had refused—he could buy mounts later, after he had retrieved Luti.

Micah had devoted most of his life to committing violence and murder, but he was not prepared for the scene of utter horror that greeted him on the battlefield near the Spring of Harod. Bedouin corpses still lay in the encampment where they had died by Israelite swords or by their own comrades' confusion. Human vultures had already severed their ears, and feathered vultures had plucked out their eyes and begun to crack open skulls and pull out the brains.

A few cries of pain arose, and the smell of smoke from the burned tents, along with the pungent sweet-

and-sour smell of rotting camel flesh, assailed the nostrils.

Old men searched through the ruins of the Midianite nation for objects to sell. They greeted Micah with hysterical cackles. A few young boys played with severed Bedouin heads while dozens of stray dogs fought over particularly choice pieces of camel flesh.

Micah hesitated only a moment, staring at the carnage, before breaking into a run toward the Amalekite tents where Luti awaited him. When he reached the tent, he was relieved to find it intact, untouched. He breathed a sigh of thanks and rushed through the tent opening. His heart pounded at the idea of seeing Luti again. Now they were free, united forever. The love into which they had so mysteriously and inextricably been drawn was about to be confirmed through eternity.

But only one slave remained in the tent. She was lying on her stomach with a spear driven through the lower part of her back. It had been sent through her body with such force that the shaft had splintered.

Micah sank to his knees, and a low moan of despair escaped his lips. Trembling, he rolled the dead woman over. When he saw it was not Luti, tears burst from his eyes. But guilt assailed him in waves. He had waited too long. He had given his loyalty to Gideon, when his first loyalty should have been to Luti. Where was she? Was she alive? How could he find her?

He ran from the tent, his sword drawn. Someone had to know where she was! Someone had to have seen her! He stood there for a long time, confused, not knowing how to begin the search. Then he realized that the only ones who might have seen her were the severely wounded Bedouins, who had been lying on the ground since the battle.

Micah searched the immediate area; there were many corpses, and he rolled each one over, hoping to find a man who, by some miracle, was still alive. He ranged farther and farther from the tent in a circular pattern. The corpses came thicker. Some had already begun to stiffen in grotesque positions. One group was particularly gruesome—Amalekites and Midianites so closely entwined in a death embrace that Micah had to use the point of his sword to pry the bodies apart. He checked each body. All were dead. Then he moved on.

"Blood!" Micah froze in his tracks. Who was calling him? Was he hallucinating? He turned and saw no one. He heard it again: "Blood! Blood!"

He realized the sound was coming from the group of Amalekite and Midianite corpses. He had been sure they were all dead, but he rushed back to the pile nonetheless and waded in.

Yes, one *was* still alive and moving. His mouth worked as he called, "Blood . . . Blood . . . Blood."

Micah dragged the wounded man from the pile and propped him up. It was Adab, king of the Amalekites, who had promised freedom but delivered nothing. Micah pressed his ear to the Bedouin's lips as Adab spoke in small gasps. "Zeeb took your slave woman and two others."

The warlord no one had been able to find! Zeeb was the last remaining Midianite threat now that Oreb and Zalmunnah were dead.

Micah grasped the Amalekite tightly. "When did they leave?" he demanded. "Which way did they go?"

Adab leaned forward, and every fiber of his being seemed to strain with the effort. He tried to answer, but it was too late. He died immediately, his eyes rolling hideously back in his head and his hand grasping like a scorpion at Micah.

Micah felt no pity, only anger that he had not gotten enough information. He angrily shoved the dead man from him. He had to think clearly now; he had to puzzle out where Zeeb would have taken the captives. It did not matter why he had taken them. Perhaps he was exacting vengeance because of the fake assassination of Gideon; perhaps he had taken the captives to ensure a source of wealth; perhaps he had taken Luti and the others because he needed slaves to cater to his needs. None of that was important now. The only thing that mattered was getting into Zeeb's mind and guessing his destination.

It was obvious the warlord would not move directly

east and attempt to cross the Jordan, Micah decided. That would have been too dangerous because the banks of the Jordan were swarming with Israelites. And he would not travel west toward the coast, because that was alien territory to the Bedouin. Going south would prove too dangerous because Zeeb would have been forced to pass through the remnants of the Israelite camps scattered near the Spring of Harod.

North, Micah judged, was the only logical move for the Midianite. Zeeb would skirt the Sea of Chinnereth on the west and cross the Jordan at its northern edge, near Almaqor. Then he would ride due east in the hope of locating remnants of the Midianite armies. That would provide the only safe and sure path to his homeland.

Micah started off using the ground-consuming jog he had developed as a bandit in the Wilderness of Judea; he could keep up that economical and far-ranging pace all day. His eyes remained glued on the ground to look for signs.

It was at Ashdod that he finally picked up the trail. The sign was clear: Someone was riding a lame camel, and from the depth of the tracks, several other people were riding one camel. The ground also showed that these captives kept falling off the beast's back. Micah stared at the signs and cursed Zeeb. His hatred was overwhelming.

Micah squinted at the sun to determine how much time had passed since he left the battle site. He guessed at his own speed and that of the party he was tracking. He had to be moving faster than they, and if all signs were correct—and if he ran through the night—he would overtake Zeeb and the slaves just south of Horbat Arbel on the western shores of the Sea of Chinnereth.

Micah ran all night with Gideon's sword balanced on his shoulder. Fatigue could not deter him. When he stumbled and fell because of the darkness, the pain meant nothing to him. He merely cursed his awkwardness, rose, and set off again. He kept his mind fixed on the image of Luti as he had last seen her. From time to time he muttered, "Soon, my beloved, soon. I will be with you soon, Luti."

The dawn's light revealed fresh tracks. He was close to his quarry, very close. The lame camel was moving slower, and the captives' pace was Micah's only hope. He ran faster now, and the sweat poured down his body. His eyes gleamed as he passed over the fresh tracks. And then he saw his quarry, camped at the edge of a gully.

Micah dropped to the ground and crawled. When he was but twenty yards away, he stopped. The lame camel had been slaughtered, and Zeeb was cutting away chunks of its flesh and dropping them into a small fire. Behind the warlord sat the three exhausted slaves, who watched the cooking fire hungrily. Micah's eyes welled with tears when he saw the face of his beloved. She was alive.

There was no time for subtleties, for tactics, for strategy. Micah stood up and walked directly toward the Midianite warlord. When he had halved the distance, he stopped, raised Gideon's sword over his head, and called, "Look at me, you filthy dog of a Midianite. Study my face before I kill you."

Zeeb jumped up and ran to the side of the dead camel, where his long, curved sword lay in its scabbard. He drew the blade and flung the scabbard away. His face was twisted with hatred.

"I have taken the head of your one-eyed dog Oreb," Micah shouted as he approached, "and now I will take yours."

The Midianite warrior crouched low and held the long blade in front of him. Micah could see the deformed right hand grasping the hilt, like a jackal fastens on to an antelope. For a brief moment Micah felt afraid. This man was a formidable warrior and strategist.

"Micah! Be careful!" Luti called.

Micah steadied himself and charged his adversary. Zeeb parried the blow with such strength that Micah was sent sprawling into the dust. He rose quickly, spitting out dirt and still holding his sword. He charged again, and this time the two blades met. Again and again the swords clashed. Grunting, cursing, sweating, digging into the ground with their heels, the opponents hacked futilely at each other until their arms grew weary and neither could raise his sword anymore.

Micah dropped his first. Zeeb followed. They would finish this contest to the death with their bare hands. Micah dived at the Midianite's feet in an effort to upend him. But Zeeb sidestepped and kicked Micah in the stomach, knocking the wind out of him. In the next instant, Zeeb was upon him, his powerful hands circling Micah's throat.

Micah thrashed mightily. His fingers sought the Bedouin's exposed eyes, but Zeeb's grip grew tighter. Micah felt his life beginning to slip away. And then with one last mighty effort he hooked his left thumb into Zeeb's right eye and pushed with all his might. Zeeb screamed as the dislodged eyeball rolled away. The warlord, fueled by his agony, turned onto his side.

Micah dived on top of him and drew Zeeb's chin back so the throat was exposed. He twisted the Bedouin's head then sank his teeth into Zeeb's naked throat, bit through the Adam's apple, and crushed the windpipe in a single paroxysm of blood and gore and gurgled screams. Then Micah rolled off him and listened with grim satisfaction to his enemy's death rattles.

At last, panting hard, he turned toward Luti and gave her the salute of victory. But she sat with her eyes averted and her arms wrapped around herself as if she could not bear the sights and the sounds of her rescue.

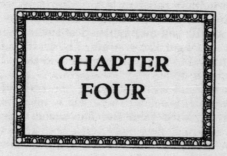

CHAPTER FOUR

Abbasiyah, Coast of Lebanon

From her balcony, Tirzah, propped up with pillows on the divan, could see far across the water. The Great Sea was placid and stunningly blue. The view soothed her, and the afternoon sun felt warm on her body.

"Would you like something to drink, madam?"

Tirzah turned slowly toward the voice and smiled. It was Nagil, a servant who had traveled from Canaan to be with his mistress the moment he had heard the news that she was dying.

"No, Nagil, I am fine," she replied.

He walked to her side and made certain she was covered properly. In fact, she was not fine. She was very weak and nauseated, and severe pains shot through her legs from time to time.

"Nagil, come close," she said.

The servant obeyed.

"Do you remember my instructions?" she asked.

"As regards to burial?" he replied. "Yes." Tears came to his eyes. He was a gentle man, and he held his mistress in highest regard. "Madam, you will be buried next to the prophetess Deborah."

Tirzah smiled, patted him on the hand, and stared out to sea again. She felt her life draining away moment by moment. It had all happened so fast—the fever had struck her in Tyre like a sword. The fever had broken, but she was still feeling progressively weaker. The damage had been done.

She was not afraid of dying—she had lived a long and interesting life—but there was so much unfinished business . . . with Talus and Theon and with those in Canaan who still depended upon her. There were so many conversations she wanted to have and so many things she still wanted to understand.

Shouts from the floor below broke into her reverie.

"Please see what all that nonsense is," she whispered to Nagil.

The servant started for the stairs but had not taken two steps when a young man burst through the doorway.

"Talus! Is that you?" Tirzah asked, staring at the disheveled, wild-looking young man. He was streaked with sweat and dust.

Talus nodded and came quickly to her side. "Forgive me for coming here like this. I know you are ill, and I have no right to impose upon you again after I abused your hospitality in Tyre."

"Sit," she said gently. "I have nothing but affection for you, and there is much I must tell you."

"And I, you."

Before Tirzah could say another word, Talus blurted out the whole sad story about Cotto—how he had gone to murder her and avenge Nimshi . . . how he had been swept off his feet . . . how they had stolen the Phoenician gold and journeyed to Megiddo . . . how she had convinced him to return to Tyre, only to betray him . . . how he had escaped. When he had finished, he stared at Tirzah. His shame was worsened by how bad she looked—the thin neck, the bulging eyes, the paleness.

"It is part of growing up, Talus," she soothed. "You should not be so hard on yourself. Good men always fall for beautiful, evil women." She laughed weakly and added, "I used to know something about that, when I was young and beautiful—and evil."

"You? Evil? I cannot believe that," Talus replied fervently.

"But it's true. Listen to me, Talus. I have much to tell you but very little time." Tirzah's face contorted in pain, and she hugged her midsection. Her face broke out into a sweat.

"You, there!" Talus shouted to the servant. "Get her something!"

But Nagil just shook his head sadly. Tirzah reached over to take Talus's hand. "There is nothing to be done, dear, by you or Nagil or anyone else. Just listen. Here, help me to sit up."

Talus and the servant raised her slightly on the divan and put two more pillows behind her back. She was breathing with difficulty now.

"I have received important information from my informants in Damascus, Talus. Khalkeus of Gournia, Nuhara's father, is alive. While administrating the shipping empire, he fell under the influence of an adviser who worships the Greek god Dionysus. He convinced Khalkeus to do the same. He joined a crazed and dangerous cult centered in the mountains of Thrace on the Greek mainland. All the treasures on Home— family treasures that belong to the Children of the Lion—were shipped to the cult's main temple in Thrace before Home was destroyed by the Phoenician raid."

Tirzah coughed deeply, and her face turned deep red. Then she fought to regain control. She sat up, using the sides of the divan to pull herself up, and finally caught her breath. "Do you understand, Talus? Khalkeus of Gournia betrayed the Children of the Lion. That treasure belongs to *you*, not to this man-god called Dionysus. That treasure belongs to all the Children of the Lion, not to the cult priests. Get it back, Talus. Get it—"

Then she fell back and began to writhe as if a

demon had grasped her. "Theon! Theon!" she
screamed, flailing wildly but weakly.

Talus jumped up and tried to take hold of her
shoulders.

"Theon is not here, Tirzah. It is I, Talus."

But Tirzah kept screaming and tried to rise off the
divan. Both Nagil and Talus restrained her. She fought
them with unnatural strength, uttered one last scream
for Theon, began to shake violently, then fell back,
limp.

She was dead. Talus took her hand and held it
gently against his face as he wept. She had been a true
friend.

He had not slept all night. Instead he had listened
to the preparations for taking Tirzah's body back to
Canaan for burial. The story she had told him was dazzling but perplexing. He found it hard to absorb the
facts: treasures, new gods, Thrace. It was too soon after
Cotto's betrayal, much too soon.

A knock on Talus's bedroom door sounded just
after the first light of dawn. It was Nagil. His face was
still wet from weeping, and he was extremely agitated.

"What is the matter?" Talus asked.

"A rider came here last night from Damascus. He
is an informer who was in the pay of the mistress. He
brought terrible news." Nagil shook his head furiously
and had trouble finding words.

Talus helped the servant to a chair. "What is this
terrible news?"

"My mistress did not die of the fever. My mistress
was poisoned. She was murdered by people in the pay
of that woman Nuhara. The informant also brought
word that it was the very same Nuhara who convinced
her father, Khalkeus of Gournia, to join the cult of
Dionysus."

He was talking so fast and in such a shrill voice
that Talus had trouble understanding him. "Please,
Nagil, calm down."

"I am almost glad she is dead so she cannot be
hurt anymore. Gods, if she were alive to hear that her

beloved Theon is next on the list! That evil woman plans to murder her own husband!"

"Are you sure?" Talus asked.

"Yes! Word came from my mistress's most trusted informant," Nagil said. "His information is consistently correct." He reached into his leather vest and withdrew three small pouches. He opened them all and poured the contents onto the bed—gold coins: brand-new, beautifully wrought gold coins.

"My mistress left this for you, Talus. Before you arrived yesterday, the money had already been set aside. I had instructions to find you after my mistress's death, explain about the treasure, and beg you to right the wrong. Now more than ever, Talus, you must go— not only to recover the fortune of the Children of the Lion but to save my mistress's beloved Theon."

Talus stared down at the coins. Once again he was caught up in the tyranny of gold. It was gold that enabled Cotto to feed her family; but it was for gold that she betrayed him. The coins on the bed would enable him to take passage on a ship bound for Thrace, in order to obtain the infinitely greater amount of money that belonged to the Children of the Lion. Where, he agonized, would it all end?

"She loved this Theon very much," Nagil repeated as if Talus's silence indicated indecision.

"Rest easy, Nagil," he said, blowing out a deep sigh. "I am no longer a child. I will go to Thrace. I will fulfill my responsibility."

CHAPTER FIVE

Desert of Transjordan

Luti and Micah rode steadily north through the desert. After being reunited following Zeeb's death, Micah carefully removed Luti's despised nose ring. Then the lovers had purchased plenty of food and water and good mounts—all bought with gold earrings, which Gideon had bestowed upon Micah for his services. They had set the two other slave women free, divided Zeeb's own magnificent gold earrings between them, and sent them on their way. Then Micah and Luti laughed and made love. They speculated about their future in Ur. Luti told him anecdotes about their son, Drak.

At night they lay in each other's arms and watched the stars. They reminisced about their first meeting those many years before and tried to recall every nuance of their feelings and actions. Neither of them had ever experienced such closeness with anyone else, and even during the daylight, as they rode side by side, it seemed as if they were spiritually joined in both passion and love.

On the third night of the journey, however, Luti began to notice a change in Micah. He had made love to her mechanically, almost as if it were a chore. And afterward he had turned away and stared moodily out into the desert. She tried to make him laugh, to interest him, to get his attention—but he was too distracted.

She nestled close to him. "What is bothering you, darling? You have been acting strange all evening."

"Nothing," he replied.

"Have I said something to offend you?"

"Of course not. I treasure your every word."

She played with a lock of his hair. "I want to share everything with you, Micah. That includes your fears as well as your triumphs."

He stared at her, hard eyed, as if evaluating her capacity to absorb the truth.

"I mean that, Micah. Please tell me what is disturbing you."

He nodded. "I am beginning to feel strange. Every mile we ride toward our new life in Ur means I am yet another mile farther from Canaan. I am beginning to wonder if I shall ever see that land again. The idea makes me uneasy . . . and thoughtful. I feel I have betrayed the land of my birth."

Luti's hand caressed his troubled face. "Micah, you owe nothing to that land. It owes nothing to you. What has it been for you but a scene of bloodshed and death? Your parents are dead; the influence that the Children of the Lion once enjoyed with the Israelites is gone; Nimshi hasn't contacted you in years and, for all you know, may be dead. Nothing remains there for you."

Micah was about to reply when he suddenly held up his hand for silence. Even in the darkness Luti could see the concern in his alert eyes.

"What's the matter?" she whispered.

"Smoke. From a campfire," he whispered back.

Luti held her face up so that her nostrils could catch the desert breeze. She sniffed but smelled nothing.

"Stay here. Don't move. I'll be back soon." A moment later he vanished into the night.

Luti waited, her heart thudding with fear. Everything had been going so well, so smoothly. And now this! She listened for any sound of movement, but she heard nothing. And then, for the first time, she caught the faint scent of burning wood. Micah had been correct. She huddled in her blanket, waiting.

He returned as suddenly as he had disappeared. "There's a Bedouin camp not far from here," he told her. "They're Midianites, maybe survivors from the battle. I can't know for sure. But there are six of them." He paused, considering. "Still, we're a bit too far north for Midianites, unless they're trying to contact some other tribes, looking for new, more powerful allies after their defeat."

He walked quickly to his mount and pulled Gideon's sword from the saddlebag.

"What are you doing, Micah?"

He ignored her question. "Stay close to the camp, Luti. I'll be back in a little while." He melted into the night again.

"Wait!" she called loudly.

He strode back to her angrily. "Keep your voice down!"

She stared at him. He had transformed in front of her eyes into the bandit Blood.

"Tell me where you are going with that sword, Micah."

"I'm going to the Bedouin camp, and I'm going to kill them all."

"Micah! Are you mad? Leave them alone. They have done nothing to us."

He sneered at her. "Either I kill them, or they will kill us. It is as simple as that." She could see his hatred and the blood lust rising. It was as if she were watching a monster emerge from the cocoon of a butterfly.

"Don't go, Micah, please. I don't want the father of our son to be tainted with any more bloodletting. I won't let you go!" She took hold of his sword arm. He shook her off and started to leave. She grabbed his arm again, in a stronger grip. "Please, Micah! You can't do this. You can't."

"Are you crazy, Luti? Have you learned nothing about the cruelty and unfairness that exists in this world? You've been a slave once. Do you want to risk your freedom again for the sake of your precious naïveté?"

He threw her violently to the ground, and when her head cleared she saw the point of the sword at her throat. Micah seemed like a wild man, about to drive it into her flesh. Their eyes met. A muscle at the side of his face began to throb. And then his whole body trembled.

"Drop the sword, Micah. Everything will be fine. Drop the sword!" The weapon dangled from his fingers, then fell from his hand and glanced harmlessly off Luti's foot.

He looked shocked and disoriented, as if he could not believe that in a fit of rage he had almost murdered the woman he loved, the mother of his child. Ashamed, he buried his face in his hands.

Luti stood and rushed over to him, then wrapped her arms around his neck. "You have been fighting for too long, Micah. You have been killing for too long. Something like this was bound to happen. You can't expect to change your whole life in three days."

He gently separated himself from her. He walked to where the sword had fallen. After picking it up and holding the blade with both hands, he bent it out of shape and then let it fall to the ground.

"Listen to me, Luti," he whispered. "I pledge to you and to whatever god is in heaven that I will never again pick up a sword in anger. Do you hear me!"

Luti wept. "I hear you, Micah."

Micah walked to his blanket and lay down. Luti lay down next to him. They rested together like that for a long time.

"I want to make a confession to you, Micah. Do you remember the hawk you told me about? The one that fed you and led you through the wilderness? That hawk was sent by me."

He turned and stared at her, astonished. "What

do you mean? How can you send a hawk anywhere? Are you a magician?"

"Yes, I guess I am, Micah. And you may be one, too. I am telling you about the hawk only to illustrate that the strange mark both you and I bear—the paw print of the Children of the Lion—signifies more than just the ability to make and, in your case, to use weapons. We are more than craftsmen and killers. We have many wonderful gifts. Some of us are able to see directly into the mystery of animals and birds and the heavens themselves."

She waited for a response from him. There was none. She leaned over. He was fast asleep.

CHAPTER
SIX

Sinai Wilderness/Mitla Pass

Time and place no longer meant anything to the twins. They were transported in secrecy. They never knew where they were going or where they had been. Cloth hoods covered their faces; their hands were bound behind their backs.

The only things they knew for a certainty were that they were in the back of a donkey cart and that it was very hot. The relentless sun baked their scalps through the cloth hoods.

Their clothes were in tatters, and their bodies were encrusted with the filth of weeks of traveling by boat, cart, or on the backs of small powerfully built horses with shaggy manes. But at least Gravis and Hela were still together. Anything else would have been unbearable. They could withstand all hardships except separation.

Now, as the cart jostled them, as their parched mouths cried out for water, as their raw, bleeding

335

wrists became ever more chafed from the ropes that bound them, they resorted to one of the tricks that had enabled them to survive.

It was a game—a simple yet challenging game. One of the twins would imagine a person, object, or concept. To win, the other twin would have to identify the person, object, or concept without asking questions or being given clues. Winning depended upon successful psychic transference.

Young Hela initiated the game that day. She remembered a wild horse she had once seen in the mountains of Home. It was a beautiful white horse, small but perfectly formed. She had seen it for only a few moments before it vanished into the trees. But it had been the most elegant creature she had ever laid her eyes on.

She leaned back against the hard side of the wooden donkey cart, relaxed, and brought the memory of it back into her mind. She began to concentrate intently on its form, on the powerful chest and legs, on the gracefully arched neck, on the lovely face.

Hela knew that Gravis would not have to be told that a game was in progress. The sudden tensing of her body beside his and the intrusion of her thoughts into his mind were enough to tell him that she was engaged in a mental retrieval.

Hela smiled beneath the hood. She had the horse's image fixed. It was as if the horse existed again, to be seen, to be touched. She waited for a response from her brother. She could not hold the image with that intensity for too long.

Then she heard Gravis drumming his fingers along the wooden side of the cart. The sound was an imitation of a horse's hooves on the hard ground. She nodded, reached out, and touched him lightly on the shoulder.

The cart lurched to a sudden stop, sending the twins slamming against each other and then onto the floor. Unhurt, they righted themselves quickly.

They heard the driver leap lightly into the back of the cart. He pulled off the twins' hoods, untied their hands, then jumped down and, without a word, ran off.

The sudden light was temporarily blinding until their eyes adjusted. They looked around: They were in a barren, sunbaked wilderness plain. Massive rock formations bordered the plain. These cliffs seemed to reflect the sun with a thousand different colors— browns and reds and purples and yellows.

The twins' eyes focused slowly because they had been hooded for so long. At last they could identify what had been a blur. What they saw was unbelievable. Gravis rubbed his eyes and took a tight grip on the side of the cart. In front of them, lined up in rows, were Egyptian charioteers fully bedecked in war plumage. Magnificently embroidered multicolored banners were rippling in the wind. Weapons and vehicles alike glistened in the harsh sun. The horses were prancing in place.

It was an astonishing, fearful sight. Neither Hela nor Gravis had ever witnessed such a display. But their shock was only momentary.

"What will be will be," Hela whispered. She took her brother's hand so lightly that it did not appear that they were touching. At the physical contact, the strange calmness returned to their eyes.

One of the chariots spun toward their cart and stopped only a few feet away. A powerfully built man stepped down from the chariot and approached them. The authority of command was written over his face. Scars from past battles marked his body. He bowed low in front of them and held the position for a long time. Gravis and Hela quickly glanced at each other.

Then the soldier straightened and said, "I am Ma-Set, commander of the Harishaf Chariot Brigade. We are returning from the Wilderness of Judea, where we destroyed the bandit Blood and his men. Our destination is Egypt. The moment we set foot on the soil of our homeland, the Egyptian army will rise up and destroy the hated pharaoh, Ramses the Third, because he has brought our beloved country to ruin."

Then Ma-Set fell to his knees, leaned forward, and placed his brow on the hard ground. He rose, prostrated himself, rose again, then went down for the third time, holding the position for a long time. Behind him, the formidable chariot brigadiers stood motionless and silent. The only sounds were the snapping of the pennants in the hot desert wind and the stamping and snorting of the restless horses.

Again the twins exchanged glances. Gravis opened his mouth to speak, but a quick shake of Hela's head silenced him.

When Ma-Set looked up, his face was glowing, and his eyes were bright with worship. "It is a great honor," he said, "to be in the presence of Osiris and Isis—the divine brother and sister gods who once ruled Egypt. I promise you this day that soon you will rule once again in our beloved land. I pledge to you my life and the lives of all the men in the brigade."

He stood and signaled with his hand. Dozens of soldiers leaped down from their chariots and brought food, water, silk garments, amphorae of cool wine, and even milk to the donkey cart. They piled the items in front of their newfound god and goddess.

Gravis and Hela watched impassively. Even in their tattered garments the twins exuded a glow of perfection. Their golden hair and their androgynous and identical beautiful faces seemed to reflect the sun, sending brilliant beams of light to dance and sparkle around the wheels of the chariots.

Hela waited until the soldiers had deposited their gifts and stepped away, taking care not to turn their backs on their newfound deities.

Then she bent and dipped her hand into a jar of milk. She cupped some of the liquid in her hand and brought it to her brother's mouth. Gravis lapped the milk from his sister's hand.

"Everything is possible," she whispered in his ear.

CHAPTER SEVEN

Canaan

The woman was naked except for the remnant of a
Bedouin robe, which sat crazily atop her head. Gideon
dribbled the wine slowly over each of her nipples and
then began to lick the liquid off. She laughed and
arched her back boldly. Around him, the revelers
cheered and laughed and applauded. Purah stood by
Gideon's side and refilled his master's bowl with good
wine from an enormous goatskin, which the servant had
balanced over his shoulder.

The raucous Israelite victory celebration had been
going on for hours, and with each passing minute it
increased in intensity and outrageousness. Huge bon-
fires lighted the night sky, and hundreds of lambs,
calves, and kids were roasted for the continuing feast.
The aroma of sizzling fat was heavy in the air.

The moment Gideon and the young woman cou-
pled on the ground, the onlookers began to chant Gideon's name in time with his thrusting hips. Finally he

released his partner and, spent, rolled along the ground
and called for Purah to pour more wine down his
throat. His servant obeyed without bending over.
Until the stream's angle was adjusted, wine splattered in Gideon's eyes and hair. The Israelite leader
sputtered and hooted with laughter at the servant's
terrible aim.

Then Gideon staggered to his feet and held up his
hands for silence. But the crowd guffawed and clapped
and called his name. They were too drunk to be quiet,
and Gideon was too drunk to care. He shouted over
them, "I want to thank this beautiful woman, and I
want to thank all the other beautiful women I'm going
to have during this night and the next night and the
next night."

Gideon sidestepped unsteadily, and someone tossed
him a staff, which he dropped, retrieved, and used to
prop himself up. The revelers cheered him again, and
someone hurled a cooked lamb's head at him. It
bounced off his shoulder, leaving a grease smudge.

Unaware something had hit him, Gideon continued, "And most of all, I want to thank all of you. You
have my blessings. Tell your children that you knew
the greatest Israelite warrior of all time!" Gideon
started to whirl and prance, dip and bow, while roar-
ing out, "I have conquered Midian! I have killed
Zalmunnah."

Again the crowd chanted his name.

Purah watched his master's drunken self-adulation.
It was strange, he thought, how quickly Gideon's
behavior had deteriorated. The overly nervous lout had
become a devout warrior of Yahweh, and Purah had
hoped the change would be permanent. Now, however,
he had become a boasting fool who wanted songs written about his prowess. The change had begun the
moment he took the gold earrings. Next he developed
a craving for strong wine. Then he desired women.
True, there had been no love lost between Gideon and
his wife; but his sudden womanizing seemed limitless.
And now he wanted to be known as the greatest warrior
of the Israelites—greater, Purah thought with disgust,

than Joshua. Gideon had completely forgotten that it was Yahweh who defeated the Midianites—not the pathetic band of three hundred recruits.

Gideon was babbling on, describing the great battle, explaining how he had tricked the Midianites and how he had broken the most ferocious army that ever faced the Israelites.

Gradually the crowd thinned as the listeners tired of his boasting. They moved off to indulge in the free wine, free food, and the uninhibited sex that the victory celebration offered.

"Purah! Purah!" Gideon called when he realized that no one was listening to him anymore.

"Yes, I am here," Purah replied, taking his master's arm and guiding him to a quiet place where he could rest.

"They love me, don't they, Purah?"

"Yes, sir, they do love you."

"They know what I have done for them, don't they? They know that I restored their dignity and their freedom."

"Yes, sir, that they know."

Gideon sighed and let himself be led by Purah, who gently lowered him to the ground near a fallen tree. "I want you to send me another woman—a younger one this time."

Purah tilted the large wineskin and gave his master another long drink. "Yes, sir, I will bring you more women soon. I will bring you all the women you want, and they all will be young and beautiful."

Gideon nodded happily, closed his eyes, and within seconds was fast asleep.

Purah knew exactly how much wine Gideon had drunk, so he knew that Gideon would be asleep for a long, long time.

The servant laid the wineskin down on the ground, next to Gideon. Then he hurried to the largest enclosure, where the revelers had tethered their mounts. He searched in the darkness for a strong young pony, and when he found one, he silently cut its hobbles and led it out. He knew he would have it back before its owner—whoever he might be—recovered from the drunken frivolity that he had come for.

Once outside the camp, Purah mounted the pony and rode swiftly north. His goal was the village of Yesud, at the southern end of Hula Valley. That village was the perfect rendezvous spot because it was approximately halfway between Gideon's home and Tyre. Yesud was due east of Tyre and due north of the Spring of Harod.

It was not yet dawn when he reached the well of Yesud, but even in the near darkness Purah could see that the man who had asked to meet with him had arrived; he could discern the distinctive Phoenician traveling carts and the Sea Peoples guards who rode beside them. All were silhouetted against the predawn wash of color lightening the night sky.

But the moment the tall stranger stepped into view, Purah became frightened. The Phoenician facing him was obviously a wealthy, influential man. His robes were shot with gold threads, and his guards looked well trained.

"My name is Navan," the tall man stated. He motioned to his guards, and they began to unload some things from the carts. "Please do not feel concerned. Let me begin by giving you something as a token of my good faith." Navan handed Purah a small leather pouch. "Half your payment. The other half is in Tyre, deposited in your name at the Port Bank."

"Thank you," Purah said. The heavy feel of the pouch and the Phoenician's words calmed his fears.

"Please join me for some conversation and refreshments," the Phoenician invited.

Purah hesitated. There was no reason for him to leave immediately. He would have plenty of time before Gideon recovered enough from his hangover to miss him. Purah shrugged, then nodded.

The bodyguards had set up a small table near the well. On it, Purah could see bowls of fruit and fresh-baked bread. He joined the Phoenician at the table.

"We hope you will be willing to provide us with new information that will prove helpful to us," Navan remarked.

Purah said nothing.

Navan plunged ahead quickly. "Ah, Purah. We know you are a good and loyal servant—better than your master deserves. You need not worry about hurting your own people. We Phoenicians bear no ill will toward the Israelites. We knew that eventually they would rise up against the Bedouins and be successful. No people can endure that kind of treatment for long. But for our own business interests it is important that no one people achieve ascendancy here. So I am afraid, dear man, that the joy of the Israelites must be short-lived. That is why you must continue to work for us. Mutual cooperation will, I assure you, be to both our benefits."

Purah replaced his half-eaten apple on the plate. He could not eat food provided by a man who would like to see the Israelites crushed. On the other hand, Purah rationalized, Gideon's lifelong immaturity before Yahweh's intervention and his repulsive behavior following the battle led the servant to believe that his own years-old loyalties had been misplaced.

"What are you planning against the Israelites?" he asked the Phoenician.

"I plan nothing," replied Navan. "The Philistines, however . . ."

"Are they going to invade the countryside?" Purah asked, horrified. He had a mental picture of well-armed legions of Philistines suddenly leaving the gates of their city-states along the coast of Canaan and striking inland.

"No, my good man." Navan laughed lightly. "No invasion is imminent. The Philistines have other concerns, which are more immediate, on their minds right now. I am giving you a long-range picture. I am merely explaining why we will need your services."

These Phoenicians were too subtle for him, Purah decided. The longer he spoke with Navan, the less he understood. He started to rise, but Navan gently pushed him back. "Wait, Purah. I have brought some other refreshment for you; it may be more to your liking than that apple."

A moment later Purah found himself staring at a beautiful dark-haired woman who had materialized beside him. She was pressing her breasts and hips against him, as if she were an old friend or an old lover. "Hello, Purah," she said softly, in a low voice. "I hope we can get to know each other. I have heard of you. My name is Cotto."

CHAPTER EIGHT

Eastern Slope of Mount Sardis/Thrace

"The ceremony will be starting shortly, Nuhara," Khalkeus said. "We must go to the temple grove."

"We have time, Father," Nuhara replied.

She wondered whether she should tell him what she was planning. He was aging very fast, and his passion for the new god Dionysus seemed to know no bounds. In fact, it was all he talked about, all he dreamed about. Even their treasure, which had been surreptitiously transferred from Home and carefully stored in the vaults beneath the temple, no longer interested him.

Nuhara wondered also whether he should be included in the negotiations that were about to start with the priests of Dionysus. The priests held the keys to the treasure storerooms and wanted what they considered to be their rightful share. Nuhara wanted to keep some of it to do with as she pleased.

"Where is Theon?" Khalkeus asked as he stroked his graying beard.

345

"He stayed in the village with the horses and the rest of the baggage."

"What about the twins? Theon doesn't believe he will ever see them again."

"What's this sudden concern about Theon and the children, Father?" Nuhara asked sharply. "He is a liability to us. He always has been. As for the twins, I'll find them."

"Theon is your husband," Khalkeus said as if he were admonishing a child.

Nuhara grimaced. In his old age the pirate had become ethical. He seemed unaware that his new god, Dionysus, wanted ecstasy, not morality, from his worshipers.

"Father," she said with elaborate patience, "Theon will find the twins quickly once we retrieve the treasure. Money can accomplish all things. But Theon cannot be trusted. We've known that for years. He is not the man he purported himself to be."

"None of us is," her father replied gently, looking anxiously toward the temple in the distance.

"Do you remember the pact we made, Father, on Home? We agreed that we cannot let sentiment sway us. We agreed that in spite of your newfound devotion to religion, you must be ruthless. There is no other way. Theon has never shared our ideals and our goals, and this is more the case now than ever before. He mocks Dionysus."

"He mocks Dionysus?" Khalkeus's eyes flared with anger at the idea.

Nuhara relaxed. At last she felt assured that her father would not interfere.

"We will be rid of the fool shortly, Father. The plans have already been set into motion."

Khalkeus nodded. "Well, enough of all that. Let's go to the grove."

Nuhara took her father's arm, and together they strolled to the beautifully wooded hillside. Others were already waiting for the spectacle to begin. The air was charged with excitement. Nothing would happen, however, until the sun had set and darkness enveloped the trees, the rocks, and the luxuriant mosses, which covered the ground like a fine rug.

Finally the shadows grew longer. Slowly, inexorably, darkness surrounded them. Khalkeus kept a hand on his daughter's arm, and she could feel his growing anticipation.

The high, eerie piping of a flute filled the air, and a slender young man stepped into view. He was clothed only in goatskins. In one hand was a flaming torch. In the other was the flute. He brought the instrument to his lips.

From the darkness a magnificently formed naked man slowly came forward. He personified Bacchus, the god of wine. Wineskins were slung around his hard-muscled body.

He took his place beside the forest path.

Behind him, in a row, came twelve naked young women, each more beautiful than the one before. Their thick, shining tresses were long and unbound. Their bodies, gleaming white in the moon's glow, were coated with fragrant oils. These, Nuhara knew, were the maenads, the true disciples of Dionysus, the young women who lived only to enter the ecstatic trance.

The young flute player moved more quickly now, and the maenads, still silent, still composed, followed. As each maenad passed the representative of Bacchus, she drank of the wine. The flute's rhythm picked up, and the maenads began to run in a circle. As they snaked past Bacchus, they drank again and again of his wine.

Faster and faster they ran, their naked, glistening bodies undulating to the increasing tempo of the music. Then the maenads began to sing. It was a wild, plaintive cry, atonal and wordless.

Six powerfully built young men suddenly stepped out of the darkness. The gathered spectators gasped at the men's evident power. The moonlight cast shadows on their musculature, raising angles and planes in deep relief. They held long, whiplike vines in their huge fists. As the maenads ran past, the men flogged the women's white nakedness until blood splattered the emerald green carpet of the forest.

The speed . . . the blood . . . the wine . . . the naked lust . . . As the gathering watched in fascinated silence, one after another the maenads sank to the ground to be sexually ravaged by one another and by the young men who had inflicted their pain. Screams of anguish and joy and orgasm exploded from their lips.

This, at last, was the purpose and culmination of the ceremony: The maenads reached a height of ecstatic arousal so powerful, so all-encompassing, that they envisioned Dionysus. They saw their god; they were possessed by their god. The onlookers could not help but feel awestruck and spiritually affected by the event.

And then all was quiet. All that could be heard was the deep breathing of the sated women and men as their fulfilled bodies lay on the blanket of moss.

Nuhara found herself drenched with sweat and shaking when the ceremony was over. She turned to her father. He was lost in some distant thought. Had the vicarious ecstasy of the ceremony brought back memories of his youth, of his strivings? she wondered.

He grasped her arm tightly and said, "I must see the face of this god before I die, Nuhara! I would gladly give all my treasures on earth to do so."

Something in the old man's voice frightened her, but she said nothing.

Then Khalkeus took her hands in his, turned the palms up, and whispered, "How much blood is on your hands, Daughter?"

She did not answer.

CHAPTER NINE

Village of Estia, Thrace

Talus tethered his horse to a sapling and stared down at the tiny village. It was comprised of only seven white houses, all squat and built low to the ground, and what appeared to be an inn. A few donkeys and mangy dogs wandered lazily about. No people were in sight.

Talus took a deep breath. The deeper he traveled into the countryside of Thrace, the more deeply affected he was by the sheer beauty of the terrain—the magnificent forests, the sweet, cold streams, the brilliant wildflowers that could be found everywhere. Now, he hoped, his journey was about to end. His inquiries and the money that Tirzah had left him had led him to this village.

But he could not enter the small settlement just yet. It was very early in the morning, and a stranger's presence would be viewed with suspicion. He would need to wait until the inhabitants were up and about.

These Thracians were peculiar; they unnerved him. He was glad he had taken the time to buy a weapon. It was a battle ax with an iron blade and bronze studs.

Talus untethered his horse and led it back up the trail. He moved off the path and into a small glade, where he lay down to wait. The soft, soothing mountain air caressed his face, but his mind was a jumble of conflicting thoughts. Before he had left Canaan, yet another spy from Tirzah's network had reported in with terrible news about the family Theon had sired during his years as a sea captain. Nuhara had proved to be a crazed monomaniac. He was relieved to be alive and away from bloodstained Canaan, but the still-vivid memories of poor Tirzah and of Cotto assaulted him in waves of misery. He tried to come to terms with the likelihood that he would never banish Cotto's face from his thoughts—and that he would never find such a love again.

He drifted off into a light sleep. But within minutes he was awakened by voices on the path. He listened, alert and wary. Two men were having an argument. He crept closer to the path but kept out of sight.

"I say we kill him right now," a brawny, long-haired Thracian said.

His companion, who wore a wolf skin slung across his shoulders and carried two long swords over his back, replied, "No, it is too dangerous. We should wait here until nightfall."

"But by nightfall he might be gone. We can slip in the tavern now, slit his throat, and be out in five minutes. You saw the village—it's deserted. Everyone's still asleep."

The Thracian in the wolf skin reluctantly agreed, and the two men headed down toward the sleeping village.

Talus knew he had stumbled on a murder in progress and felt impelled to prevent it. After hobbling the horse, he followed the men at a distance. He was not completely certain why he was getting involved. After all, he was a criminal himself; he had stolen gold from the Phoenicians, and it was in his own best interests to mind his own business. But of late he had begun to remember Phorbus's stories about Iri, his father.

His father had never shied away from a fight or from getting involved in other people's problems. Talus was inspired to follow that pattern. Furthermore, his father's life had overflowed with regrets, and Talus did not want to have another man's murder on his conscience—he knew he would regret that for the rest of his days. He realized that to act in this manner in a strange country could jeopardize his mission, but he had no choice but to follow.

The conspirators reached the outskirts of the village and slipped into the courtyard of the tavern. Talus watched them quietly climb the rough steps that led to the rooms. He followed silently, his battle ax in hand.

The assassins slipped into a room. Suddenly Talus came to his senses. He realized that he had taken too much upon himself. Thracians were notorious for their bloodthirsty feuds. No, he had to get out of there. He turned to run down the steps.

A shout caused him to stop. Something jarred his memory. He knew the voice! He had heard it before! It was Theon's!

Talus ran back up the steps two at a time and burst through the door. The Thracians had pinned Theon against the wall, and the man in the wolf skin was about to draw his ugly sword across Theon's throat. Talus flung his battle ax. It landed sickeningly on the swordsman's forearm and cut through bone and muscle. The man roared in pain as his blood sprayed the walls. The would-be murderers, taken by surprise, fled past Talus; but the uninjured one kicked him savagely in the groin as he escaped.

Talus dropped to the floor and writhed in pain. He saw Theon's unnaturally pale but concerned face hovering over him. His expression registered shock from the attack and astonishment at seeing Talus. The pain began to diminish, and Theon helped his savior over to the bed.

"Thank you, Talus! But what are you doing here? I never thought I'd see you again."

"I came to find you," he replied.

Theon laughed with the full force of released tension. "Well, you found me just in time! I am forever grateful to you."

"Do you know why those men wanted to kill you?"

"Who knows? This is Thrace, and the people are violent. Maybe they thought I was carrying gold."

Talus stared at the calm, handsome face of the older man. Theon obviously knew nothing of Nuhara's machinations. Talus knew that Theon was kind and generous. A decade before, after Iri had died in an attempt to rescue his wife, Keturah, and Talus, Theon had risked his own life to journey to Troy, in an effort to succeed where Iri had failed. He understood that if Theon had not been shipwrecked, Nuhara would never have banished Phorbus, Keturah, and him to the primitive mountains of Home; Theon would have made sure they received Iri's portion of the family's fortune. And maybe his mother would still be alive. Of all the Children of the Lion, Theon was the one most dedicated to the clan and keeping its members together and safe. Talus realized that he owed no less to Theon in return.

The young man blurted, "Theon, I want to tell you everything, but I am afraid you will not believe me. Instead you will call me a fool."

"Talus," Theon said gently, "we had little opportunity to speak after the ship rescued you at sea or while we were all staying at Tirzah's in Tyre. I was confused, having just recovered my memory and being reunited with my wife. But I never thought you were a fool. In my opinion, you are a brave young man."

Theon's words had a calming effect. Talus's trembling abated; the fresh blood on the walls no longer bothered him. He did not know where to begin, so he simply forged ahead. "Tirzah is dead, Theon."

Theon's face clouded over. His body registered massive shock. He opened his mouth, but no words came. Then he shut his eyes tightly to refrain from weeping.

"She was murdered, Theon. Poisoned."

His eyes opened wide in horror. "What are you

saying, Talus? Who would murder that kind, good woman?"

"Nuhara had her murdered. And those two men who just tried to murder you were sent by Nuhara."

Theon stood and walked to the window slowly, woodenly, touching his neck and throat, which had been wrenched by the assassins. He stared out the window for a long time and said nothing.

Talus finally intruded on Theon's silence.

"Tirzah knew that Nuhara and Khalkeus had shipped the treasure from Home to the temple of Dionysus. That's why she was murdered."

"Why would Nuhara do that? And why would she want me dead?" Theon asked.

"She wanted the family's money for herself and her father, Theon. As for her other motives, perhaps she never believed that you suffered a memory loss. Or maybe you don't fit into her plans for the treasure. Perhaps she truly worships Dionysus and considers you an infidel. Or she thinks you will not be able to find Gravis and Hela."

Theon lapsed into silence again and paced the small room.

"Did you know, Theon, that Nuhara never acknowledged me as my father's heir, that she condemned my mother and Phorbus and me to a life of harsh poverty?" Talus tried to keep the bitterness from his voice but could not succeed. "That Gravis and Hela used to bring food to me without Nuhara's knowledge?"

"No, I didn't. They were small children when I was shipwrecked. And even then I saw them rarely."

Talus stood up and approached Theon. His hands were out in supplication. "I need your help, Theon. I need your strength and wisdom. The treasure now lying in the vaults of Dionysus does not belong to this strange god or to his priests. And it doesn't belong to Nuhara or Khalkeus. It belongs to all the Children of the Lion. I've suffered in my life. I don't have the strength to suffer anymore. Help me, Theon—for Tirzah's sake, if for no one else's."

Again just the mention of her name oppressed

Theon, and his eyes filled with tears. "How sad it was," he finally said, "that I loved her twice and left her twice. And both times I thought I was doing the right thing. But I believed that someday, somehow, we would meet again. Now it is too late."

"We are both alone now, Theon."

"No, Talus. We are not alone. We have the history of the Children of the Lion behind us. We are never alone."

"Then you'll help me?" Talus asked, his voice breaking with the anticipation.

"I want to help you, Talus. I want to do what is right. But to turn on Nuhara—no matter what she has done—is hard for me. Do you understand? She is the mother of my children."

Talus grew bold. He felt that Theon was balanced on the cusp.

"She is a murderess, Theon. A traitor. A thief. She looted the wealth that the Children of the Lion earned by their sweat and their lives."

Theon pressed his palms to his forehead in misery. "Yes! Yes! Everything that you say is true! I know!"

Talus did not let up. "And I will tell you now the saddest story of all. Somewhere in one of the Philistine cities are four freshly dug graves. In them lie a woman and her three young children. They were murdered before they saw their husband and father again. The name of that man was Zeno. He no longer exists; now his name is Theon, and he remembers nothing about his existence as Zeno. Nuhara hunted the family down and had them murdered because she is sick with jealousy and greed and fear and brutality!"

Theon whirled around. His face was crazed with grief. He grasped the bloody battle ax that lay on the floor and came at Talus.

"I do not lie, Theon!" he cried out, afraid that he had gone too far. "Nuhara herself told me she would have them murdered. Tirzah's informants verified that she had done so."

Theon walked to the window again and stared out. He spoke in a hollow voice. "The steps are bloody where our assassins fled. The man you struck with the battle ax will probably die. The Thracians are primitive in their medical care. Perhaps you are a murderer, also, Talus."

"That was in self-defense," Talus retorted.

"Yes, of course. It often is."

He started to pace again, from time to time throwing up his hands. Then he turned to Talus, stared him straight in the eyes, and said bitterly, "Have you ever reflected on us—on *all* of us, the Children of the Lion? Look what has happened to a once-proud family. Our home has been wiped off the face of the earth. We betray one another. We murder one another. Members of our family vanish, and no one cares enough even to look for them. Our great gifts for working metals and other materials have fallen into total disuse. Neither the upper classes nor the lower classes depend on us anymore for any kind of wisdom. Our birthmarks have become warts."

"But that is not true of you, Theon! You have always exhibited our clan's finest attributes."

Theon paused, smiled, and continued. "Well, Talus, I have always tried to be a good man. I will help you restore the fortunes of the Children of the Lion. But we face formidable opposition and may not prevail. The idea of Nuhara in league with the priests of Dionysus is terrifying. But we will try."

Talus could not contain his joy. He ran to Theon and embraced him, then danced around the blood-splattered room. He knew that he had found much more than a surrogate father—he had found a man whose whole life had been imbued with the myth and reality of the Children of the Lion. Talus knew that as long as Theon lived, he would have a home. Let the struggle begin now, in Thrace. When or where it would end, neither of them could even guess.

CHAPTER
TEN

Canaan

Miriam was frightened. She had journeyed to the west bank of the Jordan because she had heard that her brother, Gideon, was resting there after his great triumphs. She had packed every bit of food she had remaining at home to bring to him.

Rumors had reached their father's village, claiming that thousands of Israelites had gathered to pay homage to Yahweh and Gideon. She had not seen her brother since the nightmarish night when he had been expelled by their father from the village. No one else in the family—not even his wife—seemed to care as much as Miriam about Gideon's fate or well-being; and she was certain that no one else loved him as much as she did.

So she had defied the wishes of her parents and gone to seek him out. What she had found, however, were throngs of inebriated people indulging in outrageous behavior. Concerned for her personal safety, she walked fearfully through the drunken, fornicating mob and looked for her brother. She could not understand what these people were doing. Was this how they gave thanks to Yahweh? Was this the way they eased their guilt for having abandoned Yahweh for all those years when they worshiped Baal?

As she walked, men called out lewd suggestions to her. She lowered her gaze, grasped her bundles tightly, and hurried on. The shamefulness of what she saw crushed her soul. Except for her eyes, she kept her face covered and avoided anyone's touch.

She kept asking where Gideon could be found, but the answers she received were nonsensical: "He is wherever you look!"

"He is with Yahweh!"

"He is riding a dappled horse!"

It was futile to try to get any information from these revelers, so she walked on, her eyes burning from the smoke of the cooking fires.

A loud peal of raucous laughter suddenly assailed her eardrums. She turned away from it. But the laughter was so loud and came from so many throats that curiosity forced her to turn back and approach the large group of spectators who were watching something obviously very funny.

It was difficult to elbow a path through the crowd. She had gone forward only a few feet when she realized it would be almost impossible to view the hilarious spectacle. She turned and started back. But then she heard the sound of a trumpet coming from the center of the crowd. The specific series of notes froze her where she stood because only Gideon played in that manner. She knew the sound of his horn as well as she knew the contours of his face.

She turned again and fought her way to the center of the large cheering, jeering, guffawing crowd. The notes from the trumpet filled her with enormous joy. She knew she had found her brother at last!

Miriam finally stood in a spot from which she could see the spectacle. In the center of the circle, a young woman was dancing and twirling to the music. She was naked. Gold earrings by the bushelful had been dumped around her. Some were tangled in her long, dark hair.

Gideon stood near her. He, too, was naked. As he played his trumpet, other men and women leaped into the center of the circle and danced.

Miriam felt herself growing faint. She bit her lip to keep from falling and shook her head to clear it.

The naked woman next to Gideon jumped onto his back, wrapping her legs around his waist. He staggered, flung the trumpet to the ground, and loosed a gleeful, almost animallike roar. The woman jumped down, then spread herself on the ground for Gideon. The onlookers cheered as he fitted himself between her legs.

Miriam's heart pounded, and her eyes filled with bitter tears. What had happened to her brother? How could he do such things? Across the circle she saw Purah. He appeared sober and totally disgusted by Gideon's antics. Miriam tried to catch the servant's eyes but failed. She knew she had to get out of there. She turned and, hysterical, fought her way through the crowd. She used her hands and feet and teeth to get as far from those humiliating displays as she could.

Finally she broke through the far edge of the crowd. But she did not stop; she kept on running and crying. She ran until she was well outside the gathering. At last she collapsed, exhausted, in a clump of juniper bushes. There she lay and wept piteously. For the first time in her life she hated her brother and wanted never to see him again or hear his name mentioned.

"Why are you weeping, Miriam?"

She sat up, startled. A man was standing directly in front of her. He was ugly and stout and wearing a blacksmith's leather apron. Where had he come from? she wondered. A moment before there had been no one around.

"Who are you?" she quavered.

"A friend," he replied, smiling.

It was, she had to admit, an unexpectedly warm and sincere smile. Its genuineness softened his unattractive countenance.

"How do you know my name? I don't know yours."

"Ah, Miriam, I know many things. And you'd be surprised by the number of people I know."

"Please leave me alone."

"I am a friend of your brother's."

"I have no brother," she retorted, heartsick from what she had seen.

"He loves you very much, Miriam."

"Oh, yes," she said acidly. "He loves me, and he loves Yahweh, and that is why he is now drunk and doing ridiculous things. I had heard wonderful news about him. I thought that Gideon, the good-hearted idiot, had grown up at last, that I could be proud of him and convince him to come home with me." Bitter tears stained her cheeks. "But obviously the rumors were untrue. He's the same stupid fool he always was— except not as lovable because he had the chance for dignity but threw it away."

She stood up and brushed off her clothes. "Please leave me alone."

"I will leave shortly," he said. He smiled at her again. "I want to show you something first. Please look at my hand."

She stared at his empty palm.

He closed his hand, and when he opened it, a beautiful red-topped mushroom rested in his palm. It was so perfectly formed and so obviously fresh that Miriam gasped in spite of herself.

He laughed and tore the mushroom in half. Then he ate one half and gave her the other. She looked into his face closely, and the trustworthiness she found there prompted her to eat quickly.

"That was delicious," she said. "I have never seen a mushroom like that in Canaan."

"I know. It comes from another part of the world."

"Then how did it get here, in your hand?"

"Yahweh sent it. Just as He sent me."

She took a step back, then became rigid with fear. She realized she was in the presence of a man who was more than human but less than God. *Could I be dreaming all this?* she wondered. *Was seeing Gideon's mon-*

strous behavior too much for me, or did I imagine that, too?

"I have visited Gideon many times over the past weeks," the messenger explained, "so I thought I should pay a visit to you. You have a pure heart, Miriam, and I want to ease your pain."

"How can you do that?" she cried out. "All my love and respect for Gideon has turned to nothing."

"Your brother has performed a great task. He has shouldered a tremendous responsibility with no training or preparation. In spite of all that, he exhibited great courage. Now he is just showing that he is merely human. His flesh is weak, and he has suffered terribly. He is weary, cynical, confused. Serving Yahweh proved too much for him in the end." The angel shrugged. "He did his best, and now he's come undone."

"He's drunk," she snapped. Then she added quickly, "Oh, it is not his drunkenness that upsets me; it is the public sexual acts. In spite of his silliness, my brother always has been my idol. More than anyone else I knew he appreciated that which was beautiful, even when his sensitivity and love for music won him the ridicule of our village. But now he has made ugly the most sacred act of human life. Do you understand?"

The messenger nodded. "I am not here to excuse Gideon's behavior. But remember if you can that Yahweh demands compassion as well as rectitude. One must be brutal in order to achieve freedom from oppression; but after freedom is achieved, then mercy and compassion and love must manifest themselves."

Miriam covered her eyes with her hands and shook her head. "It's not that easy. Once, I loved Gideon and would have sacrificed my life to save his. But I cannot feel compassion for him unless you erase the memories of what I have seen. You didn't see my brother dancing naked. You didn't see the woman jumping on to his back. I knew what was going to happen next—and in front of all those people!" She could not speak anymore. She was trembling violently.

"Be strong, Miriam," the angel urged. "Yahweh blesses you and your issue." And then he vanished.

She shook her head. What had the stranger meant by "her issue"? She doubted if she would ever marry and bear children in these horrible times.

It was time to go home. Everything had turned out wrong. She picked up her bundles and began the long trek. Her weariness now felt pleasurable; it was so numbing, it prevented her from agonizing over what she had witnessed.

As she walked down the dusty road, the sky began to cloud over, and a deep rumbling of thunder presaged a storm. Finally the rains came—a short but drenching downpour that sent her scurrying to the overhanging ledge of a small series of cliffs. She pressed against the rock wall to keep dry. In spite of the inconvenience, she watched the storm with a grateful smile. The farmers were desperate for rain. And she knew that after the rain the mushrooms would appear, and she would fill many baskets for her family.

As quickly as the downpour had begun, it stopped, and the hot sun burst through the clouds. Miriam was about to start out when she heard low moans coming from the far end of the ledge. Was it an animal? She could not see—bushes obscured her view. The moaning came again. It was the saddest sound she had ever heard.

Carefully, silently, she crept toward the far end of the ledge, her hand running lightly along the cliff wall for balance.

She froze the moment she saw the wounded man, and her hand involuntarily moved to her throat in fear. It was a young Midianite. He wore the robes and gold earrings of his people. The lower part of his garment was stained with blood. His eyes were closed, and he thrashed on the ground. She realized that he was too badly wounded to pose a threat to her safety. *He must be one of the survivors of the battle,* she thought, *and he had to have crawled a long way to reach this place.*

Where were his weapons? She could see none. He probably had abandoned them in his escape. She took two steps forward. She stared at his handsome, pain-filled face for a long time. This was, she realized, one of the warriors who had visited great horrors on her people. No doubt he had murdered and tortured and maimed. But she felt no hatred for him. She felt only a curiosity.

She approached slowly, then knelt beside him. His eyes fluttered open, and he stared at her. He tried to bring his fingers to his mouth. She understood: He needed water.

Quickly she placed the bladder of water she had brought for Gideon to the Midianite's lips. He choked and sputtered on it. She pulled the skin away, ashamed of herself, realizing now that he was too badly hurt to swallow. She wetted her fingers and slowly daubed his lips, as if he were a sick calf and the water was mother's milk.

His legs, she could see, were severely cut. There were particularly deep gashes in his right leg. He had obviously lost a great deal of blood, and some of his wounds were beginning to fester. Miriam cleansed and bound his wounds, stopping only when her actions caused him too much pain. When she was finished, she tore up the loaf of bread she had brought and soaked small pieces in the water. Then, propping the man up a few inches, she fed him the pieces.

By the time she had finished feeding him, the sun was vanishing over the western horizon. Now it was too late to start out for home. She would have to stay under the ledge until morning. She sat near the wounded Midianite and watched him. She would try to sleep sitting up; that was the safest thing to do.

The Bedouin's fever-brightened eyes went in and out of focus. Sometimes they seemed to see her, and sometimes they looked through her. The frequency of his cries and moans lessened. He appeared to be breathing easily now.

Miriam closed her eyes and was almost asleep when he cried out. She awakened immediately, alert and frightened. The man had raised one arm and held it out to her.

She did not know what to do. "You must go to sleep," she told him.

All he said in response was an incomprehensible call. And he stretched his hand closer to her, straining toward her.

It was no use to deny him. She slid along the ground until she was close enough to grasp his hand. His body shuddered at the touch. His palm was dry and hot from his fever.

"Ra . . . Ra . . . ni . . . Ra," he rasped.

She understood. He was speaking a name, a common name among the Bedouin women, the name Rani. Tears came to her eyes, and she gripped his hand more tightly. This poor, wounded, half-crazed Midianite thought she was his wife or his lover.

Then she released his hand and was filled with a sudden fury at herself. Why did she feel so much compassion and forgiveness for this Bedouin, who had probably murdered dozens of her countrymen, and yet felt none for her brother?

She remembered what the messenger had said: "Yahweh demands compassion as well as rectitude."

She buried her face in her hands and called herself a fraud and a hypocrite. Everyone said how kind and gentle and lovely she was; but when she was finally tested, she found herself wanting. When her brother needed her loyalty, she had responded with vindictiveness. The messenger had been right! Human beings always fail and thus must try harder. They must try again and again to stem the wickedness and cruelty that well up in their hearts.

Miriam gazed down at the moaning Bedouin. A tremendous surge of love and compassion flooded her entire being for the unfortunate nomad, for poor Gideon, for the Israelites who danced like fools for a God they never knew, and for a God who did not want their celebration.

"Forgive me, Gideon," she whispered to the night. "Forgive me, Yahweh."

Then she lay down beside the Bedouin and held him close.

"It is I, Rani," she whispered into his ear.

He clasped her to him so tightly that his body

convulsed with pain. She kissed his feverish lips, and she slipped her hands inside his robe to touch his naked young body. And then, in a moment of both terror and joy, she realized what the messenger had meant when he had said Yahweh would bless her issue.

CHAPTER ELEVEN

City of Ur/Kingdom of Babylon

"We will see it soon, Micah," Luti said.

She grasped his hand tightly as they walked along the river path. Their long, arduous, dangerous journey was almost finished. She was becoming more and more excited at the thought of seeing her child again, of seeing her house and her servants, of showing Micah how and where she lived. She stopped abruptly, threw back her head, and laughed.

Micah looked at her, perplexed.

"I was just thinking," she explained, grinning, "how the mistress of the estate is returning in a blaze of glory." She spread her arms and twirled around. "Covered with dust, barefooted, and in tattered clothes. I look like a field hand."

"You look beautiful," Micah replied sincerely.

She kissed him quickly and resumed the pace. "There!" she said, pointing. "Look there!"

The lovers stood at a fork in the path. One path

led away from the river and up to a magnificent, high-roofed building, which dominated the view.

"That's your house?" Micah asked incredulously.

"Is it too opulent, Micah? Does it embarrass your soldier's heart?" She did not wait for an answer. Instead she pulled him toward the house.

An old man pushing a wheelbarrow on the path passed them but did not say a word. Luti suppressed a giggle. "That's one of my servants. He didn't even recognize me in these rags. Let's enter through the back, through the kitchen. They'll probably think we're beggars." She was excited, like a child returning home and knowing that wonderful gifts were waiting there. "Oh, you will love your beautiful son," she squealed. She was nearly dancing with happiness.

They circled the large house and reached the back entrance. From the yard they could see into the massive kitchen, with its open fireplaces, the large pots, and cool stone floor. From outside they could hear the sound of someone scrubbing the stones with a brush.

"Wait!" she said, stopping just as she was about to pass through the entrance.

Over the doorway, on the beautifully fitted tile mosaic that she had had imported long before from Syria, was a marking that had never been there before. She studied it carefully. "How odd! An astrological sign. I wonder who put it there? It wasn't here when I left."

"What is it?" Micah asked. "Do you know what it means?"

"It's the sign for Venus, the morning star, the symbol of the goddess Astarte, protector of Ur."

"Maybe one of your servants has become pious," Micah suggested.

"Perhaps," Luti answered, vaguely troubled. But the symbol was not enough to spoil her homecoming. "Come! We're home. We'll deal with that later."

They entered the house and walked through the kitchen and toward the inner courtyard.

"Your servants work hard," Micah noted, pointing to the kneeling boy who was diligently scrubbing the stone in one corner of the kitchen.

"Ossaf must have hired him when I left," Luti said. "There were no children on the kitchen staff." She continued toward the courtyard and pulled Micah after her.

"Mommy?"

Luti stopped short and turned. Her eyes were wide with confusion and love. It was Drak's voice.

The child dropped his scrub brush. "Mommy!" he called out again, then ran and flung himself against her, nearly knocking them both off balance.

"Drak! Drak! Oh my darling Drak!" She covered the child's face with kisses. Then she turned him toward Micah. Her eyes glistened with love and pride. "This is your father, Drak. I have brought your father to you."

The boy, obviously not knowing what to do, stared at Micah.

Micah grinned at the boy. "Hello, uh, Son."

Luti pulled him to her again, kissing him repeatedly as she motioned Micah to come closer. Then, as if recovering her sense, she stepped back and looked at her child. "Why are you scrubbing the floor? Why are you wearing those filthy clothes? And where are your shoes?"

Drak did not answer. He started to sob. Luti grabbed one of his hands and turned it over. It was red and raw, covered with callouses.

Micah gently disengaged Luti's hand from Drak's. As he knelt beside the boy, his eyes also filled with tears.

"There is no need for you to cry," he whispered to his son. "I am crying enough for both of us." Micah let his hand settle on the boy's head, and then he moved it gently down Drak's face. "I will never leave you again."

The boy stared wide-eyed at his father. "Mommy told me that you are a great warrior."

Micah smiled grimly and nodded. Then he turned to Luti. He felt overwhelmed with love for her and their child. "What a beautiful young man our son is." He turned back to Drak, pulled him close, and embraced him.

But the child shook loose, saying, "And Mommy told me that you will teach me how to use the sword and the spear." The boy then kicked the scrubbing brush angrily across the floor.

Micah kept staring in wonder at his young son. The scrubbing brush, the dirty clothes, and the child's comments meant nothing to him. All he could think of was the miracle of their meeting. This small human being in front of him was his own son—flesh of his flesh . . . blood of his blood. This child was a child of love.

"He has your face," Luti said.

Micah nodded. What she said was true. Drak was a miniature of himself. He returned to the child, turned him around, and with a tender hand parted the tattered garment. The lion's-paw birthmark of the Children of the Lion stood out fresh and vibrant against the boy's flesh.

Drak looked over his shoulder at his father. "Mommy has one, too," he said. "Do you have such a mark?"

"Yes, only it is faded now—too much blood and sand and grit has rolled over it." Micah felt his whole body begin to tremble. Could he protect this beautiful boy from the cruelty of the world, or would this lovely child see the horrors he himself had witnessed? Would the Children of the Lion ever again be able to enjoy lives of peace and harmony?

A familiar voice came from the doorway to the inner courtyard. "The child has been well treated. He is just learning how to work. He is earning his keep."

Luti wheeled, furious. Ossaf was standing calmly in the doorway. He was dressed in one of his absurdly elegant robes.

"What is going on here?" Luti demanded.

Ossaf shrugged. "It was reported that you were dead."

"Well, I'm not dead. And you will pay for your arrogance. After the kindness with which you have always been treated, was it too much to expect that you would take care of my son during my absence?"

"Please, no arguing in my house," the man requested calmly.

"*Your* house?"

"Yes. I am now the master of this house and its land."

"Are you insane, Ossaf? All this is mine!"

"It has been determined by the courts that you were a blasphemer of Astarte. You have forfeited your estate. You own nothing in Ur. You will be lucky to try to get out of Babylon with your life."

Luti trembled with rage. "It's a lie!" she screamed at him. "I was acquitted of that charge years ago."

Ossaf smiled. "I provided them with evidence, Luti . . . you don't mind my calling you Luti, do you? I showed them the toys you ordered me to carve over the years. Those terrible, blasphemous toys that hold the goddess up to scorn."

Her face went pale. She realized the Hittite had been thorough in his betrayal. She realized that he had created false evidence that could not be disputed if the courts had no inclination to question it.

"But I am a generous man," Ossaf continued. "I will allow you and your child to remain here. I will allow you to share my bed and my meals. And your son shall be as my son."

Luti pressed her hands to her ears, shutting out the sound of his voice. She wheeled and faced the far kitchen wall. Her eyes caught the glint of the carving knives hanging by their handles.

She ran to the wall and pulled one of the long knives from its holder. Then she ran back to Micah and pressed the weapon into his hand. "Kill him, Micah!" she seethed. "Kill him now!"

Micah stared at the knife in his hand. He did not move or speak.

"Did you hear me?" she shrilled. "Kill him! Protect your son. Restore what is mine!"

Micah made no move.

She began to beat on his chest with her fists. "Do you want me to be poor again? Do you want our son to grow up in the fields? Do you want me to forfeit everything? This is my home, my future, *our* future, Micah. Please! You must kill him!" Exhausted, she fell to one knee and wept uncontrollably.

Micah stroked her head gently. "I cannot use this knife, Luti. I swore that I would never do violence to another man. I swore that on everything that is holy to me and all the Children of the Lion. Forget this man, Luti. Forget this house. We'll take the boy and walk away from here with nothing but one another. That's all that matters. We will survive. We will build a new life—one that belongs to the three of us, not one that belongs to you and Drak, which I'll try to squeeze into. I'll always be an outsider here, living on your kindness. If we begin anew, we'll be happy, I promise."

Micah gently helped Luti to her feet and wiped her tears with his sleeve. Then, as Drak watched, Micah smoothed back her hair and kissed her.

Luti caught her breath with ragged inhalations and nodded, resigned. She and Drak moved away from Micah. She stared first at Ossaf, then back at Micah. Both men were insane, she decided. If she went with Micah, she would face a life of poverty. She had lived that way already and loathed it. She would be sunk once again into subsistence and despair and hunger.

If she stayed in the house and became Ossaf's concubine, she would feel degraded beyond her imagination. And if she chose that, she would betray Micah yet again.

She hugged her son so fiercely that he cried out. She stared at Ossaf again. He had the hint of a smile about his lips. Then she turned to Micah. His face was full of trust. She would have to choose now.

Luti sighed deeply and collected her thoughts. At last she held out her hand to the only man to whom she knew she could entrust her future, and that of their son. Calmly, Luti took Micah and Drak by the hand, and they walked out of the house together. Whatever hardships and terror they might face, they would face them together.

Epilogue

The Teller of Tales stared at the circle of serious faces surrounding him in the desert night. The hot, harsh wind whipped across their parched skin. There was no food left and little water. The milk in the mothers' breasts had dried up, and the wails of the infants were like knives in the heart.

"Are you suffering, my brethren?" he asked sarcastically. There was no response. His tone gentled. "Your suffering is nothing compared to what faced the once-proud house of the Children of the Lion. In every land where they once had been powerful, they were now brought low. Home was a ruin. Their financial empire was shattered. Their arts and skills in the working of metal were now only a vague memory."

The old Teller of Tales paused again and fought to maintain his balance against the wind. A man rose from the circle and offered up his rough-hewn staff, but the Teller of Tales waved him back scornfully.

"I can stand alone! And the Children of the Lion began to realize that they, too, must stand alone. In the north, in the dreadful mountains of Thrace, they would meet the most formidable enemy they had ever encountered—the priests of the great god Dionysus.

"In the south, the twins Gravis and Hela were thrust into a pantheon of divinity and thus had no choice but to oppose the kingship of Ramses and his vast Egyptian forces.

"In the east, the goddess Astarte, in her role as protector of Babylon, sought to extirpate forever the

371

occult power of the Children of the Lion—a power that, in the hands of a desperate family, worked to overturn the state."

Then he raised his hands over his head, and his voice reached a depth of intensity so penetrating that the onlookers shivered and seemed to crumble. "Hear me, O my brethren! Listen with your hearts! Forget your hunger and your thirst and your weariness, for I shall also recite to you a name that will live in your hearts for as long as you draw breath. That name is . . ."

He paused and lowered his voice, and the listeners strained to hear him. "That name is Samson, Samson the Israelite. And it is in his land—Canaan—that the greatest drama unfolded. As the power of the Philistine nation, backed by the Phoenician demons, crushed Yahweh's chosen people, the Children of the Lion were called upon to enter that bloodstained land, that land of heartbreak, that land of milk and honey where all things are possible. O my brethren, you will open your hearts to this man Samson. You will discover—"

He was too exhausted to continue. His voice cracked as he said, "But all this you shall hear tomorrow. Now I must sleep."

Children of the Lion Volume XV
TOWERS OF LOVE
by Peter Danielson

Gideon's seventy "sons," his bravest warriors, rule the land. After the commander's death, his illegitimate son, Abimelech, tries to gain power. When Gideon's family utterly rejects him, he uses Shechem, Canaan's most bustling city, as his base. With a formidable army Abimelech cuts a swath of violence across Canaan, first viciously attacking Gideon's gentle sister, then murdering the seventy, the Israelites' best and brightest, one by one.

Meanwhile, in Thrace, Theon and Talus gather a following to regain the Children of the Lion's stolen fortune from Theon's evil wife, Nuhara, high priestess of Dionysus. The men are found out, and Nuhara banishes them to a marble quarry where prisoners are worked to death.

In Babylon, Luti is ordered by the government to Tyre, to spy on the Phoenician Navan. Her infant daughter is taken hostage by the army until Luti returns with information. Micah falls in love with a dancing girl, who betrays Luti to Navan. Luti is thrown into prison.

And in the Gaza desert is the five-year-old who will save them all—little Tuk . . . silent, mysterious, able to bring the dead to life, master of the occult.

(*Read* TOWERS OF LOVE, *on sale late 1992 wherever Bantam Books are sold.*)

"FROM THE PRODUCER OF WAGONS WEST COMES YET ANOTHER EXPLOSIVE SAGA OF LEGENDARY COURAGE AND UNFORGETTABLE LOVE"

CHILDREN OF THE LION

☐	26912	Children of the Lion #1	$4.99
☐	26971	The Shepherd Kings #2	$4.99
☐	26769	Vengeance of the Lion #3	$4.95
☐	26594	The Lion in Egypt #4	$4.95
☐	26885	The Golden Pharaoh #5	$4.95
☐	27187	Lord of the Nile #6	$4.50
☐	26325	The Prophecy #7	$4.50
☐	26800	Sword of Glory #8	$4.95
☐	27459	The Deliverer #9	$4.95
☐	27999	The Exodus #10	$4.50
☐	28300	The Sea Peoples #11	$4.95
☐	28588	The Promised Land #12	$4.95
☐	29082-7	The Invaders #13	$4.99
☐	29495-4	The Trumpet And The Sword #14	$4.99

Buy them at your local bookstore or use this handy page for ordering:

Bantam Books, Dept. LE5, 2451 S. Wolf Road, Des Plaines, IL 60018

Please send me the items I have checked above. I am enclosing $_____
(please add $2.50 to cover postage and handling). Send check or money
order, no cash or C.O.D.s please.

Mr/Ms _____

Address _____

City/State _____ Zip _____

LE5-1/92

Please allow four to six weeks for delivery.
Prices and availability subject to change without notice.

A Proud People in a Harsh Land

THE SPANISH BIT
SAGA

Set on the Great Plains of America in the early 16th century, Don Coldsmith's acclaimed series recreates a time, a place and a people that have been nearly lost to history. With the advent of the Spaniards, the horse culture came to the people of the Plains. Here is history in the making through the eyes of the proud Native Americans who lived it.

☐ 26397-8	**TRAIL OF THE SPANISH BIT**	$3.50
☐ 26412-5	**THE ELK-DOG HERITAGE**	$3.50
☐ 26806-6	**FOLLOW THE WIND**	$3.50
☐ 26938-0	**BUFFALO MEDICINE**	$3.50
☐ 27067-2	**MAN OF THE SHADOWS**	$3.50
☐ 27209-8	**DAUGHTER OF THE EAGLE**	$3.50
☐ 27344-2	**MOON OF THUNDER**	$3.50
☐ 27460-0	**SACRED HILLS**	$3.50
☐ 27604-2	**PALE STAR**	$3.50
☐ 27708-1	**RIVER OF SWANS**	$3.50
☐ 28163-1	**RETURN TO THE RIVER**	$3.50
☐ 28318-9	**THE MEDICINE KNIFE**	$3.50
☐ 28538-6	**THE FLOWER IN THE MOUNTAINS**	$3.50
☐ 28760-5	**TRAIL FROM TAOS**	$3.50
☐ 29123-8	**SONG OF THE ROCK**	$3.50
☐ 29419-9	**FORT DE CHASTAIGNE**	$3.99
☐ 28334-0	**THE CHANGING WIND**	$3.95
☐ 28868-7	**THE TRAVELER**	$4.50

■ ■

Available at your local bookstore or use this page to order.

Bantam Books, Dept. LE 10   414 East Golf Road, Des Plaines, IL 60016

Please send me the items I have checked above. I am enclosing $_____ (please add $2.50 to cover postage and handling). Prices are $1.00 higher per book in Canada. Send check or money order, no cash or C.O.D.'s, please.

Mr/Ms._____

Address_____

City/State_____Zip_____

Please allow four to six weeks for delivery.

Prices and availability subject to change without notice.   LE 10 12/91

GIDEON—The celebrated warrior and prophet becomes a hero to his people, but it will take more than a miracle to walk free into the promised land . . . and it will exact the greatest price mortal man has ever paid. . . .

ZALMUNNAH—The king of the Bedouins—and their most bloodthirsty warlord—he vows death to his hated enemies . . . and won't rest until the Holy Land is drenched in Israelite blood. . . .

LUTI—Ruled by mystical powers she does not understand, the beautiful sorceress and Child of the Lion tries to find her beloved Micah, but is sold into brutal bondage. . . .

NIMSHI—Treacherous and deceitful, he will betray his own brother for Phoenician gold—and a terrible revenge. . . .

TALUS—The offspring of a proud, once-prosperous family, he is now an exile among the people of the sea—until he escapes the Island of Death and becomes dangerously obsessed by a seductive Israelite dancing girl. . . .

COTTO—The exotic, dark-haired beauty uses her body to tempt men to terrible deeds. Ruthless and ambitious, she plots to infiltrate the powerful Phoenician army—and to destroy anyone who stands in her way. . . .